# THE
# WOLF
## AND THE
# WOODSMAN

# THE
# WOLF
## AND THE
# WOODSMAN

## A NOVEL

## AVA REID

HARPER Voyager
*An Imprint of* HarperCollins*Publishers*

THE WOLF AND THE WOODSMAN. Copyright © 2021 by Ava Reid. All rights reserved. Printed in Italy. No part of this book may be used or reproduced in any manner whatsoever without written permission except in the case of brief quotations embodied in critical articles and reviews. For information, address HarperCollins Publishers, 195 Broadway, New York, NY 10007.

HarperCollins books may be purchased for educational, business, or sales promotional use. For information, please email the Special Markets Department at SPsales@harpercollins.com.

Harper Voyager and design are trademarks of HarperCollins Publishers LLC.

A hardcover edition of this book was published in 2021 by Harper Voyager, an imprint of HarperCollins Publishers.

FIRST HARPER VOYAGER PAPERBACK EDITION PUBLISHED 2022.
FIRST HARPER VOYAGER COLLECTOR'S EDITION PUBLISHED 2025.

*Designed by Paula Russell Szafranski*
*Map design by Nick Springer / Springer Cartographics LLC*
*Title spread art © @uniturehd/stock.adobe.com*
*Leaves art © Shutterstock*

Library of Congress Cataloging-in-Publication Data has been applied for.

ISBN 978-0-06-343962-7

25 26 27 28 29 RTLO 10 9 8 7 6 5 4 3 2 1

Many runes the cold has told me,
Many lays the rain has brought me,
Other songs the wind has sung me—
[ . . . ]
Shall I bring these songs together
From the cold and frost collect them?

—*The Kalevala*, Elias Lönnrot
(tr. John Martin Crawford)

Half-Sea

Rodinya

KALEVA
Lake Taivas

Kuihta

SZARVASVÁR

Völkstadt

Élet River

FARKASVÁR

Little Plain

Keszi

Forest of Ezer Szem

Black Lake

Kingdom of Régország

Király Szek

AKOSVÁR

Great Plain

Empire of Merzan

Map copyright © MMXXI Springer Cartographics LLC

# THE
# WOLF
## AND THE
# WOODSMAN

# CHAPTER ONE

The trees have to be tied down by sunset. When the Woodsmen come, they always try to run.

The girls who are skilled forgers fashion little iron stakes to drive through the roots of the trees and into the earth, anchoring them in place. With no gift for forging between the two of us, Boróka and I haul a great length of rope, snaring any trees we pass in clumsy loops and awkward knots. When we finish, it looks the spider web of some giant creature, something the woods might cough up. The thought doesn't even make me shiver. Nothing that might break through the tree line could be worse than the Woodsmen.

"Who do you think it will be?" Boróka asks. The light of the setting sun filters through the patchy cathedral of tree cover, dappling her face. Tears are pearled in the corners of her eyes.

"Virág," I say. "With any luck."

Boróka's mouth twists.

"Though I suspect halfway through their journey the Woodsmen will tire of her babbling about weather omens and dump her in the Black Lake."

"You don't mean that."

Of course I don't. I wouldn't wish the Woodsmen on any-one, no matter how much they lashed me, how meanly they chided me, or how many hours I spent scraping their cold gulyás out of yesterday's pots. But it's easier to loathe Virág than to worry I might lose her.

The wind picks up, carrying the voices of the other girls toward us, as silvery as the bone chimes hanging outside of Virág's hut. They sing to make their forging gift stronger, the way the great hero Vilmötten did, when he crafted the sword of the gods. As their song falters, so does their steel. Almost unconsciously I move toward them, bow and arrow shifting on my back. Instead of listening to their words, I look at their hands.

They rub their palms together, gently at first, and then with greater ferocity, as if they might scour their skin right off. By the time the song is done, each girl is gripping a small iron stake, as slick and sturdy as any that might come off a blacksmith's blazing forge. Boróka notices me watching—notices the look of jilted longing she's seen on my face a hundred times before.

"Ignore them," Boróka whispers.

It's easy for her to say. If Isten, the father-god, cast his smiling face down on the woods right now, he would see a mottled rainbow of gray and tawny smeared against the green bramble. Their wolf cloaks gleam even in the ebbing sunlight, the individual hairs turned almost translucent. The teeth of the dead animals, still fully intact, form an arc over each girl's head, as if the animal were about to eat her. Boróka's wolf cloak is a bleached ochre—a healer's color.

But when Isten saw me, all he would see is a cloak of plain wool, thin and patched with my own lazy threadwork. I can always feel the humiliating weight of it, clothed in my own inferiority. I turn to Boróka to reply, but then I hear a hushed giggle behind me, and the smell of something burning fills my nose.

I whirl around, my hair trailing blue fire. Biting back a yelp, my impotent hands fly up to try to smother the flame. It's all they want from me, that wild-eyed panic, and they get it. The fire is out before I know it, but my throat is burning as I march toward Katalin and her lackeys.

"I'm terribly sorry, Évike," Katalin says. "The skill of fire-making is hard to master. My hand must have slipped."

"What a pity that you find such a simple skill so difficult to perform," I snap.

My comment only earns another chorus of laughs. Katalin's hood is pulled up over her head, the wolf's mouth twisted into an ugly snarl, eyes glassy and blind. Her cloak is precisely the same color as her hair, white as a carp's belly, or, if I'm charitable, the winter's first snow. It's a seer's color.

I want to tear her pristine cloak off her back and make her watch as I drag it through the muddy riverbed. A small, mute part of me wants to hang it over my own shoulders, but I know I would only feel like a fraud.

"Perhaps I do," Katalin says with a shrug. "Or perhaps I can have another girl make my fires for me, when I am the village táltos."

"Virág isn't dead yet."

"Of course it won't be you, Évike," she presses on, ignoring me. "It will have to be someone who can light more than a spark."

"Or heal more than a splinter," Írisz, one of her preening wolf pack, speaks up.

"Or forge a sewing needle," Zsófia, the other one, adds.

"Leave her alone," Boróka says. "None of you should be so cruel, especially on a Woodsman day."

In truth they're no crueler than usual. And, of course, they're right. But I would never give them the satisfaction of admitting it, or of even flinching when they enumerate my failures.

"Évike doesn't have to worry on a Woodsman day, does

she?" Katalin's smile is white and gloating, a perfect mirror of her wolf's. "The Woodsmen only take the girls with magic. It's a shame none of her mother's skills are in her blood, or else we might be rid of her for good."

The word *mother* burns worse than blue flame. "Keep your mouth shut."

Katalin smiles. At least, her mouth does.

If I think hard about it, I can almost feel sorry for her. After all, her white cloak is given, not earned—and I know how ugly a seer's duties can be. But I don't care to show her the sort of pity she's never shown me.

Boróka lays a hand on my arm. Her grip is reassuring—and restraining. I tense under the pressure of it, but I don't lurch toward Katalin. Her eyes, pale as a river under ice, glint with assured victory. She turns to go, her cloak sweeping out behind her, and Írisz and Zsófia follow.

Hands shaking, I reach for the bow on my back.

The rest of the girls spend their days honing their magic and practicing swordplay. Some can perform three skills; some have mastered one exceptionally well, like Boróka, who's as useless at fire-making or forging as I am, but can heal better than anyone in the village. Without even the feeblest glimmer of the gods' magic, though, I'm relegated to hunting with the men, who always eye me with discomfort and suspicion. It's not an easy peace, but it's made me a mean shot.

It doesn't come close to making up for being barren—the only girl in Keszi, our village, with no aptitude for any of the three skills. No blessings from Isten. Everyone has their own whispered theories about why the gods passed me over, why none of their magic pooled in my blood or grafted white onto my bones. I no longer care to hear any of them.

"*Don't,*" Boróka pleads. "You'll only make everything worse—"

I want to laugh. I want to ask her what could be worse—would they strike me? Scratch me? Burn me? They've done all that and more. Once I made the mistake of swiping one of Katalin's sausages off the feast table, and she sent a curtain of flame billowing toward me without hesitation or remorse. I sulked around the village for a month afterward, speaking to no one, until my eyebrows grew back.

There's still a tiny bald patch in my left brow, slick with scar tissue.

I notch the arrow and pull back the bow. Katalin is the perfect target—an impossible mound of snow in the gold-green haze of late summer, bright enough to make your eyes sting.

Boróka lets out another clipped sound of protest, and I let the arrow fly. It skims right past Katalin, ruffling the white fur of her wolf cloak, and vanishes into a black tangle of briars.

Katalin doesn't scream, but I catch the look of sheer panic on her face before her fear turns to scandalized anger. Though it's the only satisfaction I'll get, it's better than nothing.

And then Katalin starts toward me, flushed and furious under her wolf's hood. I keep one hand steady on my bow, and the other goes to the pocket of my cloak, searching for the braid curled there. My mother's hair is warm and feels like silk beneath my fingers, even though it's been separated from her body for more than fifteen years.

Before she can reach me, Virág's voice rings out through the woods, loud enough to startle the birds from their nests.

"Évike! Katalin! Come!"

Boróka thins her mouth at me. "You might have just earned a lashing."

"Or worse," I say, though my stomach swoops at the possibility, "she'll scold me with another story."

Perhaps both. Virág is particularly vicious on Woodsman days.

Katalin brushes past me with unnecessary force, our shoulders clacking painfully. I don't rise to the slight, because Virág is watching both of us with her hawk's wicked stare, and the vein on the old woman's forehead is throbbing especially hard. Boróka takes my hand as we trudge out of the woods and toward Keszi in the distance, the wooden huts with their reed roofs smudged like black thumbprints against the sunset. Behind us, the forest of Ezer Szem makes its perfunctory noises: a sound like a loud exhale, and then a sound like someone gasping for breath after breaching the surface of the water. Ezer Szem bears little resemblance to the other forests in Régország. It's larger than all the rest put together, and it hums with its own arboreal heartbeat. The trees have a tendency to uproot themselves when they sense danger, or even when someone ruffles their branches a little too hard. Once, a girl accidentally set fire to a sapling, and a whole copse of elms walked off in protest, leaving the village exposed to both wind and Woodsmen.

Still, we love our finicky forest, not least because of the protections it affords us. If any more than a dozen men at once tried to hack their way through, the trees would do worse than just walk off. We only take precautions against our most cowardly oaks, our most sheepish poplars.

As we get closer, I can see that Keszi is full of light and noise, the way it always is around sundown. There's a different tenor to it now, though: something frenetic. A group of boys have gathered our scrawny horses, brushing their coats until they shine, and braiding their manes so they match the Woodsmen's steeds. Our horses don't have the pedigree of the king's, but they clean up nicely. The boys glance down at the ground as I pass by, and even the horses eye me with prickling animal suspicion. My throat tightens.

Some girls and women polish their blades, humming softly. Other women run after their children, checking to make sure there are no stains on their tunics or holes in their leather shoes. We can't afford to look hungry or weak or frightened. The smell of gulyás wafts toward me from someone's pot, making my stomach cry out with longing. We won't eat until after the Woodsmen have gone.

When there is one less mouth to feed.

On the left, my mother's old hut stands like a hulking grave marker, silent and cold. Another woman lives there now with her two children, huddling around the same hearth where my mother once huddled with me. Listening to the rain drum against the reed roof as summer storms snarled through the tree branches, counting the beats between rumbles of thunder. I remember the particular curve of my mother's cheek, illuminated in the moments when lightning fissured across the sky.

It's the oldest hurt, but raw as a still-gasping wound. I touch my mother's braid again, running my fingers over its contours, high and low again, like the hills and valleys of Szarvasvár. Boróka's grip on my other hand tightens as she pulls me along.

When we reach Virág's hut, Boróka leans forward to embrace me. I hug her back, the fur of her wolf cloak bristling under my palms.

"I'll see you afterward," she says. "For the feast."

Her voice is strained, low. I don't have to fear being taken, but that doesn't mean seeing the Woodsmen is easy. We've all done our own silent calculations—how many girls, and what are the chances that a Woodsman's eye might land on your mother or sister or daughter or friend? Perhaps I'm lucky to have very little worth losing.

Still, I want to tell Boróka how ferociously glad I am to have one friend at all. She could have slipped in beside Katalin, another cruel and faceless body in a wolf cloak, hurling their barbed words. But thinking that way makes me feel small and pitiful, like a dog nosing the ground for dropped food. I give Boróka's hand a squeeze instead, and watch her go with a tightness in my chest.

Virág's hut stands on the outskirts of the village, close enough that the forest could reach out and brush it with its knotted fingertips. The wood of the hut is termite-pitted and crusted with lichen, and the reed roof is flimsy, ancient. Smoke chuffs from the doorway in fat gray clouds, making my eyes water. Her bone chimes rattle violently as I step through the threshold, but I haven't paid enough attention to her lectures to know whether it's a good omen or not. A message from Isten, or a warning from Ördög. I've never been sure either would look favorably at me in any case.

Katalin is already inside, sitting cross-legged on the ground beside Virág. The hearth is blazing, and the room is dense with woodsmoke. My own straw bed is crammed in the corner, and I hate that Katalin can see it, the one small and shameful thing that is mine and mine alone. The herbs garlanding Virág's wooden shelves are ones that I picked myself, crawling belly-flat on the forest floor and cursing her with every breath. Now Virág beckons me toward her, all six fingers of her wizened hand curling.

Unlike other girls, seers are marked at birth, with white hair or extra fingers or some other oddity. Virág even has an extra row of teeth, needle-sharp and lodged in her gums like pebbles in a muddy riverbed. Katalin was spared these indignities, of course.

"Come, Évike," Virág says. "I need my hair braided before the ceremony."

The way she calls it a *ceremony* makes me flush hot with anger. She may as well call it a burial rite. Yet I bite my tongue and sit down beside her, fingers working through the tangled strands of her hair, white with power and eternity. Virág is nearly as old as Keszi itself.

"Shall I remind you why the Woodsmen come?" Virág asks.

"I know the story well," Katalin says demurely.

I scowl at her. "We've heard it a hundred times before."

"Then you'll hear it a hundred and one, lest you forget why Keszi stands alone and untarnished in a kingdom that worships a new god."

Virág has a propensity for morbid theatrics. In truth, Keszi is one of a handful of small villages pockmarked throughout Ezer Szem, bands of near-impenetrable forest separating us from our sisters and brothers. Keszi is the closest to the edge of the wood, though, and so we alone bear the burden of the Woodsmen. I tie off Virág's braids with a strip of leather and resist the urge to correct her.

I could recite her whole story from memory, with the same pauses and intonations, with the same gravity in my voice. More than a century ago, everyone in Régország worshipped our gods. Isten, the sky god, who created half the world. Hadak Ura, who guided warriors toward their killing blows. And Ördög, god of the Under-World, whom we grudgingly acknowledge as the creator of the world's more unsavory half.

Then the Patrifaith arrived, borne by the soldiers and holy men that marched north from the Vespasian Peninsula. We speak of it like a disease, and King István was most horribly afflicted. Spurred by his nascent and feverish devotion, he spread the Patrifaith across all four regions of Régország, killing any man or woman who refused to worship the Prinkepatrios. Followers of the old gods—now called by the new, derisive term *pagans*—fled into the forest of Ezer Szem, building small villages where they hoped to keep their faith in peace, and armoring themselves with the old gods' magic.

"Please, Virág," I beg. "Don't make me hear it again."

"Hush now," she chides. "Have the patience of the great hero Vilmötten when he followed the long stream to the Far North."

"Yes, hush now, Évike," Katalin cuts in gleefully. "Some of us care very much about the history of our people. *My* people—"

Virág silences her with a glare before I can lunge toward her and show her how much damage I can do, magic or not. Almost unconsciously, my hand goes to the other pocket of my cloak, fingering the grooved edges of the golden coin nestled inside. For the briefest moment I really do love Virág, even with all the scars from her lashings latticed across the back of my thighs.

"No fighting today," she says. "Let's not do our enemy's job for them."

She smiles then, extra eyeteeth glinting in the firelight, and the smoke rises in dark clouds around her, as if it's streaming from her skull. Her mouth forms the shape of the words, but she never makes a sound: her eyes roll back in her head and she slumps over, newly plaited hair slipping from my hands like water.

Katalin lurches toward her, but it's too late. Virág writhes on the floor, her neck bent at an odd angle, as though an invisible hand is twisting the notches of her spine. Her chest rises in ragged spasms, breathing dirt—her visions look like someone being buried alive, the fruitless, manic struggle as the earth closes over your head and your lungs fill with soil. Katalin chokes back a sob.

I know what she's thinking: *It could be me*. The visions come without warning, and without mercy. I feel the barest twinge of pity now, as I gather Virág's head into my arms.

Virág's eyes shut. The quaking stops, and she lies as still as a corpse, dirt matted in her white hair. When her eyes open again, they are thankfully, blessedly blue.

Relief floods through me, but it vanishes again in an instant. Virág pushes up from the ground, seizing Katalin by the shoulders, all twelve of her fingers clawing at the fur of her wolf cloak.

"The Woodsmen," she gasps. "They're coming for you."

Something—a laugh or a scream—burns a hole in the cavern of my throat. Katalin is frozen like the trees we tied down, helplessly rooted in place, her mouth hanging slightly ajar. I don't think the realization has hit her yet. She's trapped in that cold, arrested moment before she feels the blade between her shoulders.

But Virág isn't frozen. She gets to her feet, even as she trembles with the ebbing of her vision. Whatever she saw still shudders through her, but the lines of her face are carved deep with determination. She paces the floor of her hut, from the moss clotted in the doorway to the flickering hearth, her eyes trained on something in the middle distance. When her gaze finally snaps back to Katalin and me, she says, "Take off your cloak."

I glance down at my own woolen cloak, brow furrowing. But Virág isn't looking at me.

"My cloak?" Katalin clutches the collar of it, right near the curve of the wolf's open mouth, suspended in an immortal howl.

"Yes. And go fetch a forger."

Virág is already rifling through the salves and tonics on the shelf. With a flustered nod, Katalin hurries out of the hut, leaving her beautiful white cloak pooling on the dirt floor. The sight of it jolts me from my stupor; I snatch it up and hold it up to my cheek, but it feels wrong, as empty and bodiless as a ghost. My mouth tastes like metal.

"Virág, what are you going to do?"

"The Woodsmen want a seer," she says, without looking up. "Keszi cannot spare one."

I don't have time to wonder at her words. Katalin bursts through the threshold again, Zsófia behind her. When she sees me—holding the wolf cloak too—she sucks in a haughty breath, pinched nose flaring. I want to believe that Katalin brought Zsófia just to spite me, but she really is one of the best forgers in the village.

"You must have known it all along," Katalin says wretchedly. "You must have known they wanted a seer."

"I suspected," Virág admits. "But I couldn't know with certainty. I also thought they might perish on their route. I thought perhaps the king would change his mind. But a vision is a vision. Now we don't have much time."

I open my mouth to say something, anything, but Virág's fingers jerk roughly through my hair, smoothing the knots and tangles. I let out a feeble noise of protest. There's a slow panic seeping into my belly.

Virág uncaps a small vial and pours its contents into her hands. It looks like white dust and smells sickly sweet. She works the mixture into my hair as if she were kneading dough for fried flatbread.

"Powdered asphodel," she says. "It will turn your hair white."

"Surely you don't expect the Woodsmen to be deceived by a bit of dye," Zsófia scoffs.

My stomach twists, sharp as a knife. "Virág . . ."

She doesn't say anything. She doesn't look at me. She turns to Zsófia, instead.

"The Woodsmen are not expecting Katalin," she says. "They are merely expecting a seer. Still, you will need to forge some silver."

With an enormous, persecuted sigh, Zsófia leans over and begins to sing—too quietly for me to make out the words, but I know the tune at once. It's the song of Vilmötten. Before doing his great deeds and making deals with gods, Vilmötten was a bard, wandering from town to town with his kantele strapped to his back, hoping to make enough coin for bread and wine. That was the part of the story I liked the best—the part where the hero was just a man.

It's the same song that my mother used to sing to me, cocooned in the safety of our shared hut while thunder and lightning skimmed across the black summer sky. Before I became Virág's reluctant ward.

Before the Woodsmen took my mother from me.

I've only felt fear like this once. It comes back to me in flashes, the memories I've buried down deep. My mother's hand, slipping from mine. The dull gleam of her gray cloak as she vanished into the woods. The lock of hair she'd pressed into my palm, mere moments before she left me for good.

I try to cry out, but the sound gets strangled somewhere in my chest, and comes out a half-formed sob.

I don't care that I'm weeping in front of Katalin and Zsófia. I don't care that Virág might lash me for it; I don't care that this is precise, damning proof of what a coward I really am. All I can see is my mother's face, bleary in my fifteen-year-old memory, fading, fading, fading.

Virág grabs hold of my chin. Through the rheum of tears her mouth is set, her eyes hard.

"Listen to me," she snarls. "We all must do what we can to keep the tribe alive. We cannot allow the king to have the power of a seer. Do you understand?"

"No," I manage, my throat beginning to close. "I don't understand why you want to march me to my death."

Virág lets go of me with a sharp breath, defeated. But the next moment, she's thrusting a small piece of polished metal toward me. I stare at my own face within it, slightly warped by the curves of the forged mirror. Katalin's face hovers behind my own, two polar stars in the darkness of the hut, our hair gleaming like new frost. Mine is not quite white—more of a dingy gray, sooty as liquid steel.

Perhaps it's close enough to swindle a Woodsman, but that's where the similarities end. I'm short and thick-limbed, while Katalin is willow-tree tall, her narrow shoulders shooting up like a proud, thin trunk all long fingers and delicate wrist bones. Her skin has a milky translucence, the blue veins faintly visible, like a webbed leaf shot through with sunlight. My hair is—*was*—a reddish brown, as if my mother's russet mane had been wrung out like water and sieved down to me, my eyes a murky green, my mouth small and scowling. My nose and cheeks are perpetually pink, and there's a grid of whiskery scars across my chin from running face-first into a thicket.

I expect to see her preening, glowing. But Katalin's lovely face looks as horror-struck as mine. In this moment only, we are perfect mirror images of each other.

*Charlatan,* I want to say. *An hour ago you wished I would be taken.*

I reach down to touch the braid in my left pocket, but it brings me no comfort this time.

"Évike." It's Katalin's voice, small and hushed like I've never heard it before. I watch her in the mirror, but I don't turn around. "I didn't mean—"

"You did mean it," I say, my jaw clenched. "Or else you're a liar. What's worse, a liar or a monster?"

She doesn't answer. I expect Virág to reprimand me again, but even she is silent now too. Zsófia's singing has trailed off, the last note of the melody still yet to be hummed. In the quiet space left by her unfinished song, I hear it—the sound of hooves on the ground.

The villagers are gathered into neat rows, backs straight and chins held high as they stare into the mouth of the woods. Women and girls in front, men and boys behind. All blades are sheathed, all arrows held flush in their quivers. The mosquito-flecked evening settles over us like thick linen. Virág leads me through the very center of the crowd, parting the girls in their pristine cloaks. The women and girls all have two faces—the wolf's and their own. Their human faces are schooled into masks, stoic and silent, and even the youngest know well not to shiver. But as I pass between them, their lips purse and their eyes widen. Boróka lets out a tiny gasp, and then claps her hand over her mouth. I can hardly bear to look at her.

And then I can only look at the Woodsmen.

They step forward, through our cowed and impotent trees. Four of them, on obsidian horses, each mount's breast branded with the seal of their holy order. Each Woodsman wears a dolman of finely embroidered silk, and over it, a black suba, the same shaggy woolen cloak favored by herders on the Little Plain. It almost makes me want to laugh, to think of the Woodsmen as humble shepherds. They carry no swords, but there are great steel axes hanging at their hips, so heavy it seems a miracle that they don't topple sideways off their horses.

How did my mother feel, when she saw the horrible glint of those axes?

Three of the Woodsmen have close-cropped hair, mangled scalps visible beneath the tufts that grew back scraggly and uneven. As boys, they grow their hair out long, and then cut it on their eighteenth name days, the same day that the king puts the axes in their hands. They burn all their long hair in a bonfire, sparks and awful smell shooting up into the night sky. It's their sacrifice to the Prinkepatrios, and in return, he promises to answer their prayers.

But real power requires more than hair. My gaze travels to the fourth Woodsman, whose hair is longer, curling in dark ringlets against the nape of his neck. A leather patch is drawn over his left eye. Or the hole where his eye should be.

Only the most dedicated and pious boys part with more than their hair. An eye, an ear, a pink sliver of tongue. Their littlest fingers or the tips of their noses. By the time they're men, many of them are missing tiny pieces.

Every muscle in my body is coiled like a cold snake, tensed with a thousand unmade decisions. I could run. I could scream. I could stammer out the truth to the Woodsmen.

But I can imagine what would happen if I did: those axes swinging through the crowd, slicing through flesh like shears through silk, bone crumbling into pith. Blood dyeing our wolf cloaks red. I remember that my mother went in silence, without tears in her gaze.

I touch her braid in the left pocket of my trousers, the gold coin in my right. I had just enough time to take them before Katalin swapped her cloak for mine.

The one-eyed Woodsman leans close to his compatriot. I can scarcely hear the words he speaks, but they sound something like: "Bring her."

"Igen, kapitány."

For all my newfound bluster, my heart is still pounding a frantic beat. I lean close to Virág, my voice a low, furious whisper. "This won't work. They'll figure out I'm not a seer. And then they'll come back for Katalin, or worse."

"The journey to the capital takes half a moon at best," Virág says, oddly serene. "Enough time for visions to change."

Her words hurt worse than a thousand lashes. I want to ask why she bothered raising me after my mother was taken, only to throw me up as a shield against the Woodsmen at the first opportunity. But I can't say any of that with the Woodsman approaching. And then it occurs to me, terribly, that perhaps I've answered my own question: I was raised like a goose for the slaughter, just in case this moment ever came.

The Woodsman stops his horse mere inches from where I stand and looks down, eyes passing over me as if I were a piece of livestock fettered for auction. "Is this the young seer?"

"Yes," Virág says. "Five and twenty years old and already half as skilled as me."

My cheeks flush. The Woodsman glances back at his captain, who gives one swift, curt nod. Of course he wouldn't ask her to prove it; only a fool would try to cheat the Woodsmen. Then he says, "Get her a mount."

Virág grabs hold of the nearest girl, a young healer named Anikó, and gives her a hushed command. Anikó slips through the row of villagers and disappears. When she emerges a moment later, she's leading a white mare behind her.

The Woodsman slides off his own horse. From the satchel on his hip, he produces a small length of rope. It takes me a moment to realize that he means to bind my hands.

*Were my mother's hands bound, when they took her?* I can't remember. I'm shaking like a sapling in a winter storm.

The Woodsman bends over slightly as he binds me, and from this vantage point, I'm struck by how young he looks, younger even than me. Not more than twenty and the king has already made him a monster.

When he's finished, he takes the mare's lead from Anikó and draws the horse over to me. It's clear that I'm supposed to mount her, but my hands are tied and my knees feel too weak to support my weight.

"Get up, then," the captain says, sensing my hesitation.

My gaze sweeps across the clearing until I meet his eye. It's as black and cold as a new-moon night.

I'm stunned by how quickly the fear floods out of me, leaving only loathing in its wake. I hate him so much that my breath catches. I hate him more than Katalin, more than Virág, more than I ever hated the fuzzy idea of a Woodsman, just a dark shape in my worst dreams. Even though I know he's not nearly old enough to have done it, I hate him for taking my mother away from me.

None of the villagers move as I scramble clumsily onto the mare's back, trembling as if I've been wracked by a vision myself. I can't help but scan the crowd, searching for tearful eyes or grieving mouths, but I only see their impassive masks, pale and blank. Boróka alone looks like she might weep, but her palm is pressed over her lips, fingernails carving bloody crescent moons into the skin of her cheek.

I've long given up on any of them loving me, but I still ache at how easy it is for them to hand me over. I'm a good hunter, one of the best in the village, even if I can't forge my own arrowheads. I spent years doing Virág's drudgery, even if I muttered curses the whole time, and I killed and cleaned half the food on their feast tables.

None of it matters. Without a lick of magic to my name, the only thing I'm good for is a sacrifice.

Now mounted on the mare's back, I grip the reins with numbing fingers. Zsófia styled a section of my hair, grudgingly, into a dozen tiny, intricate braids as thin as fishbones, while the rest hangs down my back, newly white. The wolf cloak sweeps over my shoulder, and I remember all the times I yearned to have one of my own. It feels like Isten playing his cruelest joke.

"Come on," the captain says, voice sharp.

And that's the end of their visit. They come, they take, they leave. Our village has paid its tax—a cruel, human tax—and that's all the Woodsmen want. The cold brevity of it all makes me hate them even more.

My horse trots forward to join the Woodsmen where they stand at the edge of the woods. Their long shadows lap at our village like dark water. As I approach, I hear a fluttering of leaves, a whisper on the wind that sounds almost like my name. More likely it's my wishful imagination, hoping for even a word I could believe was a farewell. The trees do speak, but in a language we all stopped understanding long ago, a language even older than Old Régyar.

I meet the captain's pitiless gaze. I don't look back as my horse crosses the threshold from Keszi into Ezer Szem, but the trees shift behind me, knitting together into a lacework of spindly branches and thorn-limned vines, as if the woods have swallowed me whole.

# CHAPTER TWO

've never been inside the forest at night. As soon as the sun goes down, we don't venture farther than the thin perimeter that surrounds Keszi, where the trees bloom green in summer and shed their leaves in autumn, and we certainly don't wander into the true woods, the thick tangle of forest behind it, seething and dark. Here the trees do not abide by the laws of the gods, to change with the seasons or to grow straight up, slender branches straining toward the sky. We pass trees in their full spring display, lush with verdant leaves and needle-thin white flowers, and then trees that are rotting and dead, blackened all the way down to the roots, as if they've been struck by vengeful lightning. We pass trees that have grown twisted around each other, two wooden lovers locked in eternal embrace, and then others still that bend backward toward the ground, as if their branches are aching toward the Under-World, instead.

I scarcely even think to fear the forest. I am too busy fearing the Woodsmen.

Although I don't care to, I learn their names quickly enough.

The young blond Woodsman who bound me is Imre, the rugged older one with a bow and quiver strapped to his side is Ferkó, and the surly Woodsman behind me is Peti. Whenever I dare to glance over my shoulder, I see Peti staring daggers into my back, almost certainly wishing he could put an ax through it. Eventually I stop looking behind me at all.

"When are you going to dazzle us with your magic, wolf-girl?" Imre asks as we pass by a copse of trees that bear fleshy, foul-smelling fruit the shade of cloudy river water.

I stiffen. *Wolf-girl* is one of their many names for us, but I find it more unbearable than any of the others. After all, I have no magic, and I've done nothing to earn the cloak that hangs spuriously on my shoulders.

"I can't choose when the visions come," I reply, and hope he doesn't notice the way my face burns with the lie.

"A lot of use that is. Don't they teach you a way to call your visions?"

His casual tone frightens me more than Peti's livid silence. No conversation should be easy between predator and prey. "It's not something that can be taught."

"Ah." Imre's blue eyes gleam. "Just as we in the Holy Order of Woodsmen are not taught to hate all pagans with the greatest passion. The loathing is in our blood."

My grip tightens around the reins, stomach roiling. "You must hate me, then."

"Certainly," Imre replies. "But unlike the dullard on your other side, or the simpleton behind, I'd rather pass the time by talking than staring into the darkness and waiting to die."

"Perhaps the rest of us would rather die in silence," Ferkó mutters.

"The Woodsmen do not fear death," Peti speaks up gravely. "The Prinkepatrios welcomes us to eternal glory."

"Only if you die with honor. And I intend to run away screaming the moment I see so much as a pair of eyes in the dark."

"That's not funny," Peti growls, bringing his horse to a canter so he can give Imre a steely glare.

"Don't worry, Peti. I was only teasing. I promise to protect you when the monsters come."

Peti's ear tips turn red. "You're going to tease your way to an early grave."

"Better to die young with a smile on my face than live a long life without laughter."

"If you really believed that, you wouldn't have become a Woodsman," Peti says.

"Quiet." It's the captain's voice. I haven't heard him speak since we entered the woods, and he's quieter now than I expected, almost like he's embarrassed of his authority. Of course I haven't dared to ask his name. On the rare occasions that his soldiers do speak to him, they refer to him only as *kapitány*. He hasn't fixed me with murderous stares like Peti, or tried to goad me into terrifying conversation like Imre, but I fear him worse than both of them put together. Despite the softness of his voice, his missing eye speaks of one thing—a fierce devotion to his god, which means a greater hatred for pagans and wolf-girls than either of these shorn men.

The captain halts on the path. We skid to a stop behind him, and I peer down at the ground, half expecting to see a mangle of entrails or the corpse of something freshly slaughtered. But it's only a circle etched in the dirt. I might have believed it was an accident, maybe an animal dragging its tail on the ground behind it, but then I look again. Farther down the path are cloven prints, and then beyond that, the unmistakable stumbling tracks of a barefooted man. Looking at it makes me feel dizzy and sick.

The footprints lead us away from the circle and toward a tight grove of oak trees. Their leaves are brown, dead, curling like Virág's ancient reed roof. The trunks have the same circle etched into them, and their roots are fetid and black. The smell of spoiled meat blows past us.

"Shall we investigate, kapitány?" Ferkó asks, drawing his ax.

The captain is silent as he glances around the grove. He turns his head fully to either side, so he can examine it all despite his missing eye. For a moment, his gaze lands on me, and my stomach turns into a cold, dark pit.

"No," he says. "Let's move on."


By the time we stop for the night, I have planned my escape seven times.

Leap off my horse and disappear into the trees before the Woodsmen can think to stop me. Cut the rope around my wrists on a sharp rock and flee back to Keszi. Pray to Isten that the Woodsmen die in the forest somewhere and never come to find me. Pray the king doesn't decide to punish all of Keszi for my ruse and burn our village to the ground like his great-grandfather, Saint István, did to the rest of the pagan tribes.

I would rather stare down the awful rotted heart of the forest than face the Woodsmen and their axes. I know it makes me a coward, and perhaps also a fool. But my mother's fate is a flitting bird I refuse to follow. I can't swallow the thought of the Woodsmen killing the little part of her that's left in me, the facsimile of our shared blood.

We are finally allowed to camp in a small clearing, gridded by a copse of birch trees, their pale skin half-shed. Spirals of birch paper are littered in the dead grass, and there is still the faint but unmistakable scent of meat left out too long in the sun. Peti and Ferkó scout the area for safety, axes drawn. I can't help but eye the bow and quiver on Ferkó's back, muscles twitching with deep-rooted memory. I will never shoot an arrow again. Imre collects logs and dry leaves for a fire, and sets them on the ground in front of the captain. I stand pressed to my mare's flank, wrists still painfully bound.

The captain removes his gloves and clasps his bare hands

together. For a moment I think he might start to pray, and want to turn away in revulsion. But he only utters a single word: "Megvilágit."

He says it almost as if it were a question, or a polite request, the same deferential tenor to his voice that shocked me before. And then a fire roars to life in front of him.

I cannot help the sound of alarm that slips out from between my lips, nor the accusation that follows it. "I thought Woodsmen decried all acts of magic."

"It's not magic," Imre says, stoking the fire with a birch-striped tree branch. "It's faith. The only powers we have are what Godfather Life gives us. We ask, and He answers."

"Does he always answer?"

A shadow darkens the captain's face.

"He rewards loyalty," says Imre. "The more devotion you prove, the greater powers He grants you. I don't think He has ever refused a request from the Érsek."

I meet his gaze, shivering, wanting to ask who the Érsek is but not sure I can risk another question.

"The Érsek is the highest religious authority in Régország," Imre says, preempting me, "and the king's closest confidant. Király és szentség, royalty and divinity. Think of them like twin pillars that hold up the kingdom."

I would rather not think of them at all. There's no place for wolf-girls in such a kingdom. As the captain's fire burns, I remember all the times I tried to light one of my own. How many hours I spent hunched over Virág's hearth, desperate to will a weak little flame onto my fingertips. Virág would stand above me, arms folded crossly, repeating the same adages that had never done me any good before.

"In order to perform the skills, you must know the origin of them," she'd said. "Do you remember the story of how Vilmötten first made fire? Late one night, Isten tossed a star out of the sky. Vilmötten watched it fall down to the Middle-World and sink into the sea. He dove into the water after it, hoping to rescue the star and win Isten's favor. When he reached the bottom of the ocean, he saw that the star was bright with blue flame, even underwater. He could not hold it and swim at the same time, so he put the star in his mouth and swallowed it. And when Vilmötten returned to the surface, the star was still breathing inside him, and he could summon fire without a flint."

"I know the story," I had snapped. "I just can't do it."

Virág would sigh and shake her head, or if she were in a particularly bitter mood, order me to scrub her tunic clean as punishment for my failure and my foul mouth. But after a while she gave up watching me crouch futilely over her hearth, and I gave up trying to do magic at all. Fire-making was meant to be the simplest of the three skills. If I couldn't manage that, how could I ever hope to forge metal or heal wounds?

I had always thought that somehow she was playing me for a fool, like there was some secret she and the rest of the women knew and were all gleefully keeping from me. I knew the stories as well as any of them, but it still wasn't enough. It was better than thinking that I'd been cursed, or that there was something strange and ruinous in my blood.

I want to reach for the gold coin in my pocket now, but my hands are tied. On the other side of the fire, the captain is laying out his mat. There's a small knife strapped to his boot, right below the crook of his knee, steel handle glinting in the firelight.

"The area looks clear, kapitány," Peti says. "I'll take first watch."

I wonder if he means watching me, or watching for something in the woods that we could never hope to see before it kills us. *Ezer Szem* means *thousand-eyed*. If you stare long enough into the darkness of the forest, eventually something will stare right back.

Exhaustion has begun to eat away at my fear, eroding it

like the riverbank after a rainstorm. There's no way to tell how long we've been in the woods, but my body aches as if I've been riding for a day or more. Imre and Ferkó pad down beside the fire, resting their heads on their packs.

The captain looks at me expectantly, his single eye unblinking. When I don't move, his fingers go to his ax, and he draws it with an odd, mortified hesitation, like he can't quite gauge the weight of it in his hands. *Stupid,* I think of my own evaluation. He and his blade have both been honed for killing pagan girls like me.

He closes the space between us in three long strides. I imagine the trajectory of his ax—the arc it would have to follow to meet my throat. But perhaps I can better estimate the danger by looking in his eye. It's angled downward, lashes casting a feathery shadow across his cheekbone.

Without speaking, the captain thrusts the hilt of his ax against my back, right between the blades of my shoulders. Through my wolf cloak and my tunic beneath, I can feel the press of the wood, its muffled meanness. The captain swallows, throat bobbing.

My legs tremble as I lower myself to the ground. I wonder if he recognizes the fettered hatred in the grit of my teeth, or if he only sees my white-faced fear. I wonder if it brings him pleasure, to see me on my knees. I don't breathe again until the captain returns to his own mat, even if his one black eye is still watching me.

I'm supposed to sleep. But my gaze keeps drawing back to the blade on his boot.


Night falls differently in Ezer Szem. The wind goes silent when the sun goes down. The shadows mottle themselves into shapes that look like claws and teeth. After a few hours, the fire is smoldering, more ash than flame, and I can't see farther than a few feet in front of me. I can only hear the soft, sleeping exhales of the Woodsmen and the crackle of dead leaves as something moves behind the tree line.

I can't steal the captain's knife without waking him. But maybe I can slip away while they're asleep and vanish into the darkness of the woods. I'll take my chances with monsters. The Woodsmen are worse.

Jaw clenched, I push myself up onto my elbows, then my knees. I shimmy onto the balls of my feet and stand, wincing as my sore muscles arch and bend. I take two preliminary paces backward, pausing to listen for the sound of someone stirring. Nothing. I turn to face the cold, solid blackness.

I haven't gone more than fifty paces away from camp when something catches the collar of my cloak. A scream boils in my belly, but I swallow it down. I try to adjust my eyes, to see what awful creature has gotten ahold of me. But all I can hear is heavy human breathing. A hot, mortal hand grazes the skin of my throat.

Out of the darkness, a lantern blazes gauzy and yellow, il-luminating a crescent of its face: a stubbled chin and nose red with broken blood vessels. It's no monster. It's Peti.

I let out a breath that sounds like shaky laughter. My escape plan is foiled before it's even begun, and I'm a daft, doomed fool. "What are you going to do with me?"

"What our captain doesn't have the piety to do," he says, and draws his ax.

I realize at once that I've made a terrible mistake. There's nothing human about Peti's face at all. His lips pull back into a snarl, showing all the icicle points of his teeth, and even the whites of his eyes are burning, stitched through with red.

The lantern falls to the ground, the light half-obscured by dead leaves. In the muffled glow I see the flash of Peti's ax, and I roll out of the way, almost too late. With a furi-ous howl, Peti leaps on top of me, pinning me to the grass. I struggle against his weight, but he's too strong and my limbs are flailing uselessly as he grits his teeth and pulls a dagger from the shaft of his boot.

Sweat clings to his face in a sickly sheen, cast a livid green by the lantern light. Peti is breathing hard, his heart pounding wildly against our adjacent chests, like someone is hammering on the door of my rib cage. Animal instinct edges out the fear. Driven by a mad, frantic desire to live, I lift my head and sink my teeth into his ear.

He screams, and I jerk back with as much force as I can. Blood spurts through the air and lands in thick strands on my wolf cloak, on Katalin's beautiful white wolf cloak. Peti rolls off me, sobbing and clutching the side of his head.

I spit muscle and sinew out of my mouth and wipe his blood from my face.

"You wanted a wild wolf-girl," I say in a strangled voice that doesn't sound at all like my own. "You got one."

"Not me," Peti groans. "The king. He hasn't—he won't do what needs to be done. He'll let his country burn before he rids the country of the pagan scourge."

His words chill me. I tell myself they're the ramblings of a madman with one fewer ear than most. But my moment of bewilderment gives him an opportunity. He's on top of me once again, blade flush against my throat.

"You don't deserve the dignity of a swift death," he growls. The knife digs into my skin. Not deep enough to kill, but enough to draw a collar of beaded red around my neck. Enough to make me stammer out a sob and squeeze my eyes shut. At least I can choose to die without looking at his face, terrible and stupid with bloodlust.

Then his weight vanishes from my chest. I open my eyes to see the captain lift Peti's body off me and throw him to the ground, limp and boneless. For a moment, my heart staggers with relief, almost gratitude, before loathing takes hold of me again. I hate the cold blackness of the captain's eye and the sharp cut of his jaw even as he pulls Peti off me.

Peti cowers under the gleam of the captain's ax, weeping.

"Your orders were to bring the wolf-girl to the capital, not to mutilate and murder her," the captain says, raising his voice over the sound of Peti's wailing.

"Király és szentség!" he bawls. "The king only commands half my loyalty. I must do what is right by the one true god, and by Nándor—"

"It was the king who put the ax in your hand," the captain cuts in, but I see something that looks like panic dart across his face. "You betrayed the Crown."

"What about her?" Peti raises a trembling finger and points at me. "She dishonors the very name of Régország with her filthy pagan magic."

The captain's gaze flickers briefly over me, an unreadable expression in his eye. "Her fate is for the king to decide."

Imre and Ferkó both come running, hair mussed and axes in their hands.

"What's going on?" Imre demands.

"She bit off my ear," Peti whimpers.

"You tried to kill me," I remind him, my voice shaking.

"Traitor." Ferkó spits on the ground in front of him. "You know the king's orders."

"And should I follow the orders of a king who defies the will of God?" The wild, wheeling look of desperation in Peti's eyes fades. For a moment there's something more lucid about him, blood trickling from the ruin of his ear. "When there is another who ought to wear the crown, and will honor the Prinkepatrios in his reign? Nándor—"

"Don't." The word huffs out of the captain's mouth in a white cloud. "Don't say his name again."

Imre's brows pull together, but his grip on the ax doesn't slacken. "You know the punishment for treachery, Peti."

Weeping again, Peti doesn't reply.

The captain glances between Ferkó and Imre. "Hold him down."

Together the Woodsmen lurch toward him, and Peti howls. They wrestle him onto his back, pinning his arms flat, limbs spread-eagled. I watch and watch, horror building in my chest. The captain stands at Peti's feet, hairs rising on his black suba. In the lantern light, Peti's face is slick with tears.

Imre kneels on Peti's hand, keeping his arm pressed to the ground. He unsheathes the knife from his boot and thrusts the hilt of it into Peti's mouth.

"Bite down," Imre says. I realize with a start that his face is damp too.

A word of protest rises in my throat, but I remember the mad, monstrous look on Peti's face as he pressed his blade to my skin, and the word dies before I can speak it.

The captain brings down his ax in a neat arc, right below Peti's left shoulder. The swift scything of the ax ruffles the hairs of his suba, and when the blade buries itself in the earth, they lie flat again.

For a long moment, the forest is silent. Ferkó and Imre get to their feet. The captain lifts his ax, the sickled edge of the blade dripping something viscous and black. With bleary, languid movements, as if he's just been woken from slumber, Peti shifts on the grass, raising his head. When his torso rises, his arm doesn't come with it.

I see the white knob of bone jutting from his shoulder, and the jewel-hued mangle of flesh, red as overripe berries. I see the ragged flaps of skin draped over the sudden termination of his arm, fluttering limply in the scant breeze.

The knife falls out of Peti's mouth. He screams, louder than anything I have heard before. My stomach clenches like a fist and I double over, palms pressed against the damp earth, retching.

# CHAPTER THREE

Peti weeps through the night, without ceasing. After Ferkó takes a heated blade to his shoulder, Imre packs his wound with strips of burlap and leather, and fistfuls of dry leaves webbed together by sap. I watch them, huddled by the vanishing fire, my mouth still tasting of bile. The captain stands over Peti's lost limb and clasps his hands, whispers his deferent prayer. Blue-white flame streaks across the length of his severed arm, bright as the tail of a comet. Peti's fingers melt like nubs of candle wax. His knucklebones puddle in the dirt, some strange white flora. I think I might be sick again.

A pitiful dawn creeps over the forest, the pinks and golds of sunrise strained through the dark latticework of tree branches and bracken, squeezing out their color. All that reaches me is a bleached yellow light. It falls on my shaking hands, nicked with tiny scratches from palm to fingernail, and the splatter of dried bloodstains on my wolf cloak. It falls on the captain, turning his black suba silvery with dust motes. It falls on Peti, his chest rising in fits and starts, every breath a violence. His white lips part with a guttering moan.

"You're going to bring every godforsaken monster in Ezer Szem right to us," Ferkó growls. He nudges Imre's knife toward Peti with the toe of his boot. "Bite down on this, if you must."

Peti doesn't reply. His eyelashes give a limp, moth-wing flutter.

Neither the Woodsmen nor I have slept. The wound on my throat is still wet, and it opens whenever I try to speak, so I keep my lips pressed firm. I am focusing on quelling the roil of my stomach when the captain stalks toward me, dead leaves crunching with every step.

"Stand up," he says.

My heart stutters as I rise to my feet. Now that I know the king wants me delivered to the capital unharmed, I ought to feel emboldened. But the memory of his blade swinging through Peti's arm ebbs some of that nascent bluster. A vow to the king still seems a flimsy shield to put between the captain's ax and me.

"I suppose I should thank you," I say, throat dry. "For saving my life."

Without meeting my gaze, the captain says, "I find no glory in saving wolf-girls, and I don't uphold my oath for your gratitude."

Anger burns in my chest. The Woodsmen are as pious as they are cruel, and any vengeance they may want to have upon me is tempered by their stupid devotion. "You must regret it, then."

"I didn't say that." He gives me one swift, probing glare. "And you may very well have managed without my help. You bit off Peti's ear."

I feel a little flush of shame, only because I have confirmed Woodsman stories about pagan barbarity. But then I remember the arc of the captain's ax, the patch over his missing eye, and the shame dies as quickly as a snuffed candle.

"I thought that missing body parts make the Woodsmen more powerful," I say. "Perhaps he should have thanked me."

"There is no such thing as the power of the Woodsmen," says the captain. "There is only the power of the Prinkepatrios as it flows through us, and we are His humble servants."

"We in Keszi don't fear servants. We fear brutes with axes."

I wait to see if my needling has stuck him. But the captain just arches a brow. He doesn't speak like a brute with an ax. His voice is measured, and his words have an easy eloquence. A particularly clever soldier, I decide. But a soldier all the same.

"You must also fear the wrath of your gods," he says finally, "if you dare to stray from their righteous path."

"No," I reply, taken aback. "Our gods don't ask us for perfection."

Just as we don't expect rhyme or reason from our gods. They're fickle and stubborn and heedless and indulgent, like us. The only difference is that they burn whole forests to the ground in their rage, and drink entire rivers dry in their thirst. In their joy, flowers bloom; in their grief, early winter frost edges in. The gods have gifted us a small fragment of that power, and in turn we inherited their vices.

From what I understand, the Prinkepatrios has no vices, and it would be blasphemy to even suggest such a thing. But how did a perfect being create something as imperfect as humans, so prone to caprice and cruelty? And why does a perfect being demand blood from little boys?

I look at the captain—really look at him—for the first time. He has the olive skin of a Southerner and a long nose with a harsh break at its bridge. But there's nothing harsh about the rest of his face. It's shockingly youthful, smooth except for the faint stubble bruising his throat and chin. When he turns and I see only the untarnished half of his face, it's almost regal, the kind of profile you might find on a minted coin. I imagine that if he lived in Keszi, Írisz or Zsófia might drag him down for some furtive coupling by the riverside, and he'd come back with a sheepish, knowing smile on his swollen lips. But I can't see the left half of his face without wondering morbidly what lies beneath the black patch, and how he ever summoned the strength to pluck out his own eye like a crow picking over a corpse. Or wondering if that sort of dedication disgusts or impresses me.

What would I have plucked out, to be able to call fire?

"That's just as well." The captain seems to notice how intently I am staring at him, and he lowers his gaze. There's even the barest flush on his cheeks. "Your gods may be mere illusions crafted by the demon Thanatos, but they do grant you potent magic. Why didn't you use your magic against Peti?"

I detect no trace of suspicion in his voice, but my skin prickles all the same. "I—my hands were bound. I couldn't summon it."

The captain nods slowly, lips pressed together. For a moment I can't tell whether he believes me or not. And then he says, "Give me your hands."

Instinctively, my fingers curl into my palms. The rope is still chafing against the tender skin on the insides of my wrists, leaving a rash of red.

Behind us, Peti moans. Very carefully, the captain looses the rope, giving it just enough slack for me to wriggle my hands free. Before the prospect of escape even flits through my mind, the captain's fingers close around my wrist. The pressure of his grip fills me with a mute, terrible fear, freezing me in place.

He turns to Ferkó and Imre. "Get him up."

The two Woodsmen bend over Peti, hefting him to his feet. Peti gives a gurgling cry, spittle foaming in his open mouth. Through the skeins of leather and the mesh of dead leaves, there is a slow seep of blood flowering from his shoulder, like the beginnings of a spring ice melt. Clearly the captain's attempt to cauterize the wound went poorly. My stomach dips.

Ferkó and Imre shuffle Peti toward me, and the captain takes his good arm. I realize what's happening only a heartbeat before the captain loops the other end of my rope around Peti's hand, joining us at the wrist.

A stammer of revulsion tips past my lips. "You can't—"

"I can't have you trying to escape again," says the captain. I don't think I'm imagining the note of regret in his voice, nor the dark pall that casts over his face, but it does nothing to calm the fury and horror boiling in my belly. What little gratitude I had toward him for saving my life slivers away, like a crescent moon turning new. His dainty flushes and proud nose, the pliant tenor of his voice—all of it is a veneer for his barbarity. I would rather Peti, with his frothing hatred, his openly bared teeth. With my free hand, I touch the wound circling my neck, blood pooled in the hollow of my collarbone. I've already seen the worst of what he can do.

The captain turns away from us and stalks toward his horse. I watch the bulk of his retreating back, measuring my breaths. With my gashed throat, my loathing aches even more to swallow.

I feel a tug on my rope. Peti has bent at the waist, coughing blood.

I took for granted the life of the forest, unsettling as it was, all those mightily twisting oaks and globular gray fruits. Now all the color has been drained from Ezer Szem. The bark on the trees is dull pewter, and all the foliage has fallen away, leaving the branches gnarled and bare. Even the ground beneath our feet feels firmer, colder, as if the horses are walking on stone instead of dirt. There's no tree cover, but I still can't see the sky—a frigid mist has stolen over us, blanketing our convoy in a nearly impermeable haze.

Peti rocks against my chest, groaning. We have both been propped on the back of my white mare, Peti in front of me, his knees braced around my horse's neck. His hand fists her mane, knuckles pale. Where our wrists are joined, I can feel the cold slickness of his skin, as if he's been doused in filmy pond water.

All around us, the forest has gone silent. Where there was once the crackle of dead leaves or the faint patter of footsteps, now there's nothing, not even the whispering of wind. My heart is a riot, but my stomach is pure ice. I think that perhaps the forest is showing me what a fool I am, to forget my fear of it in favor of the Woodsmen.

"Wolf-girl," Peti whispers. His head rolls backward, onto my shoulder.

"Don't," I bite out. "Don't speak."

"Do you know what will be done with you?" Peti presses on. I can't see his eyes, but the back of his neck, the skin of his jaw—it's all a marbled gray, the color of lichen on a log. "When you reach the capital. The king, the weak heathen of a king . . . no, not him, his son . . ."

I straighten my back, trying to shift his weight off me. "Do you mean the prince?"

The king has a bevy of bastards, but only one true-born son. The black prince, we call him, an epithet that's more like an elision, a beat of silence between breaths. We in Keszi know so little of him, only that he's the offspring of Régország's long-dead and much-loathed foreigner queen, a footnote in the folk tune that we call the Song of the Five Kings.

*First came King István, his cape as white as snow,*
*Then his son, Tódor, who set the North aglow,*
*After there was Géza, whose beard was long and*
*    gray,*
*Finally, King János—*
*And his son, Fekete.*

"Not the prince," murmurs Peti. His breath curls, white with cold. "His other son. His *true* son. Nándor."

My shoulders rise. It's the second time I've heard that name. I remember the shadow that fell over the captain's face when Peti invoked Nándor before, and I glance toward him now. His horse is several paces ahead, wreathed in mist, just a black smear in the haze of gray.

"Nándor," I repeat, skin prickling. "What does he mean to do with me, then?"

Peti's mouth opens and closes mutely, like a carp washed up on the riverbank. He leans over the side of the horse and retches, blood and bile splattering the path.

My vision ripples. The smell of him is worse than anything, worse than his clammy touch, the rimy gleam of his skin, worse even than the black stain soaking through the tangle of dead leaves and burlap on his shoulder, his makeshift bandages. Worse than the stomach-clenching sensation of looking for his arm and realizing with a start that it's not there, the morbid blank space of it. Peti smells like the green rot of damp wood, mold-slicked, dying. I try to hold my breath.

He mumbles something in Old Régyar, raising his good hand, and mine along with it, to wipe the sick from his chin.

Revulsion snares in me like a fishhook, twining with something lower, worse. I remember one of Katalin's cruelest and cleverest tricks. We were both girls then, not long after my mother had been taken, and she asked me to play a game. My heart had leapt at her invitation, eager for even the unlikely prospect of friendship. She told me to go hide somewhere in the woods, and she would look for me. I bedded down in a snarl of bracken and dug a small hole for my chin in the dirt. I waited and waited, until the patches of sky visible between the fingers of briar and the swaying willow fronds turned a deep, glossy blue. The chill of dusk lay over me like a second cloak, and all of a sudden the shadows of the trees looked like gaping mouths and the bramble holding me was not a cradle but a cage. I fled from my hiding place, thorns snatching at my clothes, and stumbled weeping into Keszi.

Virág was baffled by my tears. "Why didn't you just come out?"

I blinked helplessly at Katalin, too shaken to speak.

She blinked back at me, cunningly guileless. "I looked for you everywhere. I couldn't find you."

I only understood later why it was such a flawless ruse. She'd left no evidence of her wicked intent, no wound I could point to and say, *See, she hurt me.* When I tried to articulate my pain, I'd only seemed like a jabbering child. Why hadn't I just come out, after all? Everyone knows the forest is dangerous at night.

Watching Peti die against me feels like waiting for Katalin in the woods. It's my own revulsion and terror, my own misplaced pity and guilt that's wounding me, nothing more. I hate the captain for binding me to my own helplessness. I hate him so much that it's a heat unfolding in my chest, livid and breathless.

All of a sudden, my horse stops. She presses close to Imre's black steed, ears pulled flat against her ivory head.

"Do you hear that?" Imre asks. His pale lashes are clumped with tiny pearls of ice. In the distance, almost too far away to notice, there is a slow, measured rustling.

"It's Peti," Ferkó says, bringing his horse to my other side. "The monsters in the wood can hear him moaning from miles away. It's drawing them out of their dens and—"

The captain circles back toward us, hand on his ax. There's a sprinkling of white in his dark curls, a coronet of frost.

"Keep quiet," he snaps, but his throat is pulsing.

Peti stills against me. We say nothing as the rustling grows louder. Closer. I can feel my mare's chest heaving between my thighs. Imre draws his ax and Ferkó draws his bow and we all push together, a single mass of huge human prey.

The fog spits something onto the path in front of us. All four horses rear, whinnying madly, and Peti slides off my mare, pulling me down with him. I land on my back against the hard, cold earth, too shocked to even scream.

"Stop!" the captain cries.

"It's a chicken," Imre says.

A solitary hen is pecking its way across the path, oblivious to the chaos it has created. Its feathers are as shiny as polished obsidian. Even its beak and comb are black.

I can't help myself. I start to laugh. I laugh so hard that my eyes water, even as my mare trots anxious circles in the path, snorting in reproach. Imre is laughing, too, and the sound chases the remnants of fear from my heart and melts the ice in my belly. The captain looks at me as if I've grown seven heads.

"Is that the worst you have to offer?" Imre asks the woods, once his hysteria has subsided. "A black hen?"

The dead trees whisper an unintelligible reply. The captain leaps down from his horse, boots thudding. I push myself onto my elbows, a knot of panic rising in my throat once more.

But the captain doesn't approach me. He kneels beside Peti and removes one glove, pressing two fingers against the column of his throat. The gentleness of it knocks the breath from me, and I have to remind myself what it is that I've seen: the gleam of his ax in the dark, the swift certainty of his fingers as he yoked my wrist to Peti's.

The captain lifts his head. There's a wet sheen over his black eye, like the pond on a starless night. "He's dead."

There's no more laughter.

We see three more chickens on our route, while the fog begins to thin and the forest grows sparser around us. As we press on, the trees give way to grassy flatlands, and black pieces of night sky dagger through the mist. The glaze of frost melts from our hands and faces. When I get my first glimpse of the lake, it's all I can do to stop myself from leaping off my horse and bounding toward it, so grateful to be out of the woods.

The Black Lake stretches all the way to the horizon, wisps of fog hovering over its surface like steam hissing out of a pot. Beneath the mist, it glitters darkly under a white sliver of moon, the reflection of the stars speckling its surface. It looks like a pool of night, and I almost believe I could dip my hand into the water and pluck out a jewel-bright star for myself.

"It's beautiful," Imre whispers. Ferkó sinks to his knees, whispering prayers in the Old Tongue, eyes closed as the wind sweeps across his reverent face.

"It should be a safe place to camp," the captain says, unmoved.

I don't expect such exuberance from him regardless, but I can tell Peti's fate is tempering his relief. After Peti died, the captain laid one hand over his face, brushing his eyes gently shut. He pulled his legs straight, ankles touching, and placed his good arm over his chest, in some awkward approximation of slumber. It was too stiff to be real sleep, too self-consciously pious, just like the captain himself. Seeing it filled me with my own awful grief, knowing I would have no such ceremony of my own. There would be no one to close my sightless eyes or worry over the position of my limbs. If my body even survived my death, that is—no one in Keszi knows what the king does with his wolf-girls. Only that they never come back.

Then the captain clasped his hands, whispered his prayer, and Peti's body went up in flame and smoke.

Now I watch the captain climb down from his mount and kneel before the Black Lake. He removes his gloves and dips his bare hands in the water. His penitence pricks me like a thorn. Will the captain grow somber and grim after my death too? I doubt it very much. Among the Woodsmen, I imagine a wolf-girl being killed is cause for great cheer.

Imre tugs the end of the rope snarled around my wrists, leading me toward the beginnings of their campsite. There is already a bed of cold wood, and a cast-iron kettle, rusted around its edges. We will have to boil the water before we can drink it. The Black Lake is touched with salt, as if Isten carved out a hole in the earth and then poured the ocean into it to make Régország its own tiny, landlocked sea. Beyond it is the Little Plain, a scraggly prairie flecked with salt flats and occasional stretches of marshland, spilling out beside the tributaries that carve the land like a cracked mirror. It marks the western edge of Farkasvár, the region containing Keszi, which King István made when he diced up old tribal territories into tidy new districts and installed a preening count to rule over each one.

The captain lights a fire on the bank and Imre sets his kettle over it. He boils tough game and vegetables for stew, the onion stinging my eyes but making my belly whine. With the captain's brutal pace, I haven't eaten at all since leaving Keszi.

It should be unthinkable to share a meal with the Woodsmen. I don't want to acknowledge that we have anything in common—even something as small and silly as liking this stew. It's the same kind of lean meal we would eat in Keszi, scrounged together in the dead of winter when our stores have nearly been emptied. It reminds me of home, and I don't want the Woodsmen poisoning my memories. Along with my coin and my braid, and Katalin's wolf cloak, they're all that I have left.

But I'm hungry. Every bite of the stew feels treacherous, and I think, suddenly and viciously, of Katalin. *My people,* she said. Virág had stopped her before she finished, but I know what she would have said. That I don't belong in Keszi. That half my blood is tainted, and I'll never really be one of them.

A true wolf-girl would have refused the stew. She would let herself starve rather than making nice with Woodsmen.

My relief at making it out of the woods is corroded by the knowledge that we are growing closer to Király Szek. Closer to my end. I only have the vague shape of it in my mind, the icy claw of fear around my heart, the taste of blood on my tongue. I would rather know how I will die than spend the journey wondering whether it will be by blade or by fire.

"What do you expect is waiting for you when we reach Király Szek?" I ask carefully. "A personal commendation from the king? A festival in your honor?"

Imre snorts. "I'm just hoping one of the other soldiers hasn't stolen my cot."

"Is this your first mission, as a Woodsman?"

"My first into Ezer Szem. We go all over Régország, many places other than the woods. I suppose the name *Woodsman* is a bit misleading."

I want to ask what they do when they're not fighting monsters or abducting wolf-girls, but I'm not sure I will like the answer. So instead I say, "I thought that's what the king's army is for."

"The king's army has been tied up on the border for twelve years. There are scarcely enough soldiers left to guard the capital."

I draw an uneasy breath. I don't like thinking of the Woodsmen doing the work of regular soldiers. It's more difficult to loathe them if I imagine they are fighting only for gold, hoping to one day go home to their families.

"Don't look so disappointed," Imre says, noticing my startled expression. "Most of us are still God-fearing men. Some more than others."

"Like Peti."

Imre gives an embattled sigh. "Peti was not a particularly pious man; he was only a wide-eyed simpleton, an easy mark for those with cunning tongues. He believed, as many other desperate peasants have been led to, that the presence of pagans in Régország is the cause of all our kingdom's ills."

This startles me too. We have the occasional bad harvest in Keszi, or the especially bitter winter, but we can only blame ourselves for that, or our fickle gods. Some years, Ördög is stronger, and sickness claims more of our people. When Isten manages to wrest back control, however—like the sun rising after a long night—we have bountiful, verdant springs, and a glut of new baby girls.

Of course, some years the Woodsmen come, and that is far worse than a bad harvest, or even the wiles of Ördög.

"What sort of ills?" I ask.

"Mostly the war," says Imre. "I've heard the front line is soaked with Régyar blood. Merzan seems to grow stronger every day."

News of the war rarely makes its way to Keszi. I know only the barest facts: three decades ago, King Bárány János married a Merzani princess in an effort to forge an alliance with our powerful neighbors to the south. It worked, for a time. She even bore him a son. But Merzan was too ambitious and Régország too stubborn. When the queen died, any hope of peace perished with her.

"It's better not to agonize over such things," Imre says finally. "The war is going badly. The winter will be long. If Godfather Life wills it so, He must have a reason. We are trained to serve, not to ask questions."

I remember how the fire roared to life in front of the captain, so sudden and sure. Any wolf-girl would have marveled at such a fire, easily as impressive as the work of our best fire-makers. We would have called it power, magic. They called it piety. But what is the difference, if both fires burn just as bright?

The wind sings through the cattails, blowing fog from the lake. The false stars dotting the surface of the water wink like celestial eyes. Ferkó has already bedded down for the night, and soon Imre rolls over to join him. The captain, whom I did not see eat a bite of stew or swallow a sip of water, folds his arms in front of the fire. With the smear of the woods at our backs and only the pale, empty stretch of the Little Plain before us, it is finally safe for our whole convoy to sleep at once. But

I stay awake, warming my sinful pagan body by the light of Godfather Life's flames, battling the heaviness of my eyelids.

The captain's knife is glinting on his boot. Perhaps I can still be a true wolf-girl tonight.


By the time the Woodsmen have fallen asleep, I can barely shake off oblivion myself. Exhaustion has crowded my head like a flock of screeching birds. My vision is blurring and sharpening by turns, making me dizzy. When I hear a rustling in the bramble to my right, I scarcely even jump.

It's the same hen from the woods, feathers black as a slick of lake water, pecking its way toward me. Fear has turned my throat raw, so I swallow hard and mutter, "Stop scaring me."

The hen cocks its head.

Then it explodes.

At least, that's what it seems to do. There's a flurry of feathers, a puff of smoke that reeks worse than the rot of Peti's wound. And when the air clears, something that is not a chicken stands before me.

The creature looks almost human—just human enough to make my breath catch. Its gray-green skin is pulled taut over its spine and rib cage, the bones close to breaking through. Its head dangles perilously on a scrawny neck, black tongue unfurling over a row of blade-sharp teeth. Its tongue lolls on the ground as the creature crawls toward me on all fours, hissing and groaning. Its eyes are not eyes at all. They are twin clusters of flies gathered on its gaunt face.

I scramble back toward the fire, a scream rattling in my chest. Three more creatures are creeping through the brush, the hairs on their ridged backs bristling in the cold air. They crawl towards Ferkó and Imre, nosing the wet earth blindly, steered by scent alone.

I do scream, finally, when one of the creatures takes a bite out of Ferkó's skull.

The creature swallows a hunk of flesh and muscle, blood streaming onto the grass. Ferkó's skin flaps in the wind like a blown dress, exposing the plank of bone beneath it, right below his eye socket.

Imre jerks up with a start, but he doesn't have time to shake off the bleariness of sleep. Another creature lunges at him, its teeth in his throat. The gurgling sound he makes as he chokes on his own blood is worse than the sight of it, worse than watching the creature chew his red muscle and swallow.

My own creature circles me in a lazy, curious way, as if trying to decide whether I'm worth the effort of eating.

The rope on my wrists has loosened enough that I can slip it off with my teeth, but it doesn't do me much good. I have no weapon, only the blackened logs of the fire to my rear and the useless wet grass beneath me; Ferkó's bow is blood-drenched and much too far away. The monster knuckles another step forward. It has human hands with ragged yellow fingernails.

"Please," I gasp. "Isten . . ."

But it's been so long since I've prayed that I can't remember what I'm meant to say. *Let me light one fire,* I think desperately. *Let me forge one blade, and I'll never feel sorry for myself ever again.*

None of that happens, though. Instead, the air whistles as the captain brings his ax down on the creature's back. There's a crunch of bone and the monster drops to the ground, crumpling like a poorly pitched tent.

Fear and panic roar in me as loudly as river water in a rainstorm. Amidst the churning of it, the chaos, I can only remember one thing—my hatred for the Woodsmen. I lurch to my feet, half-stumbling, and snatch the captain's knife from his boot. I lift it over my head, angling for a killing blow.

"Are you mad?" the captain bellows. He dodges my knife easily, then whirls and cuts down another creature, its face caving in beneath the blade of his ax.

The other two creatures abandon Ferkó and Imre and pace

a tightening circle, herding us toward the lake. I step down into the cold water, my arm shooting out to keep my balance, and find myself back-to-back with the captain. We move farther in until I am drowned up to my waist, and the beasts are paddling toward us, the flies that are their eyes buzzing plaintively. Their teeth are red with Woodsman blood.

One of them springs toward me, out of the water, and I duck down, letting it land thrashing on top of me. I bite back a scream as its mouth closes over my shoulder blade. As quickly as a braid of pain laces down my arm, a sudden flood of anger edges it out. I'm infuriated that I might die so banally, not by the swing of King János's blade, but snapped up in the jaws of some nameless monster. From this vantage point, I stick my knife between its protruding ribs and give it a vicious twist. The monster falls back with a squeal, wound leaking.

The captain is wrestling his own creature, which is still fighting even with its left arm nearly cleaved from its body. The arm hangs on with only thin strands of muscle and sinew. The captain swings at the beast but misses. His movements are clumsy; the ax seems too heavy in his hands, and for a moment I'm stunned by his fumbling ineptitude. The creature manages to tear a chunk of fabric from the captain's dolman, leaving a swath of his bronze skin exposed.

The Woodsman spins wildly in the water, his head moving rapidly from left to right, trying to make up for his blind spot. Acting on instinct, I shift to guard the captain's left side, and when the monster lunges again, both of our weapons meet in the very center of its chest, metal rasping against metal. With a shriek, the creature falls back into the lake.

For one long moment, its body is wracked with terrible spasms. Blood pools in the water around it, dark and sickly, reeking like the green rot of Ezer Szem. Then, abruptly, the splashing stops. The flies cease their buzzing. There is only the sound of the captain breathing raggedly, and the crooked beat of my own heart.

We crawl back to the shore, the stars still winking with their wretched cheer. I collapse onto the bank, my cheek pressed to the cool grass, watching the captain through half-shut eyes as he falls beside me. Damp from the water, my hair drapes over my wolf cloak and onto the ground, patches of brown streaked through the vanishing silver dye. The captain rolls over to meet my gaze, chest heaving.

"Te nem vagy táltos," he manages, eye wide as he takes in the sight of me, chestnut-haired, unmasked. *You are not a seer.*

"Te nem vagy harcos," I shoot back between ragged breaths. *You are not a warrior.*

"No," he agrees, cheeks flushing faintly. "I'm not." With great difficulty, he pushes himself to a sitting position and holds out a gloved hand. "Bárány Gáspár."

# CHAPTER FOUR

I stare at the captain through the spider web of wet hair, come loose from all its careful braids, and try to make myself swallow his words. The Song of the Five Kings thrums through my head, the melody simple, familiar. We call the prince black—Fekete. But that's not his real name.

I push my hair back and struggle to read the captain's face. Not the captain. The prince.

I can only stammer out a single word of my own. "Why?"

"You'll have to be more specific than that."

My throat is raw from screaming and choking on lake water as I pulled myself to the shore, and my voice comes out hoarse, nothing like the snarl I want it to be. "Why did you lie to me?"

He regards the wound on his chest, the throbbing etch of the creature's claws. Where strips of his dolman have been torn away there are three long gashes, ruby-hued and new.

"I didn't lie to you," he says after a moment. "You never asked my name."

"You never asked mine," I snap back. "And you never

asked me if I had visions. If you're not a liar, then neither am I."

Gáspár fixes his gaze on me, weary. "What's your name, wolf-girl?"

I press my lips together. I consider lying, or at least staying silent, making him work for it. But I'm too exhausted to do any of that.

"Évike," I say. "My name is Évike."

"And you are not a seer."

"No." I lift my chin. "No, I'm not."

"Do you have an ounce of magic at all?"

"No, but—"

"Then the old woman is the one who lied to me." Gáspár shakes his head. "What greater insult than to send the king the only wolf-girl he would have no use for?"

I'm well accustomed to these sorts of slights, but the words still sting, and coming from a Woodsman no less. "How about the insult of stealing us in the first place? Besides, I'm not as powerless as you think. You wouldn't have survived those creatures without me."

"We wouldn't have faced the monsters at all if you had been able to see them coming. Ferkó and Imre would still be alive."

"I told you; that's not how it works," I bite out. "Seers don't choose their visions. The visions choose them."

Yet my gaze wanders to where their ruined bodies lie. Ferkó's face is split open like ripe fruit, a maw of pink flesh and slivers of bone. Imre's heart sits on top of his chest, mottled with bite marks, still weeping rosy spurts of blood. I know they're my enemies and that I should revel in their deaths, but my stomach roils when I look. When I think of how terrible their last moments were, I feel a jolt of pain between my shoulders.

And grieving dead Woodsmen pains me even more.

Gáspár gets to his feet and dips his ax into the shallow water, washing the creature's congealed blood from the blade.

His knife is still in my hand, fingers clenched so tight that it hurts to let go. I know he's not a warrior by the way he turns his back to me: I could have the blade to his throat before he even turns around again.

But it's a terribly ridiculous plan, more absurd than any of my previous imaginings. The Woodsmen are faceless soldiers, bred to be prey for the forest's monsters. Their deaths are nothing for the king to blink at, and certainly nothing to punish Keszi for. But the death of a prince—

"You can't go back," I start. "You won't survive the woods alone, and Virág is too old to make the journey to Király Szek. She's the only seer in the village."

"I'm not going back." Gáspár stares into the grid of trees, shadows oily and black between their trunks. "And I'm not going to Király Szek. I won't return to my father with only a useless, impotent wolf-girl."

The familiar anger coils in my chest. "You're just as useless yourself, with that ax. Are all Woodsmen such poor fighters, really?"

"Woodsmen are trained to kill monsters with axes," he replies, drawing himself up with a sharp breath. "Princes are trained to fight their human enemies with sword and tongue."

I let out a noise of derision. If I had any doubts he was the prince, his haughty, petulant look would have quashed them. His words seem like rehearsed court drivel. But I don't think squeamish princes with silver tongues are supposed to be Woodsmen at all. They're supposed to sip wine behind the safety of city walls while other, lesser men die for them.

"Then why are you traipsing around Farkasvár with that massive blade at your hip?" I challenge.

I feel a quiver of satisfaction at how quickly his haughtiness drains from him. Gáspár averts his gaze, face darkening.

"I could just as soon ask why the things you call gods chose not to bestow you with magic," he says slowly. "But I'm not interested in knowing the minds of demons."

To any other wolf-girl, it might have been a great insult. But what do I have to thank the gods for, besides short winters and the green promise of spring? My perfunctory faith hasn't prevented Virág's lashings, or Katalin's vicious taunts, or stopped the Woodsmen coming to take me. I'm better off praying to Ördög for a swift and painless death.

Or perhaps I should not be praying to the pagan gods at all. My hand goes suddenly to my right pocket, fishing for the gold coin, and relief pools in me when I close my sticky fingers around it.

I push myself to my feet. Keeping the dagger clenched in my fist, I walk toward Gáspár and stand on his right side, so he can look at me with his good eye.

"What will you do, then, Bárány Gáspár?" I ask. "Kill me where I stand?"

He meets my gaze and holds it. Too long. His black eye is burning and I hate him with a renewed ferocity. I hate him for being a slave to his father's worst impulses, for his ax and his black Woodsman's suba and for tying me to Peti, but most of all I hate that I was so afraid of him, that he made me feel dead before I even was.

No more. His fingers tense on the handle of his ax, but I don't flinch. I've seen him fight. I'm no skilled warrior myself, but if it does come to blows, I'll win.

In the end Gáspár doesn't lift his weapon. He blinks at me, slow and diffident, and asks, "Do you know the myth of the turul?"

I stare at him blankly, mind racing around the question. It's so unexpected that my grip almost slackens on the knife. It would have been a good trick, if he'd meant to kill me. When I've regained my composure, I reply, "Of course. It's one of Virág's many stories. But why does a Woodsman concern himself with pagan legends?"

Gáspár reaches beneath the collar of his suba and pulls out a pendant, hanging on a silver chain. He unwinds the chain from his neck and hands it to me. It's a small disc of hammered metal, stamped with the seal of the Woodsmen—the same seal that adorns his horse's breastplate armor. In the foreground, there's the symbol of the Prinkepatrios, a three-pronged spear, but behind it, engraved so faintly that I have to strain my eyes to see it, is the outline of a hawk.

"The king is very interested in pagan legends," Gáspár says. There's a heaviness to his voice. "This one in particular."

"And why is that?"

"Because he craves power more than purity, and he wants a way to win the war." Gáspár loops the pendant back around his neck, letting it fall beneath the wool of his suba again. "What did your Virág tell you about the turul?"

The memory of her telling is perfectly lucid, crystalline, and it shines in my mind like a bit of broken glass. The myth is not one she speaks of often, not without some prodding. It was after one of my many failed attempts to make fire, and she'd been feeling magnanimous. Instead of scolding me, she sat me on her knee and tried to teach me the origin stories: how Vilmötten had rescued Isten's star from the sea, how he had followed the long stream to the Far North, how he had forged the sword of the gods.

"These stories are the origin of our magic," Virág had said. "You cannot ever hope to perform any of the three skills unless you understand where they come from."

I ticked the skills off on my fingers: fire-making, healing, and forging. Each more difficult and elusive than the last. But there was a fourth skill, one that I could never even hope to master. One prized far beyond the rest.

"What about seeing?" I had asked. "What is the origin of that?"

For once, Virág didn't leap at the chance to tell the story. Her eyes didn't gleam with the same blue fire they always did when she spoke of such things, buoyed by her fierce love for our people. Instead, her eyes seemed oddly hollow, like two dark empty wells, and in the soft glow of the hearth, her face looked especially old.

"Vilmötten was exhausted from his long journey," Virág began. "He wanted to return to his home and rest, though he was uncertain what would wait for him when he arrived at his village. And that was when he saw a great bird with feathers the color of fire dart through the flat gray sky. It seemed to be beckoning him to follow. So he chased after the bird, until finally he watched it roost at the top of a very tall tree. It was the tallest tree he had ever seen, and its broad trunk knifed through the very clouds.

"Vilmötten began to climb. He climbed for what might have been days. And when he reached the top, he realized that the turul had led him to the tree of life—the tree whose branches cradle the Upper-World, the realm of Isten and the other gods. Its trunk forms the axis of the Middle-World, where he and all other humans lived. And its roots reach all the way down to the Under-World, where Ördög and his immortal bride make their home among the gnats and fleas and dead human souls."

I made a theatrical gagging sound and wrinkled my nose, but still felt a bit sorry for the fleas. Though they were a great bother to us, especially in the summer, I didn't think they deserved to be aligned with Ördög and his army of corpses.

"Hush now," murmured Virág, with none of her usual fervor. "From where Vilmötten sat, he could see for miles and miles, to the very edge of the world. And then he saw even further. He saw what had been, and what soon would be."

"What did he see?" I demanded, but Virág wouldn't answer me. She only said that when Vilmötten returned to the ground, he felt very much alone, because he had seen things that no one else ever could. He decided not to return to his village and instead to continue wandering, both blessed and cursed by what the turul had shown him.

I liked that story, and I often begged Virág to tell it again, though she almost always refused. I liked that even with all his power and glory, Vilmötten was lonely too. Nursing a sour, half-surrendered sort of hope, I'd scaled the tallest tree I could find outside Keszi, trying to glimpse a trace of flame-bright feathers.

"The myth of the turul is the origin of our seeing magic," I say to Gáspár, swallowing the bitterness of the memory. "The magic of Isten made manifest. Is that the power the king craves?"

"He's convinced that it's the only way he'll ever defeat Merzan. With its magic"—his mouth twists around the word—"he could see their every move before they made it. Which route their soldiers will take, how to ambush them on the way. The location of their supply line and where best to cut it. My father would know their war strategy before the bey even picked up his quill to write the missive."

Thinking of the turul that way, as a weapon in the king's bloody war, makes my stomach chill. Even worse when I realize what it means for Keszi. "That's why he wanted a seer."

Gáspár nods, and I watch his brow furrow faintly with disgust. It's holy disgust, which their god commands them to feel whenever they speak of pagan myths or the potential utility of wolf-girls. "He believes the powers of a seer might be able to keep the Merzani army at bay until he finds the turul."

Anger laces through my veins with such a force that it shocks me, even now. That ancient memory and any comfort it held winnows away, something black curling its edges. "The king makes a good show of hating the pagans, all while craving our heathen magic. He's a hypocrite."

Gáspár is looking down at his wound. Blood is trickling along the hem of his dolman, and his one eye is trained on it with a sort of helplessness that coaxes a drop of pity from me. I banish it as quickly as I can.

"Yes," Gáspár says finally. "He prays every day that God-father Life will forgive him for his duplicity."

Up until now, he has spoken only of Bárány János as the king, the great feared ruler of Régország whose hands are dark with pagan blood. But now he speaks of Bárány János as his father—a man who is not beyond redemption. It shouldn't move me. It should make me want to put the knife through his good eye. Instead, my chest tightens.

Gáspár is still looking down at his wound, and at that moment it strikes me, what he plans to do. "That's why you're not going to Keszi. You're going to help me find the turul."

This time, I can only give a mirthless laugh.

"I thought you were a clever soldier," I say. "But it turns out you're just a stupid prince."

"I know where it is," he says with such a petty, wretched stubbornness that if it were anyone else, I might have liked him for it. If he were anyone but a Woodsman. "It's in Kaleva."

I scoff. "And what makes you so certain?"

"Because the Woodsmen have been searching the other regions for months and haven't found even a trace of it. It has to be in Kaleva."

So that's what the Woodsmen are doing when they're not slaughtering the monsters of Ezer Szem or ripping us wolf-girls from our village—chasing after mythical creatures that they aren't supposed to believe in. I wonder how they manage to keep their faith in spite of it, how they aren't swallowed up by the king's ungraceful artifice. Something deeper than material reward or mortal glory must be driving them, or else the king would have more to worry about than the Merzani army. Gáspár is staring narrow-eyed at me, a challenge in his gaze.

"That's the stupidest logic I've ever heard," I say at last.

Gáspár's shoulders rise around his ears. "What would you know? A wolf-girl from a tiny village, who's never set foot outside Ezer Szem—"

"More than a pampered, one-eyed prince," I cut in. "For starters, you don't know the turul is in Kaleva. Just because some inept Woodsmen can't find it in those other places doesn't mean it isn't there. Besides that, you'll arrive in Kaleva just as winter sets in. Your archer is dead, and if you're as incompetent with a bow and arrow as you are with that ax, I don't expect you'll survive very long."

A wind sweeps in from the lake, and my damp hair ripples across my face. Gáspár stares and stares as his suba ruffles like a raven's black feathers, looking smaller somehow, even though he must be a head taller than me.

"Is there nothing you wouldn't do for your own father?"

His question is a blow to the back. For a moment, out of pure, breathless spite, I reconsider my decision to kill him.

"I wouldn't know," I reply hotly. "I've never met him. My mother was a pagan, taken by Woodsmen when I was ten years old. My father was a Yehuli tax collector."

"The kingdom doesn't collect tax from Keszi."

"Not anymore." Not money, anyway, since his father landed on the strategy of stealing wolf-girls. "But there used to be Yehuli tax collectors sent along with a Woodsman convoy. That's how he met my mother."

Gáspár frowns at me. I shouldn't care whether he thinks I'm lying, but with a bit of my own stubborn petulance I shift the dagger to my right hand and reach into my pocket with my left. I hold the gold coin out to him with slick, shaking fingers, thumb brushing over its engraved surface. There are Yehuli letters printed on it, but I can't read them.

"My father minted that coin himself," I say. "It was a gift to my mother, and she gave it to me before *your* father's men dragged her to her death."

Gáspár inspects the coin with great interest, the furrow in his brow smoothing. His lips part slightly, and for a moment I can believe he's only a young man, not the black prince or a Woodsman killer. He looks up. "This coin was minted in Király Szek. Do you know your father's name?"

"Zsigmond," I reply. "Zsidó Zsigmond." It's one of the

only things I *do* know about him. My mother rarely spoke of him, and when she did, it was only in a hushed, shameful whisper. The Yehuli do not worship the Prinkepatrios, but they are better loved by the king than the pagans are, and therefore almost as distasteful to those in Keszi. That the king employs them as tax collectors and financiers and merchants, the sorts of jobs that Patritians consider sinful, only deepens that loathing.

In the eyes of the pagans, the Yehuli are traitors, slaves to the Patritian tyrants, and willing ones at that. Katalin's words ribbon through my head, years and years of bitten slurs.

*Your blood is tainted, that's why you're barren.*

*Isten would never bless Yehuli scum.*

*You were born to lick the Woodsmen's boots.*

I feel a sudden flush of shame, and quickly tuck the coin back in my pocket. I've never shown it to anyone before, and I'm not sure why I've shown this Woodsman now.

I expect Gáspár to say something derisive about the Yehuli, too, or ask why I bothered holding on to the coin for all these years. But instead he looks at me with a queer scrutiny. "And you're a fair hunter?"

"A great one," I correct, smug, until I understand why he's interested in my hunting skills at all. "But I'm not coming with you. I'd rather be eaten alive in Ezer Szem than freeze to death in the Far North."

"If you don't come, I'll have no choice but to take you to Király Szek," he says. "And you can explain to the king why your old woman tried to deceive him. I'll warn you, he doesn't take kindly to pagan tricks."

"Only to our magic," I return bitterly, but my heart is pounding. "You wouldn't dare show up at the capital with your whole party dead and only a useless wolf-girl in tow. The king would be furious, and how will *you* explain that?"

"I can't," he admits. "In that case, then, you'll have to hope that his anger at me outweighs his contempt for the pagans of Keszi." Gáspár's voice is even, and I can tell it's more of his courtly rhetoric, every word as smooth as river stones. "He wouldn't have to turn your village to ash to make his point. Just a few calculated kills—perhaps the old woman of yours? You said it yourself, she's too frail to be of use to him."

The rage I feel at his words is stitched through with confusion. For so many years I've cursed Virág for her lashings, loathed Katalin for her relentless cruelty, loved no one in Keszi except Boróka. But I'm not proud of my hatred. After all, if I don't belong with the pagans, I'm not certain I belong anywhere.

My hand moves from the coin to my mother's braid, shuddering with anger.

"Or I could just run away," I say, defiant. I consider the knife in my grip again, and how it might feel meeting some soft, vulnerable part of him: the fleshy crook of his knee, the inside of his thigh. Somewhere painful but not fatal—a wound that would keep him from hungering after me.

"Then you'd seal the fate of your village for sure." Gáspár lets out a breath, running a hand through his dark curls. Mussed like that, he looks less like a Woodsman, and nothing at all like a prince. "Besides, if you care even a twitch for your father's people, you should be more eager to keep the king in power. There are others in Király Szek who pose a threat to the Yehuli."

Peti's livid face floats up at me, the name that he choked out between the blood and bile in his mouth. "Do you mean Nándor?"

Gáspár gives a tight, silent nod.

"Your brother," I say.

"Half-brother," Gáspár says, too quickly. "And if you think my father is a pious fanatic—he doesn't have even a fraction of Nándor's fire, or his gift for beguiling crowds. He gives his sermons in the street, gathering his followers who want to blame the pagans or the Yehuli for Régország's misfortune. It's not an unpopular sentiment in the capital, especially with the Merzani army at our door."

His voice catches when he says *Merzani*. I wonder, with a prickle of guilt, whether the epithet "black prince" has more to do with his Woodsman garb, or with the stain of his Merzani blood. I wonder if he ever touches the contours of his own face, trying to find some memory of his mother in them, and feels equal parts relieved and distressed at the result. We kept no mirrors in Keszi, but I would spend hours kneeling at the riverside, watching my reflection crease and wrinkle like it was an embroidery on silk, puzzling over whether my nose belonged to my mother or my father, and what it would mean either way.

There was no answer that didn't hurt to swallow. I almost tell him that, before I remember that he's no friend of mine.

"Nándor's not the prince," I say. "You are."

Gáspár's mouth goes thin. For a moment, we're both silent enough to hear the gentle lap of lake water, a frothing collar along the shoreline.

"It's not nearly as simple as that," Gáspár says with a note of finality. "The line of succession matters little when there are thousands of peasants rallying for you, and a sect of Woodsmen whispering your name, and the king's council weighing the pros and cons of sedition—not to mention the Érsek praying every day for you to take the throne."

His voice sharpens as he speaks; by the end, it's as whetted as the blade of his ax. Gáspár's fingers tighten around the handle of it, and though I knew he held the fate of my village, of my mother's people, now I realize with a stutter of alarm that he might hold the fate of my father's too. I think of Peti's lip curling back, and the lambent whites of his eyes gleaming as he arched over me in the dark. I feel the sting of the wound on my throat. It stills me with terror to imagine how vicious the man he worshipped must be.

Yet an old hesitation quivers up. Perhaps I have no right

to worry over the fate of the Yehuli when the only slender threads yoking me to them are a coin I can't read and a father I can scarcely remember.

"But you're the prince," I say again, this time with a mortified uncertainty. "And your father, the king . . ."

"Does not wish to name a bastard to succeed him, but the pressure mounts with each moment, with each Régyar soldier slain on the front line," Gáspár finishes. His gloved fingers are slick with blood—his own. "In less than a month Király Szek will celebrate Saint István's Day, which Nándor has taken to claiming as his name day as well. If there's any moment for him to make his challenge, it will be then."

My head clouds. Suddenly all my forgotten weariness surges back, and I take a breath to steel myself against the blurring at the edges of my vision. "You think that Nándor will—what? Try to kill the king on this holiday?"

"There's a contingent of Woodsmen who support his claim, and from what I can tell, several members of the king's council, and of course the Érsek. He has the support. He needs the opportunity."

I let out a breath. "And is the king sipping wine and practicing his needlework while the whole city rises up against him?"

"The king has his own fetters." Gáspár's voice is flat. "But he's the best hope for Régország's survival, and for your own people—pagan and Yehuli both. I'm sure you would prefer to hand over one wolf-girl a year than see your whole village slaughtered and burned, or the Yehuli expelled from the city."

His words knot in me, a particular coil of bewilderment and fear. All my life I've hated nothing more than the Woodsmen, except the king, like one of the shadows that moved along the tree line outside Keszi, too dark and distant to see. To hear he might be my savior, to imagine that I might even play a small part in keeping him on the throne, makes my stomach lurch with a dizzying revulsion.

"The turul," I say slowly, trying not to think of Virág as I do. "You think it will give your father the power to subdue Nándor? To end the war, even?"

Gáspár nods. His jaw is set, and he's staring at me with a flint-eyed intensity that seems to startle us both when I finally meet his gaze.

"Fine." My fingers clench around the coin in my pocket. "I'll go with you. I'll help you find the turul. But you have to do something for me too."

"If you help me find the turul, you're free to return to Keszi, unharmed."

I shake my head. It's not enough. "*And* no one will be punished for my deception."

"Fine," Gáspár echoes.

"One more thing," I say, even as my pulse quickens. "I want to know what the king does, with the girls and women that he takes."

Gáspár blinks at me, nose flaring with the beginnings of a protest. His lips part, then close again. It's several moments before he moves at all, but when he does, it's to hold out his hand.

"All right, wolf-girl," he says. "You have a deal. No harm will come to you or to your village. And when we find the turul, I'll tell you what happens to the pagan women who are brought to the capital."

I have to let go of the coin to take his hand. His grip is firm, and his gloves are soft to the touch. Someone must have slaughtered a newborn calf to make gloves so soft. When I pull my hand away, there's blood crusted into the creases of my palm.

"You're going to follow Peti to his grave if you don't cover your wound," I say, my voice odd-sounding. I don't want him to mistake my practical scrutiny for genuine concern.

Gáspár looks down at the trio of gashed lines on his side, then back up at me. "Are you a healer after all?"

"No," I tell him, trying not to flush at another reminder of my inadequacy. "But my—Virág taught me how to dress a wound."

He raises his shoulders with a sudden inhale, fast and sharp. "You could have helped us dress Peti's, then. You could have saved him."

What little camaraderie I might have felt puddles out of me. "Why would I have helped to save the life of a man who tried to kill me? And if you didn't want him to die, you shouldn't have cut off his arm!"

"The punishment had to be levied for treason," Gáspár says, voice low.

"All your grave proclamations make you sound like Virág," I snap. "Do you enjoy being as dramatic as a hundred-year-old pagan hag? You could have cut off his head, instead. At least then he wouldn't have suffered, and I wouldn't have had to watch it."

A beat of silence passes between us. Gáspár takes a step forward, and I wonder for a moment if I have given him enough reason to forget our bargain and put a blade through my back anyway.

He stops himself before he reaches me, fingers curling to a fist. "You don't understand, wolf-girl. Taking Peti's arm was a mercy, to spare both his soul and mine. Now he must face the judgment of the Prinkepatrios for his crime, and my soul is blackened with his death."

I stare up at him, openmouthed. "So it's the fate of your own soul that has you so troubled? You'd rather make a man suffer than bear the guilt of killing him? You're right—you won't survive a day in Kaleva without me."

"Killing is a mortal sin, especially killing a man of the Patrifaith." Gáspár's eye is thin as the mark of an arrowhead. "Better to wound than to kill, and better to suffer than to die before confession. Peti will never be absolved, and the Prinkepatrios will punish him in the afterlife."

I choke down a noise of derision. "But the Prinkepatrios has no compunctions about kidnapping wolf-girls. And binding me to a dying man, making me hear every gasp of his pain—more cruelty that doesn't require absolution."

"That was Ferkó's idea," Gáspár says, gaze lowering. "Not mine."

"Then you're cruel *and* gutless." My face is hot. "Do you always let your men guide the swing of your ax?"

"Not anymore," Gáspár says shortly. "They're dead now."

Something sinks in my belly with the heaviness of a stone. Ferkó and Imre lie by the fire, their bodies cradled in a sepulcher of blood-damp grass. The mist over the water has cleared, and there are little blades of moonlight rippled across its surface, turning it silver and bright as a mirror. From where I stand, it seems inconceivable that anyone could call the lake Black.

Gáspár stamps over to the corpses, and I follow. Before he can say a word I snatch up Ferkó's bow and quiver, swinging both onto my back. Their familiar weight is a comfort, like a song I will never forget.

"Do we have to burn them too?" I ask.

"Yes," he says, and kneels beside the bodies. His hands clasp. "Megvilágit."

A thread of flame knits down Ferkó's ruined face and over his blood-drenched Woodsman's suba. Imre's heart purples under the firelight, like a fist-sized bruise. The air fills with something feverish and awful, and suddenly my own cloak feels too heavy, my hair too warm on the back of my neck.

The forest of Ezer Szem is behind us, but the Little Plain is ahead, a scraggly quilt of grassland between us and the frozen plateaus. In the North winter has already cracked open like a quail egg, spilling ice and snow.

"If we're going to Kaleva, we don't need a map," I say. "We'll just go north until there's nowhere left to go."

Gáspár gets to his feet, the wound on his chest still leaking. Beneath the blood and the frayed strips of his dolman, his skin is olive-toned and knotted with muscle. My fingers squeeze around the hilt of my knife—his knife. Of course he wouldn't want me to bandage him. If the Prinkepatrios does keep an almanac of sin, I wonder how the touch of a wolf-girl will add to his tally.

A bargain between a Woodsman and a wolf-girl already seems a fragile and terrible thing. Whose god would approve of it?

I'm flushed for no reason at all by the time Gáspár marches past me, careful not to let our shoulders brush. It's not until we're both squared on our mounts that I look down at my hands again, his blood still scored across my palms.

## CHAPTER FIVE

The Little Plain skims out before us, yellow and endless, flecked by streaks of lavender thistle weed and the odd black tree. The sun filters blearily through a gauze of clouds, thin as gulyás broth. The last flies of autumn hover around our heads, humming their nasally swan songs, flitting iridescent wings. There are no other sounds, save for the soft footfalls of our horses and the wind blowing the grass flat against the loamy earth.

There's something about all the infinite open space that makes my belly feel like a gaping chasm, sheer and scraped empty. I'm used to the close cluster of trees, the choking press of bark and bramble.

"I almost prefer the woods," I muse aloud as the grass paints ruffled shadows on our horses' flanks.

Gáspár's mouth falls open. "How could you say such a thing? You saw what happened to Ferkó and Imre. Your kind really are as hard-hearted as Woodsman stories say."

I make a silent note to never be flippant around him again. But all my years with Virág have taught me how to ebb righteous anger. Turning my voice low and pliant, I ask, "What were those creatures by the lake? Do the Woodsmen have an inventory of everything they kill in the forest?"

"They were monsters," he says flatly. "Some Woodsmen call them lidércek. It doesn't matter. There's no use giving a name to evil."

His cold, superior tone rankles me, especially after all the prattling about the blackness of his soul. "Do you call a hawk evil when it snatches up a mouse to eat? Do you call a fire evil when it burns your logs to ash? Do you call the night sky evil when it drinks down the day? Of course not. They are surviving, like the rest of us."

I'm surprised by the ferocity in my voice, and by how much I sound like Virág.

"I don't think the hawk is evil," Gáspár says after a moment. "But I'm not a mouse."

"And thank Isten you aren't," I say. "Mice don't have the luxury of passing moral judgment on every living thing they come across. Mice just get eaten."

Gáspár stiffens on his mount. "The Prinkepatrios demands moral fortitude from all of His followers. It's the best we can do to mold ourselves to His image."

"And he rewards you with feeble, fire-making magic?" I can't even light a match myself, of course, but if the price of Woodsman power is being honor-bound to some morose, pitiless god who demands purity and perfection, I'm not sure it's worth the cost. Our gods ask for very little by comparison: smiling emptily through Virág's interminable stories, sacrificing wood fowl by the riverside—wretched tasks that I railed against with every breath, though both are preferable to parting with my pinkies or my little toes.

"He rewards us with salvation." Gáspár's face is stony, but there's a hitch in his voice. "Not that you would understand such a thing."

"I'm glad I don't," I reply, skin itching angrily. "I'm glad I don't live my life at the mercy of a god who takes body parts from ten-year-old boys."

Gáspár angles his body away from me so that I can only see the unmarred half of his face, and the brief pall of shame that flits across it.

"If we continue this way," he says slowly, "it will be a very long journey."

My knuckles are white around my horse's reins. After a moment I let my muscles relax, shoulders slumping beneath my wolf cloak.

"Fine," I say. But in my head, I think, *Stupid prince.*

The night seems hazy and incomplete on the plain, nothing like the dense blackness of the woods. Gáspár's lantern swings out long shafts of light, knifing a path through the grass. Farther ahead there's another light, just a filmy orange smudge on the horizon. I glance at Gáspár, a look of uncertainty passing between us. Finally, he gives a small, curt nod, and we continue toward the light, which throbs brighter with every step.

A series of tents is set out against the murk and darkness, craggy triangles like the fins of some spectacularly large river carp. There's a cluster of pale gray cattle, horns twisted as hugely as tree roots. A mop of a dog with coiled fur whines as we approach, wet nose twitching. Inside the knot of tents is a massive hearth, flinging its orange light, and above the fire is a spindly stick sculpture, carved roughly to resemble the Prinkepatrios's three-pronged spear.

"I don't think we can beg their hospitality," I murmur. The fire coughs out sparks that look like a flock of molten insects.

"Of course we can," he says. "I'm a prince. Better yet, a Woodsman."

Before I can reply, one of the tents' flaps open. A woman comes dashing out. Her hair is gathered into a limp brown plait, streaked through with gray, and her eyes are wild, wheeling.

"It's a Woodsman!" she cries. "Godfather Life has answered our prayers, we are saved!"

More tents part, calfskin fluttering. Men and women filter out, chasing their children. It's a poor village, I can see that at once—most of the children wear homespun tunics, pitted with tiny holes. The men's coats are pulling at the seams. Their obvious desperation embarrasses me, because I've never thought to wonder about the plight of small villages like this one—villages not unlike Keszi, but without magic to dull the jagged edges of hunger and scarcity.

Gáspár, holy as he is, looks down at the woman with nothing but compassion, no artifice at all in his eye. "What has happened here?"

"We have been afflicted by a terrible evil, Sir Woodsman. We—" The woman stops, gaze fallen on me. Horror and repugnance pull dark clouds over her face.

"Perhaps it was this wolf-girl!" someone in the crowd cries out. "Look, there's blood on her cloak!"

*Peti's blood,* I think, anger rising in my throat. *The blood of one of your blessed killers.* My hand goes to the dagger in my pocket, but I find the length of my mother's braid first, like some small animal slumbering.

"That's impossible," Gáspár says, his voice gentle but firm. "The wolf-girl has been under my watch since she left her village. She is not your monster."

*Not your monster, but a monster all the same.* I reach past my mother's braid and grasp the knife, chafing under all these Patritians' flint-eyed stares.

"Please, Sir Woodsman," the woman goes on. "An early frost killed all our crops and half our herd, and now our people are vanishing too. It must be a monster, drawn out of Ezer Szem by the smell of our blood. Last week, Hanna wandered off and never returned, but we found her handkerchief floating red in the water. Then Balász—we found nothing but his scythe and hoe. And last night, little Eszti left the village to play and still hasn't come back. We've found no trace of her at all."

The hairs rise on the back of my neck. The only living things we saw on our journey were grousing crows, but for all I know, the crows are as illusory as those black hens: ready to bare their teeth and claws as soon as the sun goes down.

"And have you kept your faith staunchly?" Gáspár asks.

"Yes, sir," says the woman. "Our fire has burned steadily all this time, even without much dry wood to stoke it. This cannot be a punishment from the Prinkepatrios, or else he would have taken our fire too. It must be the work of Thanatos."

The villagers murmur in troubled assent, and Gáspár's concerned expression shifts to something more severe, with harder lines and sharper edges. I'm poorly informed about the Patrifaith, but I know that Thanatos is something to be feared above all else, something that tempts the good followers of the Prinkepatrios to evil and sin.

And after listening to all this, I want to laugh at their Patritian fairy tales. Humans don't need some shadow-demon to tempt them; we are imprudent enough on our own. Even Isten and the gods are driven by greed and lust, prone to snatching stars from the sky and ravishing maidens by the riverside.

Yet Gáspár says, "I will speak to the head of your village. I will search for the monster that's hunting you, and I will kill it. But it's already dark outside. We'll need lodging for the night."

His seamless switch from singular to plural surprises no one more than me. The woman's eyes narrow as she stares me up and down. The villagers whisper and whisper, the men nervously stroking their beards. I open my mouth to protest, but the smiling glint of their scythes stops me. I don't know if I can risk even a word in front of these Patritians.

"Fine," the woman relents. "But you must understand, Sir Woodsman, that we are rightfully suspicious of sleeping beside a wolf-girl."

"Of course," he says. "She will be under my careful supervision for the duration of our stay. I am bringing her to work as a scullery maid in the fortress of Count Korhonen. She is exceptionally docile for her kind."

It takes all of my restraint not to tackle him off his horse, especially when he gives me a furtive nod, as if warning me not to imperil his lie. There's the faintest quiver in his lips, just the sister of a smirk. The woman beams.

"It's so wonderful when heathens find a way to atone for their sins," she says. "Godfather Life is merciful, and he may accept her as a servant after all."

I stare at Gáspár with near-murderous intent. We both leap from our horses and make our way through the crowd of villagers. They part easily for us, either out of respect for the Woodsman or terror at their imaginings of my pagan magic. Of course they have nothing to fear except the small dagger and my clumsy wielding of it, but I smile at the villagers, showing all of my teeth.

The head of the village is Kajetán, a young man with a fox-red beard and a ruddy face to match. I'm taken aback by his age, by his unlined brow. I expected every village head to be as wizened as Virág. But if Kajetán is not near Virág's age, he is at least half as ornery.

His tent is the largest in the village, swooping and sun-blanched on its eastern-facing side, but he doesn't even offer us a cowhide rug to sit on. Instead, he sulks on his own cowhide, hackles raised beneath his white suba.

"Tell them, Kajetán," the woman, Dorottya, urges. "Tell them about the evil that has been stalking our village."

"There is nothing more to tell," Kajetán says, dipping into a bucket of well water with a rusted tin cup. He lifts the cup to his lips, drains it, and goes on. "There have been disappearances. An old woman, a young man, and a little girl. But I doubt the Woodsmen will be of any help—there are no tracks to follow, no bodies to bury. Besides, we can scarcely afford to spare any food for two such visitors. Winter is coming. I don't need more hungry, wanting mouths."

I glance sideways at Gáspár, waiting for him to respond. Waiting for him to introduce himself as Bárány Gáspár, and to enjoy the look of humiliation on Kajetán's face when he learns that he has refused lodging to none other than Régország's true-born prince. Gáspár lifts his chin.

"I understand your apprehension," he says. "But I will not leave good, pious people to suffer. Give us lodging for one night. We will hunt for our own food, and tomorrow, I will find and kill your monster."

Kajetán makes a noise in the back of his throat. "What makes you so sure you will be able to find it?"

"Godfather Life sent me to this village for a reason," Gáspár says. "It is His will that I am fulfilling, and therefore I cannot fail."

"Are you saying that you are holier than us?" Kajetán's eyes are burning, but for all his brazenness, there's dirt clotted in the wool of his suba. "That you will succeed where we have failed because Godfather Life has given you a greater blessing? We are not Woodsmen, sir, but I'll not have you question our devotion to the Prinkepatrios."

"Kajetán," Dorottya murmurs. A warning.

Gáspár takes a step toward the headman, who has risen to his feet. He lays a hand on Kajetán's shoulder and says, "I have sacrificed much, to be as blessed as I am."

And then I swear that he turns the scarred half of his face into the firelight. Kajetán meets Gáspár's eye with defiance, but the bluster drains out of him quickly. His gaze drops to the floor.

"One night," he mumbles. "But I want the wolf-girl bound."

I won't make the same mistake twice. When Kajetán comes toward me with a rope, I thrash and scream so loudly that they all freeze like frightened chickens. I'm glad to be spoiling Gáspár's story, his assertion that I'm a particularly pliant wolf-girl, mute and malleable, a rare jewel among my kind. I don't want to think of myself as apart from them, even if it's all a calculated tale. I won't let the Woodsmen take that from me too.

By the time they finally get the rope around my wrists, my cheek is bruised and I am still screaming curses. Gáspár is pale-faced with misery. Kajetán is seething. As Dorottya leads us to an empty tent, she is careful to give me a wide berth.

"This tent was Hanna's," she says. "Of course, it's empty now."

I try not to let the grief in her voice temper my rage.

"Thank you," Gáspár says. "Your hospitality is deeply appreciated."

"It's quite small," she says.

"It's fine." He gives her a tiny nod. "May Godfather Life keep you."

"May Godfather Death spare you," she replies, in the instinctive, visceral way of an adage oft-repeated. Then she ducks out of the tent, leaving Gáspár and me alone.

As soon as she's gone, I turn my livid gaze on him.

"Get this off me," I growl.

Gáspár regards me with pursed lips. The ghost of his smirk is still maddening me. He stands across the tent, arms folded, and says, "You'll have to show a bit more repentance than that."

"Repentance?" I lurch toward him; if my hands were unbound, I might have put them around his throat. "Don't needle me with your Patritian nonsense, especially not after you've volunteered me to fight a monster."

"*You* don't have to fight it," Gáspár says. "I doubt the villagers would welcome your help anyway."

"As if *you* could do a lick of damage without my help." I twist my wrists futilely, furiously. "You beseeched me to aid you in finding the turul by Saint István's Day, and now you've happily agreed to linger for who knows how long in some nameless village, to fight some monster you can't be sure even exists. What are you trying to prove?"

Gáspár's brow draws down over his eye. "And what have you proven, wolf-girl, except that you're precisely like the heathens that these villagers fear? Vicious, wild, ungoverned by morality or good sense? There's nothing to gain by confirming everyone's worst assumptions about you."

Spitefully, I laugh. "There's nothing to gain by trying to prove them false either. I could have been the most humble, abasing wolf-girl you've ever seen and it wouldn't have changed a thing. Do you think Saint István stopped to measure each pagan's character before he cut them down with his sword? Do you think he cared how toothless their smiles were?"

Gáspár's jaw sets, and he doesn't reply. I think of the way his voice caught on the word *Merzani*. I wonder if he's spent half his life with his belly to the ground, lowing to every man or woman who curled their lip at him. The thought mollifies me, dulling a bit of my blade-sharp anger.

"Will you please untie me?" I ask finally, teeth gritted.

I watch his shoulders slacken with a sigh. Gáspár crosses the tent in a single pace and begins to loose the rope around my wrists. "I'll have to put it back in the morning, you know."

"I don't care. Do you know how hard it is to scratch an itch when your hands are bound?"

"I don't, actually."

I flex my newly freed fingers with a scowl. "Lucky you."

The tent *is* small, cowhides and wool pelts heaped around a small hearth. Gáspár clasps his hands to light a fire, and it paints our murky, moving shadows against the tent's calfskin walls. I lean closer, letting it warm my cheeks and my freezing pink nose.

Still not willing to make peace, I say, "I'm not convinced that this arrangement is preferable to spending a night on the plain."

Gáspár gives me a dour look. "You seem to be enjoying the fire, though."

"We could've had a fire there too."

"But not a roof over our heads."

"You just wanted an excuse to imagine me as a scullery maid. Scrubbing floors in penance for my impiety." I let out another laugh: shorter, humorless. "Is that really why the king takes girls from Keszi? To clean his chamber pot?"

"No," he says. "And you would make a poor scullery maid."

"Pity. Now I'll never be redeemed."

"You could be." Gáspár's black eye is on me, with a sudden intensity that makes my face heat. "Godfather Life does not consider anyone beyond redemption."

"And what of Godfather Death?" We learn very little about the Patritian faith from our village in the woods, but I'm glad I know enough to prick at him.

"You don't understand. They're one god—two halves of the same whole. Godfather Life is the bestower of mercy, and Godfather Death is the arbiter of justice. Both justice and mercy have their place, and I know Godfather Life would grant the latter to you and your kind if you wished to change your ways."

"Two sides of the same coin." As I speak, I turn my father's coin over in my hand, tracing the unreadable symbols on each side. Yehuli script on one, Régyar letters on the other. Gáspár watches me, unblinking. "Your god can keep his mercy. Perhaps you should ask me for mine, since you just damned us both to fighting a monster."

"I couldn't ignore their plea," Gáspár says, shaking his head as if my reticence disappoints him terribly. "I took the Woodsman vow. Even if I hadn't—it's the right thing to do."

Ever the noble Woodsman. I think of the way he refused to reveal himself, how he accepted Kajetán's rebuffs and impudence, and it angers me all over again. What's the point of having power if you balk at every chance to wield it?

"I'm tired of this honorable Woodsman pretense," I tell him. "You're a prince. Act like one."

"You wouldn't like it much if I did."

"Why not?"

"Because I'd gag and bind you for talking to me the way you do."

My mouth goes fiercely dry. I feel stupid for treating him like an acquaintance, like an ally, like anything but a Woodsman. I remind myself again that he's far too young to have taken my mother.

But he might as well have.

"Is that your brand of justice?" I ask him blackly.

"Not mine, wolf-girl. The king's, perhaps." His voice is light, but there's a furrow in his brow. "And you may have noticed I've not gagged you yet."

*Király és szentség.* The words that Peti spluttered as Gáspár's ax loomed over him come flickering back to me. I go stiff at the memory: royalty and divinity are twin blades to cut through pagan flesh. Gáspár slips off his suba and rests his ax against the wall of the tent. He lies down on a silver cowhide, facing the fire instead of me.

I stare at the black outline of his body, light pooling on each crease in his dolman. I should only be thinking about his ax and his horrible missing eye. But instead I am wondering why he cares so much for his oath and so little for his crown. Why he seems to suggest that it's easier to be a Woodsman than a prince. I curl onto one of the cowhides on the other side of the tent, closer to the fire, and sleep claims me before I can begin to wonder why I am thinking of him so much at all.

# CHAPTER SIX

By morning, frost lies over the Little Plain, a garland on each blade of grass. The sky is seething and gray, clouds swollen, all of it a bad omen. These are signs that Virág taught me could portend a monster, but Gáspár and I can find no trace of one.

The plain isn't like the woods—there are no tree holes to hide in, no shadows to conceal the presence of something large with fangs and claws. No prophetic smears of blood or masticated piles of bone. As we trace a two-mile perimeter around the village, tents swaying scantly in the distance, Gáspár's shoulders coil with frustration.

"I don't understand," he says. "People don't simply disappear."

"I know," I say. The forest could swallow things up, but not the plain. "Maybe they're lying."

"They have nothing to gain from lying."

"Maybe they're not thinking of the proper sort of monster. Virág once lived in a village with a woman who was married to a dragon and didn't even know it."

Gáspár thins his mouth. "A dragon is a beast."

"If girls can be wolves, can't men be beasts?" I ask. That silences him, so I go on. "A woman was married to a man that she loved very much, even though he was from a different village. Their village was a peaceful one, so it shocked no one more than her when, one day, the village's children began disappearing. Their parents searched for them desperately, but they could only find the barest traces of hair and bone, and their baby teeth. And then the woman noticed that her husband began to act strangely. And she realized that she could not remember the name of the village he was from, or how she had met him at all.

"Thinking that she might weep, the woman went out to sit under a citrus tree. The leaves began to rustle overhead, and she looked up, her face shifting from sadness to horror. Do you know what she saw there?"

"The bodies of children," Gáspár says flatly.

"No. She saw her husband's seven heads, hidden there among the branches, their eyes closed, as if they were sleeping."

I half expect him to scoff at my pagan nonsense, the way I laughed baldly at his Patritian tales. But his face is open, almost expectant. "And what happened then?"

"The woman rolled all the heads up into her arms and took them to her husband, to confront him. He began to weep at the sight of them, and then he showed her the bodies of the children he had taken, all the meatiest parts picked clean. Still weeping, he said that he had cut off his heads in order to marry her, and that he had only killed and eaten the children so that he might not be tempted to eat her, instead."

"Did the villagers band together and kill the dragon?"

"How terribly Patritian of you," I say. "No, the woman kept her husband's secret, and she fed him the tender hearts of baby lambs."

I enjoy the scowl on his face, and ignore the homesickness

winding in my chest. The memory of Virág's words is sharp and sweet all at once, like the taste of a sour cherry. I remember sitting cross-legged on the floor of her hut, my fingers twined with Boróka's, listening as she filled our heads with stories of man-dragons and trickster gods.

By midday, Gáspár has made no good on his promise to slay the monster. I try not to gloat too much, but our stomachs are growling. Although game is scarce on the Little Plain, most of it chased into early hibernation by the wind and the nascent snow, with Ferkó's bow I manage to kill a lithe hare with black-tipped ears. I skin and gut it quietly while Gáspár plucks up the bow and quiver himself. If I were more charitable, and Gáspár less stubborn, I would have offered to hunt for him. But my goodwill has evaporated after so many hours of pacing wind-chapped through the plain, and despite our bargain I think he is still loath to accept help from a wolf-girl.

He pulls back the string of the bow against his cheek with great effort and lets it snap forward. The arrow wobbles out of its notch like a bird in drunken flight, and then spirals to an early demise at my feet. I can't help it—I laugh.

"I hope you make a better prince than you do a Woodsman."

Flushing, Gáspár snatches up the arrow. He leans close to me, chest swelling, and in the cold daylight I can see pink rivulets of scar tissue furrowing from beneath his eye patch. The dark lashes on his good eye are quivering, like he can scarcely be convinced of his own boldness.

"I am still a prince," he reminds me, voice low. "And you're a trifling wolf-girl."

I can't find it in me to be ruffled by his bluster; if anything, he's only proven that even my most artless jibes can rile him.

"Then it must hurt to know how much you need me," I say. "How you couldn't survive without me."

Muscles tensed, I brace myself for his rejoinder. But Gáspár's eye only narrows further, storm clouds bruising across his face.

"Your life still depends on my survival. If the prince perishes on your watch, you'll be the one to pay for it. Tell me, wolf-girl, who belongs to whom?"

He speaks of the prince as if he were someone else, someone he knows but not very well. I wonder again why he seems to despise power as much as I desire it. But it only makes my heart flutter with anger, real anger, more than just preening spite.

"My life is worth much less than yours," I snap. "If it now belongs to you, then you struck a poor bargain."

Gáspár draws a breath. "If only it were just your life. I'll remind you that you staked the future of your whole village on this bargain, trusting me to protect it from my father's wrath. If you fail, their lives will be forfeit too."

His words crackle over me like lightning. Once my rage abates, I'm flushed with shame. He's right—I've done a terrible, stupid, selfish thing, binding myself and my people to this prickly Woodsman. My gaze wanders to his ax, and I think how it would look cleaving the soft column of Boróka's throat. I stare down at his hands, wrapped up in their black gloves, imagining that they were the hands that dragged my mother into the forest's open maw. Worse, though, is the truth: that I might have summoned Keszi's death omen myself.

"Fight your own monster, then," I bite out, tearing away from him. "Hunt your own rabbits, and uphold your own silly oath."

I don't care how futile my words are, or how petulant my voice sounds. I trudge back toward the village, dead rabbit swinging from my fist, and don't look back. If Gáspár calls after me, I don't hear him.

It takes the better part of an hour to reach the cluster of tents. My mortified anger is welling up in me like a knot of unshed tears. The dog with coiled fur nips at the hem of my cloak, whining. It has so much fur that I can't find its eyes, just its black twitching nose. A scrawny sheep bleats at me nervously, as if it can't tell the wolf on my back is dead. The silver-gray cows chew their cud, oblivious.

My hands are meant to be bound, but Kajetán is nowhere in sight, so I impale my rabbit on a stick and hoist it over the fire. I stand several paces back, arm crooked across my brow, and still the light and heat make my eyes water. Such a fire will keep the village warm through a whole winter on the plain, where, at night, it can grow as cold as Kaleva. I feel a prickle of satisfaction when I remember that this is the Prinkepatrios's holy fire, and now it's being used to fill a heathen's belly.

I crouch outside of Hanna's hut to eat my rabbit, tossing the dog its liver and shriveled purpling heart. I pull apart the greasy dark meat with my hands and swallow the gristle without chewing. I've even sucked the marrow out of rabbit bones before, in the middle of one of our leanest winters, but I'm not quite so desperate now.

When I'm finished, I lick my fingers clean and take out my father's coin. I've traced the symbols a hundred times, trying to make meaning out of their etched lines the way a hungry man might try to draw milk from a stone. There's a profile of King János on one side, with his royal nose and exuberant mustache. I try to find Gáspár's face in the gilt rendering of his father's, but I can't see any resemblance and then I'm vexed with myself for sparing it so much thought.

"Is that a forint?"

I look up with a start. Dorottya is standing over me, at least an arm's length of careful distance between us. Her hair is tied back under a red kerchief. But she's eyeing my coin with great interest, and I curl my fingers around it, throat tightening.

"I don't know," I say. I'm embarrassed to admit I'm utterly unfamiliar with the units of Régyar coin. Back when the king did collect tax from Keszi, we paid him in forged silver and rabbit furs, bundled onto the back of the Woodsmen's steeds. "It's gold."

"Then it's an arany," Dorottya says, craning her neck at

the coin. There's a hopeful glint in her eyes that makes me equal parts suspicious and sad. "It's worth two dozen pieces of silver, maybe more. I've only seen a gold piece once before."

I glower at her, waiting for some vicious punch line. Waiting for her to accuse me of theft or some other pagan treachery. But she just regards me thoughtfully, cupping her chin in her hand.

"For a long time we had no coins here at all," she says. "Then, some years ago, merchants from Király Szek came and bought up all our skins and blowing horns and wool. The merchants said they would buy all the wares that we had, but they would pay us in silver. So we had to wait until those merchants came back, because none of the other villages would take the silver, and they charged us more and more for their wares with each passing year."

A quiet, ugly feeling simmers in my belly. "Were those the king's merchants?"

Dorottya nods. "I saw a man with a coin like that once, queer script and all, a Yehuli man. He wasn't a merchant, though—he was a tax collector."

It takes a moment for the weight of her words to settle on me. "You met a man with a coin like mine?"

"Yes," Dorottya says, forehead creasing.

I can't help the eagerness in my voice when I lean forward. "Did you learn his name?"

"No. He was a tax collector from the capital, that's all I know. When he came, he took half our silver, and even a calfskin rug. The king keeps these Yehuli men like vipers in a sack, and then looses them all on us once a year."

My hand closes in a fist around my coin. Her words have dredged up some strange hurt in me, but I don't know if I have the right to feel wounded by slights against the Yehuli. "It seems like you should blame the king, for foisting his coins on you in the first place."

"The merchants said that all of Régország's neighbors are

using gold and silver for their buying and selling now," Dorottya says. "King János wants to follow their example and mint his own royal coins."

I have never thought much of Régország's neighbors, the Volkstadt to the west and Rodinya to the east. They are only more Patritians, with peculiar accents but the same pious loathings. While I am puzzling over what she has said, Dorottya takes her leave. She slips silently into a small throng of villagers who have gathered around the fire to warm their hands. Kajetán is not among them. I wonder what kind of headman stays inside his tent all day, swaddled in calfskins, while his villagers till the fields and tend to their anxious sheep. Likely the same kind who refuses the aid of a Woodsman.

Gáspár emerges from behind the pen of gray cattle, bow strung over his shoulder and his hands empty. His failure at hunting should bring me some sort of perverse joy, but my lips only purse as he approaches, like I've bitten into something curdled with rot.

"Did you cook the rabbit?" Gáspár asks, toeing the heap of tiny bones at my feet.

"Yes. It was good practice for my stint in the kitchens of Count Korhonen's keep."

"You are terribly stubborn," he says.

"You aren't much better."

Gáspár inclines his chin. "Either way, it's no good arguing with every breath. The nature of a bargain, regrettably, is that we belong to each other."

He flushes a little as he says it, and inside my boots, my toes curl. Gáspár chooses his words carefully and crossly, the way I would comb the trees outside Keszi for the largest and least-bruised apple. I wonder why he has chosen these words now. Perhaps he is only being as wretchedly reasonable as ever, but still my mind stammers around the thought of us being bound together.

I sigh heavily, mouth quivering as I try to keep it from forming a scowl. "I suppose you'll want me to feed you, then."

I think he almost smiles, but he catches himself. A smile would look odd and terrifying on his face, like a wolf trying to dance, or a bear plucking the strings of a kantele.

"Was Dorottya berating you?" he asks.

There's a note of concern in his voice, or maybe it's only my imagining. "No, though she did have some venomous words about the Yehuli."

Gáspár tilts his head. "I can't see how she managed to guess at your bloodline. You don't have much of the Yehuli look."

"She didn't. She recognized my father's coin." I stare up at him, remembering King János's engraved profile, all dull-eyed and weak-chinned. Gáspár's eye is bright and keen, his jaw as sharp as the edge of a blade. He must have more of his mother in him. "*Is* there a Yehuli look?"

"Many people say there is." He lifts one shoulder, his gaze still on me. "Something in the nose, or the brow, perhaps. There were several Yehuli men at court, tax collectors and moneylenders. None of them had your nose or your brow, and certainly not your eyes."

I blink at him. "My eyes?"

"Yes," he says, curtly and with a hint of embarrassment. "They're very green."

My stomach quivers with the pulse of a thousand tiny wings. It's an odd feeling, not unpleasant. "Is there a Merzani look, then?"

Gáspár goes silent. I wonder if I've pushed him too far, if this brief moment of peace will snap beneath us like a rope bridge over churning waters. After a moment, he says, "I don't know. My mother was the only other Merzani I've ever met."

"And do you take after her?" For some reason I feel the need to pretend that I haven't studied his father's gilded image with Gáspár's face in mind, making a catalogue of their many differences.

"So they say." His voice is perfectly flat, as if the answer is a groove well worn. "I have the wrong complexion for my father's tastes. One of the counts proposed that I spend a year indoors to see if that improved my prospects."

His words almost provoke a huff of laughter, but I swallow it down. I'm not sure he would believe it was a laugh of exasperation and solidarity, and not a mockery of his pain. Gáspár looks away at last, over his shoulder at the villagers gathered around the fire. There are more now than before, their backs arched with their long day in the field, a thread of exhaustion running under all their mumbled words.

The sky has washed itself a dusky violet, the color of a bruise still aching. Bands of pink and gold stripe along the horizon, neat as the lashes down the back of my thighs. The violence of the sunset shocks me—in Keszi we only saw pieces of purple light the size of glass shards, sieved through the fretwork of tree branches. A thrill of cold air brushes up my spine. I marvel and marvel, not caring that I must look as dumb and wide-eyed as a child, and then I hear the sound of music.

The villagers' clothes look richer and finer in the firelight, as if imbued with the glossiness of woven silk. Someone's kantele starts to play, and I remember Virág's story about Vilmötten, who was wandering in the forest when he heard a lovely sound, only to find the intestines of a squirrel strung up between two trees, which he took and fashioned into a lute that sang more beautifully than any nightingale or wood thrush. Even the coil-furred dog has added its howling to the harmony.

Gáspár and I watch as the villagers form two long lines, men on one side and women on the other. I recognize the steps at once: it's the same frantic couple's dance we do in Keszi, only when we need a particular distraction from the cold or

the emptiness in our bellies. The men and women swap partners, tapping the ground and leaping in time with the kantele's strumming, laughing when one girl's skirt nearly catches
the fire.

Looking at them fills me with the worst type of loathing:
envy. If not for the sweep of grass on all sides and the black
diamond shadows that their tents cast on the earth, I might
have believed I was back in Keszi now, sulking ostentatiously
as the other girls claimed their dance partners. Only, these villagers don't live in fear of the Woodsmen or the many horrors
of Ezer Szem.

*But now they have a monster of their own,* I remind
myself. *No matter how attentively they stoke their divine
flame.*

One girl breaks off from the circle. She's pretty and soft-
looking, with Boróka's flaxen hair and the eyes of a doe oblivious to the arc of a hunter's arrow. She approaches Gáspár
shyly, and holds out her hand. There's a smear of soot on her
cheek, but even so there's something endearing about it.

Gáspár shakes his head politely, and the girl shrinks back,
crestfallen and flushing. I catch myself wondering if he's ever
touched a woman who wasn't a wolf-girl. The Woodsmen are
a holy order, after all.

I lean toward him, my voice a whisper. "You didn't need
to turn her down on my behalf."

"I didn't," Gáspár says, mouth thinning.

"Then why? She seemed your type."

Gáspár stiffens, and his shoulders rise around his ears.
I can tell I have landed on an area of particular sensitivity.
"And what type is that?"

I glance over at the girl, folded neatly back into the dancing circle, arm-in-arm with another flaxen-haired man who
looks to be her brother. I think of my own fumbling trysts
by the riverside, of the men and boys who slipped their hands
between my thighs and then begged me not to tell anyone,

*please*, after we were both sweat-slick and panting. In turn they told me that I was pretty, which perhaps was true, and that I was sweet, which certainly was not, but only when we were in the dark, alone.

"Innocent," I say.

Gáspár scoffs at me, suba shifting as he angles his body away. His face is lucent in the firelight, like a bit of amber knuckling out of black pine. I consider that I might be the victim of some trickster god's cruel prank, cursed to keep thinking of the way his skin looks burnished in the glow of the flame, or the way his jaw tenses when my taunts have hit their mark. I tell myself to stop noticing any of it.

There is a lull in the music, and one voice rises above the rest. "Where is Kajetán?"

"He must be hiding away in his tent," says Dorottya. She knifes her narrow body through the crowd. "Someone go fetch him."

"I'll go," Gáspár offers, stepping forward with altogether too much eagerness. I can tell he is desperate to leave our conversation behind. "I must tell him that I failed to find the monster."

He dips his head shamefully, and I feel a tug of guilt, regretting my own petulance, my needling. He might have found the monster after all, if I hadn't laughed at his hunting and pestered him with my stories.

Gáspár doesn't invite me along with him, but I don't want to be left alone with these Patritians, so I follow anyway. Their eyes are bright as embers in the dark, reflecting the fiery light, and their gazes trail me in a line of heat. I touch the braid in my right pocket, then the coin in my left, squeezing what little comfort I can from the ritual.

"What sort of leader leaves his people to worry like this?" Gáspár mutters as we make our way to Kajetán's tent. "The least he could do is show his face in a time of strife."

"Perhaps he doesn't want to be a leader at all. Kajetán

seems terribly young to be the headman of a village, even a small one."

"But he is their leader," Gáspár says. "And so he should act with honor."

I roll my eyes at the simple Patritian line: right and wrong, and the intractable divide between them. I can't deny there's something appealing about its directness. If only it weren't so difficult to be right in the eyes of a Patritian, and so very easy to be wrong.

Gáspár opens the tent flap, and we both step through. Kajetán's hearth is silent, his bed cold. As Gáspár murmurs a small fire to life, I walk over to the wooden table, where the bucket of water sits beside his tin cup. The bucket is nearly full, but it has a strange look to it, a thickness that water shouldn't have.

As I lean over to examine the water, the table wobbles. I frown and peer down. There's a small hole in the dirt floor of Kajetán's hut, and one of the table legs has lodged there.

"What are you doing?" Gáspár demands. "Don't rifle through a man's things like a common thief."

I ignore him. The hole is small, and black as the inside of a well. I stick my hand inside, up to the wrist, and wriggle my fingers until they catch hold of something. When I pull my hand out, what I see turns my veins to ice.

Abandoning his principles, Gáspár peers over my shoulder. "What is that?"

"It's a doll," I say.

A little girl's stick-and-mud doll, with a scrap of wool for a skirt and yellow plain grass for hair. The doll has no eyes or mouth, just a mute, unseeing mud face.

"Why would he have a doll?" Gáspár says. "Why would he hide it?"

I reach back into the hole. This time, my fingers close around something smaller, with more give. A handful of dark berries. Their violet juice colors the creases of my palm.

There's another color with it—a deep glossy red, almost black.

I drop the berries to the ground. They leave a streak of blood across the dirt. I look up at Gáspár, and when I see the horror that's come over his face, I know he understands too.

"What do you think you're doing, wolf-girl?"

Gáspár and I turn in perfect synchrony. Kajetán is standing at the opening of his tent, his face more flushed than before, freckled with broken blood vessels. His eyes have a wicked, colorless gleam.

"It's you," I whisper. "You killed the little girl. Eszti."

"Yes," he says.

"And Hanna. And Balász."

Gáspár reaches for his ax. "Then you're not only a weak man. You're a monstrous one."

"Why did you do it?" My voice is hoarse, my throat burning. "Why did you kill your own people?"

"I don't have to answer to pagan scum," he says, but there's none of the same spite in his voice—just a low, resigned loathing.

"Then answer to a Woodsman," Gáspár spits. "Answer to your god."

"You should know better than anyone that our god demands sacrifice, Woodsman. You might as well be asking after your missing eye." Kajetán gives a short, bitter laugh. "Winters on the plain are barren and long. Many would have perished anyway. It's true, we have little dry wood to keep the fire going, but flesh and bone do just as well."

I've seen monsters claw the faces from Ferkó and Imre and feast on their mangled bodies. I watched Peti die slowly beside me, breathing in the green rot of his awful wound. This is more horrible than either—I put my hand to my mouth, afraid I might be sick.

Gáspár does not look sick. Rather, he's trembling as he raises his ax. He presses the blade to Kajetán's chest, seething with gentleness, right below his collar and the pale hollow of his throat. Careful not to cut.

"Repent," he says. "Or I will render you deaf and blind as punishment for your crimes."

Kajetán only laughs again, his eyes holding the firelight. "Repent for what, Woodsman? For serving the Prinkepatrios the way He demands to be served? Better to die swiftly under a knife than watch your fingers and toes rot away with the cold, or feel your belly eating itself until there's nothing left but bone."

Gáspár's grip tightens on his ax, throat bobbing. "You are still a killer in the eyes of the Prinkepatrios. Repent to me, or you will look like the most pious Woodsman in all of Régország when I am finished with you."

"You must be mad," I burst out. "He's not sorry at all."

There's no contrition on Kajetán's bright, ruddy face or in the glassy sweep of his gaze. He looks between Gáspár and me, sneering, shoulders tremulous with silent laughter. I remember the way he ordered me bound, the way he wrestled me to the floor and put his knee in my back so he could tie me, how I felt his hot breath against my ear. I remember how his villagers cringed away from me like I was something that would eat them in their sleep, all the while their monster was wearing a white suba and living in the headman's tent. I remember the way Dorottya spoke of the king's sack of Yehuli vipers.

There are monsters, and then there are wolf-girls, and then there are wolf-girls with Yehuli blood. Now I understand: even bound and toothless, I am more odious to them than any Patritian killer.

I unsheathe my knife and lunge at Kajetán, hurling him against the wall of the tent. He stumbles but catches himself, then thrusts an elbow into my chest. Before my knife can hit its mark, all my breath floods out of me.

"Évike!" Gáspár shouts, but his voice is distant, like something I'm hearing from underwater.

Kajetán grabs me by the shoulders with such force that my knife flies from my grasp. He twists my arm and I shriek, my vision going starry with pain. There's a whirl of fabric, flashes of skin, and then I am pinned to Kajetán's chest, my own blade held against my throat.

"You ought to keep your wolf-girl chained and muzzled," Kajetán says, panting. "She'll be the ruin of you both. How long will the fire burn when her body is added to the pyre? What is the worth of one feral wolf-girl, a heathen of the highest order, to the Prinkepatrios?"

He presses his finger to the wound on my throat, opening it again under his thumbnail. I choke on another scream, tears burning across my gaze. When Kajetán takes his hand away, it's florid with the mingling of new blood and old.

"Let her go," Gáspár says. He lowers his ax, letting the blade of it thud into the dirt.

I can almost hear the cleave of Kajetán's smile, like metal rasping over metal. "What is the worth of one feral wolf-girl to *you*, Sir Woodsman? Surely the men of your order would drink a toast to her death."

"Please." Gáspár raises his hand, weaponless. "I can bring gold to your village, food—"

"No, no," Kajetán says, shaking his head. "There is nothing you can offer me that is of greater value to the Prinkepatrios than a wolf-girl's death."

And then his fingers close around my throat, forcing me down, my body bent at the waist. The blade draws to the corner of my mouth, right over my tongue, and I realize with a start what he means to do: pick off little pieces of me to burn one at a time, stretching my sacrifice for as long as it will go.

I close my eyes, but I don't feel the bite of the blade. There is only the crush of bone, the wet sound of flesh giving way. When I open my eyes, I can see rivulets of blood in the dirt, and Kajetán's fingers have loosed from my throat.

The inertia sends me toppling to the ground, and I land on

my knees, gasping. There's blood in my mouth, but my tongue is intact. Kajetán's body lands beside me like a great felled oak, Gáspár's ax wedged in his chest.

I watch as his body gives its last spasms, limbs jerking and then going still. His head lolls to the side, eyes open and terribly blank, like two pale shards of glazed pottery. His beard is flecked with blood, black maggoty clumps of it, what he coughed up as he died.

Hands shaking, I push myself to my feet. Though the wound on my throat is leaking, I can hardly feel it now. Everything is blunted, numb as a whetstone.

"Gáspár," I start, but then I can't think of what to say. His face is drawn, his chest heaving. Kajetán's blood is a wine stain across his dolman, dyeing the leather something darker than black. I can only watch as he drops to his knees and lays a hand over Kajetán's forehead, brushing his eyelids shut.

In the end, the villagers make Gáspár their hero. They stitch together their own story when they see blood splashed against the calfskin wall of the tent, Gáspár's ax in Kajetán's chest, and the doll and the berries on the ground. Eszti's mother, a young woman with a snarly dark braid hanging to her waist, holds her daughter's stick-and-mud toy to her chest and weeps. The other villagers gather around Kajetán's stiffening body.

"We must bury him," Dorottya proclaims. "And we must elect a new headman."

Naïvely I assume the villagers will vote for her. But then I remember that, bereft of magic, these Patrician women are only meant to carry children on their hip and darn their husbands' tunics. The villagers huddle together, speaking in hushed tones. When they finally break apart, it's a man named Antal who has been chosen.

His first order of business as headman is to dispose of Kajetán's corpse.

"No ceremony," Antal proclaims. "No grave."

Outside, the coil-furred dog whines hungrily.

The villagers push through the flap of the tent, but before I emerge, there's a cry so loud that it twists in my belly like a knife. Gáspár hurries forward, shoving through the crowd, and halts in front of the hearth.

The fire has gone out. Perhaps it died with Kajetán, smoldering to its ashen end as he lay bleeding on the floor of his tent. There's only blackened stone and the stick sculpture of the Prinkepatrios's three-pronged spear. All around me, the villagers are falling to their knees, sobbing and whispering prayers. Under the white sickle of the moon, their faces look pale as bone.

I wait, but Godfather Life does not deem the villagers worthy of his mercy. The hearth stays silent, cold.

"We *must* have fire!" someone wails. "We'll freeze without it!"

Gáspár shifts suddenly. From my vantage point, I can see only a sliver of his face, but I know from the slope of his shoulders and the slowness of his pace that Kajetán's death is weighing upon him already, another black mark on his soul. I am too ashamed to meet his eye, to face the anguish I have caused him with my temerity.

He kneels beside the bed of burnt logs and clasps his hands together. "Megvilágit."

A small fire blooms in the hearth, its flames murmuring, low. Not nearly enough to keep the whole village warm through the winter. I shoulder through the crowd until I am standing as near to him as I dare.

Gáspár clasps his hands again, brow furrowed. "Megvilágit."

The flames crest higher, waving and blue now, like waterweed as it ripples along the lakebed. It's only a bruised shadow of the bonfire that crawled over the logs before, hurling its light for miles.

Gáspár turns to me. "Évike, give me your knife."

I'm too dumbstruck to refuse. My knife—his knife—which I snatched back from Kajetán's cold fingers before the villagers thundered into the tent, is still befouled with blood. I hold it out to Gáspár and he takes it, blade first. All around the villagers have hushed, lips pursed, waiting.

Staring down with consummate focus, Gáspár finally removes his gloves. He rolls up the sleeve of his dolman to reveal a raised grid of scars along his wrist, ribbons of white against his bronze skin. My breath catches in my throat. It takes him a moment to find a clear spot. When he finally does, he draws my blade across his arm with a gasp, his blood splattering onto the stone.

Fingers shaking, Gáspár lets the knife fall into the grass. He clasps his hands together once more. "Megvilágit."

The fire bursts into the air with such ferocity that Gáspár leaps back as fingers of flame snatch at his suba. Sparks dapple the immense blackness of the sky. The sound of the villagers' relief is as loud as the prairie wind.

"Thank you, Sir Woodsman!" they cry. "You've saved us!"

They flood around him, reaching out to flatten their palms against his chest, to run their fingers through the fur of his suba. None of them mentions the knife, the wound. Gáspár rolls his sleeve back down to cover the blood and puts on his gloves. The flaxen-haired girl brushes her thumb along his jawline and murmurs something that I'm too far away to hear. My stomach knots with nausea.

It seems like hours before the crowd thins and the villagers filter back into their tents. Each blade of grass is a slender mirror for the firelight, making it look like I'm standing in a field of quivering flames. Gáspár kneels to pick up the knife, then walks toward me.

He stares at me without blinking, eye half-lidded. For once his jaw is slack, lips slightly parted, like all the strength has gone out of him. I can't even bear to look down at his wrist.

"Can I trust you not to be such an imprudent fool?" he asks.

I almost wish for his bristling reproach, his self-righteous sulking. Anything is better than this, the unfathomable weariness on his face. I consider telling him that I don't need a knife to be an imprudent fool, but I don't think it will earn me one of his flushing grimaces, not this time. I only nod, and he hands the knife back to me, hilt first.

My fingers curl around the cold metal, and then the wretched question bubbles out of me. "An eye wasn't enough?"

"What?"

"You already gave him your eye." My chest tightens. "Are all Woodsmen scarred like you?"

"Every one of them worth mentioning."

"Why?" I manage. "Why do you do it?"

"The Prinkepatrios rewards sacrifice," he replies. "Sometimes sacrifice comes in the form of flesh."

I choke out a laugh. The memory of my blade against his wrist is blinkering across my vision, and it makes me want to retch. "So is it justice or mercy that you should bleed for your salvation?"

"Mercy," Gáspár says. His eye is black, holding none of the flame. "In all this time, He has never asked me for my life."

# CHAPTER SEVEN

The snowflakes swirl around us, a white eddy in the air. They land in my hair, still patchy with silver dye, and nestle in Gáspár's dark curls. If I don't blink often enough, the snowflakes gather on my lashes and melt, icy water stinging my eyes. Beneath our feet, the ground is dusted with a faint layer of early frost, the black earth still bleeding through. It's as if Isten blew on a great frozen dandelion, and its downy seeds scattered throughout the pine forest of the Far North.

There are only two seasons in Kaleva: winter and not-winter. Not-winter is short and muggy, a time when flies run rampant and plants poke their flower heads cautiously out of the dirt, only to be plucked and shucked and kept for a colder, hungrier day. Calves are born and killed so their meat can be salted and saved. In not-winter, the Kalevans enjoy a few hours of weak sunlight and a brief thawing of their rivers and lakes, revealing water that's clearer and bluer than the sky itself.

Not-winter is almost over.

I lead the way through the forest, Gáspár's horse trotting more slowly behind. Since leaving the village two days ago, our conversations have been curt and perfunctory, and on his part, mostly monosyllabic. I apologize tacitly by offering him the meatiest parts of the rabbits I shoot, and by resisting the urge to badger him during his evening prayers. I'm not sure the message reaches him.

There are pinpricks of red on the snow, tracking us like tiny footprints, whispering the story of our time in Kajetán's village. Gáspár tucks his sleeve under his glove, but the blood trickles out from it anyway, with a soft pattering sound that has followed us for miles. Abruptly, Gáspár brings his horse to a halt and stares up at the sky, letting the flakes land on his face and turn to water.

I circle back to where he stands, my heart fluttering. "You've seen snow before, haven't you?"

"Not for a long time," he says, without meeting my gaze.

I frown. I always thought it snowed everywhere in Régország, even as far south as the capital. But Gáspár watches the squall of white flakes the way that I marveled at the sunset on the Little Plain, unobstructed by the dovetail of tree branches, drenching the grass in its rosy light. When Gáspár grips the reins again, I see him wince.

A long breath huffs out of my mouth, visible in the cold. "Are you trying to punish me?"

Gáspár looks up, eye flashing. "What are you talking about?"

"If you're trying to make me feel sorry about what I did, you've already succeeded," I snap. "How like a Woodsman to let himself die of blood poisoning just to prove a point."

"I'm not going to die," Gáspár says, but his voice has a bitter edge. "And I have nothing to prove to a thankless wolf-girl."

His words bank on my shoulders as coldly as the snow. "You're angry I haven't thrown myself before you in gratitude?

I'm glad to not be Patritian kindling, but Kajetán was a monster. He deserved to die."

"It's not for me to decide that a man deserves to die."

"Who better to decide than you?" Anger is coiling in me, after two long days of silent contrition. "You can conceal yourself in your Woodsman garb, but you're still a prince."

"Enough," Gáspár says. There are fangs in his voice. "Kajetán was right—you'll be the ruin of us both. You think the Woodsmen are righteous, but you're the one who tried to cut a man's throat because his villagers made some callow slights about the pagans and the Yehuli. Do they not teach wolf-girls that sometimes it's better to sheathe their claws?"

My blood is pulsing, my cheeks so hot I almost forget we're standing in the snow at all. "That's all I've been taught, Woodsman. My entire life. To endure their slights and swallow my loathing. Did you agree with the count who told you to stay indoors, or the courtiers who turned up their noses at you? If you did—well, you must be the stupidest prince who's ever lived. All that talk of quiet obedience is for their benefit, not yours. They don't have to go to the effort of striking you down if you're already on your knees."

I can tell right away that I've pushed too far. My voice drops off, like a stone kicked down the cliffside. The wind bristles between us, howling. Gáspár's face is hard, a shard of ossified amber in all the billowing white.

"And what did your clamoring get you?" he asks finally. "Kajetán would have cut out your tongue."

I part my lips to reply, then press them closed again. I think of the scars striped down the backs of my thighs, and Virág's reed whip quivering like the plucked string of a lute. I think of Katalin's blue flame, her white crowing smile. I think of the forest knitting itself shut behind me, and Keszi vanishing from view. I had cried and screamed when the Woodsmen took my mother away, but that hadn't stopped them either.

Swallowing hard, I reach for my coin and clamp my cold

fingers around it. Nothing would have changed if I'd kept my mouth shut and my claws sheathed, except that I would have hated myself all the more. I might have even hated myself enough to take a blade to my skin, trying to buy my salvation with blood.

When I look at Gáspár again, my stomach turns in the silence. "Let me see your cut."

"No," he says, but there's not much fire in it.

"If you die of blood poisoning before we find the turul, I swear to Isten I will kill you."

Still, he hesitates, the wind beating his suba back and forth like laundry on a line. Then he drops from his mount. I slide off my own saddle and trod toward him in the snow.

The sleeve of his dolman is damp with blood. I roll it up carefully, my fingers trembling. One of my fingernails grazes his skin and Gáspár flinches, drawing in a breath. I try to focus on nothing but my careful ministrations, imagining that this is anyone else's wound but a Woodsman's.

The cut is small, but with the friction of his skin against the fabric of the dolman, it hasn't been given a chance to scab over. I prod at it as gingerly as I can, and it weeps red. The flesh around the wound is raised and warm to the touch, which I know from Virág's cursory tutelage is a bad sign.

A braid of fury and despair twines in me. "If I were a true wolf-girl, I could fix this."

"If I were a true Woodsman—" Gáspár begins, but he falls silent before he can finish, his voice breaking like ice over the river. Something shivers in me, not even close to hate or horror. I tamp it down with ferocity.

With a deep sigh, I tear off a clean strip of fabric from my own tunic, then hesitate. I could let him die. I could be free of him without shouldering much of the blame for it, and then I could go home. But I remember the words he spoke to me on the Little Plain: *We belong to each other.* I can't rail against this wicked bargain anymore; the animal has already been

THE WOLF AND THE WOODSMAN  99

skinned. And I suspect the king would find a way to punish Keszi anyway.

Worse still is the thought of him slumping over in the snow, veins darkening with poison, all the color bled out of his face. If I imagine him dying here, cold and alone, my throat closes almost painfully.

I wrap his wound.

Still, I'm not sure why I bother with the makeshift bandage. By the look of the snow and the cluster of storm clouds overhead, Kaleva will kill us before anything else can.

With every step we take farther north, the trees grow taller and taller, their trunks as wide as houses. The lowest layer of branches is so far from the sun that most of the wood has turned brittle and dead, desiccated needles heaped on the forest floor. But above, where the trees touch the sky, the needles are a heady green, lush with water and light and vibrant against the pale snow.

Any one of these trees could be the tree of life, and the turul could be hidden among the rimy foliage. But I can't see anything except the snow falling in dense white sheets. When I glance over my shoulder I can't see Gáspár either, just the blur of his suba, like a coal-blackened handprint on a windowpane. If he's still bleeding, the storm has covered any trace of it.

Soon the horses are pawing the ground and whinnying obstinately. We slip off our mounts and lead them through the forest on foot until we come upon a tree as thick around as Virág's hut, the wood porous and termite-pocked, smelling damply of rot. Fronds of moss dangle from the coiled roots, and lichen crawls up the trunk, the pale color of old lace. We usher our horses into the hollow space where its roots have cleaved apart, and Gáspár ties their reins to a bulbous, sturdy branch.

"We've lost so much time already," he says, frowning.

My voice rises over the baying wind. "You're welcome to keep going on your own. I'll return to dig you out come springtime."

Gáspár makes a face, but he doesn't protest. We trudge farther into the forest in search of shelter, finally pausing at the base of another tree. Its labyrinth of roots stretches over a hollow between the trunk and the earth, with just enough space for two bodies. I pause before the crevice, pulling my wolf cloak tighter around me.

Until now I've not touched him except to shake his hand to inaugurate our uneasy bargain, or to examine his wound. The prospect of being so close to him makes my stomach knot—especially because I know he's still bridling from the indignity of needing me to wrap his cut. I slip through the slender gap in the roots, loosing clods of dirt. I crawl under the tree and pull my knees to my chest. Gáspár stands outside, the wind carding roughly through his suba, unmoving. His lips are thinned and pale. For a brief moment I wonder if he's stubborn enough to stand out there all night, waiting for the snow to bury him. Then he slides between the roots and crouches in the hollow beside me.

There's scarcely room to move once we're both inside. His shoulder is pressed firmly against mine, the heat of his body bleeding through his suba and my wolf cloak. I can feel each tense of his muscles as his fingers curl and uncurl, jaw clenching. Our cold breath mingles in the small, dark space.

Gáspár's face is drawn, throat bobbing. I wonder for a second time if he's ever been this close to a woman who wasn't a wolf-girl, but I decide not to needle him about it, since he is already glowering. Outside, the wind shakes the branches with a ferocious howl.

"Who could live in a place like this?" he murmurs, almost to himself.

I don't know of anyone who makes their home so far

north except the Juvvi, who herd reindeer and build fishing lodges along the ragged Kalevan coastline. But I don't mention the Juvvi to Gáspár. When his great-grandfather, Bárány Tódor, conquered Kaleva, he made it his mission to subdue the Juvvi. Virág says that he captured one of their tribal leaders, a woman named Rasdi, and confined her in a prison until she ate her own feet. Remembering the story makes my skin prickle with anger.

"You say that Patritians consider killing to be a sin." I keep my voice even, struggling not to think of his body flush against my own. "But your Patritian kings slaughtered thousands, not caring about their own souls or the souls of their victims."

Gáspár's eye narrows. "Those were pagans who refused to bend the knee to the king and swear themselves to the Prinkepatrios. Kajetán was a Patritian. He could have repented."

"He wasn't going to *repent*," I say, mouth puckering around the word. "And you say that it isn't your right to choose whether a man deserves to die, but you *did* choose. You decided that I should live instead of Kajetán."

"I only did it because I can't survive the North without you, and my soul will suffer for it," Gáspár snaps. I can feel his shoulders rising, muscles coiled. "If I die before confessing the sin to the Érsek, I will join Thanatos for an eternity of torment."

I almost laugh at the gravelly tenor in his voice, his supreme certainty. "How can you be so sure that you won't join Ördög in the Under-World, instead?"

"Your devil is nothing more than an illusion cast by mine," Gáspár says, voice smooth now. This is only more of his courtly rhetoric, practiced and repeated. I roll my eyes.

"Ördög isn't a devil. He even has a human bride."

He scoffs. "Just like a wolf-girl to want to wed a monster."

"Csilla wasn't a wolf-girl at all," I tell him. "She was like the girls in your Patritian stories, sweet and pretty, but with a cruel mother and father. She lived by a swamp, and her parents sent her out to catch frogs for dinner, even though she didn't have a net. Csilla hunted the frogs anyway, but her hand got caught in the mud and it hardened. Try as she might, she couldn't get it free, and she resigned herself to death. Then she heard a voice, low and rumbling, from beneath her.

"'Whose white hand is reaching into the Under-World?' Ördög asked.

"Csilla told him her name, and begged him to help her. But Ördög said, 'Your hand is lovely. You must have a lovely face to match it. If you die here in the marsh, you can come to the Under-World and be my wife.'

"Csilla gripped Ördög's hand tightly. It was like holding on to a piece of winter birchwood, hard and inhumanly cold.

"'I may die here in the marsh,' Csilla said. 'But before I do, my skin will grow pale and pruned. My lips will turn blue, and my nose will fall off from the cold. I will join you in the Under-World then, but I will no longer be beautiful.'

"'That is true,' Ördög said. 'I can feel your skin beginning to wrinkle already.'

"'Give me a knife,' Csilla said. 'I will slit my throat and die while my face is still lovely and my skin is still smooth.'

"The marsh water bubbled beside her, and a bone-handled knife floated to the surface. Csilla took the knife in her free hand. But rather than slitting her throat, she reached down into the mud and cut off her trapped hand at the wrist. When she was free, Csilla ran from the marsh as fast as her cold legs would carry her. She could still hear Ördög rumbling in protest, holding her severed hand."

"Spare me your pagan myths," Gáspár says, but his eye is alight with reluctant, half-damned interest.

"Ördög didn't give up so easily," I go on. "He came to Csilla two more times after that, first as a fly, and then as a black goat. Both times she tricked him again. First, she used her own golden hair to trap him in a spider web. Then, she burned half her face with hot coals, so that she would no longer be beautiful, thinking that Ördög would leave her be."

"And did he?" Gáspár asks, quietly.

"No," I say. "You said yourself he was a monster. And a monster needs a monstrous bride."

The story of Csilla and Ördög is one of Virág's favorites, but I always hated when she told it, because the other girls would take the opportunity to pelt me with sticks and mud and try to tear out my hair, telling me I was no better than Ördög's hideous consort and that I might as well join him in the Under-World. It's different to be the one to tell the story, and I find it fills me with an unexpected warmth, like a hot coal in my cupped hand. Through the knife-thin slits between the tree roots, I can only see narrow diamonds of white.

"Are those the sorts of tales that pagan mothers tell their children to lull them to sleep?" Although Gáspár's voice is only lightly scathing, hearing the word *mother* come out of his mouth makes me go stiff with fury.

"I told you—my mother was taken by the Woodsmen when I was ten," I say coldly. "Virág was the only one telling them. Besides, I thought you might enjoy this one. Since you Woodsmen are so fond of severing limbs."

Gáspár's breath catches. I know it's especially cruel of me to bring up Peti, but speaking of mothers opens up my oldest wound, making me as vicious as wolf with a thorn in its paw.

"I lost my own mother when I was eight, wolf-girl," he says. There is the whetted edge to his voice again, wielding the revelation as meanly as a blade. "You don't need to enlighten me about that particular pain."

It was stupid of me to speak without remembering: Gáspár is the son of King János's Merzani queen, the foreign bride he wed to stave off a war with our southern rival, much to the distaste of his courtiers. She died almost two decades ago of some ghoulish fever, and war between the two nations began with the first toll of Király Szek's mourning bells. Of course, no one thought too kindly of the heir she left behind, his blood blackened with the lineage of the enemy.

I feel such a sharp, sudden sadness it's as if someone has stuck a knife between my ribs. With some difficulty, I shift to feel the braid in my pocket. When at last I do speak, my voice sounds odd, distant. "Do you remember her at all?"

"Not very much." Each word is a huff of white. His shoulders slacken against me. "She couldn't speak Régyar well. She spoke Merzani to me, but only when no one else was around to hear."

"Every day I think I'm remembering less of my mother than the day before."

The confession is out of me before I can even think to muzzle myself. Before I can think of how this Woodsman might turn it into a weapon.

"So do I," Gáspár says, after a long moment. "Olacakla çare bulunmaz."

I furrow my brow. The words are similar in their cadence to Régyar, but for all their unexpected familiarity, I can't understand them. "Is that Merzani? What does it mean?"

"'There is no remedy for what will be.'"

The adage hangs in the air, a sibilant constellation. My chest aches. I wonder what kind of Under-World life he had in Király Szek while Katalin and her friends were rubbing dirt in my face and burning off my hair.

Blue light trickles in from the narrow spaces, a silken evening streaming through the roots and the storm. "It's not the same. You have a father still."

Gáspár tilts his head. "So do you."

I have to wriggle my hands into my wolf cloak to find my coin, caught between our adjacent bodies. When I do, I grip it tightly despite my trembling fingers. "Maybe."

"More so than the other wolf-girls, I hear."

The girls in Keszi do have fathers, of course, but only in the way that flowers have seeds which sprouted them. Faceless village men who might briefly catch their eye and then look away, flushing and guilty. Courtship is limited to furtive romps in the woods or private dalliances by the riverside. Mothers raise their children alone.

I don't like thinking of it. It reminds me that our lives in Keszi are structured around survival, and extraneous things—love—are to be cut off like a fetid limb. The way Csilla left her arm behind in Ördög's marsh, or how I was carved out of Keszi too. All the village men feared that I would pass my barren bloodline on to a child, and so they were careful, when we coupled, to never risk making me a mother.

It makes me flush to think of coupling when I am pressed so close to Gáspár. But now I can only see the whorls of his dark hair, his long and regal nose, and the delicate curve of his jaw, shadowed with stubble. Once I coupled with a boy from Keszi, and his bristled face left a rash of red along my throat and chin. Sourly, I remember the girl from Kajetán's village, stroking Gáspár's cheek. I wonder if he imagined kissing her. I suspect he is far too grim and pious to think of me the way I have been thinking of him. He smells of pine and salt, not so terribly different from the men I've lain beside. I wonder if he is as ticklish behind the ear, or if his hair is as downy on the nape of his neck.

The snow piles over our tangle of roots, soft as distant footfalls. The blue evening has winnowed away, leaving only the slenderest planks of moonlight to illuminate our small hollow. That pale light lacquers to Gáspár's profile, making him look softer and younger than his twenty-five years, and hardly like a Woodsman at all.

I lean back against the weave of roots, damp with snowmelt, my hair tangling in garlands of moss. My head is so close to Gáspár's that I think our cheeks might touch and I wonder how I will sleep at all. I needn't have worried too much about it. As soon as I close my eyes, the world shudders away.

It's still dark when I open my eyes, in that bleary place between sleeping and waking. I've shifted in the night, my cheek pressed to the mangle of wood and moss. Gáspár's body is a warm crescent around mine, my back against his chest. I half convince myself I must be dreaming: clutched in this cradle of roots, Gáspár's arms braced over me like a reed roof, everything seems hazy and unreal.

Even more so when I feel his breath on my cheek. "Why do you still wear the wolf cloaks?"

"When the first Woodsmen chased the Wolf Tribe into the forest, most of them died," I reply. My voice is thick with sleep, each word a labor. "The men were warriors, so the king's soldiers killed them. It was only the women and children left. The soldiers thought that they would be eaten, or die of hunger and cold, but they didn't. Their wolf cloaks kept them warm, and they built their villages in the safety of the forest."

"That's why . . ." Gáspár murmurs.

"That's why it's the women who have magic," I finish, blinking into the filmy dark. "That's why we pray for nothing so much as we pray for more baby girls to be born."

Gáspár is silent for so long that I wonder if he's fallen back to sleep. When he does speak at last, his words shiver along my throat. "You are an oddity, then."

"That's an awfully kind way of putting it."

"Maybe it means you can be closer to our god," he says, "because you're further away from your own."

"You mean I could cut out my eye or my tongue and have power just like you?" I reply, though in this half-dreaming state, I can't truly be cross with him.

"If you really believed it. Saint István was born a pagan too."

"That's the problem," I tell him. "I never really believed I belonged in Keszi either."

Or perhaps no one in Keszi had let me believe it. Katalin with her merciless gaze and her mocking chants, the other villagers too terrified or scornful to meet my eyes, and even Virág, who saved me out of pity but never loved me—how could I hope to perform their magic when they all thought I was better off dead? Isten guided their hands as they forged or healed or made fire, but the threads of his magic that laced their wrists would never move my own. Every mean word or blistering stare, every time Virág's reed whip licked the back of my thighs, made my threads fray and fray until one day they snapped.

"You do," Gáspár whispers. His voice ghosts softly over my skin, breath dampening my hair. "At least, you seem as true a wolf-girl as I am a Woodsman."

The tree roots hold us in perfect suspension, like a body in a bog, untouched by the erosion of time. I open my mouth to reply, tasting soil and moss, but my eyelids are heavy and sleep snarls me back down into oblivion. When I wake for good the next morning, in the quiet aftermath of the snow-storm, I decide I must have dreamed it all: his gentle words, the warmth of his body around mine. But more than once, I catch Gáspár looking at me in a funny way, as if he has some sort of secret I don't know.

# CHAPTER EIGHT

We survived the snowstorm with little harm done to us, but in the three days since then, winter has truly come to Kaleva. The squirrels are bunkering down in their tree holes, bellies round and full. Foxes are shedding their russet summer coats in exchange for an ivory camouflage. The foul-tempered geese have long since gone, leaving the tree branches silent and bare. Beneath our feet, the snow has frozen into a slippery sheet of ice, too perilous to maneuver on horseback. We take our horses by their leads and walk instead, my toes clenched tightly inside my boots.

Half of me hopes to see a flash of flame-bright feathers dart across the gray sky, and the other half hopes that the turul never appears. I often glimpse other birds of prey, hawks and falcons circling the forest, eyes trained on their quarry. When I see them, I raise the bow, tracing their path through the clouds. I can't shoot, though. The birds are too lovely and noble to die by my hand, and they would make a pitiful meal anyway. I would feel no glory in their deaths.

Gáspár's eye narrows each time I lower the bow, but he

doesn't say a word. Like me, he must be silently hoping that when the time comes, I find the strength to loose my arrow.

Even without the snow, it's terribly, unfathomably cold. The sun glowers behind a milky layer of clouds, too surly to show its face. When night comes, the clouds knit together like Isten's great furrowed brow, ominously swollen, threatening another storm. I'm not sure if we'll survive the next one, but I don't voice my fear aloud. We've gone too far to turn back now. There are so many miles of snow and forest and prairie flatland between Keszi and me, the interminable distance that makes my eyes water when I think of it. I never imagined I would be this far from home, and with only a Woodsman at my side. Each step forward and our twined fate hardens, as unyielding as steel.

That first night in the tree was a prologue, only I didn't know it at the time. When our muscles are aching and the night has stitched closed over the wound of livid daylight, we build a fire and lie down several feet apart, our backs to each other. But always in the morning we wake huddled together beside the blackened wood, as if we've drifted across the ice in our sleep, bodies rebelling against the wind and the cold. Whoever rouses first quietly disentangles themselves, and then we pretend we haven't spent the night pressed against each other for warmth. This is something we can agree on without argument, but the silent pact thrums beneath every word we speak, slicker and even more precarious than our first bargain.

Despite the cold we eat remarkably well, mostly because I have no compunctions about plucking squirrels and rabbits from their dens, where they are slumbering fat and defenseless. Gáspár sulks over my barbarity as I skin and gut my kills, but to his credit, he resists the urge to upbraid me.

"What will you eat at the Saint István's Day feast?" I ask him as I fix the unfortunate squirrel on a spit, dreaming of green sunlight and sour cherry soup. "Chicken stew with egg noodles and warm fried bread . . ."

Across the fire, Gáspár snorts ruefully at me. "That's peasant fare, wolf-girl. Nothing the king would be seen serving at his feast table. We'll have visitors from the Volkstadt, and he'll want to impress them."

"Why would he want to impress them?"

"The Volkstadt has been a Patritian country for many hundreds of years," he says. "So the Volken pride themselves on being holier than we are, and their envoys always sit uneasily at Régország's court. They think we are barbarous, unrefined, and the king too lenient with his pagan subjects. My father is eager to prove them wrong."

I almost laugh. "Too lenient? Is it not enough that we live in fear of his soldiers knocking down our doors and kidnapping our women?"

"Not for some. Not for Nándor's followers."

Hearing his name again chills me. Gáspár stares at the fire, unblinking, flames darting through the cold air like serpent tongues. It's the first time he has spoken of his brother since that night by the lake, and nothing about the flat tenor of his voice invites further questioning. But I don't care.

"And what has Nándor done to earn such feverish devotion?" I ask carefully. My squirrel is blackening on its spit.

Gáspár's breath streams white in the cold. "He is charming and clever and overflowing with empty promises. He tells the desperate peasants everything they want to hear, and whispers to the courtiers and Volken envoys that he will rid Király Szek of its Yehuli scourge and cleanse the country of its pagans for good. The Érsek has claimed he is Saint István's true heir. And since the peasants and the courtiers and the Volken envoys believe him, it might as well be true."

An old, familiar anger kindles in me. "So you'd relinquish your claim just like that? Because some stuffy officials and stupid peasants believe Nándor's fairy tale?"

"I haven't relinquished anything." Gáspár's voice is sharp, hands curling on his lap. "Nándor has power that you can see and touch; it's not just a fairy tale. Without the turul, neither my father nor I can hope to match it."

It's his baldest confession yet. I let my squirrel drop from its spit. My gaze travels from his gloved hands to his face, that prince's regal profile that I've seen close enough to count each of the delicate lashes on his good eye, to wonder about the softness of his lips. For so long his missing eye horrified me—I'd thought it was a testament to his piety and hate. Now I consider perhaps it is a testament only to his desperation. If I'd been a passed-over prince, shackled by the shame of my foreign bloodline, sneered at in the palace halls, forever bathed in the golden light of my perfect brother, wouldn't I have taken a knife to my own flesh too? For all his grousing about my unabashed barbarity, Gáspár is braver and stronger willed than I have ever been.

The realization makes me regret at least half of my japes and my petulance. Flushing, I pass him the cooked squirrel, and he takes it with a steely nod. Overhead the sky is the color of forged iron, bristling with black clouds.

"We'll find it," I tell him, surprised by the certainty in my own voice. "I'll kill it."

Gáspár doesn't reply. His eye is boring into the fire again.

"Are you doubting my aim?"

"No," he says, lifting his gaze to mine. "I don't doubt you, wolf-girl."

My skin prickles, and not with cold. We eat our meal in silence, but I find it difficult to stop from staring at him. I am remembering the line of his body against mine, the sweep of his suba over me, the brace of his arms around my waist. Once I would have flinched at his proximity, or perhaps considered how easy it would be to slide my knife into his throat. Now I have to blink and grit my teeth and wheedle myself into thinking of him as a Woodsman at all.

Gáspár falls asleep first, turning his back to the flame. Even without seeing his face, I cannot stop imagining his sacrifice. The heated blade, the flash of metal, the blister of pain and the flowering of blood. It makes my throat tighten and my stomach roil. And yet for all I blanched at the gore of the Woodsman code, hadn't I relished the tale of Csilla cutting off her arm and shearing her hair and burning her face to be made into Ördög's monstrous, powerful consort?

I think about Katalin, too, pressing my face into the mud, telling me I belonged as close to the Under-World as I could get. Later, when the fun of her cruelty had worn thin and she and her friends abandoned me, I crawled into a thicket and let my cheek rest in the dirt. I pretended I could hear Ördög rumbling beneath the earth, like Csilla had. I wanted to hear him calling to me. I wanted to hear him telling me I belonged somewhere, even if it was the cold realm of the dead.

If I cannot be Vilmötten, my belly bright with Isten's star, perched in the highest tree branch, perhaps I can be something else. Perhaps I can be the favored of another god.

My whole body trembles as I unsheathe my knife. The metal is a lambent mirror that holds the firelight. I grip the hilt in my left hand, angling the blade over my littlest finger. I don't think I have the strength or the stomach to take my whole hand, and besides, I need both to string my bow. My pinky is what I will miss the least, but then I wonder if that is the right attitude for a sacrifice.

I tear off a scrap of my tunic and ball the fabric in my mouth. Then I raise my hand and bring my knife down with all the force that I can gather.

Before anything else, there is the splinter of bone, the spurt of blood. A wine stain laps at the blackened logs. The pain arrives later, with a bolt that leaves me dizzy and breathless. I bite down on the fabric, muffling a scream. Across the fire, Gáspár shifts, but doesn't wake. My eyes are stinging hot with tears.

Vision rippling, I lift my hand. There is a knob of bone protruding from my palm, like a smooth white stone. Where my finger was is rimmed red with gore, skin as ragged as the hem of an old skirt. And then there is my pinky, a slip of warm flesh in the snow. It looks so singular and pitiful, something that a hawk might snatch up and pick clean for a scant midwinter meal. That thought alone undoes me. I bend at the waist and retch.

When I have finished, I wipe the bile from my chin and straighten my back. The pain has started to ebb, leaving me raw with curiosity and desire. I expected to feel the sacrifice in my throat and my belly, like a swallow of good wine, but I only feel woozy, sick. Csilla didn't retch, or at least that wasn't part of Virág's story. Who knows if she did or didn't. I clench the remaining fingers of my left hand, knuckles cracking.

In Virág's story, she plunged her face into the flames without a beat of hesitation. I reach forward, letting the fire nip at my fingertips. It hurts, but not enough to make me pause. And my skin doesn't smolder or burn.

Now a more palpable curiosity is unfolding inside of me. I stretch my hand again, and the flames leap back as I do. I reach until I'm touching the ash-eaten logs at the base of the fire, and then it goes out, so quickly and suddenly that I gasp, as if it's been doused with water.

My skin prickles like a thousand bee stings, but there are no raised bumps of blistered flesh. The pain only exists somewhere unreachable inside me. And all that's left of the fire is the acrid curl of smoke.

It's a swoop in my stomach, a terror I can feel in the soles of my feet, like standing at the craggy edge of a cliffside. The other girls' magic doesn't work like this. They forge metal in just their empty hands; they make fire without wood or flint. They stitch new skin over old wounds. But they are touched by Isten, the creator, who never once answered my prayers. Perhaps all this time I should have been praying to a different god, the one that smothers green spring under winter snow, the one that bleaches black hair white and carves deep wrinkles into skin. The god that demands human flesh, not spilled goose blood or silver laurel crowns, for sacrifice.

Maybe it was only a matter of believing, like Virág said, and I had believed in the wrong thing. I can almost feel dark thread lacing up my wrists, pressing deep into my skin, like scars thin and dark with blood.

I hear Gáspár turn over and blink himself awake. After a moment of bleary fumbling, he murmurs a quiet prayer, and a ball of blue flame quivers into his cupped hand. He holds the fire so close that his face is soaked in sapphire light. It clings to the curve of his nose and his stubbled jaw. It pools on his lips, pressed with bewildered concern.

"What happened?" he asks, voice thick.

Very slowly, I arch my hand, slick with gore, above the coil of flame. Gáspár's eye widens, taking in what's gone from me, but before he can speak I let my hand drop on top of the fire, curling my four fingers over his, plunging us both into darkness.


A word hangs in the air between us, battered back and forth in the frigid wind. It remains unspoken, unacknowledged, and yet it's as visible and tangible as the ice beneath our feet.

*Boszorkány.* Witch.

The wolf-girls of Keszi are sometimes called witches, but it is not what the word really means. Real witches are not human: their bodies are made of sculpted red clay; their bones are twigs and bog wood. They have wreaths of swamp grass for hair and sea-smoothed pebbles for eyes. They are as old as the land itself, and they answer to no gods.

We both know I'm not a witch. Gáspár has seen me bleed, felt my skin beneath his gloved hand, the way my flesh gave against his touch. But this is a different kind of magic, one that is not for survival, like the magic of the other wolf-girls. With their magic they can outlast the monsters of Ezer Szem, endure the harsh forest winters, stay guarded against the Woodsmen who want them dead. Their magic built Keszi. Mine would see it crumble.

Some other girl might have despised it. I can almost see Katalin's delicate little nose wrinkling in disgust. But then I imagine closing my hand over her blue flame, the look of wonder and terror in her eyes before my fingers moved to her throat. My skin itches, black threads tightening.

Gáspár scowled and worried over my wound with as much prickly concern as Virág on her darkest days, every word laced through with grim judgment. When I fumbled with the bandage, he let out a deep, put-upon sigh and took the wrappings from me, winding them carefully around the gash where my finger had been.

"I'll not hear another word about the Woodsmen and our masochism," he said, brow furrowing.

I laughed at him weakly. "That seems fair enough."

He hasn't spoken since. As we press on against the wind, Gáspár watches me carefully, from a few paces away. Beneath his guarded gaze is obvious displeasure, but I can't puzzle out its source. Perhaps he is horrified by my newfound magic. Perhaps it has reminded him of the intractable distance between Woodsman and wolf-girl.

His reproach bruises me more than I thought it would. After days of huddling together on the ice, after I searched the skies for the turul until my eyes burned and my feet throbbed, he is looking at me like I am nothing more than a pagan barbarian again, something unknown and unknowable, something feral and loathsome.

I skid across the ice until we're side by side, matching my pace to his.

"You don't understand," I say. I'm not sure when I started caring whether he understands me or not. "Being barren in

Keszi—it's worse than being dead. They called me a Yehuli slave to the Patritian king. They told me to lick the Woodsmen's boots. They wanted to get rid of me just as much as they—"

I manage to cut myself off before I reveal the truth, reveal Virág and wicked Katalin. I'm shouting to be heard over the wind, my eyes damp and tear-pricked.

Gáspár stops. He turns toward me in slow, careful increments, teeth gritted so tightly I can see the pulse of muscle along his jaw. He doesn't speak.

"Maybe you think me more of a wolf than before," I press on, heart pounding, "and less a girl. But you can't look at me with your one eye as if I'm a monster for doing something terrible so I could finally have something of my own. You know what the price of power is. You know better than anyone. We're the same now."

The wind gives a blood-chilling widow's wail. Gáspár stares and stares, black hair feathering across his forehead. Then he starts to laugh.

I stare back, blinking in bewilderment. If he was trying to diffuse my rage, it worked—I'm too baffled to be angry.

"You're the one who doesn't understand, wolf-girl," he says, once his laughter has died.

Wounded by his mirth, a sickly cruelty comes over me. "So you do believe you have something in common with me after all. A trifling wolf-girl and the Régyar prince—"

"That's enough," he growls.

I haven't seen this much fire in him since we confronted Kajetán in his tent. Gáspár's black eye is cold again, pitiless, and seeing it makes me put on my own armor in return. Spitefully, I reach for the one thing I had sworn to myself I wouldn't use against him, because it would damn me too. "For such a pious Woodsman you were certainly eager to bed down with me—the cold was as good an excuse as any. It must be quite difficult to be five and twenty and have never come so close to a woman before. I'll tell you that I look just the same as any blushing Patritian girl under my cloak."

"Can you never keep your mouth shut?" Gáspár snarls, but there's a thread of misery running under his rage. His cheeks are tinged pink, and not just from the bite of the wind.

"Only if you admit that you're wrong. Admit that, in some way, we're the same." The words come rushing out with such breathless vigor that I have to stop walking and put my hand on a nearby tree to steady myself.

"Do you *want* us to be the same?" he asks, eye narrowed. "Is that the great hypocrisy the pagans want us to confess to?"

I don't know what the other pagans want. I don't know what I want. All I know is that, for the first time, I feel like I might finally crack the shiny, stubborn facade of him. Gáspár stares down at me, squinting against the wind. My eyes trace the lines of his face, the hills and valleys of muscle and bone. In the past days I have come to recognize the haughty way he draws his breaths and the stubborn clenching of his jaw, and I think of him so often I would recognize even his silhouette if he were only a painted shadow on the wall. For the briefest moment I want to run my finger down his cheek the way that village girl did, only to see how he would respond. I want to do something lewder and worse.

When I finally speak, my voice is hoarse, my throat aching. "Just tell me the truth."

Gáspár only shakes his head. He cannot guess what sort of lascivious things have been blooming red and hot in my mind. "The truth is so much less than you imagine it to be."

"That's no answer."

"I am so much less than you imagine me to be," he says. "An honorable Woodsman, a noble prince. You think I plucked out my own eye to have power, when in truth it was taken by force to strip me of it."

"I don't have the patience for riddles," I say, scowling.

"My father *cut out my eye*, wolf-girl. He cauterized the

wound himself before placing the ax in my hand. His way of saying I was better off as a Woodsman than I was as his heir."

I dig my fingers into the tree bark, wincing as the wood splinters under my nail. "But you're his only true-born son."

"And what does that matter, when the enemy's blood flows through my veins?" He gives a hollow laugh. "The peasants cried out for my father to disinherit me, and Nándor and the Érsek whispered in his ear until one day he finally picked up the knife and took my eye. Only one of the counts, the Kalevan count, ever raised his hand to try and stop it. But the rest would rather see a bastard take the throne than a prince with sullied blood. The king has four other sons, and they are all pure Régyar."

My shoulders rise and I shut my eyes, as if I can armor myself against the revelation. I wonder if when I open them I will see a Woodsman standing before me, and my fear and loathing will graft onto me like a steel breastplate. But in the darkness behind my eyelids, I can only see Gáspár kneeling, and a blade flashing, and his father blood-drenched and laughing.

"So you do the king's bidding," I whisper, "even though he doesn't think you're a contender for the crown."

Gáspár inclines his head, not quite a nod. "He doesn't think I'm his son, not anymore. He tore out my eye, which meant I wouldn't be able to do it myself. I would never have a chance to earn the blessing of Godfather Life on my own, for a sacrifice given freely. It's not a sacrifice when you're chained to the floor, screaming."

I think of his wrist, latticed with all its little wounds. I think of the way he scorned his title whenever he could and how he swallowed the name *Bárány* while Kajetán berated him. A breathtaking pain licks through me, worse than any of Virág's lashings, worse than Kajetán's thumb against my throat or even the severing of my finger.

"I'm sorry," I say, though it scarcely seems enough. "For all my stupid slights. You only deserved half of them."

Gáspár doesn't laugh or smile, and I didn't expect him to, but his jaw unclenches, just a little bit. "I understand why you won't spurn your newfound power, whatever it is. Witch or wolf-girl, I am with you. There's scarcely more than a week until Saint István's festival, and we can't turn back now."

He sets his gaze upon me, and for the first time, I see only the eye that is, black and blazing, and don't wonder about the grisly scar where the other one was. Tiny tremors of pain are ribboning from my absent finger, down my hand and up my arm, odd and phantasmal. I open my mouth to reply, but then I look up.

Without noticing, we have walked into a different kind of forest. A forest like Ezer Szem, where every rustle of leaves sounds like whispered words and every footfall on the ground might be the circling of a monster. My hand is on the trunk of a tree as broad as a merchant's cart, and when I narrow my eyes to try to glimpse the top, my head spins and I stumble back, dry-mouthed.

"This is it," I whisper. "The turul—it's here."

"How do you know?"

But I can't explain it. Perhaps I am a witch after all. Gáspár presses the flat of his gloved hand to the trunk, like he's feeling for a coded message on the bark, something etched and eternal.

The ground trembles under our feet. The tree starts to shake, too, scattering dead needles into the snow. Our horses rear, whinnying, and the reins of my white mare slip from my fingers.

As our horses gallop away, the trees around us stir like restless giants, uprooting themselves from the earth. With each tree that twists itself free, the ice splits open, revealing dirt beneath, the bruised memory of spring. The wrenching sound is so terrible that it drowns out the wind, and as the trees move, the lattice of their branches obscures even the slenderest piece of dusky sky.

A fat pine tree lumbers toward us, gruesome with knots and lichen. I leap out of the way, skidding on my knees in the snow. When I look up, Gáspár is holding out his hand. I take it, and he hauls me to my feet. The moment I'm upright, he lets my fingers fall from his grasp and without another breath we start to run.

I sprint as fast as I can, my hair and my white cloak streaming out behind me. Through the tangle of branches, I can just barely see the blur of Gáspár's black suba. As I run, I look back over my shoulders, trying to dodge the trees that hurtle past, or risk being crushed in a snarl of roots and filthy snow.

We burst through the tree line, my heart clanging like a blacksmith's anvil. The pine forest gives way to an open plain, miles of icy flatland skimming all the way to the horizon. I realize only then that the ground is no longer trembling; there's no whip of branches around my face or roots flinging out to snatch at my ankles. The trees have stopped at the edge of the valley, needles rustling as they hunker down again, planting themselves back into the earth.

I turn to Gáspár, clutching the stitch in my side. "Why did they stop?"

"I don't know." His chest is heaving beneath his dolman. "They were chasing us."

My throat is too tight to reply. I know now, without a prickle of doubt, that when King Tódor conquered the Far North he only managed to restrain its ancient magic, not snuff it out entirely. The Holy Order of Woodsmen will have many more years of bitter work to do, if they aim to erase Kaleva's magic for good.

"At least we haven't been trampled to death," I say when I find my voice again, letting out a tremulous laugh. "I was hoping for a nobler demise."

As soon as the words fall from my lips, the ice splits with a sound like nearing thunder.

I stare down in horror at the seismic crack, stretching

perfectly from one toe of my boot to the other. We're not standing on solid, snow-dusted earth at all. We're standing on a frozen lake, blue-black water seething beneath the cloudy mantle of ice.

Slowly, I raise my head to look up at Gáspár. I manage to meet his gaze, as horrified as mine, for only half a second before I am plunged into the freezing water.

Without a beat, the ice closes over my head, knitting itself back together and sealing me under. I'm too shocked to move, too shocked to even feel the cold. Gáspár pounds on the other side, his fists cracking tiny fissures into the ice, but it's not nearly enough.

Then my lungs begin to strain. The shock that kept the cold at bay is gone, leaving only frigid terror in its wake. I kick wildly to keep myself afloat while I beat my hands against the ice, each impact blunted by the torpid water.

I hear Gáspár screaming, mutedly, from above.

*I am going to die,* I think, surprised by how calm the thought is when it comes over me. Without noticing, I have stopped my pounding and flailing. My body sinks deeper into the black oblivion, the weight of my sodden clothes pulling me down. Hazily I consider trying to slip off the wolf cloak, but then I think to myself that I'll want it, wherever it is I am going. As I descend, I am faintly aware of the ice shattering overhead. Light bursts through the fractured surface in bright clear shafts before being obscured again as Gáspár dives into the water.

Roused from my bleary stupor I kick toward him, and his arm loops around my waist. My vision explodes with stars, a thousand hot, painful pinpricks, as he drags me back up to the surface. He grabs the handle of his ax, the blade firmly planted farther down the ice, and uses it as leverage to hurl me out of the water. He pulls himself up after me, and we crawl away from the hole. We don't get far. After no more than a few moments we both collapse onto our bellies, panting, gasping. Every breath feels like I am swallowing nettles.

It's a long time before I can speak again, and even after that, I can't think of what I want to say. The water is freezing onto my skin, my hair, the fibers of my wolf cloak, like dewdrops on grass. I turn over to face Gáspár, my cheek against the ice.

"You only saved me because you couldn't survive without me," I choke out, thinking of his clumsiness with the bow and arrow. The humor of it seems so distant now.

Gáspár coughs up water and blinks. "Yes," he says simply, as if he wants to scowl at me but can't quite manage it now.

The sun is dipping low on the horizon, light dripping off the edge of the world. I try to keep myself wrapped in my cloak, but it's soaking wet and colder than my skin itself. The chill has snuck into my marrow, settling against the hollows of my rib cage, too deep to exorcise.

"I want to go home," I whisper. "To Keszi."

There's very little waiting for me in the village, save for Boróka and prickly Virág. But in Keszi there's a warm bed by the fire, and now it's so bitterly cold.

"I know," Gáspár says. His hand slides across the ice and buries itself in my cloak. For a moment I think he's searching for me, but then he pulls out my knife. His fingers tremble as he rolls down his sleeve, blade glinting against his bronze skin.

"No." I reach out and grasp his wrist, feeling the raised grid of scars there. "Please . . . don't."

I can't bear to watch him do it, even if it means there's no guttering warmth. I grip his wrist tightly. It's like holding on to a rigid piece of winter birchwood, impossibly cold.

"I'm sorry." Gáspár's voice drifts toward me, soft as an echo. "If I were a true Woodsman, or a true prince, I could—"

I can't catch the rest of what he says. Through half-shuttered lashes, I stare at his face, his broken nose and dark eye, the frost pearling in his hair. He's so beautiful, I realize, and if I had the strength I might have laughed at my belated revelation. I feel oddly peaceful when I look at him, and very tired.

If Gáspár speaks another word, I don't hear it. A black tide rises and falls, pulling me quietly under.

## CHAPTER NINE

When I wake, it's to the smell of roasting meat. My cheek is pressed to a wooden floor, inches from a hearth. My wolf cloak has been removed, but I am under a heavy pelt of pale gray fur. The fine hairs of the pelt part easily when I run my finger through it, like a raft splitting river water. I don't know of any animal with fur so soft.

I sit up slowly and find myself staring into the gleaming amber eyes of a bear.

I open my mouth and close it again, but no sound comes out. The bear's hot breath clouds against my throat. Its eyes are as bright as tiny buttons stitched into the woolly mass of its head. After a moment, it turns slowly and lumbers away, paws thudding softly on the ground.

It pads across the small room to where Gáspár lies, tucked under an identical gray pelt. The bear noses his body lazily, and Gáspár sits up with a start. When he sees the bear, what little color there is drains from his cheeks.

The bear is rousing us. Is this typical bear behavior? I do not know enough about bears to say for sure. For a moment

I wonder if the bear pulled us from the ice and brought us here to its hut, which it built with its big clumsy paws, and now it's cooking meat over the fire to welcome its visitors. If there's anywhere in the world that such a thing could be true, it's Kaleva.

But then the door to the hut clatters open. A figure steps through the threshold, hefting a mound of firewood that obscures their face. From where I'm sat on the floor, I can only see the fringe of an embroidered skirt swinging across a pair of furred boots.

Gáspár rises at once, throwing off his pelt. "Who are you? Why did you bring us here?"

The firewood tumbles to the ground. The girl who was carrying it brings up a hand to wipe her brow. She looks my age or even younger, with pretty, shining eyes and pink cheeks.

"I saved your life, Woodsman," she says coolly. "If you would prefer, I could take you back to where I found you on Lake Taivas and see how well you'd fare."

Gáspár's gaze flickers to me, and a deep flush comes over him, from forehead to chin. I am so relieved to see it that I almost sink back down into my pelt. Instead I clamber to my feet, readying myself for a bolt of pain as my left hand knuckles over the wooden floor. Nothing comes. My littlest finger is still gone, but there's no more phantom ache.

"Who are you?" I press, staring and staring at the absence of my pinky.

The girl pulls off her mittens and runs a hand through her black hair, stiff with cold. She has the olive complexion of a Southerner, nearly like Gáspár's, which I had thought impossible in a place so bereft of sunlight.

"Tuula," she says.

A Northern name. But Tuula doesn't look like a Northerner. In Virág's stories, the Kalevans all have flaxen hair and ice-chip eyes, and skin as white as the snow under their boots.

"And the bear?" I venture.

Tuula looks around blankly, as though she's forgotten it's there.

"Oh," she says after a moment. "That's Bierdna. Don't worry, she won't hurt you as long as her belly is full and I'm in a pleasant mood."

Gáspár and I exchange glances.

"Lucky for you, I'm usually in a pleasant mood." Tuula nudges the bear, splayed out by the fire like an extraordinarily large fur rug.

I am too bewildered and sleep-muddled to think of what to say. My last memory is lying on the ice beside Gáspár, my fingers curled around his wrist. I think of how he dove after me without flinching and something stirs in my belly, a feather rustle like a flock of birds taking flight.

Across the room, I watch Gáspár roll up his sleeve. My throat tightens, anticipating a furrow of black rot, his veins spider-webbed with poison. But there's only a swath of clear, unblemished skin, edged by the raised white mottle of his older scars. A strangled noise comes out of me.

"How?" I choke. "How did you do it?"

"That wasn't me," Tuula says. "And there was nothing to be done about your finger either. One of the sloppiest cuts I've ever seen, and I've seen plenty. It looked like it was chewed off by a weasel."

"Maybe it was," I say, stomach lurching. I don't trust this stranger enough to offer her the truth. Ördög's threads are twitching around my wrist, but I don't know the margins and limits of my newfound magic, and I'm not sure how well I would fare against a fat, full-grown bear. Gáspár's ax rests against a woodpile on the other side of the room, over the mound of the bear's furry back, and my knife is missing from my pocket. I quickly check for my braid and my coin, and find both with a tremor of relief.

"Then what an intrepid weasel it must have been." Tuula's voice is light, halfway to laughter, but there's a gleam in her dark eyes, like the reflection of a blade flashing. "But since I did save your lives, I'd like to ask a favor of you. I've heard that Woodsmen are very keen on holding to their debts. What's your name, sir?"

Her *sir* sounds as bitter as a snakebite. Gáspár glances between Tuula and me, and then between Tuula and the bear, who, even sleeping, provokes some worry.

"Gáspár," he says finally, a hard edge to his voice. I wonder if he thinks Tuula might recognize him as the prince. I wonder if he wants her to. Kalevans are notoriously tepid toward their Southern rulers, even after nearly a hundred years of vassalage to the Crown.

But there's no flicker of recognition in Tuula's gaze. "And you, wolf-girl?"

I meet her eyes steadily. My palms are slick, but I don't want her to think I'm afraid. "Évike."

"Well, Gáspár, Évike"—she nods at each of us in turn—"will you help me slaughter Bierdna's supper?"

Tuula's hut is raised ten feet off the ground, straddling a quartet of oak trees that look like chicken legs, the way their roots are splayed into the frozen earth. We climb down on a rope ladder, which swings raggedly in the wind. I wonder how Tuula managed to haul the firewood up the ladder, much less our unconscious bodies. She's as short as I am and far leaner. I don't even try to contemplate how the bear got up there.

We haven't gone very far from the hut when something begins to take shape in the distance, two mounds in the snow, like bleary thumbprints. I squint and squint against the snarling wind. As we approach I see a pair of horses, one black and one white, lashing their tails and snorting.

My wolf hood tumbles down my back as I turn to Tuula. "How did you find them?"

"It wasn't easy," she says. "Horses tend to resist my charms."

I hold my peace about her *charms.*

Letting out a breath, I press my hand against my white mare's muzzle. She snuffs into my palm, a sound of contrition, as if she's trying to apologize for abandoning me. It surprises me how grateful I am to see her again, not just a relic from now-distant Keszi, but a means of escape, should I choose it. Tuula doesn't appear to have a horse of her own. I find myself wondering how fast a bear can run.

Gáspár has his hand braced on his horse's neck, but he's watching Tuula with a tight mouth.

We continue across the plain, toward a black mass moving in the snow. We pace closer and I see that it's not one mass but many, a shifting herd of reindeer with silvery coats. Their heads are bowed, chewing at the sparse tufts of grass that have speared through the frost. As Tuula approaches them their heads lift, limpid eyes following her in a dreamlike stupor. My skin prickles. Beneath his suba, Gáspár's shoulders tense.

Tuula's skirt blows out behind her, casting a dark shadow over the ice. She holds out her hand to the closest reindeer, and it saunters dutifully toward her, nosing her palm. Faster than an eyeblink, its legs buckle beneath it. The beast topples to the ground, its great coronet of antlers rolling unceremoniously in the snow.

"He's asleep now," Tuula says, still holding her gaze on its steel-gray ruff. "Woodsman, why don't you make it quick?"

She returned Gáspár's ax to him inside her hut, handing over the huge blade without a quiver of hesitation. It only made me trust her less. If she didn't fear an armed Woodsman, she was either marvelously stupid or unfathomably powerful. Staring at the crumpled reindeer makes my mouth go dry.

Gáspár swings his ax with a determination and precision that surprises me. Until now he's wielded it clumsily, hesitantly. Blood leaks in jagged rivulets down the snow, following the slight decline of the plain and pooling at my feet. It grafts onto the reindeer's fur, limning each silver fiber, the way Peti's blood hardened on my wolf cloak. Tuula reaches down to grasp the dead creature's antlers, and realization floods me like a trough filling with rainwater.

"You're Juvvi," I say.

Tuula turns toward me slowly. "And what does it mean to you, wolf-girl?"

I only know what is threaded into Virág's stories of heroes and gods, her blinkered histories. I know that when the first Northern scouts rode into Kaleva, they found the Juvvi already there, rows and rows of reindeer at their backs. They said the land was theirs, and that it had been given to them by the gods. As more Northern settlers trickled in, they resented the Juvvi for squandering the land, using it only for hunting and herding and fishing instead of farming. They pushed the Juvvi to the scraggly edges of the Far North, and then the Patrifaith pushed them even farther. Virág says that the Juvvi have a magic of their own, some boon from their gods to help them survive in this barren place, even when a series of Patritian kings tried desperately to snuff them out.

"It means you loathe the Woodsmen," I say finally, raising my voice over the keening of the wind. "Why did you save us?"

Tuula's gaze shifts to Gáspár, his gloved fingers curled rigidly around the handle of his ax. I see the familiar gleam of manacled hatred in her eyes, the lip curl of poison swallowed so many times. After a moment, she looks back at me.

"When I found you on the ice, I knew you would survive," she says. "You were as cold as the Half-Sea in deep winter, but there was still color in your cheeks, and your breath was warm against my hand. He was scarcely breathing at all, and his lips were bone white. He had taken off his cloak and used it to cover you. I knew that if a Woodsman had tried to give his life to save a wolf-girl, he would be willing to make peace with a Juvvi too."

A murder of crows tracks us from overhead, their cries glancing off the ice and echoing for miles. Tuula hums two lonely notes of a song I don't know and the crows descend, grasping the fur of the dead reindeer in their grizzled talons. They glide up again, the flutter of their wings like a staggered heartbeat, and lift the reindeer up to the threshold of Tuula's hut. When the crows depart again, they leave a gift of obsidian feathers, snatched up quickly and swallowed by the wind.

Tuula mounts the rope ladder, then looks back at us expectantly. I stand with my boots planted in the snow, jaw set. I'm not sure how wise it is to follow her back into the bear's den, but the empty plain spools before me for miles, blisteringly white. I remember closing my eyes against the fist clench of cold and not expecting to open them again. Better to face the bear, I decide, and wrap my hand around the first rung of the rope ladder.

I'm not sure what I'm expecting when we reach the top. Tuula offers us food and she doesn't try to wheedle the ax from Gáspár's grasp. She feeds Bierdna hunks of reindeer meat by hand, pink and raw, blood dampening the fur around the bear's mouth. Its incisors are gleaming like slender arrowheads in the firelight.

Gáspár doesn't touch his food, and he doesn't speak either. He stares into the hearth, his good eye angled away from me.

I half expected him to try to refute Tuula's story. Perhaps he thought we were both doomed and it mattered little whose heartbeat faltered first. I have very nearly convinced myself of this when my traitor body turns toward him and my traitor lips part and whisper, "Thank you."

"I didn't do it for your gratitude."

It's the same thing he told me so many days ago in the woods with Peti, and it makes me twice as angry now. "Is it another black mark on your soul, to save a wolf-girl's life? If I'm made to stomach any more of your pious glowering, I'll start to wish you had left me to drown."

"No," he says curtly, without meeting my eyes. "Leave it alone, Évike."

The beats of my name are like three pulses of light: quick, moribund. I blink and they have vanished. For a moment I think I imagined him saying it, imagined him calling me anything but *wolf-girl*. But I know I didn't imagine his body pressing along the length of mine, all those nights on the ice, or the heat of him as we slept in the cloister of roots, breathing soil. My only imaginings are what scroll across the insides of my eyelids: my hand on the column of his bare throat, thumb brushing the blade of his collarbone. I only allow my most prudish dreams to surface now. Anything more will make my stomach curl black with shame.

If Ördög were anything like the Prinkepatrios he would rescind my newfound magic, like a hawk snatching up a mouse, for thinking of a Woodsman this way. I look down at my right hand, bereft of its littlest finger, and feel his threads tighten around my wrist.

Gáspár is examining his own wrist, the soft stretch of skin where his cut had been. The memory of his confession makes my heart quicken, even more when I remember the vow I made in return.

"How many days until Saint István's feast?" I ask, my voice more uncertain than I want it to be.

Gáspár rolls his sleeve back down, still facing away from me. "Too few."

Tuula is watching us with lidded eyes as the bear licks her hand clean, its shoulder blades as huge as boulders. Its ear twitches, like it's trying to rid itself of a fly. Seeing the beast cowed like that, demure as a house cat, makes an idea take root in my mind. Tuula splayed a reindeer on its belly with just the touch of her hand, and summoned a murder of crows with two notes of a nameless lullaby. What would it take, I wonder, for her to call down something bigger and more reticent?

Something luminous with the gods' magic?

I am opening my mouth to speak when the door clatters open, letting in a vicious squall and another girl with it. She is bundled in reindeer fur, hood pulled up over her head.

The bear lurches to its feet, snuffling around the hem of the girl's cloak. Out of habit, I reach into my pocket for my knife before remembering that it was taken from me. I find my coin instead, and clamp my fingers around it. Beside me, Gáspár stiffens, reaching for his ax.

"Szabín," Tuula says, rising. "Our guests are awake. Évike and Gáspár—"

The woman—Szabín—flicks off her hood, but she doesn't stop to greet Tuula. Instead, she crosses the room in one long stride and drops to her knees in front of Gáspár. As she does, her cloak flaps open, revealing a loose brown tunic and the cord of a necklace. Its pendant, a sheet of metal hammered into the shape of a three-pronged spear, gleams with firelight in its grooves and edges.

"What are you doing?" Tuula demands. "Don't humble yourself to a Woodsman."

The revulsion in her voice is blatant, unbidden. Gáspár doesn't flinch.

"He's no ordinary Woodsman," Szabín says. Her eyes are wide and beseeching, even as Gáspár looks down at her in his blank bewilderment. "May Godfather Life keep you, my prince."

From across the room, Tuula makes a choking sound. Realization smooths the furrow in Gáspár's brow, and he offers Szabín a hand.

"May Godfather Death spare you," he says. "Do not kneel for me, Daughter."

Szabín takes his hand and rises to her feet. When he lets go, her sleeve slides down her wrist and nestles in the crook of her elbow, and I can't help but stare in horror: every inch of her skin is mangled pink and white with scar tissue, a hundred raised marks that make Gáspár's blemishes look as innocent as a bramble's needling. Tuula's face is twisted with sorrow, not shock. Gáspár's eye hardens.

Szabín quickly rolls down her sleeve to hide the scarred flesh, a blush deepening her exceptionally pale face.

"Forgive me, my prince," she says to Gáspár. "I saved you, but I cannot serve you. I am no one's Daughter anymore."

Szabín sits down by the fire, her shoulders up around her ears and her hands folded in her lap. Unlike Tuula, she looks a true Northerner: her eyes are two pools of ice-melt and her hair is pale as wheat chaff, shorn close to her scalp. It's almost like a Woodsman's. There is something harsh and roughhewn about her face, something almost masculine. From behind or in half-light, I might have mistaken her for a boy. The bear rests its black nose on the toe of Szabín's boot, eyelids drooping.

"I've seen you before," Szabín whispers, staring at Gáspár. She must not have recognized him at first, when she found him on the ice, all pale and no scowl on his face. "You came to visit our monastery in Kuihta with your father. Back then, you had two eyes."

"Things change," Gáspár says shortly.

"Yes, they do. That was when I thought I could be a faithful servant to the Prinkepatrios. I prayed every day that I was in Kuihta, every hour. Supplicants came to us for healing— fevers and boils, shattered bones. They needed my blood for it. Eventually I grew weary of bleeding for others. I wanted something for myself."

I can hardly bear to look at her now, knowing what's beneath her robes. Gáspár pulls his suba tighter around himself.

"Yet you still wear his symbol." He gestures to her necklace. "Do you still pray to Godfather Life? Does He still answer?"

"Sometimes." Szabín runs her thumb down the length of the iron pendant. "But the moment I decided to run, there was a change. He still answers my call, but His voice is distant. It used to feel as though I was whispering in His ear, but now it feels as though I'm shouting to Him across a lake in the snow."

I remember the way Gáspár's spoken prayers failed him when he tried to light the fire on the Little Plain. Perhaps each step he took farther north with a wolf-girl at his side made the threads noosing him to the Prinkepatrios weather and snap too. The thought drops in my stomach, heavy with unexpected guilt.

"Kuihta." Gáspár says the Northern word carefully in his Southerner's accent, as if it's an ember on his tongue. "That's the monastery where my brother was fostered. Nándor."

A shadow falls over Szabín's face. "Yes. I knew him well."

The air in the room shimmers, the way it does in the languid summer heat. There is a swell of silence that it seems no one wants to fill until Gáspár says, "You must have seen the moment that he began to make himself a saint."

Szabín's fingers curl around the prongs of her pendant with such rapid certainty that I can tell it's an old habit, not quite shaken. "Every Son and Daughter in Kuihta witnessed it."

"Then it's true?" Gáspár's voice is flat, but his throat bobs. "I always thought it was a story invented for the Érsek's pleasure."

"No," says Szabín. "I was there, that day on the ice."

I look between the two of them, stippled with their Patritian scars. Tuula places her hand on the flat of the bear's head, eyes narrow and sharp. "Just because we're godless heathens doesn't mean you can speak as if we're not here."

In another circumstance her remark might have made me laugh. Szabín smiles thinly. "You've heard this story before."

"Yes, but not the wolf-girl. Tell it again, for her sake. She has more to fear from Nándor than any of us."

My heart skips. Unlike these Patritians, Tuula doesn't seem one for grim theatrics. I trust the bleak tenor of her words. "Tell me."

Szabín draws a breath. "Nándor was a monstrous child, indulged in his every whim by the Érsek and his mother, Marjatta. He tormented the other children while their backs were turned, and when they came to him again, he was smiling and sweet as a lamb."

Gáspár huffs a sound that's almost a laugh. Even without looking at him, I can hear the change in his breathing, feel the stiffening of his muscles as his weight shifts on the floorboards. The keen awareness of him is both comfort and curse. I close my four fingers into a fist.

"He was fussed over," Szabín goes on. "There was scarcely a moment he didn't spend cradled at his mother's breast, or balanced on the Érsek's knee. But he was just as keen to buck their warnings. During the bitterest months of winter, we were all shut inside the monastery, for day after cold, dreary day. So Nándor roused his little rebellion, leading the other young Sons and Daughters outside and onto the frozen lake to play. No matter his moments of cruelty, we all were desperate for his favor—he had the oddest way of doing that. Marjatta said he could make a chicken bat its lashes at him while he carved it up for supper."

"Chickens are hardly the best judge of character," I say, but the words come out bloodless, no humor in them.

Szabín scarcely flinches at my interjection. "So we all played on the ice, our breath white, laughing. We didn't notice how it was groaning under us. And then when it split, it seemed impossible—Nándor dragged down beneath the surface, so quick he didn't even scream.

"We were all frozen with terror. It felt an eternity, but it could only have been a few moments before one of us ran back to the monastery for help. I remember watching the little dagger of dark water, the tiniest slit where Nándor had fallen through, waiting to see his body float up to the top. I was certain he was dead. We were all certain of it, by the time the Érsek and Marjatta came. It must have been the Érsek who fished him out, blue-white and cold as the ice itself. His lashes were frozen together, his eyes stuck shut. I was so scared that I wept.

"The other children were weeping, too, but Marjatta was screaming. She was cursing God in the Northern tongue and in Régyar and even in Old Régyar. The Érsek had Nándor in his lap, and he was praying. The ice was still creaking under our feet. And then Nándor opened his eyes. I thought for a moment I had imagined it; his heartbeat had faltered, there was no pulse in his throat. But he opened his eyes and then he pushed himself up and the Érsek took him by the hand and led him off the ice, with Marjatta following them. And the next day during our morning prayers, the Érsek said that Nándor had been made a saint."

"That's impossible," I say, too quickly, before silence is allowed to settle. I want to say that there's only one man who went to the Under-World and returned, and Nándor is no Vilmötten. But I don't think they will appreciate my pagan fairy tales.

"I saw it," says Szabín, without lifting her gaze. "We all did."

"Nándor is in the capital now," Gáspár says. "He's been there for years, gathering his support. With the Érsek's help he's turned half our father's council to his side, and a cabal of Woodsmen on top of it. I suspect that he plans to try and steal the crown during Saint István's feast."

I can hear Tuula shift in her chair, letting out one close breath. Szabín stares at him, slack-jawed. "Saint István's feast is eight days from now."

"I know."

My heart has started a feverish drumbeat. "That's not nearly enough time—"

"I know," Gáspár says again, sharply, and glares at me. I fall silent, face heating. Though I can't quite articulate why, I have a bone-deep feeling that it would be unwise to reveal our plan to Tuula and Szabín, to tell them about the turul.

"Yet here we sit with the true-born prince, who we fished off the ice alongside his wolf-girl consort." Tuula leans forward, eyes narrowing to slits. "You must forgive me for asking why you haven't ridden back to the capital to take your usurper brother's head off."

My flush deepens at the word *consort*. Gáspár's ear tips redden in turn.

"If only court politics were so simple," he says. "Nándor has drawn half the population of Király Szek to his side, not to mention the Woodsmen and counts. If their imagined savior is killed, there will be riots in the square. And the first place the mob will turn is Yehuli Street."

"What?" I wheel toward him, shock and fear like a sharp arrow in my chest. "You never said anything about that."

Gáspár inclines his head, as if holding himself against my sudden fury. "I warned you that Nándor has roused more loathing toward the Yehuli, and he will do worse if he manages to take the throne."

"Worse," I repeat slowly. My throat is terrifically dry. "Tell me what that means."

"The Patritian countries in the west have already begun to expel their Yehuli to Rodinya. I suspect that Nándor will want to follow suit—it would please the Volken envoys, certainly, to see a caravan of Yehuli trailing out of the city, and all their houses turned to ash."

A fire heats my blood and rises into my cheeks, and then I am pushing myself to my feet and shoving through the door into the cold. The rope ladder sways beneath me in the dark, and I nearly trip off the narrow ledge trying to clamber onto it. Tuula calls after me, but the wind muffles her words. My boots crunch the frost below and I curl my fingers around the bristling rope, feeling it chafe against my palm. I exhale, my breath misting in front of me, some poor effort to keep my tears at bay.

My heart is thrumming so loudly in my ears that I don't hear Gáspár coming down the ladder until he is already at my side. For one long moment, the wind unfurls across the empty plain and we both stare straight ahead in silence.

"I thought you understood," he says at last. "Nándor and his followers want to purge the country of everything that is not Patritian, everything that is not Régyar."

I had understood, but only in the vague way of what-ifs and maybes, like squinting at a blurry shadow-shape in the dark. I had made peace, as best I could, with what it meant to be a wolf-girl, to always fear that the Woodsmen might knock down your door and steal away your mother or your sister or your daughter. But I had not allowed myself to consider the other half of what I was: it hurt to hold, like an iron poker left to bathe too long in the hearth. I find the coin in my pocket and press my thumb along its grooved edge.

The wind brushes past us, blowing back my hood. I turn to gauge the look on his face: no furrowed brow, no narrowed eye, no hard, haughty mouth. His head is tilted, lips parted slightly. In the silvery moonlight, I can see the sweep of his dark lashes against his cheek. It is easy to imagine, in this suspended, silent moment, that all the Woodsman has leached out of him. He is only the man who held me in the husk of that huge tree. The man who dove into the frigid water to save me.

"If your mother were alive," I ask, pausing to draw a shallow breath, "out there somewhere, would you ever stop looking for her?"

Gáspár blinks. After another beat of silence, he says, "No. But I would hope that she was out there looking for me too."

"What if she didn't know?" I press on. "What if she thought that you were dead?"

"This is sounding less hypothetical by the second," Gáspár says, but his tone is gentle.

Hands shaking, I pull the coin from my pocket and hold it out to him.

"Can you read it?" My voice sounds thin, almost unintelligible in the wind. "There's Régyar on it."

Gáspár takes the coin and turns it over. I realize for the first time that his hand is ungloved, bare. "It only says the king's name. Bárány János. I can't read the Yehuli."

"I could," I whisper. "Once."

I hear the shift in Gáspár's breathing. "I thought you said you never knew your father."

It was just a small lie, and I'm surprised he even remembered. I shake my head, squeezing my eyes shut as if I can will all of it back to me, half-forgotten memories pulsing like distant torchlight.

"He came every year when I was young. Virág and the other women didn't like it, but he stayed with my mother and me in our hut. He brought us trinkets from Király Szek, and books. Long scrolls. When he unraveled them, they stretched all the way from the door of our hut to the hearth in the corner. He started teaching me the letters, alef and bet and gimel . . ." The memory winks away from me, but I swear I can hear old parchment crinkling. "There was a story of a clever trickster queen and a wicked minister, and when he told it he gave the minister a silly, pinched voice, so he sounded like an old woman with a stuffed nose."

I let out a short laugh, and when I look at Gáspár he's smiling faintly too. But there's something stiff and guarded in it, like a rabbit sensing a snare.

"He wasn't there, when my mother was taken." My voice grows smaller with every word. "The Woodsmen came for her, and the other men and women burned everything that he'd given us, all the scrolls and stories. I buried the coin in the woods and dug it up later."

"What about your father?" Gáspár prompts, gentle still. "Why wouldn't he come back for you?"

"Because he thought I was dead," I say. I feel the oddest flood of relief as I say it, like the power I thought the words might have is nothing but ash on the wind. "And he had every right to think it, in truth. When a woman with a young child, a boy, is taken, it's custom to leave the child out in the woods and let the cold and the wolves at him. There's hardly enough food to go around as it is, but when the child is a girl, they find enough to spare until she grows into her magic. Everyone in Keszi already knew that I had none, and wasn't worth a bit of bread from their table."

Something snaps, lightning in the air. I double over, gasping for breath, as the power of the story is dredged out of me like a clump of dead leaves, trapped so long beneath the rushing water. Bent at the waist, I cough and splutter, and then Gáspár lays his hand on my back. I can feel his fingers tensing through my wolf cloak, like he can't decide whether to snatch it away or let it stay.

"Virág saved me," I manage. "Even though I was a terrible, sullen, mean child who always had a red nose and skinned knees." Gáspár opens his mouth, but I go on fiercely before he can get in a word, "And don't tell me I haven't changed a bit."

"I wasn't going to say that."

Stomach unsettled, I reach for the coin in my pocket before remembering that he still has it, bright as a pooling of sunlight in his cupped palm. He holds it gingerly, like it's something extraordinarily precious, even though one piece of gold can't be worth very much to a prince, disinherited or not.

"You know that my father is in Király Szek," I say. The wind has lulled to only the feeblest wailing, and it sounds like an animal orphaned on the ice. "Nándor will drive him out, won't he? Given the first chance? And now no one will be there to stop it."

Gáspár hesitates. I hear his teeth come together, his jaw shifting to its familiar clench. Then he nods.

I look down at my own hands. In the moonlight, they are

pale as lamb tallow, knuckles nicked with tiny scars. There is the absence of my pinky, the black space where it once was suffused with a power I still don't understand. And then there is Gáspár, tall and silent as a sentinel beside me. If the moon slivers away and the wind picks up again with enough force to blister skin, I wonder if it will be dark and cold enough for him to want to hold me again, and for us both to promise ourselves we will break apart at the first rosy band of dawn.

"Don't be rash, Évike," he says softly, and then he drops the coin into my hand. I squeeze it so tightly that its scored edges press feathered imprints across my palm, and when I finally tuck it back in my pocket, I can still feel the heat his skin has left on it.

# CHAPTER TEN

I sleep uneasily, in a thrall of worry, belly quaking. Szabín's words are looping through my mind, and my teeth are gritted around the shape of Nándor's name. I'm shivering even under the reindeer pelt, my body contorting itself into a shape that fits Gáspár's perfectly, a flesh memory of our nights spent in the frozen forest. I glance so often at his sleeping form that I'm disgusted with myself, and I drag my pelt toward the bear, instead. A bear is an enemy I can more easily understand, and fear or loathe accordingly. Even snoring, I can see all its teeth.

A purple dawn lifts off the ice, sunrise steaming behind a haze of clouds and fog. Gáspár turns on his side, eye open, and meets my gaze at last. I feel a twitch of shame, wondering if he saw me moving and thrashing through the night. The memory of our conversation is an insistent hum in the back of my mind, like the soft lap of water against the lakeshore. I push myself up, careful not to rouse the bear, and crouch beside him.

"Seven days," I whisper. "There's still time to find the turul, but only if we leave now."

Gáspár nods and rises, a muscle feathering in his jaw. Wordless, he reaches for his ax, propped up against the wood-pile. I have gotten quite good at deciphering his moody silences and I can tell something is caught in him like a burr in a dog's coat, but I can't press him for it now. From the small hut's second room, Tuula and Szabín still haven't stirred. I raise the hood of my cloak and push open the door, cold stinging my cheeks and nose.

He starts to climb down the rope ladder, and as soon as his feet touch the ice below I follow. I haven't gotten far before I feel something snatch at my hood from above, and with a choked gasp I nearly slip from the rung. When my hood falls back I only see Szabín staring down at me, her lips pressed angrily, pendant glinting with a sharp and vicious light.

"Let go of me," I bite out. "Or are we prisoners here?"

Szabín's grip only tightens. "No Southerner has ever come to Kaleva without hunger in their eyes."

I want to reply that being from Keszi hardly makes me a Southerner, but Szabín's meaning is plain: to her, we are all Southerners. I steal a quick glance at Gáspár below, still holding fast to the ladder, and he looks back up at me in bewilderment.

"I'm already quite full of reindeer meat, thanks to Tuula," I say, and smile as sweetly as I can manage. Szabín's scowl only deepens. "What's the use of renouncing your oath, sister, if you treat every pagan you meet with wariness and reproach?"

"You are the only one I've ever met," Szabín says. She has the same muzzled disdain as Gáspár in the earliest days of our journey, when he alternated only between admonishing me for my barbarity and fretting over the state of his soul. "And you've done nothing to earn my trust."

"I've done nothing to earn my ire either," I say. The wind snarls past us with a renewed ferocity, shaking the ladder, and if Gáspár hadn't been holding it from below I might have fallen. I have the odd, unbidden feeling that if I did fall, he would move to catch me. "It seems ill fitting for someone who shares their bed with a Juvvi to curl their lip at me. Do you take off your pendant before your coupling?"

My words are enough to unbalance her, to make her hold slacken at last. I wrench myself free, leaving a few hairs of my wolf cloak behind in her fingers, and hurry the rest of the way down the ladder. When my boots touch the snow I see that Szabín is still staring at me from above, her eyes narrowed, thin as gashes.

"What did she say to you?" Gáspár asks.

"Morbid Patritian dramatics," I reply, voice short. Her words have pricked me in an unexpectedly tender place, or perhaps it's only a deeper and older ember that she blew to life. Szabín is less a foe and more a fool, for believing that a Patritian could ever live in sated, happy peace with a Juvvi. Someone's blade will swing between them eventually, or their own rages will burn Tuula's hut to the ground. There is a small part of me that bristles with the knowledge that I am just as much a fool for ever finding comfort in the arms of a Woodsman. I turn up my hood again and face my gaze forward.

In daylight, the lake is as smooth as a polished silver coin, and the reflections of the dark trees are rippled on its surface. They are warped into something smaller and more comprehensible now, a tree I could have climbed as a child back in Keszi.

I step over their reflections as we walk, the ice groaning and creaking under our feet, but nothing breaks. I can't even see the hole where I fell through, or the lacework of cracks. The ice has stitched itself back together like white silk over a black tear.

When we finish our crossing I could kiss the hard, solid ground in relief, even despite the ceaseless danger of the wood, thrumming as if with its own green-white heartbeat. Wreathed in fog, the forest is unchanged: there are the huge trees, lichen-thick and turned dark with snow melt, the frost glittering on each pine needle like strewn glass.

I remember the certainty I felt only a little over a day ago, some unnamable instinct flaring in my chest as I stared up at the tangle of branches, all knitted together like the weave of a basket, blue sky scarcely bleeding through. I feel none of that same certainty now. There is only Nándor's name gliding through my mind, and the refrain of *seven days, seven days, seven days* pattering after it like a hunting dog trailing its quarry. I press my palm against the nearest trunk, but if I ever did have some primal witch's sense, it is gone now.

Despair looses in me. "I don't know anymore. I thought the turul would be here, but now . . ."

Gáspár's expression doesn't shift; it's as if my words have glanced off him. There is only the same hard look in his eyes, as if he had scarcely expected anything less. I don't know why that, his disappointment, wounds me worse than anything.

Then, a flicker in his eye. "Do you hear that?"

I pause, balled fist falling to my side. It's the ground, not the trees, that's throbbing beneath our feet, and all of a sudden the wind has gone silent. I open my mouth to reply, but the words shrivel in my throat as a giant hand curls around the trunk nearest me, its fingers the precise color and texture of the bark. The hand twists for a moment to find its purchase, and then it wrenches the tree from its roots, flinging it upward into the oblivious gray sky.

The creature standing before me has no eyes, just two misshapen slits in the corrugated bark of its face. Its grizzled beard is made from garlands of pine needles and dead leaves, held together with sticky yellow sap. Its body is as thick as two trees, dovetailed, and its arms and legs are fat with moss and rot. A single bird circles its head, as if looking for a place to nest among the animate foliage.

I am still staring, openmouthed and dumb, when its fingers wrap around my torso and lift me into the air.

Gáspár shouts my name, those three syllables that shocked me so completely the night before, and then I hear the rasp of metal as he draws his ax. The creature turns me over in its hands, letting me slip from its grasp and then catching me again, like a cat with some curious plaything. Every time the ground comes rushing up at me my stomach roils in nauseated protest, but I am too rattled to even scream, much less try to reach for my inscrutable new magic.

I am overwhelmed only by my own desperate stupidity when the creature picks me up by my cloak, threadlike in its giant fingers, and holds me above its open mouth. Its breath reeks of burning flesh and rotted wood and a few tears prick at the corners of my eyes, futile and doomed. Gáspár's ax clangs furiously against the creature's wooden leg, and the immediacy of his action shocks me now: there's no hesitation, not like the way his blade faltered in the tent with Kajetán.

And then, inexplicably, another voice rings out sharp and clear: "*It goes without stopping, bends but never breaks, has branches and knots yet cannot grow leaves.*"

The creature pauses, letting me dangle squirming from its fingers. The bark of its face crumples like a furrowed brow. With its free hand it scratches its head, puzzled—looking, for a moment, quite human.

Tuula is a brightly colored speck in the snow. She repeats, "*It goes without stopping, bends but never breaks, has branches and knots yet cannot grow leaves.*"

The creature's eye-slits narrow. When I slip from its grasp, I squeeze my own eyes shut, bracing to hit the ground hard. But the impact is muffled, muted. I open my eyes and find myself draped across Bierdna's back. The bear twists its head around and sniffs at me, and my breath catches on the words *thank you*. When have I begun to imagine that it can understand me?

Gáspár freezes halfway in his path toward me, ax held tight, face pale. When he looks me up and down I don't think

I am inventing the concern in his eye, but he stops himself before he reaches my side.

I slide off the bear, still gasping. Tuula looks down her nose at me, arms folded, Szabín at her back. Once I can manage to speak, I can only ask, "What *is* that?"

"Just one of our pesky, awful wood giants," Tuula says. "They're very strong, as you can see, but very stupid. If you tell them a riddle, they'll be stuck for ages trying to solve it, and stand still until finally they forget what you said in the first place."

I just stare up at her, miserable and cowed. True to her word, the creature is rooted to the ground, still scratching its wooden head.

"It's a river, by the way," Tuula goes on.

"A what?"

"The answer to the riddle." Her voice hitches. "It goes without stopping, bends but never breaks, has branches and knots yet cannot grow leaves. A river. I suppose you ought to know, since you're planning on braving the woods alone. I won't relish saving your insipid life again, wolf-girl."

I swallow the insult, at least half-deserved, and get to my feet without breaking my stare. Reindeer and crows, wood giants and bears. Tuula has knowledge and magic that make the North look like water in a cupped hand, something that can be held fast and close. If she were to draw a map of Kaleva, it would be marked with paths that circumvent the monsters and moving trees, lines that cleave through danger to safety. Even the women of my village could never dream of moving through the forest with such assurance.

I clench my four-fingered hand, still pale with its untested power. Tuula is watching me with her black hawk's glare, as if she can even see into the animal part of my mind, can see the refrain of *seven days, seven days, seven days,* or the hunger in my eyes. Szabín was right about one thing—no one would come to such a bitter, brutal place unless they were desperate.

"You know where it is, don't you?" I say, pushing to my feet. "The turul."

Tuula's voice comes back sharp and quick. "The turul is not for you to find."

The briskness of her reply makes heat bloom in my chest. I stride toward her, even as the bear growls, showing her yellow teeth. "You knew we were here for the turul. All this time and you didn't say a word."

"Of course I knew," Tuula snaps. "You wouldn't trudge this far north except to make some reckless grab for power. And the Woodsmen all want the same thing. If they're not trying to stamp out the Juvvi, they're trying to steal the magic that keeps us safe from them."

I turn to Gáspár, heart pounding. He hasn't taken a step closer toward us, but his hand has gone to his ax. Storm clouds are brushing across his face.

"Why bother saving us, then?" I bite out. "Why not leave us to die?"

Tuula's mouth puckers, like she's tasted some fruit gone foul. "I told you, wolf-girl. I'm not entirely black-hearted. Woodsmen *are* human, underneath those ridiculous uniforms and all their fanatically devout loathing. I hoped that in your gratitude I might persuade you to give up this senseless quest."

Her voice is relentlessly smooth, and it makes an awful helplessness well up inside of me. Gáspár's words are circling my head like a flock of crows, my father's coin burning me through the fabric of my cloak.

"You may be content hiding here in the corner of the world," I say, and this time I look toward Szabín, too, scowling under her hood, "but there are so many people who don't have the protection of the ice and snow and magic. If the turul is the only thing that can match Nándor's power, you're damning them by concealing it."

"I'm not concealing anything." Tuula steps toward the bear, resting her hand on the breadth of its huge shoulders.

"The turul is not for you to find. And perhaps I made a mistake, not leaving you to freeze. The prince has gotten his poison into you—you might as well swear fealty to their god, too, because your village will not take you back if you deliver the turul right into the hands of the king."

Rage sweeps through me with such a viciousness that it makes my eyes water. I look at Gáspár, blank-faced, stupidly. I have tried for so long not to think of Virág, not to think of the turul tumbling out of the sky, my arrow in its breast. But I have always known, of course, the truth: that killing the turul will sever me from Keszi for good. I cannot go limping back to Virág with its blood still wet on my hands; she would let the wolves at me this time, and not feel a twitch of guilt.

I open my mouth, but no words rise from my throat. The bear huffs, moisture beading on its black nose. And then Gáspár says, "It's no use."

Words rise quickly, furiously. "What?"

"It's no use prodding her; she won't reveal the turul." His voice is hard and flat, and he gives Tuula a flint-eyed stare. "Besides, we've lost too much time already. Saint István's feast is in seven days, and if I linger any longer here, I won't be able to stop him."

"You said you couldn't stop him without the turul." In turn, my voice sounds as wavering as the wind. "We struck a bargain."

"I know."

He says nothing more, and I can only look at him: his sharp, square jaw, his skin like polished bronze. His dark lashes and petulant lips. Only he's not scowling now: his eye is steady, but almost too bright.

"It's not my fault," I manage, thinking of the Woodsmen running through our village, of all the ways that the king would find to punish Keszi. "Your father—"

"I know," Gáspár says again, in a hushed, plying tone, like he's trying to coax a rabbit from its burrow and into his trap.

"And I swear to you that I will keep my father from having his vengeance on your village, but I have to return to Király Szek now. There's no more time to waste."

The tenor of his words makes me feel child-small, my face pink against the blister of the wind. "And what am I to do?"

"Go home," he says.

For a moment, I let myself imagine it. I think of dragging myself back through the tundra, across the Little Plain, past the villagers with their pitchforks and their burning eyes, the word *witch* on their tongues. I think of facing down the monsters of Ezer Szem and bursting through the tree line, panting and gasping, and seeing only the other villagers' empty stares. Katalin will breathe her blue flame at me—but not before tearing her wolf cloak off my back. The boys I've coupled with will look away, flushing in shame. Boróka will make her wheedling protests. I can't even let myself think of Virág. And they will all hate me twice over, for not dying when I was supposed to.

And then, without my willing it, another flood of images comes volleying up. I think of Gáspár's arms braced around me inside the damp tree hollow, roots holding us in that timeless suspension. His soft, weary voice in my ear, the pine-salt smell of him. Him diving into the ice after me, and putting his own cloak around me even as he froze. My stomach folds with shame. I'd told him how much they all loathed me, how they wanted to leave me to be eaten, even confessed the awful secret of my waning grief: that sometimes I couldn't remember my mother at all. I sheathed my claws and hid my teeth for him, and now he wants me to go soft and toothless back to Virág with her reed whip, and Katalin with her fire, and all the other villagers with their pitiless gazes.

Anything I can think to say feels abysmally stupid. So I turn away from Gáspár, away from Tuula and Szabín and the infernal bear, and trample through the snow, toward the lake's pale, unblinking eye.

The way Virág's story goes, Vilmötten left his home for Kaleva, nothing but his kantele strapped to his back. He traveled for so long that he found himself no longer in the Middle-World, the mortal world, but in the Under-World, Ördög's kingdom. All around him he saw the souls of the departed, dead of illness or old age or grievous injury, their skin black and fetid, worms writhing in the sockets of their missing eyes.

No mortal had ever traveled to the Under-World and returned. Vilmötten knew that. But he began to pluck his kantele and sing, a song so beautiful that it moved Ördög, the god of death himself, to tears.

"You may go," he told Vilmötten. "But you can never return."

And so Vilmötten was allowed to enter the Middle-World again. But later, when he fell down and cut his hand on a sharp rock, he saw that the cut was not bleeding. The skin had stitched up again in an instant, tight as a drum. Vilmötten looked at his reflection in a lake of ice and saw that all his wrinkles had been smoothed, the gray on his temple dyed black and new. He was young again, and no wound or fever could harm him. Ördög, the god of death, had given Vilmötten the gift of life.

The story is the origin of the other girls' healing magic, only they are not quite as immaculate as Vilmötten. Their hair still goes silver and their skin still creases with time, just slower than others'. Slower than mine. And the healing takes something from them: I have seen Boróka's face grow paler and paler as she worked, sweat pearling on her brow, and afterward she was so tired she slept through two sunrises without waking. It almost seemed like it aged her, the work of her magic eating away at the years of her life.

As I skid across the lake, toward the dark mound of Tuula's hut in the distance, I stare down at my hand with its missing finger. I remember closing my fist over the fire, watching the flames die beneath my touch, and it occurs to me: if the other wolf-girls can make fire and I can snuff it out, it means that perhaps, where they heal, I can hurt.

I'm too afraid to wonder what it will take from me. I clamber up the snowbank, panting hard. Just past her hut, Tuula's reindeer move in blurs of silver, like clouds drifting. Their antlers are bone grails, holding cupfuls of sky. They are still nosing the ground absently as I approach, their sleek flanks rising and falling with their breath.

The threads around my wrist go taut. I reach my four-fingered hand toward the nearest reindeer, and I almost hesitate. My intent wavers for a moment, and then snaps back again, like a scale righting itself after the weight is lifted. I splay my fingers against its flank, feeling the soft give of its fur.

Moments whip past me, wind snarling. And then the reindeer rears its head and grunts and bolts away from me, but not before I see the burned mark on its side, a red blister in the shape of my hand.

The rest of the herd startles with it, bucking down the plain. I let them shoulder past me, waiting for the repercussion. Waiting for what I have done to echo, for it to reverberate in my ear like a plucked bow string. Nothing. I wait and wait, and I don't realize that I'm crying until I feel the tears freezing on my cheeks.

If it were so easy as that, I could've had power long ago. If I had known, I would have lopped off my finger in a heartbeat. I would have killed all of Katalin's blue flames, and I would never have lowed for any of Virág's lashings. I feel like a guileless child that I had to wait for a Woodsman to teach me what it meant to sacrifice. That I hadn't understood the stories of my own people until I'd spoken them aloud myself, with Gáspár listening.

*My people.* Katalin would have snatched the words right from my mouth.

I hear the shuffle of footsteps behind me. Quickly, I wipe the frozen tears off my cheeks and turn. Gáspár is pacing across the plain, wind carding through his dark hair. Something hard and hot rises in my throat.

"What an odd reversal of fortune," I say, as he halts before me. "A Woodsman chasing a wolf-girl *back* to Keszi."

"I'm not chasing you," Gáspár says. His lip twitches, like he's trying especially hard to keep from scowling. "You are not a seer. The king would have no use for you anyway."

The old wound still prickles. "I'm not a seer, but I have power. You've seen it."

"An even odder reversal of fortune." Gáspár's eye narrows. "A wolf-girl begging for a Woodsman to take her to Király Szek."

"I'm not begging you," I say. With a sudden rush of feckless spite, I add, "Would you like it if I did?"

I only said it to make him flush, and it succeeds. His ear tips turn pink, but his gaze is unflinching. "I suppose it depends on what you were begging for."

My cheeks fill with an answering warmth. I hadn't expected his rejoinder, or the way he's looking at me so intently, without blinking.

"I don't have to beg," I say. "You can't stop me. You said that if you knew your mother was alive, you wouldn't stop looking for her. My father is alive in Király Szek and Nándor has lit a fire at his feet. What else am I to do?"

A long, rough breath comes out of Gáspár's mouth, as pale as mist in the cold.

"You're a fool," he says baldly. "A bigger fool than a Woodsman who thought he might make a bargain with a wolf-girl, or who thought he might find the turul. Whatever power you have, it's not enough—it's not *nearly* enough. Nándor is a worse threat, it's true. But there is no safety for a wolf-girl in my father's city either. I swore once that I would tell you what the king does to the women that he takes."

My fingers curl into my palm. "And will you?"

"No," he says. "But I will tell you that when I was a boy,

my father had decided that my mother shouldn't leave the castle. He had a number of chambers set aside for her, and they all had iron bars on the windows. He would only come in at night, and berate her in words she didn't understand. So I would stand there, speaking Merzani to my mother and Régyar to my father, translating his slurs and her pleading, and pushing myself between them, so his blows would land on me, instead."

Shock twists through me, and then a torrent of grief. Thinking of him as a little boy almost undoes me, and I open my mouth to reply, but Gáspár speaks first.

"I don't say that to earn your pity. I am the one who ought to be pitying you, for how little you understand about what you plan to do. My father is a weaker man than Nándor in some ways, but he is hardly less cruel. If he would do such a thing to his wife, only because she was a foreigner, and to his son, only because he dared stand between them, what do you think he will do to you? The wolf-girl who swindled him?"

I shake my head fiercely, as if his words are arrows and I can keep them from hitting their mark. Shivering against the wind, I reach for the coin in my pocket. I have traced its engravings so many times that I have memorized their strokes, even if I don't understand their meaning. If it is a choice between drowning in the same river that has dragged me down a thousand times or walking into a pit of fire that has never burned me once, I will choose the flames and learn to bear it. But I cannot bear one more moment of Katalin's fury, or another lick of Virág's reed whip. Not when my father is somewhere in Király Szek, frothing at the shore like a tide missing the pull of its moon.

"Then perhaps you'll get to see me bare after all," I tell him, squeezing out the jest around the lump in my throat. "Does the king pluck his wolf-girls like roosters before he cooks and eats them?"

Gáspár just stares at me, lips parted, his eye filled with

all the hazy midday sunlight. His face wavers somewhere between incredulous and furious, and I see the shift, the moment when he chooses his mute fury: he raises his shoulders
around his ears, fists clenching at his sides, and stalks away
from me without another word.


It is dark again by the time we are saddling our horses, by the time we
have shaken Tuula and Szabín. In the Kalevan winter, the daylight hours slip through your hands like water. Overhead, the
stars are bright jewels threaded through the quilt of evening
sky. My mare's coat gleams white, her mane like streaks of
moonlight. Gáspár's black mount is almost invisible in the
night, and when he leaps on the horse's back, all wrapped in
his suba, he looks almost invisible too.

He doesn't speak to me as we set off across the tundra. I
armor myself in the certainty of my power, that red handprint
on the reindeer's flank, and the memory of my father's voice,
distant as the calling of a crow. They are enough to keep my
back straight, my eyes fixed forward and south. But around
the reins, my fingers are trembling. ·

# CHAPTER ELEVEN

Kaleva's empty wasteland slowly gives way to green: scraggly, wind-battered elms and long tracts of chewed-up grass, trampled under the cloven hooves of the wild racka sheep with their great spiraling horns. The hills bubble toward a black stretch of mountains in the distance, the outline of which I can only see if I squint and hold up my thumb to block the sun. The mountains are a natural border between Régország and the Volkstadt, our western neighbors, who, as Gáspár told me, had a head start on the Patrifaith and are much holier than us.

Gáspár has scarcely spoken to me since we left Kaleva, wind and snow chasing us south. I offer him my killed rabbits only once they're skinned and bloodless, but he doesn't answer my attempts at reconciliation with anything but a steely nod. And at night, he stamps away from me, far on the other side of the fire, lying down with his back turned. I huddle under my cloak, seething in my own stupid hurt. I know I shouldn't be hungering after the warmth of a Woodsman's embrace, but a part of me wants to rage at him anyway. If I showed him the scars latticed down the back of my thighs, would he accept my reasons for not wanting to return to Keszi? More likely he would flush and stammer at his first sight of a woman's bare skin. I sleep fitfully, if at all.

One morning, we come upon a cluster of weatherworn stones, rising out of a hilltop like jagged teeth. Lichen-covered, they are washed nearly white with time. In the center of each stone is a hollow circle, big enough for me to put my fist through. Seeing them makes the hairs rise on the back of my neck. Gáspár circles them on his mount, horse whinnying.

"Are they a pagan creation?" he asks finally, as though he can't swallow his curiosity any longer. "A site of worship for your gods?"

It's the first time I've heard his voice in days, and it makes my stomach quiver in a funny way, relief twining through with despair. I shake my head, brow furrowed. Inside one of the holes is a strip of sun-bleached fabric that might have once been red, and a smear of something dark that looks like dried blood. One of Virág's stories bristles in my mind, and I feel Ördög's threads tightening their grasp on my hand. Whoever bled here was older than the pagans. These stones were arranged by something far more ancient, something as old as the Earth when it was new.

I am so desperate to hear him speak again that a question flutters up in me, embarrassingly earnest. "Would you like to hear the story of how Isten made the world?"

Gáspár's lips thin. "I think I've heard too many of your fairy tales, wolf-girl."

Now that he's angry at me I am a wolf-girl again, and I ought to think him only a Woodsman. I should wring his kindnesses out of me like water from my hair. I should forget that he ever fell asleep with his arms around me, and think only of finding my father. But I feel like a dog with its teeth in something, holding fast and hard, knowing it will hurt too much and maybe take my teeth out with it, if I let go.

"Afraid you'll start to enjoy them?" I ask instead. If I can't win back his camaraderie, at least I can make him sulk and flush like our earliest days. Anything is preferable to this stone-faced silence.

"No," he says shortly. "And since you are so eager to die, perhaps we ought to ride faster toward Király Szek. Saint István's feast is in two days."

I stand up, brushing dirt from my knees, and try not to let his words ruffle me. Ördög has blessed me with his power, and it only takes a flicker of my will, a phantom pain in my absent pinky, to wield it. Its potential coils inside me, like a serpent under a sun-warmed stone.

"Perhaps I'll tell you anyway," I say, clambering back on my mount. "Unless you can think of some way to silence me."

"Enough," Gáspár murmurs, a low warning. His fingers are clenched tight around the reins, but he doesn't give another word of protest.

And so I speak into the green silence, wind scarcely rustling the slender elms.

"Once there was only Isten, alone in the Upper-World, his hair white with seven eternities. He did not think he could survive another one without companionship, because gods get lonely too. In his anguish, he began to weep. His tears washed over the barren land below with such vigor that they became the first ocean, made of salt and water and grief.

"But even when the ocean flowed, Isten was still alone. Yet now, as he surveyed the beautiful thing he had created, he was not angry or heartbroken. He was at peace, and that is the only time when you can make a sacrifice that works. So Isten cut out a piece of his own flesh and let it fall to the earth below. When it landed there, it began to stretch and change, until it became the first men and women of the world, sweet and pliant and peaceful.

"Isten's new world was beautiful, and only a fool would not want to live there. There was no word for *summer*, because every day was as warm and bright as the last. There was no word for *full* because not a single belly had ever ached with hunger. There was no word for *happy* because no one had ever been anything else.

"Then, one day, a woman went to wash her clothes by the riverside. She knelt on the shore and dipped her dress in the water. But as she did, her hand skimmed against a rock, sharp and slick. The water around her streamed red, and when she lifted her hand into the light, she saw that she was bleeding, even though she had no word for blood. She could not explain to herself or to the villagers what had happened, but Isten had seen it all. He thought: *I did not make rocks sharp enough to cut. I did not make human flesh soft enough to bleed.*

"Soon enough, the vegetables that the villagers pulled from the earth became black and putrid with rot. The ground beneath their feet had grown hard and white with frost. And when one villager looked at his reflection in the lake, he saw that his face was creased with deep wrinkles. The villagers had to create a word for what they saw, so they called it *despair*.

"They begged Isten for an answer to their troubles, and so Isten searched. He came down to the Earth and walked upon it like a man. He walked until he heard a rumble beneath his feet, and the rumble was a voice.

"'Hello, Father,' the voice said. 'I believe you are looking for me.'

"Isten looked all around, but he could see nothing. 'Who are you?'

"'Look below,' the voice said.

"So Isten did. He peeled back the layers of the world he had made and found there was another one beneath it that smelled of damp and rot. Flies circled Isten's head and maggots writhed under his feet. It was too dark to see anything ahead, but the strange voice still echoed around him, as if the blackness itself had a sound.

"'It's you,' Isten said. 'You are the one who brings decay to plants and flowers. You let frost lay upon the earth. You make my people grow white hair, and make their skin fold with wrinkles. You let them bleed, and you let them feel despair.'

"'Yes,' Ördög said. 'All of these things are true, and I am all of these things.'

"'How did you do it?' Isten asked. 'I did not create a world to rot or bleed.'

"'But you did create me,' Ördög said. 'When you cut out a piece of your flesh to make the world, I was born alongside it. Creation can only exist alongside destruction, peace alongside pain. Wherever there is life, I will also be.'

"Isten thought, *He called me Father.*

"Isten left Ördög's kingdom and returned to Earth, only now he called it the Middle-World, because there was another one beneath it. In this way, it became the world we know—a world where growth could easily become rot, where peace could easily become pain. A world that had a word for *happiness*, because now there was a word for *despair*. It was not Isten's world anymore."

When I finish the story, I feel breathless. Gáspár is staring determinedly at the blank space between his horse's ears, but his eye darts toward me, and I can see the gleam of reluctant interest.

"Is that all you think of death?" he asks finally. "No wonder you're so keen to throw yourself into my father's arms."

I blink at him, unmoored by his reaction. "What do you mean?"

"This god of yours, Ördög"—he says the word with a wrinkled nose, as if the very shape of it on his lips repulses him—"he doesn't subject the denizens of his Under-World to hellfire and torment, and every human soul finds its way to him when it dies, no matter how good or evil they were on Earth—in the Middle-World. What's to stop humans from doing harm, if you don't fear for the fate of your soul after death?"

On the backs of my thighs, my old scars flare. "I think humans are perfectly capable of punishing each other. What a terribly absurd question to ask, when you're sitting there with your missing eye. You should know better than anyone that people can be as cruel as any god."

"It's not about cruelty." Gáspár has finally turned to face me. "It's about power. Without power, all you have is anger and spite. Cruelty comes when you have the strength to turn your anger on someone else."

For a moment he sounds like the smooth-voiced prince again, armored in his eloquence, so stubbornly certain. I have missed this thread of petulance in him, but I will never admit it.

"Yes, I know that well," I say. "People turned their anger on me every single day in Keszi."

Gáspár goes silent again, angling his face away from me. After a moment, he says, "Is that where you got the scar on your eyebrow?"

I didn't think he'd ever looked at me closely enough to notice. My hand flies up to touch the pink slit of scar tissue, cleaving my left eyebrow in two.

I almost want to ask when he noticed, but I'm afraid it will make him put up his shield again. Instead I say, "Another girl in my village blew fire in my face. Katalin."

The shame of the confession hardly occurs to me. Gáspár doesn't purse his lips in pity, and I think about him telling me how he stood between his mother and father as a child, relaying their cruelties and enduring their blows. His jaw un-clenches, ever so slightly. "Why did she do that?"

"Because I stole one of the cabbage rolls off her plate. I think. It's hard to remember."

Gáspár's breathing hitches. "And did you often find your-self under threat of fire?"

"You already know that I did," I say, feeling heat rise in my chest. "Do you think that they drew lots to see who would be used to trick the Woodsmen? There was never a question. Never a word of protest. They all *wanted* it to be me. How would you like to crawl back into the arms of the people who cast you out to die?"

As soon as I finish, I'm flushed with chagrin. His ax and his cloak and his missing eye that terrified me—they are all a testament to his father's loathing. Coming back to save the king must hurt as much as being expelled to save Katalin. It's hard to think that it took me so long to realize that the shape of our wounds is the same.

There is no apology, no rejoinder, but the air changes between us, like sunlight beaming through the tree branches. When I catch Gáspár looking at me, his eye is narrowed and keen, as if he's trying to follow something that's moving farther and farther out of sight.

Still, we lapse back into silence, listening to the heavy pants of our horses and the sound of the river as it rushes downstream. I am about to suggest we stop and let our horses drink when a wonderful, familiar smell wafts toward me—the heady scent of boiling meat and the tangy finish of paprika, like a long breath followed by a sharp inhale.

We've eaten well in Szarvasvár—black birds and rabbits and one gamy racka sheep—but the smell of gulyás reminds me of feast tables and Virág's fried bread, the memory more of a comfort than anything else that comes to mind when I think about Keszi. As much as Gáspár mocked me for craving peasant food, he's stopped his horse to sniff the air too. In the distance, I can glimpse the green roof of a sod house.

Neither of us speaks, but we press on toward the village, dug right out of the riverbed. It's a winter village, a place where the farmers and herders retire when it's too cold for tents and the whole plain is pale with frost. Fires are burning in the windows of the houses like lighted eyes, and the smoke that wreathes out of them is curled like a beckoning hand. There are no doorways, just black holes in the sod that remind me of gaping mouths. The roofs are thatched with grass, and a seashell chime rattles in the threshold of the nearest house. The gulyás smell is almost thick enough to taste.

"It wouldn't be the worst thing, to beg some hospitality," I say, hopefully hiding my desire with nonchalance.

Gáspár is quiet, considering. "Perhaps you can have your peasant fare after all," he says, as if he has heard my earlier thoughts.

The wind rattles the seashells as we climb down from our mounts. I wonder how the villagers have managed to get them. Régország is landlocked on all sides, except for the small strip of coastline in Kaleva that clings to the frigid edge of the Half-Sea. Curiosity tugs at me, but the pull of the gulyás smell is stronger.

The interior of the sod house is cramped but tidy, as tidy as any place made out of dirt can be. Wooden shelves are notched into the wall, housing row after row of glass jars full of herbs and brightly colored spices. A table and two chairs are crammed beneath them, and at the very center of the sod house is a hearth with a big boiling pot, and an old woman hunched over it.

"I beg your pardon," Gáspár says. "We are travelers on our way to Király Szek. Could we trouble you for a meal? As soon as we eat, we'll be on our way again, and we won't ask you to show us more kindness than that."

Anyone would be charmed by such a polite entreaty, and Gáspár is dressed in the Woodsman's suba besides. The woman turns around slowly, a smile inching across her wizened face.

"Certainly," she says. "My house is always open to weary travelers, and my gulyás is almost ready. Please, sit."

The wooden chairs are a welcome relief after days riding on a saddle and nights spent sleeping against the hard, freezing earth. The woman stirs her cauldron, profile cast gold in the warm firelight. She has a sharp little nose and squirrel-bright eyes, which look almost squashed under the mudslide of her brow. She wears her hair long and loose, gray strands skimming the dirt floor.

She doesn't look much like Virág, except that they are both old enough to be my mother's grandmother, but the resemblance is enough to fill me with a low, skulking sadness. If all goes to plan, I will never see Virág again. I try to sit up a little straighter in spite of it, and do my best to emulate Gáspár's deferent tone.

"My name is Évike," I say. "What's your name?"

But the old woman doesn't reply; she just keeps stirring the pot. Frankly, of all the things she could have done to evoke Virág, her ignoring me summons perhaps the greatest guilty nostalgia. The woman doesn't seem remotely perturbed by my presence, bloodstained wolf cloak and all. Maybe her vision is going, and I look like a vaguely girl-shaped smudge.

"Have you always lived in Szarvasvár?" Gáspár asks. I wonder if he's thinking about the seashells on the door.

"I have always lived along this riverbed," the old woman says.

Closer now, the gulyás is even more tempting than before. She ladles two servings into bowls of hammered tin, lumpy with carrots and potatoes and thin strips of meat. The spices have dyed the broth red.

It hasn't been long since we've eaten—two rabbits that I shot near where we found the circle of stones—but I am suddenly ferocious with hunger.

I lift the spoon to my lips. "What is this meat?"

"Mink," the woman says.

But there are no minks in Szarvasvár. There are no minks anywhere south of Kaleva, now, because soldiers and missionaries from the south hunted them to extinction. Virág has a pair of mittens made of sleek brown mink fur, and I remember rubbing my hands across the surface of them, imagining what it might have been like to live in Régország before the Patrifaith beat down its doors.

I look down at the stew again, and I gag.

Coiled vipers and earthworms are writhing in a horrible knot. The edges of the tin bowl are greasy with mud and pitted with the corpses of fruit flies. Perched carefully on my spoon, a tiny gray toad gives a diminutive croak.

Ice in my veins, I turn to Gáspár. He's lifting his own spoon to his mouth. I launch myself across the table and knock the spoon out of his hand, tipping both of our bowls onto the ground. The vipers go hissing and skittering across the floor, while the earthworms wriggle blindly in the dirt. The mud laps at the old woman's skirt like dark water.

"What are you doing?" Gáspár demands.

I grab his chin and tilt his face toward her. "Look."

The woman is not a woman anymore, or, rather, she never was one at all. Her hair is swamp grass. Her eyes are two smooth white stones. Beneath her dress and her apron, her skin has a sheen of red and hardness that was not there before; her wrinkles are lines that someone has etched into the mud of a dried-up riverbed.

"Come eat, children," she says, in a voice like the sound of wind rasping through the cattails. "You're tired. You're hungry, and there's plenty to go around."

Suddenly, I feel very tired indeed. Gáspár slumps back down in his chair, eyelid fluttering under the weight of her enchantment.

My own eyelids are heavy, but through my lashes I can see the not-woman looming over me, hands outstretched. She has fish scales for fingernails that look iridescent in the firelight. Dirt is caulked under those nails, crumbling and black.

Her fingers curl around Gáspár's throat, and I watch,

trancelike, as his veins throb and darken, a poison threading down his neck and under his dolman. His chest heaves, and a blind panic knifes through the haze of her enchantment.

Still woozy, I reach for her, but my limbs are stiff and too heavy. I fall out of the chair, collapsing on my hands and knees in the dirt. Gáspár slumps in his seat, eye shut. The blackness in his veins is pulsing, and I can smell the green rot of blighted wood and it reminds me of Peti dying and I nearly retch. With great effort, I reach for her ankles, sturdy as twin oaks beneath the fringe of her white muslin dress.

Witches don't bleed, of course. There's no skin to blister. Ördög's magic does its work anyway: a chunk of her leg breaks off in my grasp, like the handle of a clay pot. The not-woman releases Gáspár and stares down at the wound, blank pebble eyes narrowing in impossible shock.

She reaches for me, hobbling on the crooked stump of her leg, and then I reach for the other one. Another piece of her comes away in my hand, staining my palms with red dust. She crumples, and as she falls to the ground, her clay fingers close around the hood of my wolf cloak. She smells like pond water gone green and stagnant in the summer heat. Hunks of her crumble over me, a shard of cheek and the nub of her thumb. I grasp her by the wrist and don't let go, until the roughhewn bits of her are scattered across the dirt floor.

My cloak is dyed crimson with clay-grime. I cough and splutter, pushing myself to my feet, still dizzy with the ebbing of the witch's spell. Gáspár is slumped and motionless, tarry blackness pulsing in his veins. I drag myself toward him, but then I feel a pull in the opposite direction. I turn. There's a green vine nosing out of the dirt, and it has laced itself around my ankle.

Fear closes around my heart. For the first time since killing the witch, I look around the house. The roof is not thatched with grass at all. It's hair. Human hair. The jars on her shelves are teeming with earthworms and red-bellied snakes, tiny toads and plaintively buzzing flies. In one of them I swear I see a pink wedge of tongue, still wriggling.

I force myself forward, nails scraping through the dirt, against the tug of the vine. Its thorns are goring through the leather of my boot. As the weariness sloughs off me, I manage to turn and tear the vine from its root, then scramble toward Gáspár and loop his arm over my shoulder. He feels impossibly heavy—even as I lift him and stagger toward the door, I worry that I'll collapse before I reach it.

The knife-slit of light ahead is narrowing. At first I think it's a trick of my hazy mind, but then I feel the dirt under me roiling, rising. The sod walls are shrinking in on us, so tight and close that my lungs fill with the scent of damp soil and I can scarcely breathe. No, not shrinking.

Swallowing.

Strung limp over my back, Gáspár gives me no help. My vision ripples and blurs.

I barrel through the threshold just before the sod roof caves in on us. Through the snarl of weeds and dirt, I hear the wind chimes pealing out our exit—only they're not seashells but finger bones, all cobwebbed up in black thread alongside a small child's skull. When the house crumples, the bones ring with their own demise.

All the fires in the other sod houses have gone out. A wind sweeps through, blowing yellow hair off their roofs. I collapse to the ground, Gáspár rolling limp onto his back. His eye is still shut and wind shivers into the hollow of my ear and I want to cry out, the way I did for seven days and seven nights after my mother was taken.

Tamping down the urge to weep, I tug at the collar of Gáspár's dolman, trying to see how deep the poison has gone. His chest is still rising and falling, only more slowly now, with more beats between each breath. With mounting panic, I loose the gold buttons down the front of his jacket, fingers sweeping through the fur lining. Underneath he wears a chemise of black leather, blood-slicked.

I can't get it off him without pulling it over his head, so I reach for my knife, instead. I draw a long slit down the front of his shirt, cleaving the leather in two. It opens like black petals over his bare chest. His veins are dark as pitch, cobbling in an inky swell over his heart. My four fingers close into a fist, and I realize with a flood of helpless anguish that my newfound magic will do him no good: all I can do is hurt.

I kneel over him in the dirt, hands shaking, a sob rising in my throat at how I might as well be the same girl I was when I left Keszi, impotent and weak, and then suddenly the blackness starts to recede. The way the witch's enchantment waned from me slowly, Gáspár's veins return to green. That cobbled murk over his heart quivers and fades. And when his eyelid flutters open again, I have to steel myself so I don't start weeping, this time in relief.

Now that the danger has passed, I am suddenly aware of his bare skin under my hands. His chest is bronze and well muscled, with three long bands of scar tissue running along his abdomen. The mark of the creature's claws, I remember, from what seems like so long ago by the edge of the lake. I stare down at him, blinking, and then I realize Gáspár is watching me stare and I snatch my hand away, feeling weak in the knees for far too many reasons.

He pushes himself up onto his elbows and buttons the dolman closed over his chest, though I can still see snatches of skin. A flash of his hip bone. I swallow.

"I thought you were going to die," I say, as if making some defense, though I'm not sure for what. My voice is trembling shamefully.

"What happened?" Gáspár asks. Though his face is still ashen, a stubborn pink creeps over the tips of his ears. I feel so glad to see it I almost laugh. "The last thing I remember is the woman—she wasn't a woman . . ."

He trails off, eye wandering over the mound of hair and dirt behind me. A white finger bone is knuckling out of the soil.

"A witch," I say. "She was a witch."

Gáspár shifts onto his knees, brushing dirt from his suba. When his gaze draws back to me, there's a furrow in his brow. "How did you stop her?"

I hold up my hand, splaying its four fingers, and try to pin a smirk on my face. "Ördög can do more than snuff out flames."

My attempt at a smirk falls flat, and Gáspár only frowns at me in return. I have spent so much time studying his expressions that I can tell when he's truly vexed, and when he's only scowling because he feels like he's supposed to. When he's looking at me like I am just a wolf-girl, and when he's looking at me like he wishes I were only just a wolf-girl. This time, I can see his lips quivering, as if he is trying to decide whether to scold me or to thank me, and which will damn him more.

To spare us both more of his miserable wavering, I say, "I wasn't going to let you die before you could atone for the sin of saving *my* life."

He only makes a noise of reproach, shaking his head. Gáspár rises to his feet, and after a moment, so do I. I can see the ripple of muscle in his chest as he walks, through one of the gaps between the buttons of his dolman, and I press my lips together, grateful that he cannot guess at the indecent things running through my mind. Wishing that I was not thinking such indecent things about a Woodsman at all, and certainly not after we both nearly died. I imagine him berating me for my single-minded vulgarity. I imagine Katalin sneering at my doomed, unrequited desire, her blue eyes mean and laughing. A rabbit might as well lust after a wolf that plans to eat it.

Gáspár climbs back onto his mount, watching me as I

straddle my silver mare. His expression is unreadable, but he cannot miss the flush on my cheeks. I have long since given up waiting for his gratitude when he brings his horse close to mine, their flanks nearly touching, and says, "Thank you, Évike."

I am so surprised to hear my name on his lips that I can't think of how to reply. The wind unspools over us, howling softly. I give a stiff nod, holding my chin up, and then Gáspár urges his horse forward, toward the river's edge. I hold the echo of his voice in my mind for a moment, and then follow after him.

# CHAPTER TWELVE

The afternoon light wends its way across the sky, the sun pale and cloud-wreathed. The Élet River foams beside us, carrying water all the way from the Half-Sea, through Kaleva, and past our southern border with Merzan. We have seen more winter villages along the riverbed, their sod houses like rock outcroppings, small windows orange with firelight, but we have taken care to avoid them, diverting our path through the scraggly brush instead. Gáspár has lapsed back into silence. I don't know what has rattled him more: that the witch nearly killed him, or that I saved his life.

Our horses' footsteps are hushed in the soft, damp soil. There is only the low churning of the river, oddly companionable as it threads through the slopes and valleys of Szarvasvár. In the aftermath of our encounter with the witch, a giddy relief has cracked open inside me, muffling many of my previous fears. I keep thinking about the way her body came apart in my hand, hunks of red clay and dust, still painted into the creases of my palm. Having spent so long being afraid, sublimating myself to the magic of the other wolf-girls, this sudden fearlessness is like a song that begs for singing, the words and the melody bubbling up in me boldly, loudly.

I let my muscles unclench from the back of my mare, belly gnawing with hunger. When I suggest to Gáspár that we stop so I can hunt, he gives me a morose stare.

"You can't possibly have an appetite after that," he says.

I consider telling him that he sounds as waspish as Virág, since the comparison always makes him scowl, but thinking of her or anyone in Keszi makes my throat tighten, all that bold certainty curdling like sour milk. "If I'm to die Király Szek, as you're so certain I will, I would like to die with a full stomach."

His face darkens. He has never appreciated my black humor, but it seems to rankle him differently now, when I speak with a flippant smile about the possibility of my death. Now it doesn't make him flush with anger, only go thin-mouthed and silent.

"We'll have to get a bit further down the river first," he says finally, voice curt, "if we're to arrive in time for Saint István's feast."

I bite my tongue on a reply. Though I've mentioned it in jest, I have not truly allowed myself to think of what awaits me when we reach the city; I have only held on fiercely to my coin and to the conviction that I will be able to find my father, and of course protect myself with my magic. If I let my mind wander long enough to consider so many grisly possibilities, fear will wither me up like a wildflower that has been cut and I will walk into one of the sod houses and wait for the soil to close over my head.

"We ought to stop for water at least," I tell him. "You look woozy."

He does scowl at that, but he doesn't argue. We bring our horses to a halt and leap down, boots soundless in the wet soil. I lead my silver mare toward the water to drink while Gáspár kneels at the riverbed. It's true enough that I wanted to stop, but I wasn't lying about Gáspár's appearance: though hours have passed since we left the witch's house, his face looks particularly pale, and there is a fold of worry between his brows that makes my stomach twist with a mirrored concern. It seems almost impossible to remember that I had been so terrified of him once, that I had wished him dead. He removes his gloves and dips his cupped hands into the water, shoulders bowing. In the early days of our journey I would have considered how easy it would be to put a knife between his shoulder blades while his back was turned. Now I am looking only at the way that water clings to his lips, almost iridescent in the late-afternoon light, delicate as drops of dew.

I bend beside him and lift a handful of water to my own mouth. I think of my trysts by a different riverside, the one near Keszi. Mostly quick and shameful, my knees in the dirt so our eyes would never meet, sometimes brusque enough that it bloodied the insides of my thighs. I imagined that when the same boys took Katalin to the riverside, they had her like an oyster strokes out its pearl, delicate and slow, and when they finished, they helped her brush the dirt from her cloak and untangle the dead leaves from her hair. Gáspár wipes his mouth with the back of his hand and squints through the light, watching me. It is frighteningly easy to envision him on his back in the dirt: he would be as fumbling and gentle as a fawn, I think, and afterward anxious to conceal any bruises he had left.

Of course, he would sooner curl his lip and bristle at a wolf-girl's touch. Since leaving Kaleva behind, there's no need to anchor each other against the cold, and if he'd felt my hands run over his bare chest, he would have leapt away from me with a start.

The question rises in me anyway. "Are Woodsmen forbidden to wed?"

Gáspár's shoulders lift, and I hear him draw in a breath. "Yes. It's a holy order—none of the men are permitted to take wives, or to father children." He hesitates, a breeze feathering his black curls over his forehead. "Why?"

"Because I know you Patritians have your silly laws," I say, almost regretting it even as I do. "Laws that forbid you from coupling outside of your marriage bed."

I expect Gáspár to make a noise of reproach and stand, flicking my question off his back like a horse ridding itself of a fly. Instead he blushes profoundly, all the way from forehead to chin, but he doesn't look away from me.

"Of all our laws, that one is perhaps the most frequently violated," he says. "Most of the Woodsmen are boys of eight or nine when they first make their vows. They don't know what they're promising when they make them. I suppose it's easier that way, never knowing what you have to live without."

Even I am flushing by the time he finishes, but I don't want to shrink back and give up what ground I've gained. Gáspár is still looking at me, a remarkable feat of cultivated tolerance. A fortnight ago he would have skulked off into the woods or threatened to gag me.

"So I ought not pity you too much," I say, wiping my damp hands on my cloak. "Since you've never known the touch of a woman, I suppose you only dream of gold and of glory and of one day wearing your father's crown. What else is there for men to desire?"

Gáspár's lips quiver. For a moment I think he will scold me after all. But he only says, "I was made a Woodsman when I was twenty. I had plenty of time to consider what I would be living without."

I blink at him, unable to summon words. I suppose I could have guessed, from the clumsy way he wields his ax, that he was bereft of the typical Woodsman training, but I hadn't thought to calculate exactly how long he's worn the cloak. Five years only, far less than most of his fellow soldiers, and scarcely long enough to scrub the impieties of manhood off him. Knowing this, and thinking of the nights we spent pressed together on the ice, makes my heart leap into my throat. Perhaps I shouldn't have considered him so prudishly detached from the same desires that have plagued me these past weeks, that have dogged me both sleeping and waking.

I am silent for so long that finally Gáspár rises, stalking back toward his horse. The amber light of the waning sun pools on his chin and along the bridge of his nose, making him look like something engraved in gold, though far younger than his father's profile on my minted coin. My cold brush with death had brought me to the dizzy, half-conscious revelation that he was beautiful. Looking at him again now, backlit by fire instead of ice, I come to the same epiphany, my stomach twisting in defiance of my brain.

Slowly, I rise to my feet and follow him. The dark is quickly chasing the light from the sky, like a wolf after a white lamb. The teeth of dusk are grinning up over the clouds and snarling jaggedly around the sun, and in the patches of shadow the river looks like something to be afraid of, cold and depthless. I look back at Gáspár, his face still suffused in sunlight, as if the shadows can't touch him at all.

A languid, mosquito-flecked evening falls over us, and the Élet River begins to weave through one of Régország's rare forests. We follow its labyrinthine path, darting like a silver blade between copses of dark oaks and dense, raveling thickets. Animals with yellow eyes blink at us from their tree holes, and red-tipped birds cast winged shadows onto our path.

This forest is unlike Ezer Szem—it is full of only mortal, comprehensible dangers like lurking wolves and steep, hidden ravines. The absence of obvious peril forces my mind to wander onto other things: the hazy shape of the capital, still distant and unreal, and Nándor, whose face is little more than a pale smudge, like a print on a windowpane, and of course my father's coin, somehow warm enough that I can feel it suffusing heat through my cloak.

Gáspár steals frequent glances at me, tight and nervous, as if he's afraid I'll vanish when his head is turned.

"It's not too late, wolf-girl," he says. There's no malice in the epithet, but not for lack of trying—his brow is furrowed with the effort of barbing his words. "We're two days from Király Szek. You can still go back to your village."

If I am a wolf-girl again, then he is a Woodsman, though there is more misery than ire in my voice when I speak. "I've already told you there's nothing for me there. I can count the rest of my years there in lashings, Woodsman, and loveless, bloody couplings by the riverside. You must truly loathe me, to want to damn me to such a cold life."

I say the last bit with more cruelty than I thought I could muster, and just because I want him to flush. He does, and then abruptly his face hardens.

"You are being unrepentantly stupid," he says. "You might return to Keszi shameful and cowed, but with your heart still beating in your chest. Whatever magic you do have, it doesn't matter. Király Szek is no place for a wolf-girl who values her life as you claim to. Your mother and all the other women my father brought had magic, and none of them survived the capital either."

"And what about you?" I demand, blood pulsing thickly now, almost bewildered by my own sudden fury. "If Nándor has as much power as you say, you are no less stupid than I am for thinking you can survive him. You ought to flee east and find some obliging Rodinyan lord with a pretty daughter you can wed, and then he can raise his armies against Nándor. You would be safe there."

Gáspár gives a laugh, humorless and short. "Because, unlike you, I care for others besides myself. Your people, pagan and Yehuli both, would be damned in the meantime. And I would leave my father to die in my absence like a coward."

"Maybe you should care for yourself a bit more, then! Your father has earned none of your unbending loyalty," I say sharply. "You are a wiser and gentler and more courageous son than he deserves."

We both fall silent then, wind scuttling through the branches. My face heats with the feeling that I have confessed something I ought not have confessed, not when we are robed in a hundred years of boiling hatreds and both staring down the end of his brother's blade. Gáspár draws in a breath, and I brace myself for his response, but he only lets it out again, wordless.

"If I were you, I *would* leave him to die," I say, just to fill the unbearable silence, though even as I do, my chest tightens. Virág's face, Boróka's face, even Katalin's face float up at me. If I succeed in finding my father, it means I will never see them again.

"I know," Gáspár says, quietly.

And then neither of us can bear to say any more. Gray-washed evening light is falling through the tree cover, the path before us quilted with planks of sun and shadow. My vision is glazing over the endless thatch of trunks and coils of bramble when I see something move behind the trees. A flash of white skin among the evergreen leaves—something small and mortal-looking.

I glance at Gáspár, his eye flashing. In our shared second of silent indecision, a cry rings out from the brush. It is a human cry, and that makes our choice for us. I dig my heels into the horse's flank, and my mare bolts through the tangled bramble. The pounding of hooves on the ground tells me that Gáspár is close behind.

The chase ends as quickly as it started. The figure has stopped inside a copse of willow trees, lithe branches swaying in the scant breeze, their fronds gossamer as a widow's mourning veil. I jerk the reins and my horse skids to a halt.

There is nothing inhuman about her, I realize with a long

breath of relief. No red-clay skin or unseeing white eyes. In fact, it's very apparent how human she is, because she wears no clothes at all. A curtain of dark hair falls over her breasts, its color stark against her ivory skin. The soles of her feet are black with dirt.

I only notice her eyes as I slide off my horse. They are bluer than any eyes I have ever seen, bluer than Katalin's, which inspired one of the village boys to compose a keening ballad in their honor. As children Boróka and I had cried ourselves laughing about that preening youth, even as we both tacitly wished he would sing about our eyes.

These eyes, though—there would be no songs written about their beauty, only their haunting pull. They are spangled bright with tears, even though her lips are a pale unfeeling line. Bewildered, I try to marry the anguish in her gaze with the pitiless cut of her mouth, like knitting together the hides of two different animals. Gáspár's boot steps fall on the ground behind me.

"What's happened, miss?" he asks, reaching out one gloved hand to bridge the space between us and the girl. "Why are you in the woods alone?" He leaves unsaid the question of where her clothes are, but I can tell by the pinking of his cheeks that he has not managed to entirely avert his eye.

The girl lifts her head, almost shyly, settling her bright-blue eyes upon me. For a moment I'm stunned in the path of her gaze, like a deer catching a hunter's downwind scent, even as my heart clangs in my chest. She turns to Gáspár, and her stare roots him there too.

Then she speaks. It's not a language I recognize; it's not even that *old* Old Régyar. I don't think it's a language made for human ears. It sounds like leaves rustling in the wind, or the ice of Lake Taivas fracturing beneath my feet. Words spill out of her mouth as her lambent blue eyes water, and I realize that we were both terribly wrong—she isn't human either.

Her colorless lips curl into something that resembles a smile.

Trembling, I reach for my knife, but my fingers won't move the way I want them to. My gaze is tethered to her, and I can't pull it away. She speaks again, the crackle of flames in a dying hearth, and I hear Gáspár choke something out. It sounds like my name, though I can't be sure.

She moves toward me in a flash of white, pale lips parting. Inside her mouth is red and berry-bright. I don't notice her teeth, rows and rows of them, slender and sharp as needles, until they are on my throat.

I can only manage a muffled gasp of pain as her teeth glide through my skin, right above my collarbone. My vision goes starry, then white. She releases me, jaw unlatched, a flap of my skin hanging over her bottom lip. Snakelike, she swallows it whole, with a gory slurping sound.

There's a slow trickle of blood pooling in the hollow of my throat. Still frozen, my caged heart throbbing its panicked beat, I watch her lean forward again, mouth opening, her lips jeweled with my blood.

And then she crumples. Her body ripples, all her willowy limbs going limp. She tips to the ground, Gáspár's blade in her back, and once she hits the dirt her body fissures open, a spew of ruby-gilded rot and droning black flies. They crawl all over the mangle of her face, split down the middle into neatly mirrored halves, and eat away at the flesh still clinging to the vault of her rib cage. Sensation returns to me slowly, with one staggered breath and then another, and all I can do is watch the flies devour her.

Gáspár lifts his ax, the edge of it slick with blood and rot. "Are you all right?"

I touch the wound on my throat. There's a muted jolt of pain as I do, something fuzzy and far-removed. I nod, still mostly numb. "Was she . . ."

"A monster," he says. "Just like the witch in the sod house."

Virág has told stories of girl-shaped creatures that move behind the tree line, shadowless, their feet leaving no prints upon the earth. Their targets are guileless hunters and unfortunate woodcutters who roam the forest at dusk, alone. I can only guess that her power was not enough to hold both of us at once. I almost want to laugh, manic with relief, and then, abruptly, with chagrin: I should not have believed that old magic was stamped out everywhere but Keszi.

"Your forests are just as dangerous as mine."

He snorts in acknowledgment.

I draw in another breath and let it out, shakily. Gáspár stares at me, brow furrowed with concern, eye darting from my face to the small wound on my throat. I watch something red drip from the corner of his mouth.

"You're bleeding," I say.

He lifts a gloved hand to his lips, and his fingers come away damp. Frowning, he looks back at me. "So are you."

"I know," I say, touching my neck wound. "It's nothing."

"No," he says. "Your mouth."

I wipe my lips with the back of my hand, staining my skin. There is something gathering under my tongue, and I let it dribble out, onto my chin. It's as dark and glossy red as boiled cherries, with a sweet-sharp taste.

"Juice," I say, in a voice that sounds nothing like my own.

Gáspár's lips and chin are smeared with it too. I feel a coiling heat in my belly, unexpected and strange. The edges of my vision are still blinkering as I take a step toward him, fingers clenched.

He stares down at me, gaze wavering. I like seeing the puzzlement on his regal prince's face, his flushing indecision. "Let me look."

Then he reaches toward me and sweeps the hair from my neck, leaning closer to examine the wound. The pain of it has ebbed entirely. I can only feel the gentle pressure of his fingers against my throat and my jawbone.

"It's nothing," I say again, and this time my voice is little more than a whisper. "I can do worse to myself."

As if to prove the point, I hold up my left hand, looking odd and skewed with only four fingers. Gáspár removes his hand, letting my hair fall back against my throat.

"You're worse than any monster, it's true," he says. He gives a soft laugh, but his eye is solemn, humorless.

Ordinarily I might have chafed at his words. Now I only feel a small quiver go through my chest, a heady pulse of thrill twined with fear, the way the air grows thick and close before a storm. "And why is that?"

"You have the uncommon ability to make me doubt what I once thought was certain," he says. "I've spent the last fortnight fearing you would destroy me. You may still."

I laugh then, too, a sound without an echo. "I think you are forgetting yourself. You're a Woodsman and a prince, and I'm a trifling wolf-girl. All my life I've been terrified I'd wake to see you at my door."

Gáspár swallows. I see his throat bobbing, skin streaked with that red juice. He lets his ax slide from his grasp, thudding softly to the ground. Then he raises his hand and tugs at the clasp of his suba, letting it pool around his feet.

I stare at him then, unarmed and uncloaked, though still with that stubborn set to his jaw. I remember looking at him down beside the lake outside Ezer Szem, when we were both panting and slick with monster blood, hatred burning a hole in my belly. The memory cleaves open without my willing it, and another flowers from the black space: him holding me in the hollowed tree, his gentle breath in my ear. The nights on the ice, anchored in the warmth of his body. Him wrapping my wound with such vexed tenderness, like he couldn't believe the stirring of his own hands.

I step closer to him, toeing the abyss. I could slit his throat; there's no blade or mantle to stop me. Maybe they'd throw a feast in my honor if I came back to Keszi with a Woodsman's head.

My hand curls around the hilt of my knife. "Would you let me destroy you, then?"

"It would be just as well," Gáspár says miserably. "I should be struck dead, for wanting you the way I do."

His words brush something inside of me, like flint touching tinder. That unnamable heat, coiling and strange, hardens into a feeling I can name: *want*. All my lewd imaginings come roaring up at me, those guilty moments of wondering how he would look pinned between my thighs. Gáspár's gaze doesn't lift from me, his black eye burning with perverse agony.

I let go of the knife and clasp my hands on either side of his face, knuckles white. And then I bring my lips to his.

Even still, I half expect him to lurch away from me. I feel the moment of his shock, the shiver of hesitation, and then he answers my kiss with such ferocity that I'm the one shaken. I taste the juice in his mouth, again sweet and sharp at once, and when a drop runs down his chin I catch it, smirking when he quivers under the sweep of my tongue.

Gáspár raises his hands from his side and circles them around my waist, pulling me flush against him. My body remembers the shape of his, from so many nights curled together on the ice, and it responds with fevered instinct, pushing him until he stumbles back against the trunk of the closest willow tree.

I break the kiss only to catch my breath, hands still clutching at his face. He looks particularly beautiful like this: newly kissed, his lips swollen and his cheeks flushed, Régország's true-born prince profaned under my touch. I let my fingers skate across his cheekbone, hesitantly, until my thumb brushes the leather patch that covers his missing left eye.

"I want to see," I whisper.

"No," he says, face hardening. But he doesn't jerk back or push away my hand.

Light as a moth's wing, I lift the patch from his eye and slide it back over his head. A web of scar tissue spreads over the skin below his empty eye socket. But there's no horror, aside from the stomach-drop moment of searching for something and finding it isn't there. It's nothing like seeing the ravaged skin of his wrist, or the way I used to feel, sick and uneasy, when I wondered what lurked beneath the patch. Gáspár loosens his grip on my waist, lifting his arm so he can cover the hole with the heel of his hand. It's quick as a reflex, like the action has been ground into him.

I move his arm away. Then I kiss him, right on the place where his eye should be.

"Stop it," he says, body tensing around mine.

"You'll have to find some other way to occupy my mouth then," I say, smiling as lasciviously as I can, and still tasting red juice between my teeth. My vision has funneled to just his face and body, the forest shuddering away in my periphery.

Gáspár slides his hands around my neck, under my hair, careful not to brush over my weeping bite. He presses his mouth to mine again, our teeth knocking together as my lips part, and his tongue slipping between them.

I grasp the back of his head, and his mouth lifts from mine for a moment, to trail across my jawline, his stubble prickling my chin. I make a small, clipped noise of protest as his lips trace the faded scar on my throat, so gently it's almost like an apology. Briefly I remember him pulling Peti off me, his voice cold and furious, the swing of his ax, and then that shudders away too. I can only feel his lips on my throat, and my stammered protest turns to a moan.

His certainty shocks and thrills me, especially as he parts my thighs with his knee. I run my hand along the hem of his dolman, fingers tracing over the coiled lines of the scar on his abdomen. Under my hands his muscles flex, hips rolling, and then he tenses again, like he's embarrassed of his own eagerness. When I shift I feel him more urgently against me, and I'm overcome with wanting more.

It's nothing like my awkward fumbling with village boys that left my knees raw and my lips bruised. All his desire is knitted through with tenderness, and for a moment I wonder if he *did* manage to have much practice, before his father cut out his eye and put the Woodsman cloak on his back.

"Am I the first woman you've touched, pious Woodsman?" I ask, more curious than mocking, my fingers working against the waistband of his trousers.

He doesn't reply, but his face darkens, and then he kisses me again, both our mouths sweet with red juice. All this time I'd wondered if his holy order had stripped from him the lusts and passions of manhood, and now I can feel the proof of his desire stiff between my thighs. I draw his hand up over my breasts and he groans, so visceral and unbidden that it makes my own desire throb in response, guiding his hand under my tunic, over my bare, prickling skin.

And then, suddenly, he stops.

I hardly have time to react before he pushes me away. I stumble backward, his name hanging off my stupid, gaping lips, while Gáspár puts his hand over his mouth, shoulders rising and falling in heated silence.

Just like that, the fog lifts. My vision swells and I can see the grid of trees behind him, the lacy veil of willow branches and their faint susurration. Moonlight beams down through the canopy, washing the whole clearing cold and white. The edges of everything are sharp again, and my blood is ice.

"It was an illusion." Gáspár's hand drops from his mouth, revealing the stain of juice on his chin, drying dark in the cool moonlight. "Some enchantment of that creature."

My mind tries to close around the possibility, memories fluttering like the wind among dead leaves. I remember my fear turning to want as quickly as the sweet juice pooled in my mouth, like a sickly poison that fevered my blood. Perhaps it *was* the echo of the creature's enchantment, lingering after her death like some scent on the air, before the breeze carried it away. My gaze travels to where her body had been. There's nothing left but a desiccated jawbone, porous with accelerated time.

But it had only loosened me, like good wine. My brain and body had been my own, my recklessly roaming hands and the traitorous pulling between my thighs. Senseless and shameful, but I can't shake the ebbing of my desire even now, the juice still stinging my lips.

"Do you think some dead creature has the power to move your mouth and tongue?" I ask, choking on a laugh. "Perhaps her poison put the thought in your mind, but you were hardly some limp little puppet. In fact, limp might be the very last word I'd use—"

"Quiet," he snarls, his face as red as I've ever seen it, eye narrowed and coal black. He fishes his patch off the ground and fixes it around his head again. "If you speak of this to anyone, they'll only call you mad."

The ice-edged cruelty to his words makes my breath catch. I watch as he pins his suba back on and picks up his ax. With his jaw clenched and his eye angled away from me, he looks every inch a Woodsman again, the same dark shape that once appeared only in my most terrible dreams, and certainly never in my lustful imaginings.

"And how does this add to the tally of your sins?" My voice is shaking, tunic still slung low across my collarbone, baring one of my breasts. I pull it up again, flushing, as the sting of his rejection begins to settle. "When you bow at the feet of the Érsek, will you ask Godfather Life to forgive you for kissing a wolf-girl? What about all those nights you spent holding her against the cold? There was no dead creature to move your limbs then."

His fingers curl around the handle of his ax. For a moment

I think he will raise it against me, even after all of this, the miles we've put behind us, our frigid days in Kaleva, after he blackened his soul to save my life. But Gáspár only looks at the ground and then shakes his head.

"It was enchantment," he says again. "Why are you clamoring to convince me otherwise? You're a wolf-girl; I'm a Woodsman. You said before that I was no more than a monster to you. This is a shame for us both to share."

What little reason his words have is lost in the boil of my rage. Hearing him speak like the silver-tongued prince again, with his rigid courtly eloquence, sends me to the bitterest, meanest place I know. I scarcely hesitate before opening up my most ancient wound again, so I can make him share in its hurt. "I'm no true wolf-girl. You've known it since that night on the Black Lake. I've already turned my back on my village—I'm not some dumb, struck dog who runs back to its vicious master for another lashing. And you're no true Woodsman, either, except for your blushing piety and your slavish dog's devotion to the father who only ever showed you the end of his blade."

Gáspár flinches, but it is not enough to make me regret the cruelty of my words. I rub the red juice from my lips and try to will down the hot coil of tears in my throat. Perhaps I wanted to kiss him to prove how little I cared for my people, for my mother's braid in my pocket, her life ended by some Woodsman at the behest of his father. Perhaps I wanted to forget that between here and Király Szek I am not pagan, not Yehuli, only some stupid girl with her hand in both pockets, finding comfort in cold, dead things. Maybe I wanted his touch to erase me.

Or perhaps I wanted the opposite: maybe I wanted his kiss to give me shape, to see how my body transfigured under his hands. I don't know who I have been with him these past weeks, indulging every perverse instinct, killing fat, slumbering rabbits and openly professing to loathe my own people. My most spiteful self, and perhaps my truest.

Gáspár meets my gaze, his black eye pooling with moonlight. He runs a hand through his dark hair, the same hand that grasped my hip like he could not bring me close enough. His face is so hard that, for a moment, I am almost ready to believe it was nothing but enchantment after all, just the red juice in our mouths. But when he speaks, his voice is thin with anguish.

"What would you have me do?" he asks. "You have already ruined me."

## CHAPTER THIRTEEN

near where the Élet River finally snakes through Király
Szek, the land smooths and flattens, and green grass
turns flaxen where it marks the edge of the Great
Plain. The Great Plain swallows up nearly all of Akosvár, and
the capital, too, the wide, fertile grassland that the Merzani
are currently trying to conquer and burn. But there are no
enemy fires burning on the horizon, just the dark swell of our
shared silence, almost tangible. Neither of us has spoken in
nearly two days.

My anger fizzled early, and in its absence, there came a
pall of despair, all my blustery certainty withered like a stalk
of wheat. The silence has given my mind the chance to run
its worried circuit, returning only a hopeless augury: I have
damned myself entirely, having chosen to walk right into the
arms of the enemy. And our encounter with the creature has
cost me even the meager protection of Gáspár's proximity. He
walks several yards ahead of me, showing me only the back
of him, his shoulders stiff under his suba. When we reach the
city, I suspect he will leave me for good.

My belly fills with an embarrassed, lurking hurt. I should not be mourning the loss of a Woodsman's goodwill, or thinking hungrily of his touch. Pagans don't have a ritual of repentance like the Patritians do, a cheek-to-the-floor confession, but I was always made to pay for my mistakes in other ways. Now I almost wish for lashings, or to be tasked with Virág's most odious chores. I wonder if there is a Yehuli way of killing your guilt and burying it. Perhaps I will learn soon.

Or perhaps I will be dead first. Gáspár stops suddenly, his horse's tail bridling. I come to his side slowly, the way one would approach a dog that was keen to snap. Seeing his profile, amber cast in the midday sunlight, makes my stomach clench like a fist. There is still a bruise on his throat in the shape of my mouth, stubbornly violet.

"What is it?" I manage. My voice is hoarse from disuse.

Gáspár's gaze lifts, but he doesn't quite meet my eyes. I remember the way my thumb brushed across his cheekbone, my lips against his eyelid. I wonder if he is thinking of it too. His jaw is set hard, and when he speaks, it is with a Woodsman's steel edge.

"This is your last chance," he says. "Turn back and spare yourself."

He has done all he can to keep his words from betraying concern, his eye cold and unflinching. But I have seen enough of his dogged pretense to recognize it, the calculated falsehood of his ambivalence. I know the way his mouth tastes now. I have heard him moan into the shell of my ear.

"I'll turn back if you will," I say. "I'll go back to Keszi and face my lashings if you flee to Rodinya and find some amiable lord to shelter you. How is that for a bargain?"

Gáspár doesn't reply, and I didn't expect him to; he turns away from me and spurs his horse onward, following the line of the river. I urge my mare slowly after him, face burning. It is the memory of tenderness that wounds me more than the desire. I have desired many men who had me brusquely and were afterward too ashamed to meet my eyes. But I have never wanted to kiss their wounds, or bare to them any of my own. I had thought myself truest when I was skinning baby rabbits and seething with vicious hatreds, but perhaps that tenderness is true too. I wonder how tender I might have been, if I had not lived cowering under the threat of Virág's reed whip, forever menaced by Katalin's blue flame.

But that matters little now. I ought to slough off any tenderness like old dead skin. It will only leave me soft-bellied and spent when we reach Király Szek. The river churns beside me, the foaming crests of the waves iridescent when they catch the sunlight. Gáspár has gone so far ahead that I can scarcely see him now, unless I raise a hand to shield my eyes and squint against the glare.

I have never deserved less to wear the wolf cloak over my shoulders, but a memory rises in me anyway, stinging and sour, like a swallow of saltwater. If Gáspár were speaking to me, I would tell him one last story: Once, Vilmötten *did* slay a dragon—not the one who loved a human woman, I don't think. But this dragon was a man with seven heads, too, and he rode into battle with full mail on the back of an eight-legged horse.

Vilmötten was not a warrior. He was only a bard who had been granted the favor of the gods. He wondered how he might slay such a creature, with nothing to his name but a five-stringed kantele, which made music, not war. Isten told him he must forge a sword.

"But how?" Vilmötten asked. "I have no steel to melt, and no skills as a smith. Besides, what kind of blade could slay such a monster?"

"The sword that you make with the blessings of the gods," Isten replied. And then he clipped off one of his fingernails and let it fall to the Middle-World below. It was thick and heavy as steel, and carved with the magic of the father-god himself. And because the nail had been a sacrifice, death lived inside it also.

Vilmötten had the power to make fire, thanks to the star he had swallowed. While he worked, he sang. He sang a song of battle (the words of which have been forgotten, or maybe just forgotten by Virág). When he finished his forging, the song ended too.

Vilmötten's sword looked like nothing special. It had a bronze hilt and a silver blade. But when he held it up to the sky, a bright flame burst across the length of it, as if someone had struck the blade with a piece of flint. He slew the dragon with his sword, cutting off all seven of its heads in one swing. The sword was coveted across all of Régország and the lands beyond, but when Vilmötten sailed away to the realm of the gods, the sword was lost.

I have no gleaming sword forged from a sliver of Isten's nail; I have only my own untested magic, and Király Szek is filled with a thousand dragons, all of them men in disguise. Still, I let the words twine silently through my mind, as if I might make a weapon of them. Virág's stories never comforted me when I was sitting at her hearth, knees pulled to my chest, aching with the labor of her chores and chafing under Katalin's cruel stare. Now so many miles from Keszi the familiar words gird me like battle mail, and it seems like a trickster god's mean joke: that I should yearn for her solace only as soon as I have forsaken it. I reach for my mother's braid, red as a fox's pelt and smooth from all my years of stroking. I wonder if Gáspár has kept any relic of his mother. I wonder if I will ever have a chance to ask him.

I draw my hand to my lips, still swollen with the memory of his touch, and then urge my horse forward after him.

Two miles out of the capital, the sky ceases to be blue.

We stand on a small hill outside of Király Szek, wind bristling past us. A mass of seething clouds is gathered over the city, thick and low-hanging, lush with unshed rain. It casts the city in a grayish half-light, almost like the murky reflection of the real Király Szek rippling on the surface of a lake at dusk. It almost comforts me, that black mantle of storm clouds. Maybe a torrent of rain will come down and wash the festival-goers out of the streets.

If Gáspár takes particular notice of the looming clouds, he doesn't comment on them. I let my gaze sweep across the horizon, ambling over the palace belfry and down again to the sloping roofs of the houses. The city is an earthwork, banked with mounds of soil to fortify it against a siege, but I can see even from a distance the beginnings of a stone wall around the old wooden barricades, higher in some places than others. It looks like a project recently undertaken, perhaps in anticipation of the Merzani army. The Élet River gashes the city in two, a shock of silver-blue cleaving east from west.

The outer layer of the city is a scruff of farmland, squares of yellow wheat alternated with tracts of green and red paprika plants, each pepper gleaming like a ruby scythe. A long black road daggers through the farmland, terminating at the main city gate. And, of course, because it's festival day, the road is glutted with travelers: devout men and women making their pilgrimage on foot or on horseback, slogging toward Király Szek to pay tribute to the memory of the nation's first Patritian king.

A braid of fear and anger coils in my chest, burning like an old scar. Gáspár leads me down to the road, where we join the throng of Patritians, all a chaos of protests and muttered prayers. Their eyes glint from their dirty faces like knife-points, bright and sharp, gazes fixed toward the gate and the palace that knuckles over the old wooden walls. None of them seems to notice that a wolf-girl has entered their procession.

"You have certainly chosen the most treacherous time to arrive in Király Szek," Gáspár murmurs, and I hear the bridled worry in his voice. "There is no worse day to be a wolf-girl in the capital, when Patritian zeal reaches its fever pitch."

I only stare at him as our horses jostle through the crowd. A fury deep in my marrow has been pulled to the surface, like an old ship dredged up out of the sea. "There is no day where it is safe to be a wolf-girl in the capital. Don't forget that you meant to bring me here as a prisoner. Is there still blood on the city walls where your Saint István displayed his trophies?"

Gáspár blinks at me, a pale flush ghosting across his face. "I didn't know that story had found its way to your village."

"Of course it did." My four fingers curl around my horse's reins, tight enough to turn my knuckles white. "Do you think we just sit around a fire, mindlessly repeating the legends of our great heroes and gods? Every boy and girl in Keszi learns the story before they're old enough to talk: how King István nailed the hearts and livers of the pagan chieftains to the gates of Király Szek. How he paraded them proudly to his visitors from the west, so they could see how holy Régország had become."

Gáspár looks pointedly away, but his hands, too, tighten on their reins. "You shouldn't have come here."

I don't argue with him. My head is a snarl of storm clouds, mirroring the sky above. Perhaps that is all it means to be pagan: to fear having your heart or liver cut out. In that way I am no different from the other wolf-girls with their easy magic and their mean smiles, no matter what Katalin or the gods might say.

The roiling of the crowd carries us through the gate. Király Szek stinks badly enough to make my eyes burn: smoke chuffs from every open window and door, from all the wooden houses that topple over and run into each other, like clumsily felled trees. The streets are made of hard, dry earth, and they cough up yellow dust with every footfall. All my life I had imagined the city would be clean and bright like a forest in the snow, and its people as fat and sated as bears in their winter dens. But Király Szek is blatantly ugly and so are its citizens. Their gums are crammed with teeth as rotted as the crumbling belfries, their jowls sagging like their own wind-beaten roofs. From somewhere farther away I hear the sound of a bell tolling, and a blacksmith's bellows, and a torrent of curses piping from some merchant's grizzled mouth. The procession flows left, in the direction of the palace, but I draw my horse to a halt, bewildered and breathless and my ears ringing.

Gáspár pauses, too, and raises his voice over the din. "If you want to find your father, you'll have to go to Yehuli Street. It's—"

But I don't hear the rest of his words. All I can see are twin smudges of black in the distance, two figures on obsidian mounts barreling through the crowd. Woodsmen.

Beside me, Gáspár stiffens. The Woodsmen are angling toward us, their eyes pinning me in place like thrown darts. Gáspár leans toward me, and in a fierce whisper says, "Don't utter a word."

I choke out a laugh, lunatic with terror. "Do you really think I have plans to reveal our tryst, you fool? As much as it brings me pleasure to know that I've imperiled your purity, I'm more concerned with keeping Woodsman axes out of my back."

Gáspár presses his lips together, looking mortified.

"Besides," I bite out, "if you want to convince them you've kept your oath of chastity, you might consider covering the bruise on your throat first."

He flushes the shade of a sour cherry and tugs at the collar of his suba. In another two beats, the Woodsmen reach us, the rough wind flinging their cloaks this way and that. They are both freshly shorn, with lean faces like foxes at midwinter. One of them is missing his left ear.

Gáspár nods at each of them in turn, hand still braced on the nape of his neck. "Ferenc. Miklós."

The one with the missing ear, Ferenc, narrows his eyes.

"Bárány. You've been gone too long. The king has been asking after his wolf-girl for more than a fortnight, and your brother is nearly done biding his time."

It shocks me how casually they address him, Régország's true-born prince, but I try to keep from making my dismay plain.

"I know," Gáspár says. "I have the wolf-girl now, and I'll take her to the palace as soon as the feast is done."

The other Woodsman, Miklós, glances between Gáspár and me. I can feel the coldness of his gaze leaching through my wolf cloak, like a beam of icy moonlight. "Where are the other men? Peti and Ferkó, Imre . . ."

Abruptly, Gáspár's face shutters. His shoulders rise around his ears, swelling as if with guilt. For a mute, shameful moment I almost want to heft the burden from his back to mine, take the blame for their deaths, even if it will damn me further in front of these Woodsmen. But Gáspár speaks first.

"Dead." His voice is flat. "Ambushed by monsters as we journeyed from Ezer Szem. The wolf-girl and I barely survived."

All at once, as though moved by invisible threads, both Woodsmen press two fingers to their chests. Their eyes close penitently. When they open them again, Ferenc says, "Three good Patritian men dead, and for what? So the king can have his—"

"Careful," Gáspár says shortly, and Ferenc falls silent at once. "Your blades are still sworn to my father as long as he sits the throne."

"Yes, and we'd prefer he stay there, despite his affinity for pagan magic," Miklós says, cutting another glare toward me. "Nándor has only grown more insufferable in your absence, Bárány. He's like a child, and this city is a toy he doesn't want to share. He'll be loath to see you again, but I think the shock of it will be enough to shake him loose—for now. You ought to get to the palace as quickly as you can."

A knot of fear curls in my throat, but Gáspár doesn't flinch at his words. "I'll go as soon as I've dealt with the wolf-girl. If you can find Count Korhonen, you may be able to stall Nándor."

Ferenc dips his head in assent. He and Miklós draw back their horses, and the crowd sweeps them away like driftwood on a river, streaming toward the palace. As soon as they're gone, Gáspár turns to me, his face hardening all over again.

"I'll take you to Yehuli Street," he says—perfectly smooth, save for the flicker in his eye, like a candle flame seizing in the wind. "I'll leave you there once you find your father."

I nod, not trusting myself to speak without weeping, or else saying something damningly stupid. The same bell tolls again, a gonging that echoes through the ground and vibrates through my fingers and toes. The wind carries the smell of ash and smoke toward us, and I loop the reins twice around my hand, driving my horse against the current of the crowd.

Yehuli Street is as silent as a winter morning in the woods, before even the foxes rouse white-coated from their dens. Wool stockings and muslin dresses hang out on lines that stretch from window to window, fluttering emptily, like clothespinned ghosts. I had expected to feel some bolt of recognition, the illumination of instinct long-buried, my memory struck up like a match. But I feel nothing. Yehuli Street spools out before me, each squat gray house the same as the last, like pale fingerprints against the darkening sky.

"Where is everyone?" I whisper. The silence feels precarious, and I don't want to be responsible for breaking it.

He frowns at me, jaw set sharply. I am keeping him from his task, but I can't bring myself to care, not when my mouth has gone dry and my heart has stirred to a manic beat.

"It's a Yehuli holy day," he says. "On this day their god forbids them from working."

"And are all these houses . . ." I trail off, gaze running down the length of the street, edged by hovel after hovel.

"Yehuli houses. They are forbidden from occupying any other part of the city that the king himself has not ordained."

The wind snarls through my hair and blows the fur of my wolf cloak flat. I feel unspeakably cold. One of Katalin's chants burrows its way into my mind: *Yehuli slave, Yehuli scum, Yehuli bow to anyone.*

"Do you know where my father lives?" I ask, voice small.

I see the moment that Gáspár's face softens, his jaw losing its whetted edge, and then the instant when it goes hard again, like he has only just remembered that he is supposed to loathe me.

"No," he says. "You'll have to knock and see."

This is where he would take his leave, disappear down Yehuli Street and let fate decide what will become of me. But Gáspár only sits stiffly on his mount, back straight as a blade. A swell of fierce gratitude and painful affection rises in my chest, but I swallow it back down.

I leap off my horse, blood roaring hot in my ears. The direness of the situation occurs to me all over again, my mind racing with thoughts of disembodied livers and hearts, Virág's desperate warnings. Here in Király Szek my wolf cloak may as well be a death shroud. Every moment that I am without my father is an opportunity for a Patritian to take my head off.

All furious panic, I hurl myself to the nearest door and pound on it rudely, then stand back, chest heaving. After a few moments, the door lurches open, ancient springs squealing. A squat woman blinks at me from the threshold, a gilt-edged book shoved under her arm.

"What's the meaning of this?" she demands—angrily, and I don't blame her. I must look half-mad in my wolf cloak, tunic still stained with red juice. I force my numb lips to move.

"I'm looking for Zsidó Zsigmond," I say. "Is this his house? Do you know—"

The woman lets out a chortling laugh and slams the door in my face.

It all happens too fast for me to feel any way about it. My mind hardly registers her rebuff before my legs are carrying me to the next house. I hear Gáspár slide off his horse, and by the time the second door clatters open, he is right behind me.

"I'm looking for Zsidó Zsigmond," I say, before the man can speak. "Is this his house? Do you know where he lives?"

The man has long curling black hair, laced through with threads of gray. When he opens his mouth I see that one of his teeth has been set in silver. I reach for the coin in my pocket, ready to hold it up like some mute, useless offering.

"We are all *Zsidó* here, girl," he scoffs. "*Zsidó* is the name the Patritians gave us, so they wouldn't sully their Patritian mouths by speaking in our tongue."

And then he closes the door without another word. Knees quaking, I turn slowly toward Gáspár. A flush of red goes through my face, my throat tightening with a coil of shame and anger.

"Why didn't you tell me?" I demand. "Did you want me to look a blundering simpleton, some insipid wolf-girl you dragged out of the woods to civilize?"

For a moment, Gáspár doesn't reply, only stares at me with a tight mouth. There's a familiar glint of misery in his eye.

"I thought you knew," he says finally. "I didn't realize how little you'd been told about the Yehuli and how they live here."

I don't want to hear any more. I turn on my heel, cheeks still burning, and march up to the next house. Paint is peeling off the wood in long tongues of red, and something that looks like a silver scroll is hammered to the door. It's stamped with more Yehuli letters that make my eyes water and my mind glaze over, like staring at a bleary shape on the horizon.

Another woman opens the door. She has chestnut hair braided neatly as a string of garlic, her eyes wavering between green and hazel. I can see rough, vague mirrors of my own features in hers—the reddish tint to her hair, the pointed nose, the small, worrying mouth—and in that suspended instant I manage to convince myself that I have found my father's house, and that she is an aunt or a cousin or maybe even a sister.

"Is this Zsigmond's house?" I ask, voice squeezed tight with hope.

The woman shakes her head, sadly.

"Not on Shabbos," she whispers, and then closes the door.

Her rebuff needles through my numb resolve. I have to draw in another quick breath to keep from whimpering, though I know Gáspár sees the anguish on my face. He reaches toward me, gloved hand open, and then abruptly draws back. The clear retraction of his kindness nearly unravels me. I held him so fast and so close and with such desperate fervor that he will never touch me again, like when you pluck an apple too soon and it rots before you can eat it.

When I reach the next threshold, I no longer hear Gáspár's footsteps behind me.

The man who answers the door is young enough to be my brother, but I can find none of my features in his. He wears an odd white hat, almost like a woman's bonnet, and it skews sideways, the string come loose behind one of his ears. He gawks at me for several beats before relenting to my reedy voice and wide, desperate eyes.

"Please," I say. "Do you know where I can find Zsigmond?"

The boy's face goes wan. "Didn't you hear? Zsigmond was taken to trial outside of the king's palace. Nándor had him arrested, for working on the Patritian holy day."

I charge back into the procession of festival-goers as the storm clouds churn and roil overhead. Once there, I am swept up in a current of pedestrians, shouldering from market stall to market stall. Saint István's feast must be the biggest market day of the year. People stream around me, coins clenched in dirty fists, arms curling around loaves of bread and long coils of smoked sausage. My poor, jostled mare kicks out her hind legs and topples a stinking bucket of trout heads to the ground, eliciting a curse from the fishmonger. Someone is selling fat sacks of red paprika, and the smell of it cuts through everything else, stinging like salt in a wound.

Gáspár shoves through the crowd and manages to catch one corner of my wolf cloak, yanking it right off my back.

"Have you gone absolutely mad?" he snarls. "The people in this city are God-fearing Patritians, and on this, the holiest day, they are riled to the peak of their zealotry. They would line up at the gates for a chance to prove their faith by killing you, especially the men—to them you are a pagan before you are a woman."

Even without my cloak I am an oddity in the crowd, among the dour Patritian women with their covered hair and downcast eyes. I can scarcely hear my own voice over the ragged, vicious pounding of my heart.

"What else would you have me do?" I bite back. "Nándor has my father."

"I would have you not be a fool," Gáspár says—harshly, but there's a desperate, pleading look in his eye that makes me pause, drawing in a furious breath. "If you charge into the palace like this, you'll damn both of us *and* your father."

*Both of us.* He's afraid that I'll reveal him, as a failure who brought back the wrong wolf-girl, or worse, as a failure who kissed that wolf-girl and bared his throat for her to latch her teeth into. My fear and hurt hardens into fury, and I no longer care about my dignity or his.

"Is there really nothing more precious to you than your purity?" I spit. "You've spent too many nights lying beside a wolf-girl to flush and fret over it now. I don't have any plans to reveal you, so save your miserable spluttering. If you're right,

THE WOLF AND THE WOODSMAN 201

one of your prized, pious killers will put a blade through my back first, and your secret will die when I do."

Gáspár holds my wolf cloak limply, the wind ruffling his hair across his face. Unlike the other occasions when I have spoken of our tryst or his compromised chastity, no color rises to his cheeks, and his eye is narrowed thin as an arrow slit.

"Do you really think that's all I care about?" he demands. "If you're really so keen to damn us both—"

"No," I cut in, thinking of cut hearts and my mother's braid in my pocket. "Not both of us. You are still a Woods-man, a prince. His son. The worst thing your father took from you is an eye."

With difficulty, I turn my horse and maneuver her through the crowd. In the distance, the castle looms like a great dark bird, but it casts no shadow because there is no sun. The crumbling stone of the Broken Tower is a pale gash against the charcoal sky.

The narrow street opens to a courtyard, penned by a gate of black wood. Here the festival-goers are packed so close, straining over one another's heads, that I can't inch my horse any farther. I slip off her back and shoulder through the crowd, past good Patritian women with white bonnets and Patritian men with grim, sweat-stained faces. The smell of fried bread drifts past me, mingling with something fouler and worse.

I elbow past a weaver woman with six teeth, who scowls at me and claws at my arm in retaliation. I scarcely feel the swipe of her nails. I push and push until I reach the very front of the crowd, staring out at the square courtyard with its filthy gray stones. In the center is a huddle of Woodsmen, and a Yehuli man between them, and he is standing on the corpse of a killed pig.

My stomach lurches at the sight and smell of it. I raise a hand to my mouth, bile crawling up my throat.

The man's arms are bound behind his back with a long, frayed rope, taut with his pulling. He wears the same odd white hat as the boy I saw on Yehuli Street. From where I stand all I can see is a slivered fraction of his face, pale as a waning moon. He has a long nose and woolly gray brows, and his chin is raised defiantly, as if he can't even see the gore on the ground beneath him.

There are two more men in the courtyard. One is hunched with age, swaddled in the dull tawny robes of a Patritian holy man. He blinks his small, bright eyes like a little brown mole, fingers curling around the iron pendant at his throat.

The other man is far too young to be king, but that is not the thought that dominates me in the moment. All I can think is that he is the most beautiful man I have ever seen. He is no older than Gáspár, sweet-faced and almost boyish, wearing a dolman dyed the color of a velvet-dark evening. His auburn hair curls loosely to the nape of his neck, luxuriant, as if it's mocking the shorn heads of the Woodsmen beside him. He has the dewy complexion of an opal newly polished, and blue eyes that gleam beneath feathered golden lashes. When he smiles, it etches crooked dimples into his cheeks, the kind of small flaw that throws the rest of his face into breathless relief, every other feature made lovelier by comparison.

The man circles my father with the lithe grace of a hawk just before it snatches its prey.

"What do you say, Zsidó Zsigmond, to these charges?" he asks, sounding terribly pleasant, as though he were inquiring to a merchant about the price of some coveted ware. "Do you confess that you were indeed working on the last Lord's Day?"

"I am *paid* to work on the Lord's Day," Zsigmond says. "Commissioned by your own father to—"

I don't hear the rest. Gáspár has shoved his way to my side, his hand closing around my wrist.

"You need to leave," he rasps. "If you only heed my warning once in your life, wolf-girl, please sheathe your claws now."

My four fingers curl into a fist at my side. Ördög's magic is there, coiled like a snake ready to strike, but the ragged desperation in Gáspár's voice stills me, just for a moment, as the crowd pushes around us.

"These sorts of trials aren't unusual," he goes on, quickly, now that he's gotten me to falter, "but they make a mockery of the very notion of justice. Yehuli men and women are charged with a number of invented, flimsy accusations, and then paraded around in chains for the crowd to gnash their teeth at. It's an easy way to win the favor of peasants who loathe the Yehuli."

Ice edges into my veins. "And the pig . . . ?"

Gáspár lets out a breath. "Yehuli scripture forbids them from eating or touching pig."

And then I think I really will be sick, with the smell of the pig's blood and viscera stiff and heavy in the air, and Nándor's gloating voice running over me like water in a stream bed, and I grab hold of Gáspár's arm to steady myself. He tenses under my touch but doesn't jerk away.

"He can't," I manage. "Please—you have to say something. You have to stop him."

"Your father is in no real danger, at least not yet," Gáspár replies, but a swallow ticks in his throat. "Our protestations are better spent at the king's feet, or later, when there's no audience to preen for. Nándor won't abandon his fun while there are half a hundred peasants looking on, cheering for a Yehuli man's debasement."

The evenness of his voice, the pinched-nose rationality of his proposal, makes my vision glaze with fury. Nándor might as well be Virág, standing over me with her reed whip, or Katalin—they have the same gleeful venom in their eyes. I let go of Gáspár's arm as brusquely as I can, hoping to leave marks.

"Will you only move to prevent injustice when no one is watching?" I ask, with as much meanness as I can muster.

"It's no wonder the people prefer Nándor—at least he's not a coward."

"I suppose a coward is anyone who acts with forethought, who doesn't hurl themselves into the jaws of the beast only to prove their own heroism?" Gáspár's eye is as black as pitch. "Surviving in Király Szek is a test of shrewdness, not of bravery. You will not last long here unless you understand that."

There is an undercurrent of desperation to his words, even concern, but I am too angry to be moved. I have done plenty of kneeling. It has never earned me any mercy. The crowd's chanting rises, louder, like a flock of birds taking flight into the gray sky, and Nándor smiles and smiles as pig's blood soaks my father's boots.

"Stop!"

The word shudders out of me, unbidden, before I can think to prevent it. And because I've already started, I say again, "Stop, let him go!"

The onlookers go quiet. Nándor's eyes lift, scanning the crowd until they find me—his lambent, laughing eyes. He considers me for a moment, blinking once, and then his gaze shifts, landing on Gáspár.

"Is this an illusion of Thanatos?" he asks, and then pauses, although it is not a question anyone is supposed to answer. "Or is it my brother back again, with a wolf-girl by his side?"

Nándor leaves my father and strides toward us. Instinctively, my hand goes for my knife, but then I remember that it's gone, along with my braid and my coin.

My four fingers open, unfurling like a flower, as Nándor nears. If he reaches for me I will grasp him first and see what Ördög's power can do, but here before all these Patritians, and four Woodsmen guards, I realize with a slippery feeling in my stomach that it will not be enough. It can't be. The beautiful man stalks toward me, his eyes searing right through my skin, and I think I finally understand Gáspár's dire warnings.

Yet, when Nándor does pause in front of us, he scarcely

seems to glance my way at all. Instead, he wraps his arms around Gáspár.

"Welcome home," he says, voice muffled against the fur of Gáspár's suba.

Gáspár says nothing. He is rigid inside Nándor's embrace, his brother's mouth hovering far too close to the bruise on his throat. A weight settles on my chest, my breathing short and quick. Gáspár disentangles himself as soon as he's able.

"This must be the wolf-girl Father wanted," says Nándor. He clasps his hand under my chin, his long fingers stroking down my cheek. "She's rough-looking, like all wolf-girls, and a bit plain-faced besides."

His thumb curls over my lip. I cannot look anywhere else, trapped in his bewitching viper's stare. I think of biting off his thumb, like I did Peti's ear. I imagine watching him scream and fumble for his missing finger amidst the spray of blood and the stuttering pain. But it is precisely that stupid, vicious instinct that will get me killed faster.

Still, I jerk my chin away, my four fingers clenching.

"You know that Father wants his wolf-girls unharmed," Gáspár says, smooth-voiced and princely again, the same tenor to his words that always made me bristle and scowl. His eye reveals only a quick glimmer of unease.

"I also know that Father wants his wolf-girls silent and cowed," says Nándor. He blinks toward me. "You've charged into the palace courtyard in the midst of our Saint István's Day celebration, looking every inch a barbarian, more wolf than girl. Tell me, what do you care about the fate of this Yehuli man?"

I could kill him. Or, at least, I could try. Ördög's threads twitch around my wrist. But even if I succeeded, if he burned up like a lightning-struck tree under my touch, I would not escape the city alive. And what then? Keszi would be punished for my crime, and so would the Yehuli as soon as the king figured out I was one of them.

In this moment I am nothing at all to this brilliant would-be prince, worth less than the muck on his boots—and yet whatever I do next will decide the fate of two peoples, a whole village and every house on that long gray street.

My mouth opens mutely, then closes again. After all the weeks I spent upbraiding Gáspár for his deference, the easy way his knees buckle and his head bows, I realize that he is, in fact, cleverer than me. What kind of idiot bird pecks at its master between the bars of its cage?

A terrible fear settles over me, heavy as my missing wolf cloak.

"Very well then," Nándor says. "We deal with wolf-girls the same way we deal with Yehuli merchant scum."

And then the crowd is chanting, screaming, spittle foaming in their open mouths. I am reminded of the black snapping jaws of the wolves that skulk around Keszi, on the deepest, coldest winter days, watching and growling and waiting for someone to wander too far into the woods.

I waver between shrinking back and leaping forward, and in that manic, seizing moment of indecision, I manage to meet my father's eyes over the broad sweep of Nándor's shoulder. They are as blank as two tide pools at midnight, no starry pinprick of recognition in them. I am staring at a stranger. I am going to die for a man who doesn't even know me.

Gáspár's voice arcs over the din. "The wolf-girl is Father's prize. He'll be the one to decide what to do with her."

But Nándor only raises a beckoning hand. The Woodsmen descend, all at once, like a murder of crows coming down on a corpse. Everything that follows, I see only in flashes: a billowing black suba—not Gáspár's—and the metal glint of an ax. Nándor's incandescent smile. My spooked mare charging the crowd, sides heaving, whinnying through her flared nostrils. A Woodsman's gloved hand jams against the back of my throat, forcing me to the ground, my hair grazing over the filthy cobblestones.

I look up again, with difficulty. Nándor is pacing toward my mare, making hushing sounds. She stills, letting him place one hand on her muzzle, and the other on her broad neck.

"What a lovely beast," he murmurs. "Her coat is pure white. There are no other horses in our stables with such a coat. I do appreciate a unique, unblemished beauty."

A Woodsman's ax slides between my shoulder blades. "Where shall we take her, my lord?"

If they call him lord, I wonder, what do they call the king?

"Where we take all the wolf-girls," Nándor says, his voice hitching with impatience.

The crowd is still chanting, the words all running together, until I can't hear anything but dull, oblivious noise. I stare through the matted tangle of my hair at Nándor, watching as he takes my horse by the reins and leads her toward the palace door. The storm clouds seethe overhead, glowering as if they were Isten's great black brow. A strain of murky light beams through, catching on Nándor's hair, on the sweet curve of his jaw, whiter than my mare's pelt. I remember what Szabín said, about him floundering up out of the ice and then standing again as if his pulse had never stopped its pounding.

I am almost ready to believe it now. There is ice in his eyes still, like his death has lived with him all the years since.

I cannot twist my neck far enough to see Gáspár's face, but he is by my side, unmoving and silent. From the waist down he looks like any other Woodsman, dressed finely in his black suba and his embroidered leather boots. There are flies hovering over the pig's carcass, circling the bloody gouges where someone has stabbed out its eyes. And then I hear my father's footsteps, fading, as someone leads him away too.


The Woodsman throws a hood over my eyes and takes me on a dizzying journey through the dungeons. I almost want to laugh when he peels back my blinds: they are dark and damp, the ceilings slick with sour water and the walls clotted blue-white with mold, but they are nothing worse than that. I have been imagining some peculiar torture, designed specifically for wolf-girls.

He thrusts me into the cell and shuts me behind the rust-gritted bars. I hear his suba ghosting through the foul puddles as he goes, ascending a flight of crooked stairs and leaving me alone in the greasy smear of dimming torchlight.

I slide to my knees in the mud and grime, my cheek against the mold-speckled wall. Even after everything, I am surprised by how easy it is to cry. I cry so hard I'm certain someone will come slit my throat to shut me up, and by the time I finish I'm half praying that they do, as I'm imagining my mother in this same cell. My mind conjures its vague memories of her body, contorting them into a shape that matches my own. Small, cowed, kneeling. I almost think I will find a clump of her soft red hair buried in the muck, or a white clavicle bone.

I fall asleep that way, curled around my mother's ghost.

# CHAPTER FOURTEEN

É vike."

I wake to the sound of my name and to Gáspár standing outside of my cell. He has my cloak draped over his arm, the wolf looking limp and more dead than usual. I wipe the grime from my face and stand, knees quivering under me.

"I brought this for you," he says, holding my cloak through the bars.

In the oily gleam of lantern light, his face looks cleaved in two: one half dewed in gold and the other cached in darkness. His good eye is shadow-drenched, so I have to read his expression by the clench of his jaw, the white line of his lips. Torchlight leaps off his ax blade, glinting wetly.

Very slowly, I take my cloak from him. I search its pockets, but my knife is gone.

"I had to take it." His voice is sharp enough to scythe through the bars. "I can't worry about you trying anything so abysmally stupid again."

"How utterly noble of you."

My words glance off him like arrows off a steel breast-plate. He doesn't shift. My braid and my coin are still inside the pockets, but they feel leached of their warmth. When I run my finger along the grooved edge of the coin, all I can think about is my father's blank-faced stare and the alien shape of his nose and mouth. We could have passed each other oblivi-ously in a crowd.

"Have you finished with all your snarling outrage, then?" Gáspár asks, and not kindly. "I told you what would happen if you came to the city. If you provoked Nándor."

"You were planning to bring me anyway!" I burst out. "If your men hadn't been killed, if you hadn't figured out I wasn't a seer, you would have brought me right to your father's feet and let him do what he wished to me. When did you begin to have compunctions about seizing girls and trussing them up for the king like sheep to the slaughter? Was it after you knew the taste of my mouth, or after you felt the shape of my body under my cloak?"

I expect it to rattle him, and it does, but only for a mo-ment. A grit of his teeth chases the flush from his cheeks.

"If I wanted you to die, I would have let Peti kill you. I would have let you drown under the ice. I wouldn't have tried to stop you from tearing into Nándor's false trial," he says. "I could have left you to Miklós and Ferenc. If they weren't bound by oath to serve my father, do you know what they would have done to you?"

Hearts and livers on the city gates. I think of the crowd closing in around me, the spittle foaming in their open mouths. My five-fingered hand curls around the iron bars. It doesn't matter how sharp my claws are; I can't cut a thou-sand throats.

"You've not an ounce of good sense," Gáspár goes on, in his pinched-nose prince's voice. Despite everything, I can tell a part of him relishes the opportunity to castigate me. "Don't you realize what you've done? Half of Király Szek has now seen you for a vicious wolf-girl, and Nándor looks more vindicated in his loathings than ever."

I know there's truth in his words, but all I can feel is hurt and toothless anger. I might as well be back in Virág's hut, my thighs stinging with her lashes.

"You could have done *something*," I bite out. When I remember his stony silence, the way he watched the Woodsmen drag me away without lifting a hand to stop them, it burns worse than a hundred billows of blue flame. "You didn't say a word against Nándor once he had me. You told me I've ruined you, but you're clearly still the same selfish princeling you've always been, dressed in your delusions of piety. Well, I apologize, my lord. I'd take back every kiss if I could. Lucky for you, once I'm dead, the secret of your broken oath will die with me, and you can go back to pretending you're the purest, most honorable Woodsman alive."

I'm not sure how much of what I've said is honest and how much of it is my bitter floundering, hoping at least one of my cruel barbs will hit its mark. Gáspár draws in a short breath, throat bobbing, and then steps sideways into the light. His eye is pooling with venom, but it's a poor guise for grief. Even though I ought to feel satisfied that my thorns have stuck in him, my blood is cold as ice.

"You don't understand," he says, each word a labor, as if he truly does think I'm too simple to grasp their meaning. "If Nándor had even the barest suspicion that I might care for you at all, he'd torture you to death or madness, just to feel like he was taking something from me."

I stare and stare at him, gulping my fury. I think of the way he held me through the long nights in Kaleva, or the way his lips moved so gently against my throat, but it all makes me want to weep again when I see how he's looking at me now, as if I'm hopeless and doomed.

"You've done a good job pretending," I say. "Even I'm quite convinced."

His mouth twists wretchedly. "You'll have a much easier time pleading your case in front of my father. He tolerates pagans, unlike Nándor."

The word *father* runs me through like a sword. "Where is Zsigmond?"

Gáspár doesn't look at me. The flickering torchlight leaps from wall to wall, bounding after shadows. Finally, he says, "Nándor is still having his fun."

A blind and furious rage comes over me, like a fissure of pale lightning. I lunge toward him, the bars rattling vainly between us, tears beading at the corners of my eyes.

"Why come back at all, just to keep your head down and follow orders like some weak, worthless Woodsman?" I snarl. "What kind of prince bends silently to the wills of his bastard brother? What kind of prince stands idle and dumb as a struck dog while his people—and yes, the Yehuli *are* your people, no matter what you believe—suffer? You're no better than any other soldier who tears mothers from their children."

"Enough," Gáspár spits back. "You would be dead already, wolf-girl, if I hadn't—"

He stops himself, mouth snapping shut. In the time he has been speaking, I have reached out and grasped his wrist, the space between where his sleeve ends and his glove begins and where his bare skin is latticed white with scars.

"I don't need a knife to wound you," I whisper.

Gáspár doesn't move. His gaze meets mine, through the cell bars, black and steady. I see a glimpse of the man I knew on the ice and in the woods again, that bridled fervor and swallowed pain.

"Do it, then," he says, without a trace of fear. It's the first time I've witnessed this courage from him since we reached the city.

I have the briefest instinct to reach for his throat, where

the violet memory of my kiss is still throbbing, but I'm not sure whether I mean to smother him with my tenderness or with my hate. I let go of his wrist, skin prickling.

"Keep one promise." My voice is trembling so terribly that I have to swallow hard before going on again. "Tell me what your father does to the wolf-girls that he takes."

Gáspár's gaze lowers, torchlight leaving his eye. For a long moment there is only the sound of water dripping from the mold-slick walls, and, more distantly, another prisoner's chains rattling. Bastioned inside my wolf cloak, I wrap my arms around myself, like there is something that needs to be held from breaking apart, or breaking out.

"I'm sorry," Gáspár says finally. And it is his refusal, this smallest of betrayals, that hurts worse than anything.

He sweeps out of the dungeon, his suba gathering a patchwork of shadow and light, leaving me alone.

I can't tell how many hours have passed when another Woodsman comes for me, but I have already resigned myself to dying. He's the same Woodsman from the courtyard, with a bald head like a bruised peach and a mangled, half-missing nose. Beside him is a slip of a girl, shaking and thin as an icicle, laureled in her homespun servant's clothes. She stares at me meekly over the rim of a bucket, her halved face like a white moon rising.

"You're the worst I've seen yet," the Woodsman says.

I don't know if by *worst* he means ugliest, or if by *worst* he means filthiest, or if by *worst* he means wickedest, or if perhaps it is all three. I scarcely have the energy to curl my lip at him.

"Lajos, don't rile her," the serving girl protests. I can tell she is not concerned with wounding my feelings, merely afraid that I will lash out at her in my rage. I can hardly blame her for that: I must look worse than I smell, and I feel like something chained and hunted and hungry.

"Wolf-girls aren't capable of being hurt, Riika," chides the Woodsman. "They're soulless things, no gentler or wiser than the animals they wear."

But Riika is still staring at me wide-eyed. She has a Northerner's name and a Northerner's blanched complexion, as pale as a peeled apple. It's a long way from here to Kaleva, and I feel sorry for her in spite of myself—mostly sorry that she has been given the unfortunate task of wrangling me.

"It's a waste of water to wash her," Lajos says. "But it would be a great insult to the king, to present her to him in such a state."

I consider wounding him, killing him, but it's a fleeting thought. It won't help me escape, and it will only prove how loathsome I am to those who already loathe me. I sit still and silent in my cell as Lajos flings open the door and Riika approaches me with no more bravery than a skittish wood mouse. I can almost see whiskers twitching.

"Please," she squeaks out. "He'll be furious if you don't . . ."

She sets the bucket in front of me and then scuttles behind Lajos's back. I dip my hands in, watching motes of dirt flake off my fingers and drift through the water like dead flies. The water is cold enough to sting, but I scrub my cheeks and my nose and even the grime caked behind my ears. Why not die with a pink, shining face?

Did my mother have a chance to clean her face before they killed her?

There's a bone-toothed comb for my tangled hair and a new tunic made of bristly wool that I know will be too small and too tight, so I shake my head. Riika chews her lip and looks like she might weep, so I put it on anyway, blinking numbly as a seam splits up my thigh.

"You don't look like a monster," she whispers, almost to herself.

I think about how many times I woke, sweating and

screaming, from nightmares about Woodsmen with gleaming sharp teeth and claws beneath their black gloves, and wonder if good Patritian girls like Riika have dreams about wolf-girls eating them.

"Let's go," Lajos says shortly, prodding me with the blunt edge of his ax.

This time, no one pulls a hood over my eyes as Lajos leads me barefooted out of the dungeon. We turn down long hall-ways that curve as wickedly as viper tongues. Small square windows wink star-glutted light—in the time I've spent in the dungeon, evening has withered into night. Finally, an arched doorway opens like a scowling mouth, bearing us into the Great Hall.

Feasting tables have already been laid out with cooked swans, their necks curling like white-gloved hands and their beaks still intact; a whole roast boar gumming a green apple, its side split open to reveal a stuffing of dried cherries and link sausages; two enormous pies molded to resemble twin crowns; bowls of red-currant soup the color of a lake at sunrise. Gáspár was right—there's no peasant fare here.

The Patritian guests rise as I enter, whispering like a sibilant tide. The women all have their hair covered, in headscarves or rheumy veils or silly boxed hats, and each man wears a silk dolman, cinched at the waist with a woven belt of red. The men in Keszi wear the same embroidered belts to ward off de-mons from the forest, who confuse the red with blood and think their would-be victims already dead, and I want to laugh seeing these pious Patritian men wearing them, too, until I re-alize I am the evil thing they are trying to keep at bay.

My gait must have faltered, because Lajos gives me an-other vicious shove.

Iron chandeliers wheel overhead, candle flames blinking at me like the thousand eyes of Ezer Szem in the dark. My heart is a riot as I fix my gaze on the dais ahead, where a long table has been set out and laid with white cloth. There are six chairs girding the table, and at the very center, knuckling out of the white like a tree in the snow, is a carved wooden throne.

For now, the throne is empty. But in the threshold behind the dais, a cluster of figures emerges. Three boys at first, the youngest no older than twelve, each dressed in a dolman of emerald green. One has a Northerner's frosted hair, nervous as an albino fawn, skittering-bright under a hunter's stare. One has chestnut hair like mine, curling maniacally around his overlarge ears. The last has hair the color of beechwood, shot through with streaks of darker brown. The king's young bastard sons, all born of different mothers.

Nándor strides in behind them, and the guests all leap to their feet so quickly they trip and scuffle, like a flock of bejeweled birds, squawking out their blessings and prayers. He wears a dolman of ivory and gold, and I wonder if he put it on after he wrung my father's blood from his hands.

I didn't let myself think of seeing Gáspár here, but he comes last through the archway, head bowed, eye following some invisible path toward the dais. His black dolman is buttoned all the way to the line of his jaw, obscuring the bruise I left on his throat. He takes a seat at the very last chair, farthest from the throne, beside the boy with beechwood hair, and gives his younger brother a gentle smile that steals the breath from my lungs.

I want him to lift his gaze and find me in the crowd, Lajos's ax in my back. I don't dare make a sound, but I stare at him as if I can will him to stare back, to see what his cowardice has done.

Lajos prods me to the corner of the chamber, where I am half-hidden behind a wrought-iron candle holder. I wonder again if my mother stood in this very spot in the king's Great Hall, knees trembling as she waited to die. The thought passes through my mind like wind thrashing open the flap of a tent, leaving me ragged and ruined. I blink furiously, wishing that

I could cry and be comforted—I would take even Virág's per-functory comfort, her six fingers stroking roughly through my hair—but I won't let these Patritians see me weeping.

Nándor rises to his feet, and the tittering guests fall silent at once, like a candle being snuffed.

"Now arrives your king," he says. "Heir to the throne of Ave István, blood chieftain of the White Falcon Tribe and all its lands, and blessed by the gentle hand of the Prinkepatrios. Kneel for him and for your god. Király és szentség."

"Király és szentség," the guests murmur, and then fold to their knees.

I have spent all my life hating the king so fiercely, so blindly, that when I finally see him, I don't know what to think or how to feel. He could not have been as monstrous as my imaginings, because even the worst monsters, like drag-ons, look only like men. King János is neither tall nor short, neither fat nor thin. He has the look of a man who grew his beard long and gray for the precise purpose of hiding a weak chin. He wears a dolman of exquisite gold, and over it a velvet mente with a furred collar and sleeves that drape all the way down to the stone floor.

I almost don't notice his crown. It's a funny thing, oddly skewed, a bleached color somewhere between yellow and white. It's not the grand coronet I envisioned, knobbed with precious stones. It's made up of a thousand tiny pieces tacked together, and I can't tell what they are until I look down at my own hand, feverishly clutching the hem of my too-small tunic.

King János wears a crown of fingernails.

In the gauze of candlelight, I stare at the nails on the king's crown. There are infinitesimal slivers of blood between each one, where bone was peeled away from skin. I try to find my mother's fingernails among them, but it's too dark and I've forgotten what her hands looked like, much less her nails. Were they long and elegant, like Katalin's? Short and bitten to nubs, like mine? Did they wait to take her fingernails until after they killed her, or did they flay them off while she was still alive, shucking them like insect shells, so they could hear her whimper?

King János lifts his hand, his own fingers gnarled with golden rings. The cold candles lining the feast tables blossom with flame, wicks cringing black. A murmur rises from the guests, something appreciative but guarded, the way a warrior might admire a compatriot's particularly gruesome kill. The king brings his hands together, rings clattering, and knives and forks and spoons glimmer onto the tables in front of us, silver dinnerware shining bright as blades.

He's *forging*.

I've never seen a Woodsman do it before, and not even a whisper of a prayer has left the king's lips. The guests are flashing their eyes now, like prey animals at the mouths of their burrows.

The room starts to shrink away, candlelight pinwheeling through my darkening vision. My heart thrums like the pulse of blood behind a bruise. I try to count how many wolf-girls have been taken from Keszi. One every two or three years, for all the years that János has been king. It tallies to twelve girls, not including me.

Twelve girls. Ten fingernails each. Is it enough to cobble together into King János's bone crown? Enough to leach the magic from his victims' cold skin and give the king the power that he craves?

The king takes a seat and coughs into the luxurious sleeve of his mente.

"Now," he says in a phlegmy voice, once he has finished, "bring in the counts."

I push myself onto my toes, still feeling the thrust of Lajos's ax between my shoulder blades, and wait to see more men come swathed in silk and velvet. But the first man who enters is dressed plainly, in a pagan's brown tunic and woolen cloak. The recognition gives way to terrible grief, like the first bite of an apple before you taste the curdle of its rot. He is wearing a grand headdress of antlers, and two men beside him are leading a massive buck, its own antlers sawed to sad nubs. The deer strains and strains against its bounds, fur matted with blood where the rope has cut in.

My stomach floods with ice. Szarvasvár was once the land of the Deer Tribe, and its count is the great-grand-nephew of a tribal chieftain. He is dressed precisely like a tribal chieftain now, even though so many laws have been passed since, to forbid the worship of our gods.

The deer is brought in front of the dais, before the king. Its eyes are twin pools that hold the candlelight, black as a new-moon night. A Woodsman with a missing ear steps away from the wall, ax held aloft.

Blood arcs over the white tablecloth, narrowly missing the king himself. It kisses the sleeve of Nándor's dolman, like a napkin dipped in wine. As the deer slumps over, the guests come alive again, a scale toppled over and then righted again with the weight of a second, identical stone. Their approval whisks through the air.

The Woodsman drags the deer away. My eyes are burning, my throat is burning, and then the next man comes in, the count of Kaleva, dressed in a black bear cloak, escorted by some pitiful shaved mongrel that could be Bierdna's brother or sister. The bear makes its frantic, desperate honking sounds, fighting until the Woodsman's ax comes down and even after, against the choke of blood and the quivering splay of its limbs.

The count of Farkasvár is next. I know his face without ever having seen him before, and he is draped in a russet wolf cloak. I can barely look at the shorn, whimpering dog that the soldiers drag in after him, the thing that no man with eyes could call a wolf. Its bald tail lashes, teeth grinding against the leather muzzle.

I have seen things die before. I have killed them myself, birds and rabbits and mean, hissing badgers with their white-planked faces that had the audacity to steal from our winter vegetable stores. I have even seen a man killed and watched the light drain from his mad, manic eyes. I can't watch this. I squeeze my eyes shut, but when I do, Lajos prods me sharply in the back, and then grips my head with his gloved hand, turning my face toward the dais.

The wolf dies howling. By this time, blood has soaked the stone floor so thoroughly I know it will take some serving girl a day and a half to clean, scrubbing on her hands and knees until her own palms are soaked too. I try to meet Gáspár's gaze, but he is looking down at his goblet, his empty plate. He has one hand over his younger brother's eyes.

Even though I know what's coming next I have to raise my hand and bite down on my straining knuckles to keep from crying out. The count of Akosvár sweeps in wearing a cloak of white feathers, candlelight streaming off each one. He carries the golden cage himself, and inside it is the plucked falcon, shuddering and scrawny, looking like someone's supper. I sob against my palm, tasting my own salt-damp skin.

The count of Akosvár is not the true heir of the White Falcon Tribe. Hardly anyone remembers that Saint István was born with a pagan name (which has now been struck from any record books and almanacs, and is forbidden by Régyar law to be uttered aloud), because his grandfather, a pagan, was the blood chieftain.

The king clears his throat, but he doesn't speak, only nods.

Nándor is looking on with bright, glassy eyes. They are blue rimmed with an even paler blue, like frost ossifying around a window frame. He plucks a knife from the table, forged by the king only moments ago, and steps lightly off the dais. The falcon beats its bald wings, shrieking hoarsely.

Nándor wedges the knife through the bars of the cage and twists it into the bird's naked breast.

The falcon dies slowly, pooling pink at the floor of its cage like a baby bird in its nest, made small again in its death. Tears come streaming down my cheeks. Nándor tosses the knife to the floor, where it clatters against the blood-slick stone. He lifts his chin to the heavens and to the Upper-World.

"Let the old ways die," he says, "and the false gods with them."

# CHAPTER FIFTEEN

midst the murmurs of approval, the tear-stricken prayers, Nándor turns and fixes his eyes on me. They are terrifying in their two-toned blue, pale and bright as quartz glinting out of a cave mouth, as if the ice has never left him. Lajos gives me a cruel jab with his ax, and I stumble forward in front of the dais, in front of Nándor, on my knees. Voices hum in my periphery, as nasal and oblivious as insect wings. I try to pull out a word, a phrase, something small enough to bite down on. *Monster,* from one woman in a white box hat. *Heathen,* from a man in a smoky-gray dolman. From a dozen more: *justice, justice, justice.* Godfather Death will have me slit open like a crow on an augur's workbench.

"Your people cry for justice," Nándor says, looking to his father. "Will you answer them?"

The king stares at him for a moment. But instead of nodding assent, he says, "Come here, my son."

Shoulders slackened, Nándor returns to his place at the table, but I catch the corner of his mouth puckering, almost turning to a frown. His finger strokes along the edge of his empty plate. I remember that Gáspár said he would make a move against his father at Saint István's feast, and I find myself measuring the distance between Nándor's hand and his knife. Not that it matters very much—I will be dead before I witness any monarchs falling.

"Gáspár has brought this wolf-girl on a long journey from Keszi," says the king. He pauses, wiping his sweat-dewed forehead. "She is not a seer, I am told, but she may prove to have strength in one of the other three skills."

Some of the nails on the king's crown are cracking, yellowing. Eventually they will sliver into nothing, and he will need more warm wolf-girl bodies when they do.

"Father—" Nándor begins, but the king holds up his hand.

"Bring me a lump of coal and some kindling," the king says.

The Woodsman with the missing ear vanishes for a moment, and then comes back laden with coal and wood. I only recognize him now as the same Woodsman from before, the one who spoke with Gáspár: Ferenc. He drops the wood in front of me, scowling, and then grabs my hand and pries it open, pressing the coal into my palm. Disgust carves long furrows into his cheeks and brow.

"Now, then." King János draws himself up, blinking down at me. "Show me what magic your gods have granted you. Light a fire with this wood."

The king has brown eyes, not blue, and his face is nearly as ugly and aged as Virág's, but I could swear in this moment he looks like Katalin, dangling death over my head while demanding the impossible.

I pick up one of the pieces of wood and run my finger down the splintering length of it. I do it twice, three times, until the king makes a disgruntled noise and shakes his head.

"Not a fire-maker, evidently," he says. "Then take that coal, wolf-girl, and turn it into iron or silver."

The coal is still clenched in my four-fingered hand, black-ening the rivulets of my palm. King János has seen pagan magic before; he has watched a dozen wolf-girls cower before him this way, like cattle on an auction block, squirming to prove the value of their deaths. And so I start to sing, softly, just loud enough for my words to reach the king's long table.

*"First came King István, his cape as white as snow,*
*Then his son, Tódor, who set the North aglow,*
*After there was Géza, whose beard was long and*
   *gray,*
*Finally, King János—*
*And his son, Fekete."*

I watch Gáspár as I sing it, my gaze unflinching, daring him to look away. He has his arm around his younger brother, fist curling into the fabric of the boy's green dolman. There's no subterfuge on his face, no pretense of courtly indifference. His eye is gleaming with anguish, but still he doesn't speak. I won-der if he will think of kissing my throat when I die, remember-ing how he ran his lips so gently over the same skin that flowers open under his father's blade.

When I finish the song, the coal is still sooty and black.

"No talent for forging," the king murmurs. "Well, per-haps you're a healer, then. Woodsman, come here."

He beckons to Lajos, who has been pressed against the wall, half a shadow himself. The Woodsman strides forward and gives the king a low, silent bow.

"Your face," the king says.

I think I might be sick as I press my blackened hand to Lajos's cheek, to the gory remainder of his nose, the scar that cleaves his brow in two. All the while Lajos is breathing like a riled bull, his throat bobbing and his own hands closed into tight fists, cer-tainly wishing he could wrap them around my throat, instead.

But no new muscle rises up to make his nose whole again; no new skin stretches over the crags of his wicked scar. Lajos rips away from me, spitting and heaving, and I fall back on my heels, staggering in front of all the Patritian guests.

The king draws in a sharp breath. "What *is* your magic, wolf-girl?"

"Why does it matter?" My voice is hoarse and useless. "You're going to kill me anyway."

A hopeful murmur runs through the crowd. They want to see me slaughtered like a deer, a bird, a wolf. A girl.

"I cannot allow pagan deception to go unpunished," King János says. "Keszi promised me a seer, and they delivered me some barren thing instead. Would you rather I take my vengeance on your village?"

Murmurs of approval again. Nándor leans forward in his seat, eyes shifting like water under ice.

I almost laugh. I remember Gáspár giving me the same threat, on the shores of the Black Lake, both of our masks torn off. If nothing else, I will make him speak before I die.

"Did your son tell you?" I ask. "Is he the one who told you that I couldn't see?"

"My son . . ." The king's gaze turns blearily to Gáspár, and then he speaks to me while looking at him. "My son has all of Géza's wisdom, and none of István's fire."

Géza was the king's own father, who died young and sickly, and is remembered for little more than that. Even now the king's words still coax an ache into me, like a limbless, phantom pain. Gáspár swallows, and I think he might finally open his mouth, but he only looks down at his plate.

Betrayal lances through the hurt, shattering it like glass. Nándor's head whirls.

"Father, she is a wolf-girl," he says, just a thread of petulance in it. "If she refuses to repent to the one true God, and renounce her false ones, slay her here and prove that the people's clamoring for justice has not gone unheard. It is a great affront to King István's memory, to shelter a heathen here, in the very palace that he built, on his name day."

His voice goes high and reedy by the end of it, summoning renewed whispers from the crowd. *Justice, justice, justice.*

The king gives a feeble twitch, as if he is trying to right something within himself that is in danger of tipping over. "Is it true, wolf-girl, that you have no magic?"

*Yes* and *no* will both doom me, so I say nothing.

King János turns back to Gáspár. "Have you ever seen the girl perform an act of magic yourself? You said yourself she cannot see, but is she truly as barren as she appears?"

Gáspár's jaw clenches. I know this look of his, that miserable effort, like a toothless dog realizing the futility of its own bite. He may sit at the king's table, but he has scarcely more power here than I do. I think, with a rush of damned, traitorous tenderness so sudden that it frightens me, how steadily he is staring down the man who stabbed out his eye.

"Father," he says, the word low with its beseeching, "there are other ways—"

"Enough of this," Nándor cuts in. "My softhearted, weak-willed brother has grown too friendly with the pagans in his time away, and his judgment is therefore compromised. King István's memory ought to be enough to guide the swing of your blade, not to mention the will of your subjects, your people. The wolf-girl must die."

The guests purr their approval, and in that moment I hate them so much I can scarcely breathe, more than I ever hated the monstrous Woodsmen. They can see me here, see how pitifully human I am, no less human than they are, and yet they still slaver for my death. I have never wanted more to scream in fury at Gáspár, for all his stupid nobility, his impotent wisdom, his desire to save his people from Nándor. If Nándor is truly the king they yearn for, then he is the king they deserve.

Maybe I am just as much a fool, for wanting to save Keszi. Maybe, even now, I am still eating from the hands that struck me.

King János stares vaguely into the middle distance, eyes glazed. Then he says, "Bring me my sword."

I lurch to my feet, but Lajos and Ferenc are at my back instantly, axes drawn. It is Nándor who steps down the dais to retrieve the king's sword, a huge, heavy thing with a pearl-enameled hilt. Its scabbard is carved with an elaborate tracery of leaves and vines that at first I mistake for a coil of a hundred vipers, all of them devouring one another. Thorns snarl around the seal of the king's great house. Nándor places the blade in his father's hands.

"Father—" Gáspár starts, rising from his seat. Quick as a whip, Nándor stands, too, one of the king's forged knives in his grasp. Below the line of the table, where even I can barely see the gleam of it, he presses the blade against the inside of Gáspár's wrist.

"No true heir of Saint István," Nándor says softly, "would rise to stop a pagan girl from dying by his holy blade."

My heart is pounding, bile rising in my throat. I think of running, but my muscles seize as if I've been plunged into the frigid water again, ice closing over my head. I think of screaming, but my lips can only part wordlessly, sweat chilled on my brow. I think of reaching for my magic, but I can hardly feel my own hands, and that phantom ache is gone. I think of at least dying like a true wolf-girl, all vicious snarling and mouth-foaming fury, but there are already blades crowding my back.

"I," the king begins, and then has to stop and exhale shakily, "King János, of House Bárány, blood chieftain of Akosvár, heir to the throne of Saint István and ruler of the kingdom of Régország, hereby sentence you to die."

I was not half so terrified when the Woodsmen took me, or when Peti was grimacing over me, or when I watched my mother's cloak vanish into the mouth of the forest. And then something else knifes through the fear, bright as a beam of sunlight. It is nothing more than animal instinct, the rawest, most feral desire to live. The king's sword hurtles toward me, and I lift my four-fingered hand, black threads noosing around my wrist.

The blade halts against the tip of my finger, carving the tiniest slit, and a single drop of blood blooms from the cut, red as a summer-flushed rose. As the sword hovers there, in that suspended moment, it begins to rust: the steel loses all its luster and turns a dull, grainy shade of amber before flaking away into nothing.

The blunted hilt of the king's sword clatters to the ground.

"You, wolf-girl," he whispers. "What are you?"

"You said it yourself. A wolf-girl."

I stride forward, too quickly for the awestruck Woodsmen to follow, and before either of them can think of killing me, my hand is locked around the king's wrist. His flesh is dry and papery, scarless. I let my magic push out from under my skin and scrape against his—only a little wound, but enough to make him cry out.

"You wouldn't," the king rasps. "My soldiers will strike you dead, even if you do."

"I may die, eventually," I reply, "but I will go chasing you out of this world, because I will kill you first."

King János swallows. He looks like the profile of my coin if it were tossed into the forge again, the planes of his face rippling, his jaw going slack under the melting heat, his brow folding like a rotted fruit. I imagine what it would feel like to let my magic clamber up his throat, blistering all the skin from his body, to see him puddle limp to the ground just like any of the animals he ordered killed.

The king knows that I could kill him. I know that I will die if I do. A scale tips in these realizations, wobbling between our twin desires: we both want to live.

"Perhaps," the king says, quietly, holding his hand up to stop the Woodsmen lumbering toward me, "neither of us have to die today."

Nándor makes a strangled noise, though not a word escapes him.

My grip doesn't slacken. "What will you offer me, to spare your life?"

"Your village's safety," the king says. "No soldiers of mine will move against Keszi."

"Not enough." My stomach is roiling, sick with this new-found, unchecked power. *I am the warden of Keszi's destiny, now.* "I want Zsigmond released, unharmed."

"Who?"

"Zsidó Zsigmond," I say. "A Yehuli man that Nándor dragged to trial and falsely imprisoned. You must set him free and promise that no one will try to harm any Yehuli in your city."

"I have already issued missives forbidding violence against the Yehuli in Király Szek."

"They're obviously not good enough," I snap, flushing angrily. "Not with your own son undermining them."

The king closes his eyes briefly. His eyelids are thin as onionskin; I can see his pupils rolling beneath them. Then he opens them again. "I will free this Yehuli man, and to the best of my ability protect the Yehuli of this city. But now you must offer something to me. I don't suppose I can convince you to give up your fingernails."

"No," I say, stomach hitching in revulsion. I think of Nándor, his fingers inching closer and closer to the knife. I think of what Gáspár told me, that very first night by the Black Lake. *He craves power more than purity, and he wants a way to win the war.* I think of my father, soaked to the knee in pig's blood. I think, for the briefest moment, about Katalin, her face cast blue in the light of her flame. This will prove her right for good. "But you can have my power. My magic."

Confusion clusters like dark clouds over the king's brow, and then realization breaks across it bright as day. "You would swear an oath of fealty to the Crown."

"Yes." The roar of blood in my ears is so loud I can hardly hear myself speak the word. "My power is yours, as long as you uphold your end of our bargain."

"I swear by the Prinkepatrios, the one true and almighty God, that as long as you are in my service, no harm will come to Keszi or to the Yehuli man, Zsigmond." King János's arm shudders under my grasp. "What is your name, wolf-girl?"

I remember Gáspár asking me the same thing, lake water lapping at our boots. Saying it to the king now feels as if I am handing him something fragile and precious, like my own cut tongue.

"Évike," I say. "My name is Évike."

The king dips his head, swallowing my name whole. "Do you, Évike of Keszi, swear to protect the crown of Régország? To be my sword where I have none, and to speak with my voice when I cannot?"

"Yes." I am surprised by how lightly the vow leaves my lips, like an ember drifting out of a hearth. "I swear it."

"To make this a true Patritian oath, you must kneel."

I cast a glance at Lajos, whose gaze is burning holes in my back. "Call off your dogs first."

"Stand down," the king tells the Woodsmen.

Very slowly, Lajos lowers his blade. Beside him, Ferenc does the same, but I can hear him mutter something that sounds like a curse, close to treachery.

I relax my grasp on the king's wrist, Ördög's threads loosing. His skin is slick and red where I have grasped him, etched with four burn marks the length and breadth of my fingers. Keeping one eye on the king and another on the Woodsmen behind me, I lower myself to the ground.

"Father, this is madness," comes Nándor's voice, words slipped through the white grit of his teeth. There are murmurs of agreement from the guests, those who aren't too slack-jawed to speak.

The king bends to pick up the pearled hilt of his blade, long sleeves pooling on the stone floor. He closes his eyes and another blade shimmers to life, shooting out of the hilt like a tree streaming up toward the sun. I wonder what Virág would think, if she saw it, the loathsome king suffused with pagan magic. I wonder what she would think if she saw me, shoulders bent under his blade. It shouldn't rattle her at all. If she has taught me anything, it has been how to kneel.

King János lays his sword on each of my shoulders, one after the other. I can scarcely feel the press of it. All I can feel is the steadying of my heartbeat, like a wheel falling into a groove. I was cast out to the Woodsmen, but I have survived. I have come to the capital, but I have not met my mother's fate. I am alive despite so many wishing me dead, pagan and Patritian alike. I feel as if I have crawled up from some black abyss, eyes flashing and wild as light fills them for the first time. The weight of their loathing lifts from me like a loosed cloak. Here in the capital, their words and their lashes cannot reach me, and I am the one who keeps the wolves from Keszi's door. Even with my oath tethering me to the king, my life feels more like my own than it ever has before. Mine to spend as I see fit, and mine to lose foolishly, if that's what I wish.

Gáspár is staring at me with a pale, stricken face, but he no longer gets to care what I do. Nándor pushes out of his seat and stalks from the room, footsteps brisk against the cold stone. When I rise again, I can scarcely hear the Patritians weeping.

Lajos takes me down to the dungeon again, where they are keeping my father.

I retrieve my wolf cloak from my old cell—it's damp and filthy, the wolf's teeth blackened, as if by soot—but I don't put it on. It feels wrong to wear it, after what I've done, like a dress or a doll that's been outgrown. I drape it over my arm, instead, the wolf's head hanging limp and its eyes particularly glassy. No one stops me as I move in and out of the cells. Lajos doesn't lift a hand. My oath to the king has armored me, but even better than that, my display of magic has clearly cowed him. I could turn his ax to nothing in my hand. He watches me like a carp at the end of a fisherman's line, openmouthed, and flinches whenever I make an abrupt move. He looks the way I have always wanted the Woods-men to look: afraid. Lajos seems nearly old enough to have taken my mother.

My father is in the very last cell, a great distance from my own. Maybe he was there all night, same as I was, the two of us curled like mollusks against the wet, dirty floor, oblivious symmetries of each other. The thought chills and heartens me in equal measure. A bad memory shared between two people carries with it only half the pain. Now my father is drawn up neatly on the far left side of his cell, legs crossed at the ankle, face angled toward the dank ceiling. When Lajos unlatches the door, he doesn't leap to his feet. He only looks at me oddly and blinks.

Staring at him now, even in the grizzled torchlight, I can see his features better than I did in the courtyard. His eyes are a warm brown, keen and bright, drawing what little light there is and holding it. His nose is proud and almost regal; I think he would make a fine profile for a minted coin, be-tween that and the stubborn triangle of his chin. His lips are thin and terse. His hair is thoroughly grayed, which dis-appoints me—I wish I could see whether it was the same chestnut hue as my own. Zsigmond seems to chafe under my probing stare, his shoulders rising around his ears.

"Who are you?" he asks.

Suddenly my mouth goes as dry as cotton. I can't think of how to answer him, so I reach into the pocket of my wolf cloak, fumbling for my coin, and hold it out to him, fingers quivering.

Zsigmond rises to his feet, unsteadily. When he reaches me, he takes the coin with such delicacy that not even the pads of our thumbs touch. I try not to feel deflated by his balking gingerness. He watches me with one eye, and with the other, examines the coin in the scant torchlight.

Finally, he says, "Where did you get this?"

"You gave it to me." My voice doesn't have half the certainty I want it to. I wonder if he'll believe me at all. "Well, you gave it to my mother, and then she gave it to me."

"Are you Rákhel's daughter?"

Some name I don't recognize, a woman I don't know. My stomach hollows.

"No," I say, "I'm yours."

Zsigmond looks at me, long and hard. He is not much taller than I am and I can see one blue vein on his temple throbbing as he stares, reminding me, with a bitter start, of Virág. I chase the thought from my mind. His bushy brows draw together.

"It's not possible," he says. "I had a daughter once, true, but . . ."

"She's not dead," I whisper. "The Woodsmen came to Magda and they took her, but Virág—she saved me."

"Virág?"

I blink, baffled that he has caught onto her name, that *this* is the part of my story he has picked out. "Yes, the seer. She has white hair and twelve fingers."

When I was twelve or thirteen, I decided I hated him, my faceless father, who had cursed me with his alien bloodline, and I made up some story in my head that he hadn't tried to stop the Woodsmen, being a Yehuli slave to the king and all. If Virág had been able to press me with more of her superstitions, I might have believed that a trickster god has decided to punish me for my perverse thoughts, and now Zsigmond will only see me as a faceless girl, never his daughter. That sneering sort of justice is seamed through all of Virág's stories. Even still I feel wretched with guilt, especially when Zsigmond's face crumples like someone's used-up handkerchief.

"Évike," he says. "I remember now. We named you Évike."

I want him to say something like *I told your mother once that I loved that name and all three of its rough sounds,* but he doesn't. He only frowns, his chin quivering.

I should ask him about my mother. I want to know if our memories will mirror each other's, like the real moon and its reflection on the dark surface of a lake, but I don't. A more selfish question rises to my lips.

"Why didn't you come back?"

Zsigmond gives me a level look, but his fingers clench white-knuckled around the coin. "I thought that you were dead. Taken with Magda, or . . ."

He can't even say it. Hasn't he turned the words over in his head enough to know how to speak them aloud, hasn't the scene of my supposed death played on the insides of his eyelids for years and years whenever he lay down to sleep? My throat burns.

"No," I say. "I'm here." My gaze flickers to his closed fist. "My mother always said that you minted the coin yourself. Did you?"

"I did," says Zsigmond. Something almost like relief darts across his face. "My father was a goldsmith and taught me the art. I worked for the king's treasury council to create a new design for the coins made in János's image. This coin was an early model, but it was never circulated. They didn't like that it had Yehuli script, of course, even though I slaved away on the bench for hours. This must be the only one left in existence. The rest were melted down and recast in the mold of the king's proper arany coin."

That thread of bitterness in his voice soothes me more than anything else. I am almost willing to forget our mismatched features, the way he hasn't reached out to embrace me. He speaks with the same indignation that I would, the same acrimony, and with no cowing deference. Katalin was wrong about the Yehuli, I think.

While he speaks, I notice that he rubs his left shoulder, wincing. A purple bruise fingers out from beneath the collar of his shirt, and my heart plummets into my stomach.

"What did Nándor do to you?"

"Nothing worse than what he's done to others," Zsigmond answers quickly, though his eyes narrow. "He likes to do his work on Shabbos, or on our other holy days."

I almost want to laugh at the way he calls what Nándor has done *work*; it's so dry and self-effacing, nothing like Virág's theatric portents, her gloomy augury. I want to imagine that he would shake his head and roll his eyes at her dramatics, just like I always did.

"I hope you didn't have to do anything too awful to win my freedom," Zsigmond goes on, meeting my eyes.

"Only swear my fealty to the king," I say, and offer a weak smile. Katalin would smirk endlessly if she heard me say it, knowing that I proved her right; Virág would glower and raise her lash, dismayed that I have proven her wrong. Zsigmond gives a bracing nod, neither disappointed nor shocked, and then lays a hand hesitantly on my arm.

His touch eats away at some of my oldest fears, narrowing the space between his features and mine. For so long I wanted our imagined resemblance to be the reason that I looked the way I do: short and solidly built, with hair that snarled around the teeth of Virág's bone-handled comb, with small squinting eyes that watered in any weather, and a nose that always itched. I was embarrassed by the low sway of my breasts, the breadth of my shoulders. I wanted to throw my father up against their ugly words, his existence and our shared blood a justification, a shield. Now none of it matters anyway. I am miles from Keszi, and my father's hand is braced around my elbow.

Silence begins to slip between us. Zsigmond lets go of my arm. Desperate to fill the silence, to hold him here, I ask, "What does the coin say?"

Zsigmond furrows his brow. "You don't know how to read?"

He says it casually, curiously, and I can tell he doesn't mean it to hurt me, but it does anyway, because it is proof that he doesn't know me well enough to know what I do or do not know. What will hurt me and what won't. I swallow hard and try not to reveal that it has wounded me at all.

"No," I tell him, shaking my head. "No one in Keszi can read."

"Not even Régyar, or Old Régyar?"

I shake my head once more.

"Well," he says after a moment, "Király Szek will not be an easy place for you."

I haven't allowed myself to think that far, so preoccupied with my sudden freedom that I hadn't yet imagined its consequences. Suddenly I can see my life stretching out before me like a road in the dark, limned with thousands of black trees and between them, so many seething yellow eyes. Király Szek is full of monsters, too, and they all look like men. I won't be able to recognize them until their hands are at my throat.

"The Yehuli symbols . . ." I start.

"Yes, it's in our alphabet," he says, rescuing me from my incoherence. His eyes are gentle, his voice low, and I allow myself to believe in that moment that by *our* he only means the two of us, here in the dungeon, together. He turns the coin over to where the Yehuli letters show: three of them. "This is the word for truth, *emet*. What a thing is, the existence of it. And this"—he presses the coin into my palm, and then puts his thumb over one of the letters, obscuring it—"is *met*. Dead."

The letters vanish, as if with his finger he erased them, and then the coin does, too—fading to silver and then rusting into nothing. Just like the blade of the king's sword, becoming dust in my hand. I look up at him, palm now empty, gaping.

"How did you do that?"

"When something is no longer true, it is no longer real," Zsigmond says. "When we write something in our letters, it's a way of making it true, and therefore making it real. When we erase it—well, you saw what happened. If you learned our letters, you could do it too."

Virág, I think, would call it magic. Gáspár and the Patrians would call it power. I close my fingers over my empty palm, no longer feeling the coin's absence. There's only the phantom feeling of Zsigmond's hand on my arm, its steadying pressure. The memory of his coin and the king's sword, both splintering—our abilities twinned, if not our faces. Hope fills me soundly, like something bright beaming at the end of a dark road, washing all the shadows.

"If I knocked on your door," I ask slowly, "would you answer?"

Zsigmond meets my gaze. The purple bruise throbs on his shoulder, and my wolf cloak suddenly feels heavy draped over my arm, but in that moment all I can see is him nodding at me, him saying, "Yes."

## CHAPTER SIXTEEN

After Lajos escorts my father from the castle, he takes me to one of the small rooms inside the Broken Tower, that long white scar furrowing the charcoal sky. The Broken Tower is the oldest part of the castle, the stones blanched by a hundred years or more of harsh weather, and once it was the fortress of Saint István's grandfather, the chieftain of Akosvár. Old blood is dried into the floor—I can smell the memory of slain cattle and livers curdling on altars. The Patritians do no such rituals now, of course, but the Broken Tower has been left to crumble under the weight of its shameful, silent archive. The stones in the walls are loose behind the headboard of the bed; I prod one and it clatters to the ground. There's a cold hearth in one corner, and a single window, the glass marbled with rainwater.

"Am I trapped here?" I ask with a hollow laugh. "Am I allowed to leave?"

"Of course," Lajos says brusquely, not answering my question at all, and then he lets the door slam shut behind him.

What would be the point of locking me away? The king

wants me to serve him. He has enough mute and toothless wolf-girls, fettered by their deaths, watching him narrow-eyed from the Under-World.

I sleep only in short bursts, the night seamed through with dreams. Purple and green miasmas, the chuff of smoke and the jangle of bone chimes. I dream of the turul in a golden cage, its feathers shorn, my arrow lanced into its naked breast. I dream of pine trees in the snow. Gáspár's face, his lashes daggered with frost, his chest bare under my hands. When I wake, it's to the clanging of my own heart, and a honeycomb of light on my cheek. The window glass is yellow and bright.

There's a ringing in my ears, like someone has been striking an anvil inside my skull. With a shake of my head I banish the dreams, but Gáspár's face lingers a moment longer, conjuring a jolt of want between my legs. I stoke the hearth, fists clenched, and when I manage to catch a spark I sit back on my heels, letting out a breath.

I have survived the worst things I thought possible: being taken by the Woodsmen, cowering in front of the king. Now I must make some shape out of the unimaginable after, measure my new life by its margins and limits. I retrieve Katalin's wolf cloak, my mother's braid still tucked safely in the pocket, and stow it inside the trunk at the foot of my bed. Gáspár's scolding has left its mark on me—I won't invite more danger by wearing the cloak within Király Szek.

Sometime during the night, a serving girl must have come and left new clothes for me. A simple dress of plum silk, stiflingly tight in the arms and the bust, with sleeves that pool open like two wailing mouths. I make my own adjustments, tearing off the excess fabric with my teeth, and splitting a seam inside the bodice so I can breathe easily while wearing it. As I dress, I imagine Katalin's delicate sneer, the mocking gleam of her lambent blue eyes. She's no proper táltos yet, but her prophecy came true all the same: I look every inch a Patrician, a moon-faced servant to the king. I look no fiercer than

Riika. I search for my father's coin, to steel myself, but then I remember that it's gone, turned to dust by my father's Yehuli magic. Thinking of Zsigmond soothes me by some small measure anyway.

Before my chagrin settles on me, the door to my room swings open. I am caught between exhilaration and fear, half hoping it's Gáspár and then chiding myself for such a silly desire, when more likely it's an assassin or a murderous Woodsman, ready to mutiny over the king's recent bargain. As it turns out, it's something worse than either one. Nándor stands in the threshold, wearing a pale-blue dolman and an exceedingly pleasant smile.

"Wolf-girl," he says. "Will you come with me?"

His tone is cool and polite, his expression open, his eyes glassy and bright. For a beat, I imagine he could be any man, with no ice in his heart and none of my father's blood on his hands. He's so lovely I can almost believe it. But Katalin is beautiful, too, and so is the frozen lake before it fissures under you.

"Don't you knock?" I ask, curling my four fingers into my palm.

"Does a farmer knock on the barn door?" Nándor tips his head. His voice is so light, I hardly register the insult and when I do, my face heats. "Of course not. Now come with me."

"Why should I?" I bite back. "So you can torture me like you did Zsigmond?"

"I haven't tortured anyone. The Yehuli man was guilty. I punished him accordingly."

"Not guilty by the king's laws."

"Guilty by the law of God," Nándor says. "Without the Prinkepatrios, we would have no kingdom at all, and no earth to walk on, for that matter. The least we can do is abide by His proscriptions."

It was easy enough to laugh off Gáspár's pious ramblings when it was only the two of us in the woods, and even easier once I knew the feeling of his body against mine, the sweet taste of his mouth. Now, in the heart of the capital, pressed flush by all these Patritians, his words flood me with cold.

"You can't hurt me," I say. "I'm under your father's protection."

"I'm not going to hurt you," Nándor says. His lip quirks, carving its crooked dimple. "You look as sweet and pretty as any Patritian girl now. I only wished to give you my favorite view of our glorious capital."

I try to imagine what Nándor's favorite view could be: Perhaps the place where Saint István nailed his hearts and livers to the gate? The place where he slaughtered the pig before my father? I think of Zsigmond's boots trampling all that stinking flesh, tangling in the entrails, and draw in a harsh breath.

"I have no interest in anything that interests you," I tell him.

"But you are interested in protecting the king," Nándor says keenly. "You swore as much when you made your oath. You could never hope to succeed in your goal if you don't understand life here in the capital."

He is most certainly trying to trick me, but he's also right. I feel like his gaze has swept right through me, swift and clean as a scythe. He has none of Gáspár's stiff courtly rhetoric, his prince's dour oration. He sounds more like Katalin, forever devising new ways to beautify her cruelties, to code them for my ears alone, slipping her insults right under Virág's nose. And, like Katalin, he shows no sign of relenting.

"Fine," I say. "Whatever awful thing you want me to see, it can't be worse than what you've done to Zsigmond already."

Nándor beams. A knot of fear and revulsion makes my lip curl as I trail him through the castle's winding halls, narrow and viperous, until they bear us out into the courtyard. All traces of his demonstration have been erased, buried as if under a layer of clean snow. There's no blood soaked into the cobblestones, no vapor of rot lingering in the air. All I can think of is the frozen lake, sealing itself so neatly over my head. Nándor leads me farther down the courtyard, his neck as lithe and pale as a swan's under the feather of his auburn hair.

Finally, he stops. Following the line of the castle is a row of marble statues, surveying the courtyard like cold sentinels. If I caught them out of the corner of my eye, I might really have believed they were human soldiers after all. They are etched in remarkable detail, as if drawn up out of the earth by Isten himself.

"This is Saint István," Nándor says, gesturing toward the largest. "The first true king of Régország. He united the three tribes and banished paganism to the furthest reaches of the country."

Saint István's statue has been carved from marble of purest alabaster. His long cape tumbles to the ground behind him, the folds draping and crinkling like water, frozen in a moment of cold, immaculate suspension. The sword he holds in his hand is real—a simple thing, only a bronze hilt and a silver blade, speckled with rust. It must be King István's actual sword, or else they would have replaced it with something shining and new.

The old king is holding something else in his left hand, its shape distorted and bulging around his curled fingers. It takes me a moment to recognize that it's a human heart.

"The heart of the chieftain of the Wolf Tribe," Nándor says. "He had them dismembered, and their body parts nailed to the gates of the fortress in his newly united city."

I almost want to laugh at such an artless attempt to frighten me. "I know the story. Every boy or girl in Keszi hears it first at their mother's breast. You can't think you can spook me with tales of hundred-year-old atrocities. A wet nurse could tell me worse."

Nándor doesn't rise to my challenge, but his eyes narrow, almost imperceptibly, like night edging up onto the horizon. The next statue is carved of darker marble, but it grasps and holds the early-morning sunlight, making the king's cheek-bones gleam like twin knives. This man has no sword, but in his outstretched hand he grasps an iron pendant, identical to the one Gáspár wears, engraved with the Woodsmen's seal.

"Bárány Tódor," Nándor says. "Conqueror of Kaleva, he founded the Holy Order of Woodsmen. But you're quite familiar with the Woodsmen already, aren't you?"

I sense a hidden jest in his voice, something that means to carve a deeper wound. My stomach quivers with uncertain trepidation. Nándor's face was so close to the bruise on Gáspár's throat. His hand was on my lips. I wonder if he has managed to trace a line between the two, and what he will do with that realization, if he has. Nándor watches me expectantly, as though he can see me turning the idea over in my mind.

I decide not to give him the satisfaction of a reply. Instead I stare at Tódor's statue, studying the way his ivory fingers hold the pendant like a hawk's talon clutched around its unfortunate prey. The carved outline of the turul is hardly visible, obscured by Tódor's marble thumb.

"He was made a saint too," Nándor goes on, eyes still narrowed. "In every way, he was his father's son."

This time I cannot resist a jape of my own. "Was he a true-born son?"

The lovely pink color drains from Nándor's face, and it's his turn to say nothing. For a moment I worry that I have damned myself further, but I don't think there is much I could do to make Nándor loathe me more. He wanted me dead when I was mute and lowing under his father's blade, and he still wants me dead now, when I am snarling back at him and showing all my teeth.

He stares at me blackly for a moment, and then moves on without a word.

The next statue is of Tódor's eldest son, Géza the Gray. Géza's statue depicts him as an old man, small and stooped, leaning heavily on a cane and half swallowed by his dark robes. But this one is all wrong—Géza was never an old man. He lived only to early middle age before succumbing to the same fever that later killed his son's Merzani bride, Gáspár's mother. Virág told us the stories of Régország's kings with great reluctance, each word a bitter warning.

"Géza was a weak king," Nándor says quietly. "He forgot the divine mission of his father and grandfather. He let the country make peace with its heathen enemies, and even arranged the marriage of his son to a Merzani apostate. It is a blessing that he died before doing more damage than he did."

Géza's statue is a murky gray, precisely the same color of the clouds when they bunch and gather before a storm. The void of his sainthood seems obvious, somehow, like the pall of a sunless day. "If Géza was such a terrible ruler, why mount his statue here, beside your precious heroes?"

"Because it serves as a reminder," says Nándor, "of what we must not let our nation become. You were there at Saint István's feast, wolf-girl. Surely you can see that the people of Király Szek want to live in a Patritian kingdom, just like our neighbors east and west."

"If only the whole kingdom were comprised of just your admirers," I say.

Nándor's smile returns, with a sharper edge this time. "There was no kingdom of Régország before the Patrifaith, wolf-girl. You understand that, don't you? There was only a loose handful of tribes hacking each other to death on the Little Plain, scarcely able to even understand the accents of their enemies. If you and your pagan brothers and sisters even dare to call yourselves Régyar, you must acquiesce to that point, or else you ought to scrub *our* language out of your mouths and go back to garbling the old tongues of your blood chieftains."

His argument is laced through with conceits that I hardly understand, words that almost make me feel like a stranger to this language after all. It reminds me that he's spent years learning at the knee of royal tutors, and I am a wolf-girl from a flyspeck of a village who can't even spell her own name. A coil of shame rises in my throat. I fight back with the only weapon I have.

"Your mother is a Northerner," I say, remembering Szabín's story. "Régyar words must curdle in her Kalevan accent. If I'm a foreigner in this land, then you are half a foreigner as well."

I expect him to balk, to give me another baleful stare, but Nándor hardly blinks. His smile deepens. It is the smile of an assured victory.

"You think that this is a problem of blood, wolf-girl?" He lifts a brow. "Saint István was born a pagan, as you well know. Some of my compatriots wish to forget that fact, but I see no reason to efface the truth. It was his *choice* to relinquish the false gods that matters, in the end. And you pagans, the Juvvi, the Yehuli—they all have been given so many chances to do the same."

I bite my lip on a derisive laugh. "I saw what you did to Zsigmond. You wouldn't welcome a Yehuli with open arms even if he swore his undying devotion to the Prinkepatrios."

It is the same logic I have been made to swallow my whole life, the same way Boróka tried to wheedle me into keeping my head down and my eyes trained on the ground, into evading Katalin's stare and mumbling my soft-bellied deference. But I had tried kindness. I had tried sheathing my claws. It only made it easier for her to strike me down again.

"Certainly I would," says Nándor, "if his soul was truly repentant. I would even welcome you with open arms, wolf-girl—you look almost like a true Patrician already. If you stay in this city long enough, perhaps I can get you on your knees."

His casual remark blinkers me for a moment, like a trick of light. Nándor is beautiful enough that I think even Katalin would go dry-mouthed at the veiled proposal. I, too, might have been tempted by his entreaty if I hadn't just watched him drench my father in pig's blood, if all the words bracketing his guileful suggestion weren't so ugly. I wonder how many girls in Király Szek *have* fallen to their knees in front of him, babbling in reverence, pleasuring him with their promises. I will not allow myself to think of it further, and banish all the lurid fantasies from my mind. Nándor's smile is all too innocent, both of us keenly aware of the flush painting my cheeks.

Now desperate to change the subject, I turn to the final statue. It is hewn roughly in the shape of a man, but his face is featureless, his robes carved only in the vaguest lines. "Is this meant to be King János?"

"Yes," Nándor says, sounding supremely pleased with himself, and certainly noting the tremor in my voice. "His legacy is yet to be written. The statue will only be completed after he dies, when we can judge properly what sort of kingdom he has left behind. Surely you can see as well that the people of Régország want a king who will move their country further toward its Patritian ideal, rather than mingling with pagans and Yehuli, and suffusing himself with pagan magic."

His words are close to treasonous. I try to remember them very precisely, and their exact cadence, so I can tell János when I see him, but the plan dies before I even finish making it. I think of the king's rheumy eyes, trained vaguely in the middle distance. He won't see his son's sedition until Nándor's knife is in his throat.

For now, the threat is only for my ears. I clench and unclench my fingers, considering the same dismal possibilities. I could grasp his wrist and see what my magic would do to him, but Gáspár is right—I would never leave Király Szek alive, and Nándor's followers would find a way to avenge him, likely fixing their gaze upon Yehuli Street. A wind picks up, raising gooseflesh on my bare forearms. Standing perfectly still in the wash of cold sunlight, Nándor looks half like a statue himself, carved by the hand of some lonely, salacious woman, a marble cast of her most torrid fantasies. I blink, and for a moment I can see him as Vilmötten after all, golden-haired and sapphire-eyed, with long fingers made for plucking lute strings. I imagine he could sing his way out of the Under-World too.

I blink again, and the illusion fractures like glass. Nándor is no more my hero than Saint István.

As if he could hear my thoughts, Nándor wanders back across the courtyard, toward his great-great-grandfather's statue, and lets his fingertips drift across the dead king's holy cheekbone.

"They're more than just statues," Nándor says, turning to me. "A piece of the stone has been hollowed out, and the remains of our kings are kept inside. We have King Géza's finger bones, and a lock of King Tódor's hair. We even have King Ist-ván's right eye. The blessing of the Prinkepatrios keeps them from decaying, and our prayers are channeled through these vessels, their power multiplied a thousandfold."

I don't know how he can believe such a thing—that there's power in the hair and bones of some long-dead saints. But King János has proven that magic thrums in the veins of every wolf-girl, diffused down to even her fingernails. Perhaps their saints are no different, though Nándor is the first to call it *power.*

"You ought to make a crown out of your old kings' finger-nails," I say, "since you Patritians are so keen on worshipping dead things."

Nándor gives an airy laugh that makes my stomach turn. "You must accustom yourself to worshipping them, too, now that you've knelt for my father."

"I'd sooner swallow your dead saint's knucklebone," I say, giving a laugh of my own, but really I am thinking of Peti. I am thinking of *király és szentség*, the words stitching them-selves into the fabric of mind. The memory of Zsigmond's magic surges up in reply, as if hastily summoned. What would happen if I learned to write those words on parchment, and then blotted them out with my thumb? Would that erase the truth of them too?

"How very ferocious of you," Nándor says loftily. His eyes, in this moment, are perfect mirrors of Katalin's: gleaming, gloating. "You may be oath-bound to my father, but I'd caution you against forgetting what you are. A pagan girl, a long way from home, alone in a city of Patritian peasants and soldiers, with Woodsmen around every corner and down every long hall at night. The Patrifaith has lived here long before you, and it will live here long after. You are nothing, wolf-girl, scarcely even worth the mess of killing."

He wants to frighten me, but he doesn't know that I've spent all my life under threat of cold blue fire.

"I don't believe you," I say, meeting his gaze. "You say that I'm nothing, but you've already gone to the effort of trying to make me fear for my life. Did the Érsek put these words in your mouth, too, or did you contrive them all on your own? Either way, you could have left me to my own quiet demise, to flounder and fail, but you've chosen to try and terrify me instead, the way you tortured my father—"

I stop abruptly, my chest seizing. I have made a terrible mistake. Confusion clouds over Nándor's face, and then clears with triumphant revelation.

"Your father," he echoes, clucking his tongue. "I did wonder why you seemed to care so much about the fate of that Yehuli man."

It is the closest I have come to killing him, the possibility so clear and bright in my mind, like staring wide-eyed at a cloudless sun. I know I'll only damn the Yehuli, and Zsigmond, further if I do, but I can scarcely believe the stupid looseness of my tongue. I have handed Nándor a polished, whetted blade. Ördög's threads twitch, my fingers aching to wrap themselves around his delicate wrist. I know he can see the stricken look on my face, the way I have stilled like a prey animal.

Before I can reply, the sound of wood meeting metal reverberates through the courtyard. I hurry toward the noise, Nándor at my heels, and we turn around the barbican into another, smaller courtyard, closed on three sides by the castle walls. Archery targets are so stuck full of arrows, they look like wounded martyrs. Gáspár stands in the center of the square, clutching a wooden sword. His younger half-brother, the one with beechwood hair, holds his own play sword loosely in one hand.

"Use your right hand, Matyi," Gáspár says. "And lead with your right foot."

The boy switches his sword to the other hand, brow furrowing. "I don't want to hurt you."

"I think it will be quite a long time before you're capable of that," Gáspár says. An easy smile comes across his face, cheek feathering with a small dimple. The gentleness of it roots me to the ground, my stomach turning over on itself. I left any trace of that gentleness on the ice, back in Kaleva, or in the woods of Szarvasvár girded by a copse of willow trees. A pulse of anger returns in its place: Gáspár was ready to watch me die.

But I have survived, and now when Gáspár sees me, his smile vanishes as if it's been swept away by the wind. His eye runs up and down me, taking in my dress with its torn sleeves and too-tight bodice. I wonder if he will react to the visceral wrongness of it, the way I would shudder at seeing him in a wolf cloak, but he only goes red and turns his face away, and I try to convince myself that I am better off without him and his flustered, prayerful blushing. If my bruise still lingers on his throat, I can't see it—he has buttoned his dolman all the way up to his chin.

Matyi is staring openly at me, mouth slightly ajar. When he catches me looking back, he inches closer to Gáspár and whispers, "The wolf-girl is watching."

"I know," Gáspár says, and then adds quickly, "Her name is Évike. She's no danger to you."

I resist the urge to bare my teeth and snarl, just because I want to prove him wrong. I've grown so weary of meager Patritian kindnesses with their ugly underbellies, like a gleaming handful of holly berries: they look sweet, but it will kill you to swallow them. If I am no danger to Matyi, it's because I am a good wolf-girl, unlike the rest, or I am not a wolf-girl at all, and therefore nothing: just a ghost of a girl in a too-small silk gown.

Nándor strides toward them, an exuberant smile on his face. "Are you teaching Matyi the ways of the sword? Surely there's a better tutor in all of Király Szek."

Gáspár's hand goes tense around his sword, creasing the black leather of his gloves. "I can teach a young boy with no prior training."

"Do you really think you're better with one eye than most men are with two?"

Even though I haven't forgiven Gáspár, my throat still burns for him.

"I don't know," Gáspár says. I am surprised at the lightness in his voice, the almost playful quirk of his brow. "Why don't we find out?"

And then he tosses his sword to Nándor, who catches it one-handed, arm arcing up over his head. He looks expectantly at Matyi, and the boy passes his sword over, face contorting with a bewildered, weary concern that seems better suited to someone three times his age. It's hardly a surprise that Gáspár would best love a brother with the same scowling, humorless temper.

"Well, brother," Nándor says, blinking giddily, "I am not most men."

Their blades meet with a sound that reminds me of ice cracking under my feet. Nándor lunges forward, his sword wheeling wildly, as if he's hoping to get in a jab on chance alone. Gáspár falls back, blocking each blow as they come, steady. All his clumsiness with the ax seems hazy and distant, and my face heats remembering the way that I mocked him for it. He fights like a real soldier now, steel-boned and iron-blooded, only leaning heavily to the right, his head turning back and forth to cover his blind side.

Nándor retreats, the sword whirling blindly at his hip. He leads with his right foot and leaps out again, aiming his blow at Gáspár's left, where he struggles to see. Gáspár would call it a dirty trick, the low tactic of a man without honor. But I suspect Nándor would not think his honor imperiled by something as trivial as a play fight with a blunted practice sword.

Especially not if he won. Matyi has come to stand beside me, a safe distance from the scything of his brothers' blades. His gaze travels anxiously between the fight and me, as if he's trying to gauge which is the greater danger.

"You should take your brother at his word," I say, trying to smooth the rough edges of my voice, trying to wring some kindness out of me, some deep-buried instinct for mothering. But when I look at Matyi I can't see anything but a boy who will grow into a man, or worse, a Woodsman. "It's your father who hurts wolf-girls, not the other way around."

"Gáspár says you would have killed him." Matyi regards me soberly.

It feels churlish and silly to argue with a child, but anger blackens in me anyway. "Your father would have killed *me*. And then Nándor would have taken his crown, and—"

"No," Matyi cuts in, with a rigid certainty that makes him sound very much like Gáspár indeed. "That's the pagan way, to have a king choose his successor, the way the tribal chieftains chose which son they wanted to rule when they were dead. I have a tutor from the Volkstadt who told me so. In all the other Patritian kingdoms, it's the eldest son, the true-born son, who must rule by the law of God."

My eyes dart back toward Nándor and Gáspár, the air gashed by their blades. I understand now why Nándor recoiled at once when he saw Gáspár in the crowd, why his presence alone seemed to make Nándor falter in his plans.

"So he's a hypocrite," I say, pleased by my own conclusion. "If he wants to claim the throne, he'll have to acknowledge that there's something right about our pagan ways, and wrong about his Patritian ones."

Matyi lifts a shoulder, taking a slight step to the left. Perhaps my enthusiasm has made me seem more frightening, my smile showing the edges of my teeth.

"Some people say that my father's marriage was never legitimate," Matyi mumbles, cowed by my smirk. "Because Elif Hatun never made her proper conversion."

"Gáspár's mother?"

He nods.

I think of what Gáspár told me about his mother, a crumbling pillar in her palace quarters, eroded day after day by the tide of a thousand foreign tongues. Had she held on to her faith in mute stubbornness? Or had the Régyar words tumbled right out of her when she tried to take her vows, like a mouthful of rotted teeth? I wonder if that's what has cursed Gáspár more than anything: the legacy of his mother's quiet rebellion.

The rasping of wood goes silent for a moment, and I turn my gaze back toward their fight. Their swords are pressed together, faces close as they push and push, each trying to make the other crumble. It is Gáspár, finally, who falters. He lets Nándor's blade slide off his, and though he steps backward, clearly yielding, his brother doesn't hesitate. He strikes a blow to Gáspár's blind left side that sends him stumbling back across the courtyard. Nándor's sword waves like a war banner.

"A well-fought battle," Nándor says, letting his blade clatter to the ground. His auburn hair is exquisitely tousled, as if the wind took to it with gentle fingers. "But I can hardly feign surprise at the outcome. Monsters are one thing, Gáspár, but men are a far greater challenge. You'll need both eyes to fight your *mortal* enemies and win."

"You've made your point," Gáspár says sharply. Under his black dolman, his chest is heaving, and I feel a traitorous tug of affection. "At least Matyi saw a demonstration of proper swordsmanship."

At the sound of his name, Matyi dashes toward his brothers, casting me one last, glowering look of deep mistrust. I watch the three of them in tense silence, the wind carrying the smell of ash from someone's hearth and hot paprika from the marketplace, wondering if it's possible that no one else saw what I did: that Gáspár let his brother win.

It's late by the time I finally return to my room, the sky as glossy as black silk. I have endured a dinner with the king, a small feast, during which he hosted two emissaries from the Volkstadt, both wearing brilliantly colored satins with ruffled collars that looked like the plumages of exotic birds. The king tried desperately to ply them with wine and food and flattery, while they appeared mostly bored for the duration of it, and spoke brazenly to one another in their own language. The Volken tongue sounded lyrical by turns, as if they were reciting riddles and rhymes, and then became abruptly harsh, too strange and guttural to imitate. But by the end they still offered the king a thousand men each to help fight the Merzani invaders, and the king smiled and smiled even though he had a red-currant seed stuck in his teeth. Nándor looked disappointed by the outcome, and I couldn't see why. Perhaps he had hoped for more men, or for a better deal that didn't see us losing gold and silver, because the king had then quickly agreed to lease them some of the mines in Szarvasvár, which is on the border with the Volkstadt anyway.

My mind wandered, and I stole far too many glances at Gáspár, trying vainly to draw his gaze toward me. Our weeks together taught me to read his scowls and frowns, how to tell real anger from flushing pretense, how to coax gentleness from him as if with a needle, his smiles as rare and precious as blood drops. Now his expressions are more indecipherable to me than the words of the Volken men preening at my elbow. But Gáspár scarcely even looked up from his plate, lips purpling with the stain of wine.

When the Volken men pulled out a contract for the king to sign, I glanced over at it, but it was only ink splashed on a page. The king might have been signing the whole country into bondage or selling me off to the Volken emissaries, and I wouldn't have known until they were fitting me with chains.

And then, after all of that, I find a note tucked under my door.

It's a short message, and the ink is wet, fresh. It blackens the pad of my thumb when I unfold it. I can't even read who has signed it, if anyone at all. My mind tries desperately to constellate the loops and lines, but staring at it makes me want to cry like a child.

It must be Nándor, I decide. His earlier warning in the courtyard hadn't stuck, and he wanted to intimidate me further, or perhaps only punish me for daring to hold my ground against him, for smiling blithely at his barbed words. Tears prick at the corners of my eyes and then fall onto the page in hot splashes, thinning the black ink to a rheumy gray.

I will die here, I think, just like Elif Hatun, deaf to the threats whispered in her ear. Something in me hardens at the thought, all my fear and humiliation congealing into blustery courage. I crumple the note in my fist and hurry down the halls, through the barbican, and out toward Yehuli Street.

# CHAPTER SEVENTEEN

Zsigmond's house is nothing like I expect. In fact, half of me is still thinking of him as a Yehuli man, and wondering what sort of house a Yehuli man would live in, while the other half of me thinks of him as my father, and my mind paints its own misty imaginings of what sort of house my father would live in. I wonder if I will ever think of him as my father, a Yehuli man. A Yehuli man who is my father.

There is only one room, with a bed and a hearth and a table with chairs. It is not entirely unlike Virág's hut, but Zsigmond's things are finer, merchant-crafted rather than homespun. Wrought-iron candle stands with carved ivy clambering up the length. A woven tablecloth embroidered with flowers and leaves that has no moth-eaten edges. The familiarity of it chills me rather than comforts me. I realize for the first time that I want Zsigmond to be different from anything I have known before. A new father for my new life.

"Thank you," I stammer out, clenching and unclenching my fingers as Zsigmond stokes the fire. "I'm sorry it's so late. I hope I didn't wake you."

The fire crackles pleasantly, tongues of flame licking at the blackened stone. Zsigmond stands, brushing ash from his knees, and says, "You did. But I asked you to come, and I never told you when, so I should have known to expect you at any hour of the day."

I blink at him, shoulders still raised around my ears. It only now occurs to me how much I am braced for scoldings and lashings, flinching at the slightest change in pitch or the sudden tense of a fist. But Zsigmond looks at me steadily, his thick brows pulled together with concern rather than consternation.

"I need your help," I say, encouraged by his gentle face. "Someone left a note for me, in the palace. I can't read it."

A breath goes out of Zsigmond. I think I hear relief in it. I realize that he, too, has been bracing for something worse.

"Let me see," he says. And then, almost as a second thought, "Évike."

Hearing him say my name melts some of the ice in my belly. I reach into the folds of my skirt and retrieve the scrap of parchment, now bunched small and tight, no bigger than an acorn. I try to smooth it flat again before I hand it to him, but even I can see that the ink has run into a bizarre cartography, a pattern that is no pattern at all. Zsigmond squints at it anyway, holding the note up to the candlelight, ink darkening the pads of his thumbs.

"I'm sorry," he says after a moment. "I can make out a few letters, but the rest is too smudged."

I nod, a burn rising in my throat. "Thank you for trying."

Zsigmond nods back at me. He puts the parchment down on the table, and like a lunatic I almost laugh at the absurdity of it: *my* note on *his* table. Me, standing in my father's house, shorn of my wolf cloak, looking into his eyes. As a child it would have seemed a more impossible dream than seeing my mother again, or than gleefully watching Katalin pecked to death by a thousand crows. I hoarded those unfathomable dreams as I did my braid and my coin, polishing them in my mind like a mirror, seething, waiting.

"Do you remember her?" The words tumble out of my mouth almost without me willing it. "My mother."

Zsigmond's face creases. The corners of his mouth pull down, and I can hear him swallowing. For a moment I think, with no small amount of alarm, that he might cry.

"Of course I do," he says. "You must think I'm a monster, or at least an especially cold and callous man. You must have wondered why I never came back for you, or why I never tried to stop them from taking Magda."

Hearing him say it conjures an old pain, the oldest pain I know, and it makes me as mean as a limping dog.

"Yes," I say, venom lacing my voice. "I did wonder why my own father seemed not to care for me at all."

Zsigmond is silent, gaze faltering. I am glad, just for a moment, that I have cowed him. I have spent so many years coaxed out of my own pain, half convinced that I had no right to feel it. Afraid that even that would be taken from me, and the memories that came with it.

"I named you, you know," Zsigmond says finally. His voice is tight, small, as if someone has wrapped a tender hand around his throat. "*Évike.* It means 'life,' in the Yehuli tongue. I went to Keszi every year for six years in a row, and spent seven days with Magda every time. It doesn't amount to very much, and none of my family or friends here in Király Szek could understand why I was so taken with a woman that I seemed to scarcely know at all, and whose life was so different from mine. But in truth, it only took one day for me to know that I loved her. And I *did* love her."

"Then why did you leave her?" There's a dull ache in my chest, like the tick of blood behind a bruise.

"She didn't want to come with me. What sort of life is there, for a pagan woman in Király Szek?" I narrow my eyes at his words, and Zsigmond's face goes pale with chagrin.

"Never mind the Patritians—it's not looked upon well for a Yehuli man to wed a woman outside the community. And then the king removed me from my post, and I couldn't return to Keszi on my own. It was too dangerous to traverse the forest without the escort of the Woodsmen. I had been warned by that woman, Virág, that Magda's child—that our child—would be an outcast in Keszi too. But Magda wanted to keep you. There was nothing I could do."

His voice tips up at the end, edging with desperation. His eyes are starry and wet, bleary with the reflection of candlelight. I try to memorize the canvas of his face, every fold in his brow, the particular set of his jaw, so I can hold it with me and know this: for so long I thought that I was carrying the weight of my mother's death alone, but in the moment that the king swung his blade, he cleaved that pain in two. My father has carried his piece of it all these years, like a stone split down its middle, the jagged edges of his half fitting perfectly with mine.

"Tell me something about her," I say, biting my lip. "Something I don't know."

"She wanted to learn to read," Zsigmond says. He gives several measured blinks, drying his eyes. "I always brought a book with me when I traveled, so I could show her the letters. By the time she died, I had taught her the alphabet. She could spell her name."

It would have been too much, to hold this grief on my own. But Zsigmond is still looking at me, gaze clear now and starless, and the hearth floods the room with such a wonderful smoky warmth that I never want to leave it. Words float up.

"Will you teach me too?"

I am not a particularly fast learner. The night unspools over us like Zsigmond's endless rolls of parchment. The quill feels awkward in my hand, too small and thin. It doesn't make sense that two etched lines meeting in a downward point mean the sound *vee*, which, Zsigmond tells me, is the second letter of my name, but he says it doesn't matter. A long time ago someone sat down and decided that these etched lines meant something, and then everyone else agreed to it and made it true. My quill moves painstakingly across the parchment, tracing letter after letter, until I can recognize them all even upside down.

It takes hours, but once I have them committed to my mind, it all seems so simple that it makes my blood boil. Like with my magic, I feel as if I've just learned a secret that the world has been cruelly conspiring to keep from me. I write my name over and over again, five letters and three syllables that hold me like a cupped hand. É-V-I-K-E.

Zsigmond is not a particularly patient tutor. After I have exhausted three hours of his time, he returns to his own books with a sigh. I like this streak of peevishness in him, and that he trusts me enough to let it show. The books that he pores over are Yehuli holy texts, and he spends as many hours studying them as I do learning the Régyar letters for the first time.

It seems like a strange thing to me, that you should have to study from a book in order to properly worship the Yehuli god. No one in Keszi can read, and the Patritians make it sound like their god is something you ought to *know*, or else not ask too many questions about. Zsigmond scrawls questions into the very margins of his scrolls, underlining passages that he agrees with and marking up ones that he doesn't. All of it baffles me. Can you believe in something while still running your hand over its every contour, feeling for bumps and bruises, like a farmer trying to pick the best, roundest peach?

"That is the only way to truly believe in something," Zsigmond says. "When you've weighed and measured it yourself."

I wonder—stupidly, shamefully—what Gáspár would say

about that. I think he would say that God is too big for one mortal hand to hold. You would need a thousand pairs of limbs to carry it, and a thousand eyes to see it. Or something like that, in his pompous prince's voice.

A thin band of orange light lips over the horizon, and muffled words leaf through Zsigmond's window, like a plant stretching its long green vines. Eventually, there's a knock on the door. I watch from behind the table as he opens it to reveal the same stout woman who chided me from her threshold only two days ago. She pauses when she sees me, her wide mouth falling open as if it is a hatch.

"Zsigmond, who—" she starts.

"It's my daughter," Zsigmond says easily, as if they are words *he* has been practicing his whole life. A warm pleasure puddles in me hearing them. "Évike."

The woman rubs her eyes; the way she is staring at me I might as well be a smudge on a windowpane, something she wants to see past. I remember what Zsigmond said: that it isn't looked kindly upon for a Yehuli man to father a child with someone who is not of their blood.

"And you didn't think to—oh, never mind." The woman brushes by Zsigmond and sets down something on the table. It's a loaf of braided bread, shining honey-gold. She holds out her hand to me, still not quite meeting my eyes. "I'm Batya. I've been keeping your father fed for the last twenty years."

Zsigmond's lips part as if to protest, but a hawk-eyed glare from Batya silences him. I take her hand and she squeezes mine tightly, three times, like she's trying to judge its heft. Already she reminds me of Virág. Her gaze sweeps over the parchment in front of me, streaked over and over again with the five letters of my name.

"Évike," I say. My fingers are half-numb by the time she lets go.

"And will you be joining us for our celebration next week?" Batya asks, a hand on her hip. When I only stare at her blankly, she turns back to Zsigmond. "Well, you might as well invite her. You're already teaching her to read, I see. She might as well hear some of our stories, and try a bit of our food." Her eyes go up and down me again, and then she says something to Zsigmond in the Yehuli tongue, something I don't understand, and I only catch the word *zaftig*.

Whatever it is, it makes Zsigmond scowl. When Batya leaves again, my father sits down across from me and offers me the bread, so brusquely it seems almost like he expects me to refuse it. I pick off a piece and taste it. Each bite dissolves sweetly on my tongue. Zsigmond seems relieved.

"What did she say about me?" I press. "Batya."

"The Yehuli tongue is like a long hallway with locked doors on all sides," he says.

It is the first time he has been so evasive, and it mortifies me. I don't take another bite of the bread, and pick up my quill again. As dawn ladders up over Király Szek, it occurs to me that I haven't slept, and a sudden tiredness clouds my mind.

"Then teach me to open them," I say finally, more a petulant challenge than genuine entreaty. If Yehuli is an oak tree branching between us, I only want to clamber over it, or else hack it down to nothing. I wonder if he worries what Batya and the others will think, if they see his half-blooded daughter speaking their tongue and writing their words.

"Perhaps," says Zsigmond. I just stare at him, unblinking, and eventually he relents to only a few words, even though they vex me terribly. I don't know which is worse—the speaking or the writing. The sounds tear up the back of my throat, and the words are missing half the letters that I learned in Régyar. The word *ohr* makes me feel as if I'm choking on food, but when my father traces its letters into the base of his candle stand, the wick goes up in perfect light.

My vision trains on the teardrop of flame. "Could you put it out too?"

"Certainly," Zsigmond says. "Creation and destruction are two sides of the same coin."

Like Isten in the Upper-World and Ördög down below. "And can all Yehuli do magic like that?"

"All who have the patience to learn it. Our children learn to read and write Yehuli at the same time they learn Régyar, so they can study the holy text."

It seems less troublesome than lopping off a pinky, or listening to Virág's interminable stories, struggling to commit every detail of Vilmötten's exploits to immaculate memory. My heart skitters like an animal in the underbrush. I'm afraid that if I needle Zsigmond too much he will shrink away from me, or begin to feel that having a daughter is more burden than blessing. But I try one more question anyway.

"And the celebration," I say, "the one that Batya mentioned . . ."

Zsigmond gives a slow nod. "It's a holiday. Not a big one, but we will go to the temple and hear the rabbi tell the story. If you would like to come, you must let me ask Batya to borrow a dress from one of her daughters."

His easy acquiescence shocks and thrills me, but I sense a current of uncertainty beneath it. Perhaps my very presence will jeopardize his position among the Yehuli—it was the reason that my mother never took me to Király Szek to begin with. Going to the temple with my father will require as much delicate maneuvering as attending a banquet with the king. I am still not quite one of them, and I don't know if I ever will be. I brace myself against these worries, curling my ink-stained fingers into my palm, and remind myself why I came to Zsigmond last night. If I'm not careful, I will end up with a knife in my back before I can decide whether to be Yehuli or not.

Still, I don't want to leave Yehuli Street. When Zsigmond opens the door for me, I reach out and take his hand impetu-

ously, swallowing hard and waiting to see if he will squeeze
mine back. His thumb brushes across the nub where my pinky
once was, and then his other hand closes over our twined fingers, a perfect weight.

The king has gathered all his counts for a council meeting, and of course
I am compelled to be in the chamber beside him. We all sit
around an oaken table, the king at its head with his crown
of fingernails, parchment scrolls unfurling before him like
shed snakeskin. Now I can recognize the letters on them, but
my vision goes fuzzy when I try to noose them into words. I
fear how long it will take before I'm able to read Régyar, to
decipher the silent threats coiled on the table in front of me.

Although I saw them at the king's feast, the counts are
scarcely recognizable. They wear their silk dolmans now,
each as neat and bright as a lizard sunning itself on a rock. I
can only tell them apart by the small ornaments they wear on
their chest, symbols of their region: a shard of antler for the
count of Szarvasvár, a white feather for the count of Akosvár,
a tuft of wolf fur for the count of Farkasvár, and a bear's long
claw pinned to the breast of the Kalevan count. Count Furedi,
who administers Farkasvár from a great walled fortress on
the western side of Ezer Szem, gives me the chilliest of stares.
We wolf-girls are his region's greatest embarrassment.

I stare back, eyes narrowing. I wonder if he was the one
who left the note at my door, but his face betrays nothing. If
there is anyone in this city, aside from Nándor, who would
want me dead, it is Count Furedi. Nándor and Gáspár are
both barred from the king's council meetings, but their names
run quietly beneath every thread of conversation, like the
simmer of distant thunder. It quickly becomes clear enough
what side each count has chosen.

"We intercepted a missive from the Merzani bey to his

soldiers," says Count Furedi, tearing his gaze from mine. "Once they manage to cross the border into Akosvár, they were instructed to burn the crops, to starve us into submission. They know very well that winter is near."

"Of course." Count Reményi, who administers Akosvár, curls his large fingers into a larger fist. "Forgive me, my lord, but I have warned you of precisely such a thing. Already the inhabitants of Akosvár have begun to abandon their villages and flee north, seeking refuge behind the walls of my own keep. We cannot accommodate any more of these refugees, and we certainly won't be able to feed them once winter is upon us."

I remember Gáspár's words—that with each Régyar soldier dead at the hands of the Merzani army, Nándor's appeal grows. I think further of the peasants I saw at the festival, with their dirty hands and missing teeth. They seemed hardly less desperate than the people of Kajetán's village, and easy prey for a very pretty man who makes empty promises.

"We are expecting a hard winter in Kaleva," says Count Korhonen, in his lilting Northern accent. "But we trust that the guidance and the goodwill of Godfather Life will carry us through these difficult months."

"Indeed we do," comes the voice of Count Németh of Szarvasvár, who is preoccupied stroking his antler ornament. "We must thank Godfather Life for his blessings, and perhaps appease Godfather Death with a greater sacrifice. What say you, my lord?"

Although it is his council meeting, and I am his personal guard, it's easy to forget that the king is even seated beside me. He blinks, dazed, as if someone has just prodded him from slumber.

"Well, we must fight, of course," he says. "We have an influx of soldiers from the Volkstadt to furnish our armies for the time being, and—"

"Forgive me, my lord, but no soldiers will help us if God

Himself is not on our side," Count Reményi cuts in. "The Prinkepatrios will leave our country to Thanatos and the Merzani heathens if we continue to foster pagans—in our very own palace, no less. And I cannot pretend I haven't seen this."

He tosses a scroll of parchment onto the table. Count Furedi snatches it up quickly, too quickly for me to decipher any of the letters, much less knit them into words.

"It's posted on nearly every stall in the marketplace," says Count Reményi. "It is a message from some of the Patrifaith's Sons and Daughters in the capital, and many of the peasants and merchants have signed it too. They are unhappy that you've continued to allow the pagans to thrive in Keszi, and even invited one to sit at our council table."

Hearing him say it while wearing the feather of the White Falcon Tribe on his chest, while claiming his fortress and his land through the lineage of a blood chieftain, makes my veins run hot.

"We're hardly thriving," I snap. "We endure the same winters as you, only worse because the forest grows too thick and too close for us to plant many crops, not to mention worrying about monsters and Woodsmen. And in case you think that your nation is otherwise pure, I must tell you that the old magic is still alive in every forest of Farkasvár, every hill and valley in Szarvasvár, and every field of Akosvár too. We met nameless wraiths and witches on our journey here, and your own party of Woodsmen were eaten by monsters not two steps onto the Little Plain."

"And why should we believe a word of your pagan fairy tales?" Count Reményi challenges.

To my surprise, Count Németh's tepid voice rises from the other end of the table. "The wolf-girl isn't wrong, Reményi. In Szarvasvár I have peasants run out of their winter villages by women made of stone and swamp grass, and hunters and woodcutters found with their hearts carved out of their chests. What else could be the cause, if not monsters and old magic?"

"If anything, it is only more proof that God is punishing Régország for continuing to harbor heathens."

"The monsters are killing us too," I point out in a tremulous voice, scarcely able to keep from shouting. "And perhaps if the Woodsmen did a proper job of hunting them, rather than skulking around the city so they can lick your bastard-prince's boots, there would be fewer hunters with missing hearts."

Count Reményi's hand curls around the edge of the table; I hear the sound of his chair scraping across the stone floor, as though he is readying himself to stand. "It is a disgrace to God that you were allowed living into this city, much less into our council chamber. Unrepentant pagans like you will be the downfall of Régország."

I see him pushing up from his seat, but before he can get very far, a band of metal stretches over both of his wrists, locking him to the table. The king has risen, one hand on his crown of fingernails. All the color has gone out of his cheeks, and his very mustache looks limp.

"Sit," he rasps, and Count Reményi does.

Despite his gruesome coronet, the forging has taken something from him. In another moment, the metal flakes and rusts, withering into nothing. I tense my muscles, ready to spring between the king and Count Reményi, my four fingers closed into a fist. Even the animal instinct shames me. Have I become little more than a dog on a leash?

"I have made up my mind about the pagans and the wolf-girl," the king says, returning to his seat. "She sits beside me docilely, wearing proper Patritian dress; you would hardly know she is a wolf-girl at all. And you have seen what kind of power she has—what kind of power this crown grants me. The Érsek will punish the Sons and Daughters who wrote this message in defiance of their king."

Count Reményi's gaze cuts to me as he lifts a hand to rub at his wrist. For such a large man he has small, beady eyes that remind me of the weasels I would hunt for sport, not enough meat on their bones to justify the work of skinning and eating them.

"There is still the matter of the Yehuli," the chastened count says. "They overrun this city like vermin. They are equally an affront to the Prinkepatrios, with their black rituals and their false god."

I know right away that these are not his words—they are the words that Nándor has snuck into his mouth, just to rile me. I keep still, my belly churning, careful not to reveal myself. The truth of my blood will only be another strike against me, and it will only damn Zsigmond and the Yehuli further.

"The Yehuli provide important services, do they not?" Count Korhonen tilts his head. "They can handle coin so we don't have to sully our hands with it, and they can work on the Lord's Day, saving the Patritians from breaking our vows to God."

"The Yehuli god may be a false one, but at least they do worship *one*," Count Németh says begrudgingly.

I draw a breath and try to keep my voice level. "The pagans and the Yehuli are both living peacefully. They're no threat to you."

Count Reményi barks a laugh. "I trust that you haven't received much tutelage in Volken, wolf-girl, but our banquet guests were quite clear in their demands. Régország is a shield between them and the Merzani. If they conquer us, it won't be long before the whole continent is overrun by Merzan, and the Patrifaith is crushed beneath their soldiers' feet. We are not much good as a shield if we cannot even keep our own country united and pure—*that* is the threat of the Yehuli. And what is it that keeps the Yehuli here? Only their desire to leverage our own misfortune against us, as the business of moneylending is most profitable in times of greatest desperation. Rodinya has set aside a large swath of its territory where the Yehuli can live in peace, away from Patritians. They can have villages and towns all their own. Already the Volkstadt and the other countries to the west have begun sending their Yehuli to this region. Why should we not do the same with ours?"

The other counts fall silent, heads bobbing, blinking their consideration. As if buoyed by their silence, Count Reményi presses on.

"Régország is a country for Régyar," he says. "For Patritians. If we are to stand against the Merzani, we cannot risk a divided nation. Our neighbors already think poorly of Régország, and are eager to cast us as eastern barbarians. If we follow their example in banishing our Yehuli, it will improve our country's standing in their eyes."

I know these are Nándor's words too. There is a sleekness to his argument that even pulls at some part of me, making my mind splutter at the possibility. Would Zsigmond be happy to live somewhere else, in a city or town of only Yehuli? Would he give up his house, his street, even his Régyar name? The notion sits in the base of my stomach like a stone. If I were truly one of the Yehuli, I would already know the answer.

"I will think on it," the king says. His eyes are half-lidded. "Until then, I will need you all to send more soldiers to the border."

A shared murmuring passes among the counts, like wind whispering through the reeds. Count Reményi draws a breath.

"You concern yourself greatly with the threat beyond our borders, but there are as many threats inside," he says, voice steady despite the low set of his brow. "The continued existence of the Yehuli and the pagans threatens to plunge all of Régország into a heretic darkness. And yet you ask us all, your trusted councilors, to stand by and watch? The Yehuli

THE WOLF AND THE WOODSMAN 269

celebrate a holiday next week, and they will fill the streets with their unholy worshipping. What will our Volken guests think when they see it?"

Fear grips me, cold and tight. Count Reményi's words are nearly treasonous, but the king only sits up a bit straighter in his seat, balancing the crown of fingernails on his head. When he speaks, there is not much fire in it.

"It was Saint István who gave you your fortress and all the green lands surrounding it, and you are speaking now to his heir. You will give me the men I need now."

Finally, Reményi goes quiet, his hand tensing around the edge of the table. The white feather on his chest seems to bristle, even though the air in the chamber is stiff, still. I know he is thinking of another one of Saint István's heirs, one that he would like to see wear the crown instead.

"Come with me," the king says brusquely. "I must consult the Prinkepatrios."

After my sleepless night with Zsigmond the council meeting has left me particularly weary, and I don't have the strength to refuse, even if my oath would allow it. My mind is reeling with everything I have learned, and all that I still don't know. It is like the blank spaces where the Yehuli vowels ought to be, something you must be taught by someone older and wiser, if you ever want to understand how to fill the absence.

The chapel surprises me by being carved right into the cliffside. Its oaken door is wedged between two knuckles of rock, scarcely wide enough for the king and I to walk through at once. Torches are mounted on blackened stones, and candles are set in the cave's many small orifices, casting bubbles of filmy light. Green moss spangles the ceiling, a damp, breathing topography. The Sons and Daughters of the

Patrifaith scuttle through the pews, looking like little brown mice. Their shaven heads are as glossy as pearls in the recessed candlelight. I wonder which among them drew up the missive calling for my death.

Gáspár and Nándor have both joined us here, looking properly contrite. After hearing Count Reményi's ramblings I am even more loath to meet Nándor's stare, though he watches me with hawkish scrutiny, his eyes holding the pale candlelight. Gáspár keeps his face turned away from me, too, but I see his gaze flicker toward me once, so briefly I might only have imagined it.

"Some say the three-pronged spear is really a trident." Gáspár's voice, hushed as it is, still echoes through the near-vacant church. Syllables scrape the craggy ceiling. "They say that the Patrifaith began as the cult of a sea god in Ionika, but it morphed and changed as it moved further north."

"Detractors and infidels say that," Nándor replies flatly. "And princes who spend too much time reading the mad scribblings of heretics in the palace archives."

"These things should not be spoken of in a holy place," the king says, sounding almost queasy.

A narrow aisle breaches the pews, clambering over the rock and up to a large stone altar. Melting candles are heaped upon it like dirty snow. They have cooled and hardened into a single mound, needles of ossified wax dripping off the edge of the dais. Mounted above it is the three-pronged spear, or trident, of the Prinkepatrios, set in gold, and below it a marble statue, dyed pale green by a hundred years of moist air. It's of a man, entirely nude, his muscled arms coiled around the throat of a huge bull. Moss grows over his bare toes. Ivy wreathes the bull's long horns.

The statue is so curious that I can't help the question falling from my lips. "Who is that?"

"Mithros," Gáspár surprises me by answering. "He was a

mortal man granted the favor of the Prinkepatrios. He proved himself to be a great hero, so the Prinkepatrios made him immortal. He stepped into the sea and vanished, joining God in heaven."

I don't like how very much Mithros sounds like Vilmötten. As we approach the altar, I can see the bulging sinew of Mithros's bare thighs, and the appendage hanging between them. It makes me wonder how Gáspár ended up so fretfully prudish when he's spent his life worshipping at the feet of some lusty naked man's statue.

The king and his sons kneel before the altar, hands clasped. From behind, I can see only their bent backs and their hunched shoulders, their hair. The king's, gray with age; Gáspár's, his dark curls twining down his neck; Nándor's like whorls of liquid gold. They are still and quiet for several moments until the Érsek emerges from behind the altar, swathed in a cocoon of brown muslin. He totters unsteadily up the dais and blinks his wet little eyes. I remember him now—he was the man fixed beside Nándor in the courtyard, soberly watching my father stand in pig's blood.

"My lords, why have you come here today?" the Érsek asks. He has a low, nasal voice, and I am reminded of the wicked minister from Zsigmond's story, the one who ordered the deaths of all the Yehuli. In truth I can hardly imagine the Érsek doing such a thing, if only because I think Nándor would leap up to do it first.

"Today, I pray for wisdom," the king replies. "So I may learn how to set right the mistakes of the past."

"Then wisdom you shall have," the Érsek says, and he brushes his thumb against the king's forehead. He turns to Nándor. "What do you pray for today, my son?"

"Today, I pray for strength," Nándor replies. "So I may do what weaker men cannot."

"Then strength you shall have," says the Érsek, his thumb

brushing Nándor's forehead. It lingers there for longer than it should, and Nándor closes his eyes and lets out a shuddering breath. I remember Szabín's story—how he has lived his whole life with the priest whispering in his ear—and something knifes through my loathing, an unexpected and hard-won pity. How much can you blame a hunting dog for biting when it's only ever been trained to use its teeth?

My pity shrivels when the Érsek turns to Gáspár. "What do you pray for today, my son?"

"I would like to confess a sin," he says.

The air in the cave seems to thicken, and my muscles tense. The Érsek gives a nod, and says, "Speak, my son."

"I took a man's life. Two men. They were both guilty of terrible crimes themselves, but they were good Patritian men, pious and prayerful. I would like to cleanse my soul of sin."

He has not confessed to kissing me, to touching my breasts or stroking me between my thighs. I cannot see Gáspár's face, only the heave of his shoulders as he takes his labored breaths. The Érsek brushes his thumb quickly over Gáspár's forehead, barely grazing his bronze skin.

"Godfather Life grants you mercy," he says. "You have made your full confession, and you are now absolved of your sin."

As the king and his sons rise in perfect synchrony, I gape at the Érsek. For all of Gáspár's prattling about souls and justice, it takes only the touch of a priest's finger to absolve him? I wonder how the men he killed would feel about that. Before I can even give voice to my bewilderment, they each produce a small leather pouch, bunched shut with a drawstring. From the pouches, they pour out a small pile of gold coins, the carved profile of Saint István glinting on every one. They hold the coins out in their cupped hands, and the Érsek takes them, sliding each piece into a satchel of his own. He tugs the drawstring to close it, the coins rattling as he slips it into his robes. The bag forms a bulge in his side beneath the brown muslin, an answer to my unspoken question.

"The Prinkepatrios accepts what you have given," the Érsek says, bowing his head. "Where there is sacrifice, great things are sure to come."

The Érsek ambles toward the shadowed doorway, his gait now lopsided with the load of the coins, and Nándor bounds up the dais to follow him. Their faces are close as they speak in whispers. Perhaps it was even the Érsek who left the note at my door, another one of Nándor's slavering followers. The king stalks aimlessly through the pews, murmuring to himself. And then I am standing alone with Gáspár.

It's the first time we've had a chance to speak since he came to see me in my cell, and the memory of it bruises me. Despite it, I have some small instinct to tell him everything that has happened: about the council meeting, about Zsigmond. As if he can help fill some of the empty spaces. But I have quashed the instinct by the time he opens his mouth.

"You *did* survive," he says quietly.

"No thanks to you," I bite back. I think of the way he sat silently at the banquet table while the king held his sword over my head, and I feel as wretched as ever.

Gáspár holds my gaze, throat bobbing. "I tried."

"If you mean your pitiful protests at the feast—"

"No," he says, with a thread of stubborn petulance that I've found myself oddly missing. "Before the feast. I begged my father for your life, even though I thought you might be the death of me."

I remember how Nándor touched me so easily, putting his finger to my lips as if he weren't afraid that I might threaten his holiness. I wonder what Gáspár would do, if he weren't afraid. But he hasn't confessed me like a sin. He hasn't tried to absolve himself of what he's done, of what we did, together.

"Did you kneel for him?" I ask perversely.

It is not a question meant to be answered, and I half expect Gáspár to scowl at me and turn away. For a suspended moment, there's no sound in the church except the harmony of our breathing; even the trickle of water and the king's footsteps have gone silent. Gáspár stares at me without blinking, for so long that my own eyes are hot and damp by the end of it, by the time he finally says, "Yes."

# CHAPTER EIGHTEEN

After the first time I spend five straight nights at Zsigmond's house, tracing letters. It doesn't seem quite right, to call what I am doing writing, not yet. I can only copy what I see on Zsigmond's parchments; I can't conjure any words of my own. Zsigmond watches me over the top of his book, until I am yawning with every other breath and my vision is too glazed to read anything, and then he puts me to sleep in his bed, covering me with a quilt that smells of candle wax and ink and old paper, that smells like him. When pink dawn light filters through the window and lands gridded on my bleary face, I know it is time to return to the castle, to sit dull-eyed at the king's side like some exceptionally devoted guard dog. Council meetings and banquets and church visits wend past me in an oblivious litany. All day I can think of nothing except returning to Zsigmond that night.

He tells me stories of my mother, only the good ones, when she was rosy-cheeked and alive, still swollen with the distant dream of me. I tell him about Virág and her theatrically grim predictions, careful never to mention anything about lashings, trying to wring the small bits of humor out of a mostly humorless life. Zsigmond is particularly good at that; he has none of Virág's self-pitying gloom. Even when he speaks of his abuse at Nándor's hands, he makes me laugh at his depiction of the Woodsmen as sheep newly shorn, embarrassed of their nascent nudity, bleating after their prettier, fluffier master. It is only then that I feel brave enough to recall Count Reményi's words.

"During the council meeting," I start, my voice low and uncertain, "there was one count, the count of Akosvár, who said that there was a place for Yehuli where they could have towns and villages of their own. A strip of land in Rodinya that has been set aside for them. He said the other countries in the west are already sending their Yehuli there."

The lambent humor drains from Zsigmond's eyes. "They call it the Stake. It is cobbled from the worst bits of land in the Rodinyan empire, scraggly and cold, where not much good can grow. The Yehuli there live in their own towns and villages, it's true, but there are laws forbidding them from owning land and selling wares, from working on certain days, from sending their children to school. And then Patritians come from the nearby cities, to burn Yehuli houses, to kill. They don't spare even the women and children."

A lump rises hard and hot in my throat. "But doesn't all that happen here? Nándor had you arrested and tortured for working on a Patritian holy day, and now he threatens to visit violence upon the Yehuli . . ."

"My family," Zsigmond starts, and then clears his throat, amending himself, "*our* family has lived in Király Szek for six generations. We have served kings and counts. We have done everything from goldsmithing to street sweeping. We watched the city gates fall to King István's enemies and then be built back up again; we saw his coronation and murmured about it in Old Régyar with the rest of them. This is our home, as much as Keszi is yours."

"But it's not my home," I say, feeling my stomach turn and roil. "Not anymore. They cast me out to die."

Zsigmond draws a breath. I can tell he regrets his words, but he doesn't have time to apologize for them before there's a knock on the door. It's Batya, hefting two enormously full wicker baskets and a skein of pale silk draped over her arm.

My lips pucker when I see her, like I have bitten into a citrus fruit. By now I have learned enough of the Yehuli tongue to know that the first time we met, she called me chubby.

"Well, I did tell you to invite her, didn't I?" Batya thrusts the silk at me; as it folds open onto the table, I see that it's a dress. "And here is your food, as if I don't cook enough for you all the other days of the year."

Blinking, I touch the sleeve of the dress, unsure what to say. Zsigmond relieves Batya of the baskets, which are laden with more loaves of sweet bread and sacks of hard biscuits, poppy-speckled.

"Thank you," he says, kissing her cheek as his own face turns faintly pink. "Have your daughters and their husbands all gone to the temple already?"

"Yes," she says. "I told them I would make sure you've gotten out of bed and dressed yourself, and you did ask me to bring your daughter something to wear."

"What are the gifts for?" I ask.

Zsigmond opens his mouth, but Batya speaks first. "We're supposed to give two portions of food to our friends on the holiday, and at least two portions to someone who needs something to fill their bellies. We used to go around to the poorer streets in Király Szek and bring them bread, but they weren't happy to take charity from Yehuli, and then the king forbid it anyway. Zsigmond, haven't you told your daughter anything at all? You're teaching her to read—why don't you teach her to read the holy book? She looks as baffled as a newborn fawn."

It's a kinder characterization than I expected, and for all

her gruffness, Batya doesn't seem to have any compunctions about inviting me to the temple. I feel a pinprick of guilt for comparing her to Virág.

"Aren't you afraid?" The question bubbles out of me, almost unbidden. "Nándor wants you gone, the counts want you gone . . . don't you think it's dangerous, to celebrate anything?"

I wonder if Batya will find my words impolite; if she were really anything like Virág, I might have been struck or scolded. But Batya only laughs.

"If we only celebrated on the days when there was no danger, we'd never have occasion to celebrate at all," she says. "Come on now, Zsigmond, and bring your daughter. I think she would like to hear this story."


The temple is nothing like I expect either. In the Yehuli tongue, Zsigmond tells me, it is called a shul. After seeing the gray-washed houses of Yehuli Street, I anticipated a small building, made of wood or crumbling stone, room enough for only a huddle of standing worshippers. But the temple is larger than even the king's chapel, with its crags and moss and trickling water, and perhaps even grander. The domed ceiling is painted a bright clear blue, like the sky's broad cheek, freckled with stars. There are rows and rows of polished wooden benches, leading to an altar of carved marble, but there's no naked statue there—only a lectern with a book lying open upon it. A dozen chandeliers wheel with gauzy candlelight. Volutes of gold clamber up tall ivory pillars, shooting toward the ceiling like hearty, ancient oaks. Even crowded with bodies the temple seems so vast I know that my voice would echo all the way to the lectern, if I were brave enough to speak.

The dress Batya lent me fits surprisingly well, with enough room in the bodice. It buttons all the way to my throat, which is as chaste as I have likely ever been. Most of the other women my age have covered their hair with kerchiefs, which befuddles me until I see them sit down beside their dour husbands, pulling their wriggling children into their laps. A pang of awful loneliness lances through me, and I wonder if Zsigmond aches with it too. Or if he has inured himself to it after so many years, well accustomed to sitting alone in a sea of families. He leads me toward the bench where Batya sits, her three black-haired daughters beside her like ravens on a perch.

The youngest one glares at me sharp-eyed. "Mama, she's wearing my dress."

"Enough, Jozefa," Batya snaps. "You can consider it your act of charity."

Jozefa scowls at her mother, but when she turns to me again, there is only a look of curiosity on her face, pink lips bowing. "Are you Zsigmond's daughter?"

I nod mutely.

"You must have converted then, haven't you? You aren't wed." Her gaze skims me up and down, like a merchant examining a porcelain vase for its cracks. "You look older than I am. If you want to be wed—"

"Jozefa." Batya's voice cuts between us. "The rabbi is going to start."

Jozefa's lips go taut, and she faces back toward the lectern. My cheeks are hot, but it's a small flustering. There's no shame pooling in my belly. I've long since learned to tell which questions are meant only to probe and which are meant to wound. Jozefa's are dull, toothless—Katalin would have scoffed at such mundane impudence. I imagine she might have asked them of any Yehuli girl who was unwed at five and twenty, and the thought fills me with a tight, blooming hope, something like a coin clutched in a closed fist.

I expect the rabbi to be someone like the Érsek, but he is younger, with a dense beard that coils profusely, black as wet bramble. There are two candles on the lectern, and when he traces something into their stands, the wicks both blossom into flame. It makes my breath catch, the same as when Zsigmond did it.

He begins to speak, and I am deeply relieved to hear Régyar and not Yehuli. My skin prickles with the memory of Count Reményi's words, how easily he imagined the Yehuli could give up their homes and their histories in Régország, how I had even briefly entertained the same fantasy. Now it seems impossible to imagine: Régyar words spill from the rabbi's mouth as easily as water from a mountain spring. The story he tells is familiar, names and places lighting up in my mind like signal fires. There is the orphaned Yehuli girl, Esther, who was wed to a king. The king didn't know that his new wife was Yehuli, and neither did his wicked minister, who plotted to kill all the Yehuli in the kingdom. When Zsigmond told me the story, decades ago, he gave the minister a pinched voice that made me laugh and laugh. Now, every time the rabbi starts to speak the minister's name, the temple fills with shouting and crowing, sounds that blot the minister from the tale like a thumb smudging ink. I think of Zsigmond obscuring the first letter of *emet*, turning *truth* into *death*.

"Esther knew that she had been made queen so that she could help her people, but approaching the king about such things was against the law, and would lead to her death," the rabbi says. "So for three days Esther prayed and fasted and sharpened her mind, and then she went to the king anyway."

I already know that the story ends with Esther triumphant, the Yehuli safe, and the wicked minister killed. I know, too, that there is a lesson in it, like all of Virág's dire tales, but I can't tell what it is. Was Esther brave, or was she shrewd? Was the king cruel, or was he only stupid? I think Virág would say that Esther was a coward for marrying the king at all, or for not first slitting his throat while he slept soundly in their marriage bed.

A bit of grief leaches into me, like rainwater through roots. All around me the Yehuli sit with their families, shoulders brushing, hands linked together, and then there is Zsigmond and me, our thighs barely touching. Yehuli words float through the air in whispers, thin and pale as dust motes, still mostly foreign to me. I can sit in their temple and wear their clothes and even try to garble their tongue, but I am still not really one of them.

And then, extraordinarily, Zsigmond lays his hand over mine. I feel the quiver of hesitation run through his palm, and then he threads his fingers with my own. Warmth envelops me. Jozefa reaches across her mother's lap and smooths one of the pleats of my dress, of her dress, almost absently, like she has noticed one of her own hairs out of place. Zsigmond is still staring straight ahead, watching the rabbi, but when his eye flickers to me briefly, I see in it a look of exquisite peace.

After the reading, bodies flood from the temple into the street. Feast tables are laid with huge platters of triangular-shaped dumplings, thin pancakes rolled with sweet cheese and topped with the last blackberries of summer, carafes of wine, and the same hard biscuits that Batya brought my father in his gift basket, thumbprints of sour-cherry jam at their centers. Zsigmond told me this was a minor holiday, but it looks as big as any feast we have ever had in Keszi. Farther down the road, there is a man performing a bawdy shadow-puppet play, telling the story of Esther with some embellishments not fit for children's ears. The children are not listening anyway: they run through their mothers' skirts, mouths stained purple with berry juice. The girls wear paper crowns, imagining themselves Queen Esther. The dusky evening sky is banded with orange and gold.

I linger by the feast table, scarcely able to restrain myself from clinging to Zsigmond's side like a child myself. He speaks mostly to Batya in soft tones, clutching a cup of wine. I can see how each Yehuli family is like a constellation, and

Zsigmond is his own unclustered star, winking its singular light. Just like how I was in Keszi, a daughter without her mother, nothing to give me shape except my braid in one pocket and my coin in the other. I fill a cup of wine for myself and swallow it down in one gulp.

"My mother will take offense if you don't try her dumplings," Jozefa says.

I put down my glass. "Your mother called me chubby."

Jozefa regards me with a furrowed brow, as if she is trying to judge the veracity of her mother's claim. "She'll take offense anyway. And if you're chubby, then so am I. We fit into the same dress."

She takes a biscuit and eats it in two bites, smiling wolfishly. I watch her, uneasy. Batya's other daughters are older, married, with the exhaustion of three children each gleaming dully behind their eyes. Jozefa has her mother's bright, clear eyes and a face full of freckles that look scattered by an indolent hand. She is pretty in a razor-edged way; after spending so many years tormented by Katalin and the other girls in Keszi, it's hard for me to look at pretty girls and not think of the blades behind their smiles. If we were in Keszi, Jozefa seems the type who would pull my hair and sneer at me. But now she only fills my glass with wine again, and then tops off her own.

"Thank you," I say.

My voice is laced with suspicion, and she can tell. Jozefa's lips purse. "My mother says you come from the pagan villages in Farkasvár, and that your mother was a pagan. Why are you in Király Szek?"

I swallow my wine. "It's a long story."

"We Yehuli like stories, in case you couldn't tell." Her eyes are light and laughing. "You ought to get used to telling them, if you want to be one of us."

I almost say that I have plenty of practice listening, but I have done little telling of my own. "But I can't be one of you, can I? I hardly know your language or your prayers or . . ."

"You can learn," Jozefa says with a shrug. "You're not simple, are you? Even my little cousin can read the holy book, and he still thinks that black hens lay black eggs. And even though your mother wasn't Yehuli, you can do a conversion."

"Does that happen very often?" I ask keenly. "Conversions."

"Not very much anymore. But a long time ago, before the Patrifaith came to Régország, there were plenty of Yehuli men and women who married outsiders. Then they converted and raised their children here and no one could even know they were different at all. Of course, that was when we were allowed to live where we liked, and there was no Yehuli Street."

"Before the Patrifaith?" Though Virág claims to remember a time when there were no three-pronged spears or Woodsman axes flashing, it is impossible for me to conceive.

"Of course," Jozefa says. "The Yehuli lived in this city when King István wasn't even a dream in his mother's mind. Why else do you think our temple is so grand even when we can only work the days and the jobs that the Patritians allow us? Our temple was here before the Broken Tower, and long before the king carved his chapel into the hillside."

The revelation of it shocks me. All I know of Régyar history is what I learned at Virág's feet, and of course there was never any mention of the Yehuli. Jozefa watches my face flush first with bewilderment, and then with anger, thinking of the Patrifaith like a wave eating away at some pale and ancient stone.

"Why have you been so kind to me?" The question is not the one I intended to ask, but it rises up without me realizing it.

"Why wouldn't we be?" Jozefa counters, brow lowering. "Zsigmond has been alone nearly all his life; it was difficult to watch. Now he's learned the daughter he thought was dead is alive after all—why should we take offense that her mother was some pagan woman?"

"Because I'm only half—" I start, and then stop abruptly, because Jozefa is looking at me as if I really am simple.

"Some on this street might not like it," she says. "But I think it's Patritians who care more about measuring blood."

Not just Patritians. My thoughts go to Katalin, her face cast blue in the light of her flame. For all her eloquent assurance, Jozefa might be as sheltered as a fox pup in its den. Blood has power. I've seen it streaked across Gáspár's wrist, felt it drying on the backs of my thighs. I've been eating the truth of it all my life, even before I knew you could cut your arm to kindle a fire, or lop off your pinky to invite Ördög's magic inside you.

Several feet away, Batya throws her head back and laughs at something my father has said. Her eyes are gleaming. I remember how she sat with her daughters in the temple, the absence of a husband obvious to me only now.

"What about *your* father?" I ask keenly, no longer caring to be tactful. "Where is he?"

"He died when I was a child." Jozefa blinks, untroubled. "I don't remember him at all. But I do know what it's like to be without one."

The baldness of her answer almost makes me feel embarrassed for asking, and doubly ashamed for thinking that she was as soft as a kit, oblivious to any suffering. I see a different cant to Batya's smile now, and a new meaning to the way Zsigmond has laid his hand on her arm.

I open my mouth to reply, but the wind picks up then, ferrying the sound of voices down Yehuli Street. Firelight dances on the facades of the houses, and moving shadows fall upon the cobblestones. Now all my blood turns cold.

My mind conjures images of stakes and torches, bodies in the street. But I can't see any blades glinting, only a crowd gathering at the very end of the road, mostly peasants in their homespun clothes. They are murmuring, their heads bobbing like prairie mice, but there is one voice, dulcet and familiar, that rises above the rest.

"See how they celebrate while our soldiers are struck down by Merzani steel," Nándor says. "See how heartily they eat while the bey's army burns our crops in Akosvár. If you believe, as I do, that the Prinkepatrios rewards staunch faith and punishes apostasy, then how can you believe that we are not being punished for sheltering heathens in our city?"

A chorus of approval lifts from the crowd. Jozefa has gone stiff beside me, one hand gripping the edge of the feast table. Her knuckles are white. Behind me, Zsigmond's gaze passes between Nándor and me, the wine-flush draining from his cheeks.

"All this time the king has been searching for the power to defeat the Merzani and to end the war," Nándor goes on. He paces to the front of the crowd, his boot steps feather-light. "Stealing magic from pagan girls' fingernails, like some sort of impious grave robber. Perhaps the solution has been before us all this time: send the Yehuli from this city, and wipe the pagans from this Earth."

His words are openly mutinous. I scan the crowd, searching for Gáspár, for anyone who might bear witness to Nándor's treason. My heart leaps when I see a black suba, but it's not Gáspár—it's only a nameless Woodsman whose face is unfamiliar to me. My gaze lands on another Woodsman, and then another, their axes at their hips and their eyes following Nándor reverently. My vision falters, and I feel sick enough to retch.

The crowd presses around Nándor, pushing farther down the road. All the sounds of our feast have gone silent. Children are clinging to their fathers' legs, the feathers from their masks snatched up in the wind. The rabbi is mutely cradling his cup of wine in one hand and a half-eaten biscuit in the other. We are all, in this moment, part of the same constellation: dozens of stars clustered in identical terror.

Nándor breaks from the crowd. In the evening light, his

face is incandescent, torchlight flickering on the shining planes of his cheeks. He comes toward me, and Jozefa gives a tiny gasp of fear, stumbling back. I hold myself still. My heart is all roaring clamor. When Nándor finally stops, our noses are a hair's breadth apart. I can see a small, imperfect birthmark under his left eyebrow.

"Évike," he says. "What a terrible disappointment. There's hardly any trace of pagan left in you. Pity for my father—he wanted a vicious wolf-girl, and he got a slavering Yehuli dog."

He wants his words to draw deep gouges in me, deep enough to make me cower, or else rise to violence like a wolf with an arrow in its hind. Pain makes animals mean, but I must be more than just an animal now. The crowd thrums in bridled fury behind him, so many faces blank with their loathing. Ashen-faced peasants mostly, along with a handful of Woodsmen and even a few nobles in their jewel-bright dolmans. Something familiar sharpens out of the throng: Count Reményi, his weasel eyes narrowed like knife points.

"Wolf-girl or Yehuli, I know what to do with seditious bastards," I say, though my voice is more uncertain than I would like. "And I know what shackles you now, Nándor. You want to be a Patritian king of a Patritian country, but it's Patritian law that the crown goes to the firstborn son. The true-born son."

I expect Nándor to flinch, if only briefly, but he scarcely even blinks at me. His gaze wanders over my shoulder, landing on Zsigmond. My heart stutters.

"So it is," Nándor says, shifting his gaze back to me. "As long as the firstborn son lives. And you and your people may have my father's protection for now, but one man's word, even the word of a king, cannot hold against the tide of an entire city."

It's another moment before I can untangle the threefold braid of his threat, my stomach curdling with terror. Is it Gáspár's life, not his father's, that he aims to take? Does he

plan to banish the Yehuli on his own, with his faction of dis-
loyal Woodsmen? And then will he march them to Keszi too?

My four fingers curl into a fist. I've been told of Nándor's
power, but I have never seen it. I have heard him entrance
a crowd with his voice, but voices can be silenced. Hateful
instinct laces through me, and I very nearly wrap my hand
around his throat.

I stop before I even lift my arm. It will only bring violence
upon Zsigmond, upon Jozefa and Batya and all the Yehuli
behind me. For all that I lambasted Gáspár over his cringing silence, for all that I fought Katalin's cruelty, I don't rise
against Nándor now. I let his words land on my shoulders like
brittle winter leaves. He plucks the wine cup from my hand
and drains it, a stain of scarlet tinging the corners of his lips.
Then he smashes the glass onto the cobblestones, turns, and
leads his crowd away with him.

# CHAPTER NINETEEN

The street empties within moments of Nándor's departure. Food is swept off the feast tables. Children are bundled into their houses, hushed with their mothers' kisses. All that remains is the red spill of wine across the cobblestones and the shattered porcelain of my cup. Dusk has sharpened into night, and the cool air stings my cheeks and nose as I help Batya and Jozefa heft their trays through the threshold, Zsigmond following close behind.

When the door is shut, Batya collapses into a chair. Jozefa wipes her brow mutely. And Zsigmond sits down at the table, hands steepled in front of him, gaze set blankly into the middle distance. The gonged absence of sound is louder than Király Szek's church bells.

"What will you do?" I ask finally, when I can't stand the silence any longer. My voice squeaks like a wood mouse.

"What we have always done." Batya rubs one hand along her chin. "There's nothing else to do. We have weathered worse threats before. It has been particularly bad these past years, with the war, but once the Merzani are pushed back from the border, Nándor will temper himself again."

"It's not only Nándor," Zsigmond says softly. "There were near a hundred peasants there, and Woodsmen and nobles too. Is Nándor the mouth behind their prayers, or the answer to them?"

I don't know how to reply. If a fire burns your hut to the ground, do you blame the man who stoked your hearth, or the god who made the winter cold?

"Yes, and still we have endured worse," Batya says again, but I notice the way her eyes dart between my father and the doorway. "We must keep low until it passes, like we always do."

Just like King János, I think, who has only tried to patch the holes of an unsound ship. That's the problem with Patritians— they care about their legacies more than their lives. The king would let Keszi burn, would let my father bleed, would even let himself die if he could still have his statue carved in gold. If he could stay in that courtyard as a slender finger bone or a lock of hair or whitened eye.

Zsigmond nods, and says nothing more. Jozefa brushes a loose braid back from her mother's face. And then I can feel my chest start to heave, tears pricking hot in the corners of my eyes. Batya draws a sharp breath, and I flush with shame at my weakness, how easily Nándor has moved me to weep, until Zsigmond rises from his chair and puts his arms around me, tucking my head under his chin.

I almost laugh then, in disbelief and despair. All my life I have only wanted my father to hold me, but now when he finally does, it feels as if he is holding me against the wolves at the door. I wipe my tears on the collar of his shirt and say, "Virág would tell you that I was a bad omen."

Zsigmond laughs; I feel it echo through my cheek. "God has brought my daughter back to me, and whatever else has

come with her is dust on the wind. Have I told you the fable
of the rabbi and the golem?"

From the other side of the room, Jozefa groans. "Please,
my mother has told it a thousand times. I can't bear to hear it
once more."

Batya silences her with a glare, even as I think of how
I've echoed her sentiment so many times. The Yehuli, I have
learned, have as many stories as Virág. There are ash fables
for funerals, wine fables for weddings, moon fables for trying
to get your children to go to sleep at night. Thread fables are
stories that mothers tell their daughters as they teach them to
stitch, but I have no mother, so I've never heard a single one.

"It is a salt fable," Zsigmond says, releasing me. "It's what
you tell on Shabbos when you dip your bread in salt. This
story is about a rabbi who lived in a city much like Király
Szek, but where the Yehuli were not treated nearly as well.
They would close their windows and lock their doors, but
still the Patritians would come at night, to burn their houses
and loot them. The rabbi lost his own wife that way, and his
daughter was taken and raised as a Patritian in the house of
a childless lord. He watched her dark head in a crowd of Patritians with flaxen hair, watched her grow taller and lose her
baby teeth, never knowing that her real family were living
behind the gates of the city's Yehuli quarter.

"The rabbi prayed to God for an answer, and because the
rabbi was a good and loyal man who loved his people, God
whispered back. He told the rabbi his true name. The rabbi
wrote down God's true name on a scrap of parchment and
tucked it into his sleeve, so that he wouldn't forget it. And
then he left the city and went down to the riverbed, where he
began to dig in the mud. With his bare hands, he reached into
the earth and shaped a man from the clay—just the rough
outline of a man, with two holes for eyes and another hole for
its mouth. Inside its mouth, the rabbi put the scroll with the
name of God. And then the clay-man sat up.

"The clay-man followed the rabbi back to the city. He was twice the size of a normal man and four times as strong, and being made of clay, he couldn't be wounded. When the Patritians came that night, with their pitchforks and torches, the clay-man was waiting for them. Their pitchforks bent and broke against his clay body, and he extinguished all their torches with his huge hard fingers.

"The Yehuli were so grateful for the clay-man, and grateful to the rabbi for making him. And it is said that when the rabbi wanted the clay-man to be clay again, he reached into the creature's mouth and took the name of God back out."

It feels like the story of Esther: I know there's a lesson in it, but I don't understand. All I can think of is Nándor rising out of the ice like some pale hallucination, and all the Patritians dropping to their knees in front of him. I think he is both the mouth behind their prayers and the answer to them all at once.

"But there's no clay-man now," I say. "There's no one to protect you against Nándor and the rest."

"A protector doesn't always look like a creature made of mud," Zsigmond says. His dark eyes throw the candlelight like a black pool reflecting the moon at its highest peak. "You could be one of us, if you chose it."

Jozefa gives a nod, contrite. "Didn't I say so?"

I think about writing my own name, practicing each letter until the movements became as natural as breathing. The four stark lines of the É, the V a sharp little dagger, then a stiff line for I and more hard, fast strokes for K and E. I held that scrap of parchment with my name written on it so close and tight in my palm that the ink came off in my hand, but it was finally something that belonged to me and me alone.

Nándor would take it from me, and then cleave my head from my body. He wouldn't even keep my fingernails and the little power he could leach from them—he would kill any memory of me and send all the Yehuli out into the cold.

"I think I do," I say, even if they feel like the last words I will speak in the world.

Zsigmond smiles at me with such firmness it's as if he's gripping a blade. And then he leans over and whispers the name of God in my ear.

When I leave Yehuli Street, the bells are clanging in the castle courtyard. My heart clangs with them, echoing through my rib cage and up my spine. I haven't left the king alone for too long, but I wonder if Nándor seized the moment of my absence anyway. What if the bells are mourning bells? What if he took the life of his true-born brother after all? The words of his threat are still lacing through my mind.

But the crowd gathered in the courtyard shows no signs of mourning. Many of them are the same peasants who followed Nándor to Yehuli Street, and I wonder if they will recognize me, in my dress of pale-green silk, my face pink with the memory of my weeping. None of them seem to even notice me, though—they are jostling one another and standing on the balls of their feet, craning their necks to see what is taking place at the center of the throng. The gray sky seems equally unsettled, clouds rolling back and forth across it like a prisoner pacing his cell. I push past a merchant in a red dolman and a beggar man holding a silver coin in his mouth and come to the front of the crowd.

My vision blurs, glazing over the chuff of smoke from the marketplace and the sharp smell of spices in the air. I can see the dark shape of a Woodsman's suba, trotting toward the barbican on his black horse. And then, beside him, impossibly: the white blur of a wolf cloak, and a girl with hair the color of snow.

I blink once, hoping I will wake from a nightmare.

I blink again, praying it's a mirage, a trick of Király Szek's pallid sunlight.

I blink a third time, and I know with a sickening crush of dread that it's real.

Someone's cart of cabbages overturns, and the cabbages go rolling across the filthy cobblestones. In the ensuing scuffle, I dart forward across the courtyard, toward the Woodsman. I skid to a halt between him and the barbican.

It's the Woodsman with the horrible mangled nose, Lajos. He looks down his half nose at me and sneers.

"Get out of my way, wolf-girl," he says. "Nothing you can do or say will save your sister."

"She is *not* my sister," Katalin huffs.

In that moment, I can't decide whom I would rather kill—her or Lajos. From up on her silvery mare, Katalin's blue eyes are gleaming with stubborn reproach, but I notice that her hands are bound, and there's a ghost of a bruise smudged purple on her cheek. It's not quite enough to make me pity her, but a snarl of fury coils in my gut.

"The king swore," I say, going on despite the trembling in my voice, "he swore that no harm would come to Keszi!"

"*I* don't make bargains with wolf-girls," says Lajos. He kicks his horse so that it shoulders roughly past me. "I just follow the king's orders."

Looking at Katalin now, she hardly seems real. I have been so worried about Nándor's treachery that I have forgotten that the king is a tyrant in his own way. After so many sleepless nights, my belly churning with fear over what would become of the Yehuli, I have nearly let Keszi slip from my mind. Guilt and horror twine in me at once, a fiery string of pain.

I turn to Katalin. "Get down from the horse."

Katalin's gaze shifts uncertainly between Lajos and me. She's not worried about provoking Lajos, of course—she's more concerned with snubbing me and making sure I know it. But she puts one leg over her horse's saddle and then slides off it, boots hitting the ground with a muted thud.

"You don't give anyone orders, wolf-girl," Lajos spits,

leaping from his mount in one furious motion, his hand on his ax. "I don't care what sort of bargain you have with the king—you can serve him just as well when I've cut your demon tongue out of your mouth."

But the bargain is broken already and the air is cold and clear. All my fear shudders out of me, leaving only anger in its place. "I welcome you to try."

And then Lajos swings. It's a warning strike, halfhearted, but I reach out for his blade with my right hand, as soon as its movement slows enough that I won't lose the rest of my fingers doing it. In my grasp the metal peels with rust, flaking away in long strips like iron tongues, until the whole blade has crumbled right down to its shiny hilt. Lajos takes a step back, eyes widening.

"How did you do that?" Katalin demands.

"The king will punish you!" Lajos cries out as the crowd startles like spooked chickens. "You've attacked one of his loyal Woodsmen!"

"*You* attacked *me*," I remind him hotly. Perhaps I have lost all my good sense, broken the promises I made to myself to stay quiet and cowed. But the king broke his end of our oath first.

I jump as the gate of the barbican grinds open, expecting Nándor or worse. But it's Gáspár. I hate how relief stills in me when I see him, the way the warmth of a fire can make you feel sated and sleepy as it settles into your marrow. There are two Woodsmen with him, Miklós and Ferenc, but my gaze trains on him and him alone, remembering how he looked in the chapel's puddled candlelight. Remembering how he told me he kneeled.

Gáspár takes in the scene and my trembling hands and draws a breath. "What are you doing?"

"What am *I* doing?" I look between him and Lajos, gaping. "Your father broke his bargain. He promised that if I served him, Keszi would be safe from harm, and now he's brought another wolf-girl anyway!"

I see a shadow go across his face, but I can't guess at its meaning. Gáspár turns to Lajos. "When did the king order you to go to Keszi?"

"Just after Saint István's feast," he mumbles. "After the wolf-girl—"

I don't hear the rest of it. Blood pulses in my ears, loud as nearing thunder. The king didn't even blink before turning on me. He must have known all his promises were lies even as they left his lips, and I am the guileless idiot who believed them. I had felt giddy with power after bargaining for my life, not realizing that as I preened and gloated, the king was fitting me with chains.

While I am marveling at my own miserable stupidity, Lajos grabs Katalin by the arm. In my meanest, most secret imaginings, I sometimes dreamed that she would be taken by the Woodsmen and torn apart by monsters on her way through Ezer Szem, or even better, falling under the king's sword. Now my head whirls as I watch Lajos drag her away, sick with horror. I imagine the king tearing off her fingernails, one by one, like plucking the white feathers from a swan.

"Évike." Gáspár's voice knifes through the haze. "Don't do anything reckless."

I meet his eye, hands shaking. "I want to speak with the king."

I have no plan as I march to the king's chambers; it's only anger buoying me. Gáspár is a pace behind, and his words chase after me like loosed arrows.

"Consider what you want to achieve before you walk into the room," he says, an edge of pleading to his voice. "There's no use confronting him with venom and fury—you'll only get yourself thrown into the dungeons again."

I whirl on him. "And should I just be like you, instead? Swallowing every cruel word, bowing to the same man who tore your eye out? Letting your bastard brother stomp all over your birthright?"

I'm so enraged that I don't care how much I hurt him. But Gáspár only looks at me steadily, black eye unflinching.

"You swore an oath to my father too," he says.

"Yes, and it's my greatest shame," I snap, cheeks flushing.

"And don't you think it shames me equally?" I see his chest swell; for a moment I think he will close the space between us. "But you understood, as I do, that survival is not a battle that you win only once. You must fight it again every day. And so you take your small losses so that you can live to fight tomorrow. You know that my father is a slower, gentler poison."

His words bite at me like a splinter under my nail. I slow my pace, fury ebbing, despair rising up in its place. "But what should I do, then? Should I keep letting your father slip through my fingers again and again, reassuring myself that at least he is better than his bastard, until one day, without my knowing it, every single girl in Keszi is dead?"

Gáspár draws a breath. "Can Keszi not survive the loss of one girl every few years, as it has for all my father's reign?"

I consider it, even as my stomach roils. Virág will live another decade at least—she is as hearty as an old tree, which only grows stronger with its years. Another seer would likely be born in the meantime, her white hair a happy omen. And until she grew into her magic Keszi could learn to live without one, even if it meant not knowing when the frost came to kill our crops or when the Woodsmen would arrive at our door.

As if by instinct, I reach into my pocket for my mother's braid, but I remember that I am wearing Jozefa's dress, and not my wolf cloak.

"I was only one girl," I whisper. "And so was my mother."

Gáspár opens his mouth to reply, then closes it again. Guilt flits across his face, though I hadn't really meant for my words to wound him. I know that he is remembering the first time he saw me across the clearing, a bound and quaking sacrifice.

Before the memory can make me falter, I turn on my heel and shove into the king's chamber.

King János is kneeling at his bed, hands clasped. When he sees me, he leaps to his feet, reaching up to steady the fingernail crown on his head. He blinks at me mutely; there is something crusted into the corners of his lips.

"I'm not here to kill you," I say, "but it would be only fair if I did, since you broke our bargain."

The king lifts his chin, indignant. "I've broken nothing. Your village is unharmed, if not for the loss of one girl."

"That's all our village is!" I burst out. "Girls and women, boys and men. People. Would you say I left you unharmed if I cut off your arm or your leg?"

King János takes a step away from me, one hand still on his crown. "You wouldn't dare, wolf-girl. My blood would spill under the door and reveal you. You would never leave the palace alive."

But that has always been true. The moment that I entered Király Szek with a wolf cloak on my back I knew I was more likely to die than to ever step beyond its gates again. I think of how Esther spoke to the king so shrewdly, how she handled him so gingerly, the way you might eat around the spot of black in your apple. I can only try and do the same now.

"You'll kill her, then." My voice is soft, careful. Gáspár would commend me for speaking with such little venom. "Just like you did all the others. Add her fingernails to your crown."

"She is not like the others," says the king. "She's a seer."

"And what sort of power do you think her death will grant you?" My mind conjures images of Virág, writhing in the dirt. "A seer's magic isn't what you think. Their visions come at random, and what they see is never what you really want. You think her power will put you inside the mind of the bey, will anticipate his moves before he makes them, but it won't. It wouldn't be like—"

I almost mention the turul. My jaw snaps shut.

King János's eyes film over. He wanders toward the long window, his face turning gray-washed in the gridded squares of rheumy light. I can't help but think of his father's statue in the courtyard, hunched by the legacy of his failures.

"If I can end the war," he says, "then I can end what ails us here too. When food is scarce and sons are dying, the people always look for someone to blame. Nándor has pointed toward the Yehuli, the pagans. Now I am blamed for protecting them." His gaze shifts to me, a turbid look in it, like the pond water made murky by the thrashing of some fish. "Truly, wolf-girl, what would you have me do? Tell me—your counsel can be no less useful than that of my insipid advisers, who have only their own hoards behind their eyes."

His words stun me, not to mention the beseeching tenor of his voice. He is not nearly as much a buffoon as I have thought, sipping his wine, oblivious to the knives being drawn at his back. I remember Count Reményi's face in the crowd, and all those Woodsmen, black as shadows. Perhaps the king is as fettered as I am, as fettered as Gáspár, surviving in whatever shameful way he can. The truth of what the king is brings me no comfort. I almost wish I could still imagine him a monster, some seven-headed beast with lashing tongues, swallowing up wolf-girls for his supper. Now I see only a skinny dog gnawing on an old bone, already stripped of all its lustiest bits.

"Why protect them, then?" I ask, when I can manage to speak again. "Why not finish what Saint István started?"

"You already know," the king says.

And it strikes me then that I do. I have known ever since I first saw his gruesome crown, since I saw the counts in their pagan garb, trussed with feathers and draped in bear cloaks. They cannot kill the old ways entirely, or else they will lose their power. They will only take and take the parts that they like, the fingernails and the titles that their pagan blood right grants them, one girl every few years, not the whole village. Nándor told me that the Patrifaith was what made Régország, but that's not true. It is made of a thousand different threads twining together like tree roots, shooting up tall and thick, aching toward some impossible whole. Mithros and Vilmötten are like a two-headed statue, or a coin with a different face on either side.

I cut off my finger so that I could survive. Gáspár let his father take his eye so he would not cut his throat. And now Katalin must die, so that the rest of Keszi can live.

"So it is, then," I say, my voice thick with pain. "Another girl dead to keep the wolves from the door."

The king lifts one shoulder, gaze steady. For a moment, I can see a bit of Gáspár in him, like a trick of the light.

"I know you must hate me, wolf-girl," he says. "But I am certain you hate my son more."

There is nowhere else for me to go, so I return to my chamber. My mind and body feel heavy, weighed down with a thousand unmade decisions. By now the sky is black, depthless and starless. It has been mere hours since my father held me in Batya's house, but the memory seems irretrievably distant, and even though I try to summon it, I can recapture none of its warmth. All I can see is Katalin vanishing down the hall, like a white stone tossed into a well. All I can see is Nándor's face, livid gold in the torchlight.

The collar of Jozefa's dress feels stifling now, the starched wool painting a rash of red across my throat. As if moved by some invisible hand, I go toward the trunk at the foot of my bed and retrieve my wolf cloak. Katalin's wolf cloak. The wolf's teeth look yellower than I remembered. When I touch one, a tiny shard of bone comes away in my fingers. I search the pockets and find my mother's braid, coiled around itself like a cold snake. I squeeze it tight in my fist.

I remember how much I railed against Virág's decision to send me to the Woodsmen, how much her betrayal tormented me. It felt every day like a different wound, my mind forever conjuring some new way for it to ache. Watching Virág paint my hair silver in her hut, Katalin had finally gone quiet. Even she had been cowed by Virág's unimaginable coldness, a hurt worse than any she could ever cause.

If I let Katalin die now, I might as well admit that Virág was right to cast me away. That the life of one wolf-girl is no more than a brittle shield to throw up at the slightest threat or provocation. That we all have been reared only for the Woodsmen's axes.

A soft knock on the door makes me jump. But it's only the shivering servant girl, Riika, holding out a bolt of deep plum silk. When she unfurls it, I see that it's a dress, with long pooling sleeves and gold stitched up the bodice.

"The king had this sewn for you," she says. "So that you could attend feasts without attracting so much attention as a—"

The word *wolf-girl* dies in her throat. Anger steals over me, and I snatch the dress out of her hands. I toss it in the vague direction of the hearth, even though it's not lit. It flutters emptily to the floor instead, bodiless as a ghost.

"Tell him I have no use for his dresses," I spit. "If he thinks I'll uphold my end of our bargain if he doesn't care to—"

A sudden, taut cord of pain laces through my arm, splitting the gristle of my shoulder. I turn around slowly, the room tilting on an uneven axis. Riika lets a small dagger drop from her hand, the blade of it thick with my blood.

"I'm sorry," she whispers. "He didn't want me to have to do it."

I sway on my feet, the ground lurching toward me and then shuddering away again. I don't need to ask to know that she doesn't mean the king.

"What did he offer you?" I bite out as my vision starts to ripple and fray.

Riika's eyes mist. Her lower lip trembles, jutting out beneath the icicle edge of her teeth.

"Nothing," she replies softly, voice tipping up so that the word is almost a question. "He just said it would make him very happy, if I were to help him, and that Godfather Life would reward me too."

I hear the sweet melody of her voice that half sings the words, and I see the flush in her cheeks, and I know that she is in love with him. I want to scream and shake her and tell her what a fool she is, this pitiable Northern girl, for thinking that Nándor might love her back. But I am too dizzy to speak.

Pressing down on the wound with my right hand, I push past her. The pressure of my fingers only makes it worse, so I tear a scrap of fabric from Jozefa's dress and knot it over the wound, fingers slick and trembling. I should kill her, I think, but I can't bring myself to. I am as stupid as she is, for coming to the capital at all, for believing that I was strong or clever enough to survive here.

A million thoughts gutter through my mind, each more terrible than the last. I drop to my knees and scramble to find the dagger before Riika can get to it again. I curl my bloody fingers around its hilt just as the door swings open, Nándor's boot steps calm and soft upon the floor.

# CHAPTER TWENTY

I try to stagger to my feet, but Nándor places a gentle hand on my shoulder, squeezing my wound with just enough force to make me gasp. Pain blankets my vision in white.

"Stay down," Nándor says. "I like the way you look when you're kneeling."

His nails feel as sharp as knives. I draw in a breath and reach for him, but before I can wrap my fingers around his wrist, he steps backward. The inertia sends me tumbling forward, catching myself on my hands. The floor is slick with my blood.

"How terribly heroic," I bite out, "to send a serving girl to do your ugly work for you."

Nándor stands up and walks over to where Riika has pressed herself against the wall, trembling. He runs a red-dyed finger down her cheek, and her face softens like challah bread fresh from the oven.

"I have friends everywhere, wolf-girl," he says, looking at me while he grips Riika's chin. "You should have figured that out by now."

Friends in the Woodsman barracks and in the king's council hall. I remember Count Reményi's knifepoint eyes, sharpening as they found me in the dark. I remember Zsigmond shaking under Nándor's stare, and the rabbi freezing like a frightened deer, and all the Yehuli children weeping. Anger cleaves through the pain.

"Then why did it take you so long to kill me?" I manage.

"You would have been dead your first day in the city if you'd been able to read my note," he says. "I left it at your door, but I forgot that you wolf-girls are as dumb as dead fish, and can't even spell your own names."

I make a sound that's almost a laugh: it was my own illiteracy that saved me, or at least prolonged my life. He must have invited me somewhere, perhaps pretending to be the king, and waited in the dark with a knife to cut my throat. And if he'd come to my room any other evening while I slept, he would have found it empty, too, since I have spent the past five nights at Zsigmond's house.

"It won't do you any good," I say. The room, his face, all of it is blinkering with pale stars. "Even if I'm dead, the king will never name you. Not when there's still a true-born son . . ."

I trail off, stuttering in agony. Nándor pushes off the wall and crouches down before me, his blue eyes so clear and cold I can almost see the ice in them still.

"Perhaps," he says. "Perhaps not. Either way, you will not be alive to see it. Nor will you be alive to see Yehuli Street looted and empty, or your village turned to ash."

I have no doubt that he means it, that he will turn his cold fire on Yehuli Street and Keszi the moment he gets the chance. I try to remember how many Woodsmen I saw in the crowd and calculate the number that the king still has on his side, but my mind feels like a frayed rope, only a few threads away from snapping.

"The king's real heir lives," I say, though my tongue tastes like copper and my eyes are starting to film. "And while he does, you have no chance of ever sitting the throne, unless you aim to rule by *pagan* right."

I hope to see even a trace of disconcert on Nándor's face, but he only smiles, such a beautiful, pure white smile that for just a moment I believe Szabín—that a chicken would bat its lashes at him while he butchered it.

"I know you have kept a close eye on my brother, as he has on you," Nándor says. "I haven't much wondered about why, since he came back to Király Szek with a bruise on his throat in the shape of your mouth."

He knows. Of course he knows. Fear runs bleakly up my spine.

"What do you think my brother will do, when he sees your body?" Very calmly, Nándor begins untying the make-shift bandage I have knotted over my own shoulder. "What concessions do you think he will grant me?"

"Maybe he'll thank you for it." My voice is hoarse, nearly inaudible. "Then he'll never have to confess to his sin. You'll have taken care of his shameful problem for him."

"I don't think so, wolf-girl," Nándor says. "I think that my brother will weep."

And then he digs his fingers into my wound, pressing deep through flesh and sinew, nearly down to the bone. A hot, breathtaking pain bursts across my eyes, blinding me. I scream, but the sound of it is muffled by the blood in my mouth.

Gáspár was right. Nándor will torture me to death or madness, whichever comes first, just to make him falter. Even after I'm dead, I will damn Gáspár. Maybe my corpse will be the very thing that gets him killed.

Nándor withdraws his fingers. His hand is gloved in scar-let down to the wrist, but beyond that his skin is white and unblemished, as pure as the year's first snow. He draws his hand up over my shoulder, along my collarbone, and closes a fist over my left breast.

"You missed," he says, and at first I don't realize that he's speaking to Riika, not me. "I told you to aim for her heart. But I think she will die anyway—there's certainly enough blood on my shirt."

The front of his dolman is flecked with red. Against the wall, Riika has started weeping, her eyes squeezed shut.

"I'm sorry," she whispers. I don't know if she's talking to Nándor at all.

The four fingers of my right hand curl over the stone floor. Above his collar, the pale column of Nándor's throat is inches from my face, taut with muscle.

"Or maybe you'll die first," I say, drawing my lips back to show my teeth.

I raise my hand and rip open his dolman, tearing through the silk as if I have claws. I tear right down to his bare chest, just as pale and bright as the rest of him, blue veins straining under his skin like water under ice. Ördög's threads go stiff around my wrist. Black marks feather across his skin in the shape of my fingers, my touch burning *him* right down to the bone. It's a wound deep enough to kill.

Riika screams. Nándor topples back, a soft gasp escaping his lips. Blood washes over his ruined dolman, spilling onto floor like strewn flower petals, the precise color of poured wine. The light begins to drain from his eyes, a white moon slivering away, and he raises his hands. I think he might beg me for mercy and I smile at the prospect, in spite of my own dizzying pain.

Instead, he clasps his hands together and utters a quiet prayer.

The wound on his chest stitches itself back up, an invisible needle strung with invisible thread. Where his face has gone gray with lost blood it flushes pink again, the vibrant pallor of a living man. His skin is as immaculate as a frozen lake on midwinter's coldest morning. Slowly, Nándor gets to his feet.

"Didn't I tell you I was holy?" he rasps, as if death has not yet receded from his throat. "Would you like to try and kill me again?"

I search his body—what I can see of it—for evidence of sacrifice, any small ruination that will help me make sense of what I have seen. But I find nothing. No missing eye like his brother, no scars like Szabín. No lopped finger like me. He is unmarred by the toll that power usually takes.

It's more terrifying than a thousand scars.

I collapse onto my hands and knees, quashed by fear and pain, as Nándor approaches me. He grasps the collar of my dress and hurls me onto my back, my wound flattening against the stone floor. My heart thrums so loudly in my ears that I can't even hear my own scream.

"I'll come back when you're cold, wolf-girl." Nándor's voice floats above me, his face blurring and doubling behind the glaze that's fallen over my eyes. "And then I'll bring my brother to weep over your corpse. Or perhaps I'll kill him first—if Godfather Death wills it."

I try to make a sound, any sound of protest, but my lungs are like shriveled violets. I hear Nándor's boots make their way toward the door, and then a softer set of footsteps, Riika scuttling after him. My vision ripples into black. Then there is the slide of a lock.


I don't know how much time has passed, as life eddies from me. With every breath I can taste the metallic tang of my own blood, suffusing the air like a red mist. Through the lattice of my wet lashes, I can see the hearth, the stone floor, my abandoned wolf cloak and plum dress. My own arm, stretched out limply like a fallen branch, still swathed in pale-green silk.

Ever since the moment that Virág had her vision, I knew that I would die here in Király Szek, cold and alone. But how could I have known what would happen in between? The stretch of snowy road between Keszi and the capital, flecked with bright moments, like fires in the dark. Gáspár holding me in the cradle of tree roots, his breath damp and warm against my ear. All the nights we spent on the ice, and his arm around my waist as he pulled me up out of the freezing water. His mouth on mine, the red juice staining both of our tongues. The way he kissed my throat so gently that it felt like he was apologizing for any pain I had ever felt, whether it was his fault or not. Zsigmond embracing me, Jozefa smoothing the skirt on my lap, Batya feeding me challah. Seeing my own name etched on paper for the first time.

I try to hold each of those moments in my mind, like a butterfly in amber, encasing them in timeless suspension. But when I die, they will die with me. And it seems so terribly unfair, to leave Zsigmond and Gáspár, to leave Batya and Jozefa, alone with only their bitter memories, carrying a pain meant for two people.

And then, skimming underneath all these mortal contemplations, is the unadulterated animal instinct: I don't want to die. Not now, not yet, at only five and twenty.

It is stubborn, bitter strength that forces me up, onto my knees and then my feet. I clamber toward the door. Pain is dragging at me like a wet dress. The door locks from the outside, to keep me in, a cow in her barn after all. I fumble at the iron handle, gathering all my will like kindling, and then setting it alight. The handle crumbles, and with it, the lock on the other side. The door groans open.

The relief of that small victory threatens to undo me. I slump against the wall, catching my breath, trying to make my vision steady. The hallway in front of me is feathering away between strands of black.

My plan forms in my body before it takes shape in my mind. I stumble down the corridor, one hand against the wall, blood painting a streak on the floor after me. I remember the way to Gáspár's room hazily, as if I learned it in a dream. When I reach his door I half collapse upon it, my knees weakening under me.

For a moment, I hear nothing on the other side. Maybe he's not there. Maybe Nándor has already come for him. Each terrible possibility runs itself ragged through my brain, and my vision has winnowed to nearly nothing by the time the door swings open, Gáspár standing openmouthed in the threshold.

"Évike," he says, catching me before I fall.

He leads me into his room, and I crumple onto his bed. If my mind weren't so pain-addled, and my lungs doing all their work just to keep me breathing, I would make a quip about someone finding the true-born prince with a wolf-girl in his bed. Even in my head, the jest is not half as clever as I would like.

My blood leaks onto his sheets. Gáspár holds my arm in his lap, gloved hands running over my wound.

"Tell me what to do," he says, and the helplessness in his voice nearly ruins me. "Tell me how to . . ."

"Take off your gloves," I manage, eyelids fluttering.

I watch him as he does, removing each one and letting them drift to the ground, limp as shed black feathers. "Why?" he asks. "What now?"

"No reason," I mumble. "I'm just tired of you wearing them."

He lets out a breath that is half annoyance, half exasperated amusement. When his bare fingers touch my skin through the dress, I feel them shaking.

"I have to stop the bleeding," he says. His hand presses hard over my wound, and I let out a whimper of pain. "I'm sorry. It's going to hurt. Try and bear it."

The fabric of my dress is so blood-drenched that I can see the shape of my wound beneath it, wide and clenching. Gáspár pulls at the silk, but the seams hold fast. I hear panic in the hitch of his breath and then he leans over me, mouth so close to my throat that I think for a startled moment he will draw his lips over my old scar again. Instead he takes the fabric between his teeth, incisor grazing my shoulder, and pulls until the sleeve of my dress flowers open.

I remember how Imre stuck the hilt of his knife into Peti's mouth and told him to bite down while Gáspár cut off his arm. Even then, even when he was only a Woodsman to me, there was horror and regret in his eye. Now Gáspár works with a black determination, his gaze narrowed to nothing but his hands and my bare, bleeding arm in front of him. He tears strips of fabric from his bedclothes and wraps them tight around my shoulder. The pain ebbs, if only slightly.

"I don't know," he says, his voice tight. "You've lost so much blood already . . ."

"It's my hunting arm," I say quietly. Even if I survive, I will never draw a bow again.

Gáspár's face crumples. In that moment he looks so miserable that I want to apologize for every little cut I have made in him, every drop of blood my words have drawn.

"What happened?" he whispers.

And so I tell him everything: about the Yehuli holiday and Nándor's mob, about Riika and the dagger, and every single one of his brother's threats, and worst of all, about his brother's terrifying power. Gáspár's brow furrows as I speak, his lips pressing together until they are nearly white. As the pain recedes further, tidewater drawing back from the shore, I become aware of his hand against my arm, his bare knuckles brushing my skin.

"He wants to kill you," I say at last, hoarse with exhaustion. "And then he'll banish all the Yehuli, and destroy Keszi."

Gáspár's jaw sets. "It won't be as easy for him as he thinks."

"What do you mean?"

"I'm not as daft as you imagine me, Évike," he says, but his tone is gentle. "I have Miklós and Ferenc switch off guarding my door while I sleep. I don't eat anything unless I have procured it myself. When I must attend feasts, I let the wine touch my lips but I never swallow it. I know that I am what stands between Nándor and the crown, and that he will do anything to get his hands around my throat."

My mouth goes dry. "He thought that killing me would make you drop your guard."

Gáspár nods, just once, and doesn't meet my eyes.

"None of it matters now." A bolt of pain runs through me, and I shiver. "He's too powerful. There's no way to stop him. Even my magic was nothing against him."

"Then you must let the king have her," Gáspár says. "Your seer. It's not the power of the turul, but it is enough to help my father hold on to his crown."

"Katalin," I say, my voice dropping like a stone kicked off a cliff. "Her name is Katalin."

I see Gáspár's face shift from bewilderment to realization, and then, abruptly, it hardens. "The girl who tormented you. The one who gave you that scar."

His thumb brushes my left eyebrow, split by white scar tissue. Memories of blue flame bubble up, but they don't wound me like they once did, now that I know Katalin is sitting in the king's dungeon, perhaps even fettered in the same cell that I was.

"If I let her die, then I might as well admit that Virág was right," I say. The confession of it feels shameful, poisonous, but Gáspár's expression doesn't change. "That she was right to cast me out, and that all of us wolf-girls are nothing more than warm bodies. Besides, it's the same thing I told your father: a seer's magic is not what you think. It will give the king only a fraction of the turul's power."

"Évike, think of what you're saying."

"I *am*," I bite out, anger and despair washing over all the pain. "Don't you understand how much I have thought of it? If I save Katalin, I will lose any power I have in this city, any sway over the king's mind, and any ability to protect the Ye-huli. To protect my father, I . . ." I can't bring myself to admit what I am thinking: that when Zsigmond told me the story of the clay-man, he was begging *me* to be the one to save them this time. "You have no idea how much I have considered the weight of my words."

Gáspár pulls away from me, lifting his chin. For a moment, his eye is as hard as obsidian. "You think I don't understand? You were the one who told me, so long ago, that we were the same. You wielded that revelation like a weapon against me. My every action is a choice between honoring my mother and serving my father. You would be hard-pressed to find anyone who knows this strife better."

Mortified, I press my lips together. I hadn't thought he would remember my words so well, the words I hurled at him in anger, not knowing how much they would sting.

"I'm sorry," I say, staring down at the floor. "For that and a thousand other petty cruelties."

Gáspár doesn't reply, but I hear the shift in his breathing. I feel like a blacksmith, everything I know laid out in pieces in front of me, and somehow I must forge a weapon from them. But any blade that I make will be double-edged. I cannot help Katalin without hurting my father. I cannot save the pagans without damning the Yehuli. And the only thing I know that might be strong enough to stop Nándor is a hundred miles away in Kaleva, just an orange flyspeck on the gray horizon.

I don't know when I have become something so burdened by other people's hopes and loyalties and lives. It almost makes me weep to think of it, how many people will die or be thrown out if I choose wrong. My head bows over my bent knees, pain still crawling up my arm like a glut of blackflies.

"The worst thing Nándor will do to the Yehuli is banish them." My words taste so bitter I think I might die before I finish speaking them. "But he wants to burn Keszi to the ground."

Gáspár gives a slow nod. His hand inches toward mine, but it only brushes the absence of my pinky. The space between us feels smaller than it ever has. If he knelt before his father to beg for my life, it seems only fair that I should humble myself to him now.

"Please," I say. But when I raise my head, I see from the look on his face that he has already agreed.

Long shadows chase us down the hall, wraithlike fingers snatching at my wolf cloak. I don't know if Nándor has already realized that I am gone, but I can't waste the time turning around to check. I don't stop until we've reached the top of the stairs that lead down into the dungeon, and even then, it's only for a moment, to catch my breath. The wound on my shoulder is burning like a brand. I half walk, half stumble down the steps, reaching out for Gáspár to steady myself. My eyes keep fuzzing over the pinpricks of torchlight on the wall.

Katalin is in the same cell that I was, huddled against the mold-slick wall. Her pale hair is damp and tangled, and there's another bruise pulsing on her perfect cheekbone. When she sees me, she rises, eyes sapphire bright and full of embattled loathing.

"What are you doing here?" she asks, voice low. "Come to deliver me to the king? How long were you in the capital before you decided to kneel to him?"

Her cruelty makes me regret my decision, but only for an eyeblink. I cannot watch another wolf-girl die, not even Katalin. I step forward and wrap my hand around the iron bar of her cell, Ördög's threads going taut around my wrist. I close my eyes, and when I open them again, the bar is gone. I'm holding on to nothing, but my palm is orange with rust.

"How?" Katalin stutters out. "Could you always—"

"Do you think I would have endured half your wickedness

if I could?" I interrupt, gritting my teeth as another wave of pain rocks through me. "Follow me."

"Follow you *where*?" Her gaze darts between Gáspár and me. "I'm not going anywhere with you, or a Woodsman."

Anger curdles in my belly. Despite my wooziness, I reach through the bars and grab her with my good arm, yanking her out of the cell.

"I'm *saving your life*," I snap. "One more word and I'll change my mind."

Katalin fixes me with a cool stare. She slowly extricates herself from my grasp and then wipes her borrowed wolf cloak clean.

"Your hand is covered in blood," she says.

This time, I scarcely resist the urge to strangle her and save King János the trouble. I look up at Gáspár, as if to steel myself, and the resolve on his face invigorates me. When we turn to walk back up the dungeon stairs, I hear the soft padding of Katalin's footsteps behind us. She doesn't speak again until we reach the top of the steps.

"You *are* bleeding," she says, eyes wide.

I only nod, not particularly keen on explaining that I lost a battle of blades with a tiny serving girl.

"Here," Katalin says. She pushes back my wolf cloak—*her* wolf cloak—and unties Gáspár's makeshift wrappings underneath. I take a deep breath before looking at the wound, an ugly gash like an old woman's blackened mouth. But Katalin only waves a hand over it, and the cut stitches itself shut.

I am deciding whether to thank her when Gáspár jerks me back into the threshold. A Woodsman's shadow passes across the torchlit wall.

"How do you plan on getting us out of here?" Katalin demands, once the shadow has vanished.

"There's another way out of the city," says Gáspár. "Through the Woodsman barracks."

I laugh at him openly. "You must be joking."

"*He's* joking?" Katalin scoffs. "What was your plan?"

There is enough blood left in my body for me to flush.

"They've all gone now," Gáspár says, before Katalin can ridicule me further. "There are only the Woodsmen in my father's retinue, who are stationed around the palace at night, and the ones loyal to Nándor, who are still at his side. The barracks are empty."

Katalin makes a derisive sound, but she doesn't argue. And then Gáspár leads us through the palace halls and down into another cellar, this one furnished with wood and crammed full of cots. Filmy bubbles of torchlight yellow the walls, illuminating the racks of weapons. Ax blades glint in blind crescents. Every mounded shadow looks like it could be a Woodsman in his black suba, but there are no footsteps on the ground except our own. Distantly, I hear a trickling of water, and as we go on, I see the wooden floors give way to slick gray stone. Like the church, the barracks have been built into the cliffside.

We gather what we can: a bow and quiver for me, a sword for Gáspár. Katalin's mouth pinches shut as she watches; I can tell that she is repulsed by the prospect of wielding a Woodsman blade. Mercifully, she has not mentioned the wolf cloak that was once hers strung over my back. I was sure to retrieve it before we went down to the dungeon, its white fur matted with my blood. Maybe Katalin thinks me more worthy of it now.

My breath comes in white clouds as we pause at the mouth of a tunnel. Now that the pain has ebbed and my mind has cleared, there is room for all my misgivings, all my bewilderment and despair. I think of Yehuli Street and the taste of challah bread. I think of the star-dappled temple ceiling and the way my father held me to his chest. I may be damning them all.

"Évike." Gáspár's voice is stern, but not ungentle. "You have to come now. You've already made your choice."

He is right, though the thought of it makes me want to weep. I follow him through the tunnel and out the other side, stepping into the cool wash of moonlight. Katalin's hair and cloak are as pale as a dewy pearl.

Numbly, we go to the stables, saddling three black Woodsman steeds. They stomp the earth with a sound like far-off thunder. As we mount them, I stare and stare at the sweep of the landscape before us, the flat grasslands of Akosvár and the craggy topography of Szarvasvár. Beyond it, farther than I can see, winter is holding Kaleva in its white-toothed maw.

Above us, the city bells begin to sound. They are certainly spreading the word of our escape, of the missing seer, the cunning wolf-girl, the traitorous prince. Something hard and hot rises in my throat.

Gáspár's brow is as heavy as a storm cloud, but his jaw is held tight. He spurs his horse on, and Katalin and I follow, leaving Király Szek behind.

# CHAPTER TWENTY-ONE

We ride hard until dawn, when morning light glides down the yellow hills of Szarvasvár and we and our horses are all too exhausted to take another step. I half topple off my horse and kneel on the soft, cool grass. A stream of silver-blue water threads down the mountainside, and when I can summon the strength I pad over to it and take a long drink. The wind feels fierce on my face, stinging the skin that has been rubbed raw by tears.

Katalin, to her credit, says nothing. She hasn't spoken a word since we left Király Szek, though I can feel her chagrin mounting with each passing moment, her eyes narrowed as thin as knife slits. She joins me by the water, to drink and wash her hands, which are burned red with bristly rope marks from having her fingers locked so tightly around the reins. Her gaze trains on my missing pinky.

"So that's what you did," she says. "Mutilated yourself like some Woodsman."

I curl my hand into a fist, flushing. "What makes you think I did it to myself?"

"It just seems like something you would do."

"Well, you gave me plenty of practice in enduring pain," I say, but I can't imbue the words with the venom that I want. "Have you known all this time, that this was a way to get magic?"

"I suspected." Katalin lifts one shoulder under her wolf cloak; her eyes are circled with sleepless bruises. "Our magic always takes something from us, but I see that Ördög's ways are a bit more extreme."

I think of Virág thrashing in my lap, of Boróka falling into her long, impermeable slumbers. Of course, Virág would never want to highlight what magic cost us, only what we could gain, how it protected us. She talked around the truth, shrouding it in stories of Vilmötten and his great feats. But thinking of Vilmötten makes me think of Nándor, and my stomach folds over on itself, chest tightening like a vise.

Gáspár hunches beside us and fills one of the calfskin flasks hanging on the horse's saddle. Katalin draws herself up again, wiping her mouth, and levels him with a baleful stare.

"So, Woodsman," she says. "What have you been offered in exchange for helping a wolf-girl? I don't think Évike has much to bargain with, except her body."

I'm not sure if she's talking about my pinky or something else, but Gáspár goes red from forehead to chin. Either way, her barbed words make me wish, for a fleeting moment, that I had left her in Király Szek to die.

"He's not a Woodsman," I snap. "He's the prince. Bárány Gáspár. And do you know what his father would have done to you, if he hadn't helped me save your life? He would have torn off all your fingernails to adorn his crown, then slit your throat on the floor of his feast hall."

Katalin inhales sharply; she looks not quite mortified, but it's better than nothing. "Still, what does the prince have to gain from saving a wolf-girl?"

With a roiling belly I tell her everything: about making

my vow to the king, about the counts and the Woodsmen, about Nándor. I leave out all the parts about the Yehuli and my father—they are too painful to speak aloud, and it would feel like a betrayal if I did. Those moments are for me alone to hold, precious as the last ember in a bed of ash. And I cannot swallow the shame of leaving them behind. When I speak of Nándor, Katalin's lips go taut.

"I tried to kill him," I say, holding up my four-fingered hand. My voice is shaking. "His skin was burned off, right down to the bone. His blood was on the ground. But all he did was pray, and he was new again."

And he had no scars, no evidence of the sacrifice that had bought him such power. All I can think of are his eyes, the edges of them still iced and white, bright with the memory of his death. Perhaps the black, silent moment when his heart stopped beating, before the Érsek dragged him out of the water, has earned him greater blessings than any spilled blood. Perhaps what he believes about himself is true. When Vilmötten cheated death it made him immortal, too, something close to a god.

"If he's so powerful, it seems a poor choice to leave the king unguarded in your absence," says Katalin. "What's to stop him from taking the throne now?"

"Me," Gáspár says. "If he takes the throne while I'm still breathing, he's compromised all that he stands for. Patrician law decrees that it must be the eldest son, the true-born son. But even if he kills me, his reign will be plagued by doubt and uncertainty. What he really wants is for me to step aside willingly, then live the rest of my life in exile or obscurity, until he can have me killed later, when everyone has stopped paying attention."

I feel as if I've been scraped clean of anger and hate, scraped clean of everything but exhaustion. Fear. "And then he can massacre the pagans as he pleases."

Gáspár nods. A silence falls over us, the wind bristling

through the dead grass. Finally, Katalin says, "It might have been a lot simpler if you'd only left me to die."

I choke out a laugh. "Are you sincerely saying you'd rather I let the king slit your throat?"

"No," Katalin says. The bruise on her cheek is throbbing violet. "I'm only saying that you could easily have left me. It's what Virág would have done."

My mouth opens mutely, then closes again. Katalin has turned away from me, staring off into the distance, at the clouds gathering like fat white birds on the horizon. I think it is the closest she will ever come to thanking me.

"The king would not have been able to end the war with your magic anyway," I say. "He didn't understand that a seer can't choose her visions."

Katalin's lips quiver. "That's not quite true."

"What do you mean?"

"Well, sometimes visions will come when we least expect them," she goes on slowly. "But there are ways to force them. Just like cutting off your pinky—surely you remember how Virág would go down to the river."

I frown at her, trying to conjure the memory. It comes back to me in jagged pieces, just a flash of Virág's six fingers, her knees blackened with river mud. Her white hair spidering out through the water. Someone's hand on the back of her neck.

"Yes," I say, feeling my stomach fill with a slick nausea.

"So it's no perfect method, but what about the gods' magic is perfect, anyway?" Katalin runs a hand through her hair. "You can ask a question, and if you offer enough of yourself, the gods will give you some kind of hazy answer."

"But it's not the omniscience that my father imagines," says Gáspár. His eye shifts uneasily between Katalin and me. "And it's not enough to stop Nándor either."

"No," Katalin says. Her mouth twists, certainly displeased that she has agreed with a Woodsman.

I stare down at the water, the gray sky reflected on its murky surface. The clouds wash downriver. Quietly, I say, "But the turul is."

I expect Katalin to scowl, to swear. To laugh in derision at my suggestion. But she only arches her eyebrow at me, bemused. "I thought you loathed all of Virág's stories with every bone in your body."

"I didn't loathe her stories. Only that I was made to hear them so many times. And that they were coming from Virág's wicked mouth." But I don't know whether I mean the words or not. I hated Virág's stories because I never felt like they belonged to me. "Anyway, that doesn't matter. The turul will give us enough power to stop Nándor, if we can find it and kill it."

Gáspár's breathing quickens. I know he wants to argue with me, to tell me that the Woodsmen have been searching for ages and have never found a trace, to remind me how we already tried to find it and failed. He stays silent, though. Katalin blinks her disbelief.

"Even if that were true, what makes you think you can find the turul?" Her nostrils flare, and for a moment it feels like the old days again: her preening, me scowling, our shared history littered with slurs and bolts of blue flame.

"I can't find it," I tell her, drawing a breath. "But you can."

Confusion creases Katalin's perfect face. It takes her a moment, gaze traveling over me and down to the water, then back up to me again. Then she hardens, her eyes like bits of ice.

"Don't let me drown," she says.

I'm so relieved, I almost laugh. "What if this was my grand plan all along, to save you from the king's hands so I could kill you myself? I might have the perversity for such a thing, but not the forethought."

Katalin sniffs. "I could hardly blame you for having your vengeance."

And this, I suspect, is the closest she will ever come to an apology. Gáspár watches stone-faced as Katalin unpins her wolf cloak, letting it slide to the ground. She bundles her hair up onto her head, baring the pale column of her throat.

"What do you mean to do?" Gáspár asks.

"There is a way to trigger a vision," I tell him. My hands are trembling as they move toward Katalin's neck. "I never realized it before, but I know how it's done. She'll have to hold the question in her mind."

Katalin nods. Her fingers have dug into the riverbed. "I'm ready."

I nod back at her, steeling myself. Something passes between us then, lacing out between her chest and mine, a thread of tenuous trust.

And then I clasp my hand around her throat and force her head underwater.

Katalin submerges without struggle, her hair spilling from her head in pale rivulets. Bubbles foam around her. I hold her there for so long that even my arm starts to ache, and I feel the tense of her throat under my hand, and then finally, finally, I yank her up again.

She gasps and splutters, coughing up river water. Her eyes are misted, still half-white, and her body shudders violently with the ebbing of her vision. There is a reed pasted to her cheek and I have the urge to wipe it away, but I quash whatever gentle instinct has risen in me unbidden.

Wet-faced, Katalin groans. Gáspár watches in bridled panic, eye too bright. After another few beats, Katalin's shaking ceases.

"I saw it," she rasps. "The turul. Flying between the black pines, against a pure-white sky."

My heart quickens. "Are you certain? Do you know where to go?"

"Of course I'm certain," Katalin snaps. "You're not a seer, so you wouldn't understand, but a vision isn't something you can forget. Every single vision I've ever had plays on the insides of my eyelids when I try to sleep at night."

Despite the sharpness of her voice, for once I truly pity her. Katalin wrings water from her hair, fingers still quivering between the white strands. Gáspár rises to his feet, flask in hand.

"You lead the way, then," he says. "But we'll need to hurry. Nándor's men won't be very far behind."

Slowly, Katalin stands too. I take another moment before I follow them, staring up at the sky. The sun's red eye is like a drop of blood in the river, the clouds streaming sickly pink around it. My mind goes back to Zsigmond's house, and I imagine that I am sitting there with him practicing my letters, Régyar and Yehuli both. I let the image fill me up and then I let it go, scattering it like flower petals into the wind.

The snow starts falling later that day, the sky going sleek and gray. The ground mottles with new frost, crunching under our horses' hooves. The hills have begun to flatten, racing toward a distant white horizon. Somewhere farther north, the Kalevans have hunkered down for true winter, Tuula and Szabín among them. I imagine that Bierdna is running out in front of us, flicking snowflakes off her ears. I follow the dark shape of her, invisible to anyone but me, with a fierce, unblinking determination.

I worry over the prospect of a storm, but snowfall lightens and then shivers away. Gauzy ribbons of cloud wrap around the sun, and light comes straining through like milk through cheesecloth. Katalin brings her horse to my side and then nudges me, pointing wordlessly over her shoulder. I turn around. Our footsteps have frozen in the snow, leaving a miles-long trail behind us. A wave of despair runs over me.

Gáspár must see it written on my face, because he says, "Let's stop for now."

There's no way to erase the trail that we have left, and it's not snowing hard enough to cover our tracks in time, which means that Nándor's men will have a path guiding them right to us. I feel a hopeless anguish unspooling in me. I clamber down off my horse and tie her to a nearby tree with numbing fingers.

I think it might be a relief to cry, but all my tears have been spent in silence during the ride, my hood pulled up over my face so neither Gáspár nor Katalin could see. Instead, I reach for the bow strapped to my horse's back. The familiar tensing of my muscles and the twang of the bow string in my ear will comfort me better than anything else now.

"I'll hunt," I say.

Gáspár and Katalin nod their agreement, both pink-faced and grim. I move through the copse of bare, frost-dewed trees, listening for sounds of scuffling in the snow, watching for bright, blinking eyes. I catch two gamy rabbits, their patchy fur coming off in my hands. By the time I return, the sun is a band of gold along the horizon and Katalin has kindled a fire. Gáspár is whispering something to her, his mouth not far from her ear. She has a hardened look on her face, a tiny furrow between her brow.

I drop the dead rabbits by the fire and warm my hands. Katalin comes over to me, her borrowed wolf cloak sweeping up small flurries of new snow.

"What did he say to you?" I ask.

"He said he was sorry," she replies.

"For what?"

"For terrifying us all our lives," Katalin says. "I suppose he ought to apologize for it, being the prince. I could have done without his mooning eyes, though. Well, *eye*."

Something like a laugh coils in my belly, but I am too exhausted to loose it past my lips. Besides, I don't want Katalin to think that I will forgive her so easily, or that saving her life means I have any interest in being friends.

My gaze wanders to Gáspár, still standing beside the horses. We are not very far now from the woods where we encountered the beautiful girl who was a monster. I wonder if he is thinking of it too. My arm still throbs with an irregular, phantom pain, soothed by the memory of his hands pressing gently over the wound.

Katalin and I skin and gut the rabbits in silence, and Gáspár keeps his distance. Perhaps he has regretted agreeing to this plan; maybe he doubts Katalin's vision. I can't let myself think of what will happen if we fail, but my stomach churns like white water and I only manage a few bites of rabbit. Zsigmond's face keeps drifting across my mind.

Night comes over our scrubby patch of forest with a vengeance, blanketing us in a swift and total blackness. Once the sun is down, we warm ourselves for a few more heady, stolen moments before we have to stamp out the fire again. Nándor's men would see the light of it from miles away. Katalin offers to take the first watch, so I pad down beside a mangled midwinter tree, my back against the frozen bark. Sleep seems both inescapably tempting and utterly impossible.

I don't know how long it is before Gáspár joins me. His boots tread through the frost. There is only the jeweled scattering of starlight, and the pallid horn of the moon. His face holds what light it can, silver on his cheeks and the curve of his nose, the rigid line of his jaw. He stands before me and doesn't speak, so I push myself to my feet, brushing snow from my skirts.

I have so much to say to him and also nothing at all. Our breaths cloud with cold. Words constellate in my mind, sibilant and bright.

"Would you like to hear a story?"

The stories always began in the dark. Virág's six-fingered hands could make shadow puppets that the rest of us could not: turul hawks, racka sheep, stags with their huge coronets of bone. We watched their silhouettes dance across the thatched roof of her hut, fire warming our cheeks, wild-haired and wild-eyed, our noses running from the cold. The memory cows me for a moment, making something deep in my belly twist with pain.

Gáspár blinks slowly. "All right."

"I'll tell you about Vilmötten and his flaming sword." Even the name *Vilmötten* tastes sour on my tongue as I think of Nándor's body floating up from the ice, just the way the bard crawled out of the Under-World.

"I think I already know it," he says. "My wet nurse had an endless number of stories, and that was one of her favorites."

"Was your wet nurse a pagan?"

"Certainly not," he says. "The way she told it, Vilmötten prayed to the Prinkepatrios for a weapon with which to defeat Régország's pagan enemies, and all the world's nonbelievers, and so Godfather Life granted him a blade that was unbreakable, and could catch fire when he held it up to the light of the sun."

For a moment I want to tell him that it's not right, that Vilmötten was *our* hero, not theirs. But I think of the counts in their bear cloaks and feathered mantles, and of the king in his fingernail crown. You can't hoard stories the way you hoard gold, despite what Virág would say. There's nothing to stop anyone from taking the bits they like, and changing or erasing the rest, like a finger smudging over ink. Like shouts drowning out the sound of a vicious minister's name.

I ought to ask him whether he thinks we can find the turul, if we will succeed now where we failed before. But there's another question burning in my throat like a held breath.

"Do you remember those nights on the ice?" I ask. "When we almost froze to death under a pitch-black sky like this one? Did you love me then, or hate me?"

Gáspár's throat bobs in the dark.

"I hated you then," he says. "For being the only warm, bright thing for miles."

"What about on the Little Plain?" I ask. "When you killed Kajetán to save me?"

"I must have hated you then too," he says. "For making me trade my soul for your life."

I nod, but there's a burning in my chest. I'm not sure how much longer I can play this game, even if I want to know the truth more than anything. In the stories, there are always three tasks, three questions, three chances to damn yourself or to cheat death, or to win a bargain with a trickster god.

"And what about when you pulled me out of the water?" I ask. "After I fell through the frozen lake?"

Gáspár grips his own wrist, palm covering the pale tracery of scars. Silence swans over us. For a moment I wonder if he won't answer me at all.

"I think I loved you then," he says. "And I hated myself for it."

His voice flickers like a flame in the wind, sparking up and then blowing flat again. I remember precisely when I realized how beautiful he was, both of us shivering wet and drenched in cold white light. Now I feel the darkness bending and folding around us, black as a Woodsman's suba.

"But you followed me here." My own voice is a whisper. "What a foolish thing for a pious prince to do."

A breath comes out of him. "You've made me a fool many times over."

My instinct is to laugh; all of his foolishness is couched in loyalty and humility, his stubborn virtues and steadfast, noble promises. I wish I could say the same of myself. I take a step toward him, my nose level with his chin. Since we have kissed before, I know exactly how much closer I would have to move in order to meet his mouth, and how his lips would part if I did, and the low sound that I might draw out of him as he braced his arms around my waist.

Instead, I speak. "Do you love me now?"

"Yes," he says. There is some of his prince's petulance to the word, like he has to stop himself from scowling at me as he says it. Below it, a gentleness, like the way his mouth ran over the scar on my throat.

"Do you desire me?"

Before we went to the dungeons, I returned to my chamber to reclaim my wolf cloak, and to change from Jozefa's ruined dress to the new one the king had sewn for me. Gáspár had turned his back as I stripped off the pale silk, baring my skin and breasts to the stone wall, but when he turned again I saw him flushed all the way to his ear tips, his lower lip bitten and bloody.

"Yes," he says.

I swallow. "And will you follow me further into the cold?"

Gáspár's chin lifts, eye going to the star-wild sky and then back to me again. He swallows, the bronze skin of his throat shuddering in the frosted light.

"Yes," he says finally.

Something warm spreads itself through my body, deeper in my marrow and blood. It is not as quick and bright as joy, the sudden burst of flint touching tinder; it is more like an old tree set alight in the summer, fire crawling through the gnarls and whorls of all that black wood. A bit of my own petulance flowers up.

"I won't believe you," I say, "unless you kneel."

Very slowly, Gáspár lowers himself to the ground. His boots leave long tracks in the snow. He looks up at me, shoulders rising and falling, waiting.

I take another step toward him, close enough that the silk of my dress feathers against his cheek. I cup my hands around his face, my thumb grazing the edge of his eye patch. Gáspár flinches once, almost imperceptibly, but he doesn't pull away.

Gáspár's hands wander too. They go under my skirt,

running up the backs of my thighs, his fingers tracing the grid of scars there. I tense, and he feels it, stilling himself against my skin.

"Where did you get these?" he asks quietly.

"I was punished often," I say. "For talking back, for running away. I was terrible and rude and you would probably think I deserved most of them."

He manages a laugh that looks like pale smoke in the frigid air. "That sounds like the sort of punishment a Patritian would dream up."

I close my eyes. Gáspár lifts my dress up around my hips, and I gasp as his mouth skims the inside of my thigh. A thrill of pleasure rolls through me, his mouth going higher, finding its place between my legs. I let out a soft moan, a whimper. His tongue trails hotly through me. And then I drop to my knees beside him, hands clutching at his face, and kiss him fiercely on the lips.

Without breaking our kiss, I bear him down into the snow, his cloak fanning out over the frozen earth. I can only think of how much I want to be closer to him, to have him hold me against the cold like he did so many nights in Kaleva. He kisses my jaw and my throat. I wonder if he thinks of his Woodsman oath as I straddle him, his hands moving under my dress and over my breasts. His thumb brushes my nipple and I make a stammering noise against his mouth, needy and breathless.

"Will you disavow me this time?" I ask him, my hair branching over both of us, like the soft limbs of a willow tree. "Will you push me away and tell me never to speak of it again, and prattle on and on about how touching my body blackened your soul?"

I hadn't expected that old hurt to flare in me, or the way my voice shakes with each word. Gáspár's face creases.

"You've killed any part of me that was a devout and loyal

Woodsman," he says. There is pain threaded through his voice; I imagine the Prinkepatrios fading from his mind, like a moon paring away in the black sky. His hand shifts from my breast, closing into a fist over my heart. "This is all that's left now."

No one since my mother has spoken to me so sweetly, not even Virág on her warmest days, and certainly none of the men I've lain with by the riverside, who only whispered their rote flattery in the dark. Somehow it makes me want to weep. I touch my forehead to his, fingers sliding under the band of his trousers.

"Do you still pray?"

He shudders as I grasp him, eye flashing. "Sometimes."

"Pray for me, then," I say, my chest tightening, "and for my father and everyone on Yehuli Street, and for all of Keszi too."

It is treachery to ask it, to suggest that his god is as real as mine, but since leaving Keszi I have seen so many kinds of power and magic that I never could have dreamed before. I have even learned to shape the letters of my name. Besides, the worse treachery is kissing a Woodsman, and I have already done that and more.

"I will," he says. His lips graze my temple, and I hear his huff of breath as I sink myself onto him. He knots his fingers into my hair. "I will."

When morning comes, my wet lashes are clumped with frost and Gáspár is gone. I sit up with a terrible start, fear pooling in my belly before I see him hunched over the fire, several yards away. A fine layer of snow has gathered on the stubbled grass, glittering like a Patritian woman's jeweled veil. I hope that the second flurry was enough to cover our tracks.

Katalin is perched on a sharp gray rock, frost growing

over it like pale lichen. In one hand, she holds a long, shining sword, its silver blade a blinding mirror for all the snow. She must have forged it last night, wrapping it in the steady rhythm of her song.

"What?" she says when she sees me looking. "I'm not going to leave the task of killing the turul up to you."

I roll my eyes and turn away.

"Because the gods will certainly be furious with whoever does it," Katalin goes on. "I can endure some of Isten's fury, but you are already half-cursed and I wouldn't wish a greater burden on you."

My body tenses, but I don't spit back at her or scowl. As far as I can tell, this is Katalin's version of kindness.

While Gáspár waters and saddles the horses, I drag a big stick down from the mangled tree and whet one of its ends to a point. Then I find a clear patch of snow and begin to etch my letters into it. I start with my name, and the easy familiarity of it settles into my bones like good wine. Then I try more Régyar. I've never seen most of the words before, but I can match the sounds to letters. Katalin watches me with a cool, guarded interest, but Gáspár strides over and looks at the words from over my shoulder.

"Did your father teach you that?" he asks.

I nod. I concentrate and etch his name into the snow. G-Á-S-P-Á-R. I think I have spelled it right.

Gáspár smiles when he sees it, chewing the inner corner of his mouth. "You write nearly as well as my littlest brother."

I elbow him fiercely in the side. "If you teach me how to spell, I'll teach you how to shoot an arrow as well as any clumsy, one-armed child in Király Szek, which is probably the best you can hope for."

Gáspár laughs then, and Katalin laughs, too, like a preening white bird on her perch.

We pack up our campsite, burying the ashy remains of our fire and heaping snow over the dark patches that our sleeping bodies have made. But I hesitate before scrubbing away the words I have scratched into the frost. I stand there for one long cold moment, the wind sweeping ice and sharp pine smell from the north, staring at our names written there beside each other, as clear and bright as anything.

## CHAPTER TWENTY-TWO

The tundra stretches out before us like a long tract of silvery sky, cloudy mounds of snow banked on its surface. I've counted six days since we left Király Szek, and overhead, the real sky is the gray color of water that's been wrung through someone's dirty laundry, flat as a mirror without any of a mirror's luster. Small tufts of brittle grass peek through the frost, but our horses trample them as they pass, or else eat them right down to the roots. The horses are hungrier than we are. I can find the burrows of winter-fat rabbits and slumbering squirrels, but there will be nothing green here again until spring.

I try to mark the places that we have passed before, remembering a rocky overhang where Gáspár and I sheltered one night, wrapped together for warmth, or a small ravine that had once been a river, the old waters etching a permanent groove into the earth. If I stare all the way to the horizon, I can glimpse the dark silhouette of the pine forest, trees bristling against the vicious wind. Gáspár keeps a steady pace beside me, and my eyes dart to his with an animal's unconscious twitch, just to make sure he's still there. I would rather be looking at him than thinking of what we left behind in Király Szek, or about Nándor's men snarling through the snow after us, or about the dangers of the forest ahead. His presence soothes me, though only by a small measure.

Katalin has taken to her role of guiding us with a true táltos's steely determination, her horse pacing out several yards ahead of ours and her face ever forward, like an arrow aiming true. Once the sparse daylight winnows away, the sky goes dark and the snow starts to fall with such ferocity that it feels as if Isten himself is hurling handfuls of it down upon us. At the very least it covers our tracks, and we ride doggedly through it, but I begin to think that it *is* some sort of divine punishment. If Isten can read our intent, he must be trying to stop us. Katalin doesn't do very much to dispel the notion.

"There will be some vengeance for killing it," Katalin says, as we bed down to steal a few precious hours of slumber before riding on. "There must be. The gods won't let you have anything for free."

"Did you see that in your vision?" I ask, half-hopeful and half-despaired.

"No," she says. "Only the path to the pine forest where the trees grow as wide around as huts, and tall enough to brush the highest clouds."

"What is the power that's worth risking your gods' vengeance?" Gáspár's voice is level, but I see the flicker in his eye.

"The power to see," says Katalin. "To see everything. What has happened before and what is happening now in the most far-off places you can imagine and what will happen in a day or a year or even a moment. You could even read the thoughts in men's minds. That's the sort of power your father was going to kill me for, even though I don't have it. No seer does. Only the turul."

Gáspár leans back against the rock that we've sheltered ourselves beneath. I have the urge to bury myself in his chest, but I feel oddly afraid to reveal my affections in front of Katalin. Though she has nothing to gain from hurting me now, I can tell by the cut of her gaze she thinks me a traitor, a slave to the Woodsmen and the Crown. I swallow hard instead.

"It would be like burning your chapel to the ground," I say. "Or looting Saint István's corpse. Killing the turul is like defiling something sacred, something we all spin toward like a compass point."

Katalin makes a derisive sound in the back of her throat; I know she is taking offense at me comparing the turul to any of the Patrifaith's holy symbols.

Overhead, the sky is turning to a riot of color, ribbons of green and purple light wavering across it. The Juvvi believe that when whales in the Half-Sea breach the surface of the dark water, they're so elated at the sight of the stars above them that they let out streams of rainbow light through their blowholes, winking radiance into the night. The Juvvi think this a good omen, portending a bountiful fishing season, a glut of silver-backed fish squirming in their twined nets. I don't know what sort of future this portends for me.

"We can't rest for very long," Gáspár says. "Nándor's men will be close behind."

I nod, my eyes watering with the sting of the wind. I am about to lie back and rest my head on my arms when I hear Katalin gasp softly. She tips backward into the snow, little more than a heap of wolf fur and thrashing limbs, her pupils gone empty and white.

It is mere instinct that moves me, primed after so many years of watching Virág succumb to her visions. I kneel beside Katalin and roll her head into my lap, even as she flails, her mouth gaping open and then closing again silently, as if she's gasping for air.

Gáspár draws a short, sharp breath. "Is this what it's like every time?"

"Yes," I say, as Katalin's phantom hand nicks a chunk of flesh from my cheek, the bloody skin wedged beneath her fingernail. I think about how I held Virág the same way, and then how I held the secret of her writhing weakness close to me, too, so that no one else had to know the truth of what happened behind the walls of her hut in the dark. My fingers close around Katalin's wrists, pinning her arms to the ground. Gáspár grabs hold of her ankles until the shaking stops and her eyes slide shut.

When she opens them again, her eyes are blue, only wider and colder than before, as if the chill air snuck into her as the vision flooded out.

"Katalin," I manage. "What did you see?"

She flings herself up and rolls away from me, panting. "A tree, its trunk soaked in blood. And you—Évike, you were the one to kill it. The turul."

The realization is like a rush of freezing lake water. I want to fight it, to armor myself against its truth, but a seer's visions have never been wrong before. Gáspár lays a hand on the small of my back.

"I'm sorry," I say.

Katalin's eyes thin. Her white hair is pasted to her forehead with cold sweat. "What are you apologizing for?"

"Well—" I begin, but then I stop, because I'm not exactly sure either.

"I never apologized to you," she says.

Stiffening, I say, "I don't suppose you'll do it now, though."

"No," she concedes. She draws herself into a sitting position, knees against her chest, still managing, somehow, to look down her nose at me. "But I won't taunt you for making besotted eyes at a Woodsman, or even for lying with one, if that's as true as I suspect. As it is in the Upper-World, so it is in the Under-World."

Gáspár's brow furrows. "What?"

"It's just a saying," I explain wearily. "One of Virág's adages. It means that there is a balance between two things, sort of like a bargain."

Virág's name burns a hole in my tongue. On her best days, she held me in her lap and whispered her stories in my ear, and I didn't hate them so much when they were only for me, only for the two of us, and not a whetted blade that Katalin and the rest could use to wound me. If there are any threads still left to tie me back to her and to Keszi, I can feel them wearing with every passing moment, with every step that I move closer to the pine forest and the turul. Katalin's vision feels like the swing of a sword.

Gáspár must notice my anguish, because he says, "Sleep now. I'll take the first watch."

Numbly, I nod. I sink down, resting my head in his lap and letting my eyes slide shut. Dreams loose through my mind: hunting dogs with snapping jaws, the turul in a golden cage. Nándor's chest sewing up again, his wound vanishing bloodlessly. The ice ossifying around his pupils. My father embracing me and whispering the true name of God in my ear. The name was him asking me to save them, to be as shrewd as Queen Esther or as strong as the clay-man, and I am neither, just a girl shivering in the dark.

When I wake, the sky is still fuzzy and black and Gáspár's hand is cupping my cheek. I rouse quickly, shaking off slumber. Katalin has already woken and is guiding her horse toward a small patch of bristly grass, sweeping the frost off it with the toe of her boot. Gáspár stands and saddles his own horse, exhaustion etched in violet circles under his eye. My stomach clenches.

"I'm sorry you've had to stay awake so long on my account," I say, meaning it. "I hope you enjoyed at least one of your sleepless nights."

I only want to see him flush, and he does, his cheeks and ear tips pinking faintly.

"It's not just for your sake," he says. "Nándor wants me dead, too, or at least in chains. It's hard to sleep knowing I could wake with a knife to my throat."

I'm glad to hear him say that it's his fear of Nándor that keeps him from sleeping, and not regret over what we've done. Even stripped of his ax and Woodsman suba, there is still a century of gory hatreds stretching long between us, and so many gods darkening the sky with displeasure at our coupling.

"Do you ever think of letting him have it?" I ask. "This whole ugly, bloody country, I mean. Sometimes I think Nándor is what it deserves."

Gáspár's lips go taut, considering. "You mean I ought to leave him to the throne and go herd reindeer in the corner of the world?"

"You wouldn't have to herd reindeer." I try to imagine what sort of avocation might keep him occupied, him with his clever tongue and sharp mind, his carefully considered principles. "You could write treatises and dabble in poetry from the safety of your Volken hermitage."

Amusement crinkles his eye. "And what would you do?"

Once I would have been eager to abandon Régország entirely, if I'd ever had the chance and the will to leave it. But those kinds of bitter perversities seem behind me now. I have felt my father's arms circle me and heard the temple filling with Yehuli prayer; I have had a man hold me through the cold and promise to follow me wherever I go. It weighs me down, that love, fettering me to this terrible destiny. Katalin's prophecy floats through my mind.

"I don't know," I say. "Perhaps you'll have me as your scullery maid after all."

Gáspár scoffs, but there is laughter under it. "I'd rather have you as my wife."

We let it linger there in the cold, in the silence, that beautiful and impossible dream. We will always be foiled by history, manacled by blood. I know how well it turned out, his father marrying a nonbeliever, and though I feel I know myself very little now, I don't think I would relish spending my days bastioned behind castle walls. Yet Gáspár is not the frivolous type. This moment is as much a surrender as him kneeling. I want to kiss him again, my own knees weakening with another lovely capitulation.

Katalin's voice cuts through the air. "We'll have to keep moving. We're very close now, but so are Nándor's men, certainly."

A part of me wonders how they haven't caught up to us already. Perhaps they were stalled by the snow and the cold, or some other unforeseeable disaster, but it seems too much to hope for. I clamber onto my own horse and we spur on, kicking up white in our wake.

It's quiet in the forest. There are no animals scurrying in the underbrush or in the branches overhead. There are only the wind that makes the trees creak and moan like the wood-rotted roof of an old house, and the snow that falls softly through the empty spaces in the canopy, the cracked-glass splits that expose flashes of gray and white. The hair on the back of my neck is raised, and my horse's ears are pressed flat to her skull.

"Slow down," Katalin says, and I nudge my horse to a trot. "We're so close—look for a trunk soaked in blood."

Gáspár's head jerks left and right, and then his eye angles up again, toward the sky. I can tell by the girth of the trees and the impossible silence in the air that we're close to the same forest that our hunt for the turul led us to before, where the trees uprooted themselves and chased us to the lake.

My gaze fixes on something shiny in the distance. The lake is glimmering there beyond the lattice of pines, rimy with ice, like a huge pupilless eye.

I turn to Katalin, my heart in my throat. "Is this the way?"

"Yes," she says. Her knuckles are white on the reins. "Toward the water."

Deftly, we maneuver our horses through the maze of trees, stopping only when we've reached the frost-hardened bank. The lake is perfectly slick—a true mirror, false clouds gathering in white fists on its surface.

Gáspár brings his horse to my side. I can see the tension in his shoulders as he holds the memory of the ice and the cold water seething beneath it. And then I remember, too, that Tuula told us the name of the lake.

"What does *Taivas* mean," I ask him, "in the Northern tongue?"

"'Sky,'" he replies. "But what does it matter?"

"This is it," Katalin says. "It must be, but—"

I slide down from my horse, chest tight. I am thinking about Isten finding Ördög in the Under-World. I am thinking about the rabbi digging into the dirt and mud of the riverbank to create life.

"Stop!"

The word rings out, arching over the lake, but it's not Gáspár's voice. I turn around, the soles of my boots sliding perilously on the bank, to see Tuula and Szabín racing through the woods toward us. Bierdna is at their backs, her huge tongue lolling as she runs. Ice sprays up from their feet.

"Tuula," Gáspár says, when they skid to a halt in front of him. "Why are you here?"

"Me?" Her voice is thick with poison. "This is my *home*. I know why you're here, like all the Woodsmen before, and I can't let you do this."

"You don't understand," I say. "The turul's powers—

they're the only way we can stop Nándor. And if we don't stop Nándor, he will come for the pagans—including the Juvvi eventually. What other choice do we have?"

My words are dulled arrows; they bounce off her and land in the snow. Tuula's dark eyes narrow and flash.

"Find another way," she says. "The turul belongs to all of us. You cannot have it for your own."

"This is for *all* of us. Maybe the gods are willing us here." I say the words without really believing them, imagining a long red thread unspooling from here to Keszi, thin and close to snapping.

"And maybe the gods have willed me here to stay your hand."

I wonder if Tuula's mother told her the stories of Vilmötten, too, weaving them into her long dark braid. If even when the Patritians tore her mother's hand from hers, she kept the story of the turul clutched against her chest, bright and hot as a small flame. The thought nearly undoes me. I want to tell her that if there were any other way, I would do it—but Katalin's vision can't be changed and Yehuli Street might already be looted and empty.

Katalin slides down from her horse, fingers curled around the hilt of her blade. "I don't think you can stop us."

"You don't know anything, wolf-girl," Tuula says, the wind tangling with her words. "You're just like any other hungry Southerner, thinking you can tear the North apart and eat its most tender bits. You can't eat a thing that's still alive."

The bear growls, plumes of pale air rising from her nostrils.

"And what about you?" Gáspár asks, turning to Szabín. She's staring down at her ice-caulked boots, hood over her face. "Am I not still your prince? Will you betray the Crown?"

"I am already hell-bound." Szabín shakes off her hood.

"No wisdom or reason will save me now. So I will go with my heart."

Bierdna rears on her hind legs, giving a roar that ripples in the wind. It echoes in the emptiness a thousand times over, like a scrap of silk folded into itself again and again. Gáspár draws his sword.

The bear's giant paw slams into him and sends Gáspár rolling across the snow. He picks himself up, frost clinging to the black wool of his cloak, but Katalin's blade is quick, slashing across Bierdna's shoulder. The bear hardly reacts at all. There's a mean glint in her watery eyes, but it's human and familiar, somehow. It's Tuula's rage I'm seeing in her gaze, fierce but calculated.

I fumble for my hunting bow, even though it won't do me much good at such close range. Katalin moves toward Bierdna again, but the bear's claws are faster. She swipes three red lines across the left side of Katalin's face, narrowly missing her eye. Her scream is bitten back, swallowed up by the wind. Gáspár lands a wet, sickening blow in the bear's side, and Tuula screams too.

I hardly notice Szabín, standing at the edge of the brawl, has taken a knife from her cloak.

"No," I gasp out, but she doesn't hear. Szabín pushes up her sleeve and cuts right over the white mangle of scars, a wellspring of blood brimming up over the ragged flaps of skin. Then she smears the blood on Tuula's cheek.

The other girl doesn't react. Her forehead is pearling with beads of sweat, eyes as hard as flint. Bierdna's wound begins to close, slowly, blood misting into the air. I can scarcely believe what I'm seeing, Patritian power and Juvvi magic working as one. The shock of it sends Gáspár stumbling back, red blooming beneath the ruined fabric of his dolman.

Bierdna gives a throaty roar. Blood bubbles in the black pits of her nose. The cold air has turned thick and hot with the smell of it, and I turn briefly back toward the forest to see blood—Gáspár's this time—splatter across the trunk of the nearest tree. The wood soaks it in, breathing it, suffusing the blood all the way down to its gnarled roots.

Fear opens a chasm inside of me. Gáspár spits blood from his mouth. And then, like the nocking of an arrow, something fits together perfectly inside my mind.

I don't turn back again until I've taken two strides onto the frozen water. I can scarcely stand to look at Gáspár, his dolman shredded, his chest weeping red. He strains under the bear's heavy paw, searching for me. His eye widens when he sees me moving, with slow, deliberate certainty, toward the center of the lake.

"Évike, stop!" he cries. The sound shatters me like glass, but I can't turn back now. I keep going until I can feel the ice thinning. Until I can see the solid opalescence transform into watery translucence.

I take another step.

The ice gives a lurching, seismic shift under my feet, and as I am plunged into the dark water once more, all I can think is: *As it is in the Upper-World, so it is in the Under-World.*


This time, I bury all my desperate, flailing instinct and let my limbs slacken. Every inch of my body is daggered with cold, like a thousand tiny, sharp teeth gnawing at my skin. For a moment I am perfectly still, held in an icy suspension, even the sound of rushing water gone silent. I wonder if this is how Nándor felt when the black water swallowed him. If this is how Katalin felt as I held her head under the river. I wonder if I can possibly be the same, if I survive this.

*There will be some vengeance for killing it,* Katalin said. *There must be. The gods won't let you have anything for free.*

Maybe I'm wrong—maybe I've misinterpreted Tuula's

words, or missed all the meaning in Virág's stories. Maybe, when the breath burns out of my throat and the cold grows over my limbs like white moss, I will simply die. And then where will I go? Ördög gave me his magic, but will he welcome me into his kingdom? Or have I betrayed him already with my treasonous yearnings, my love for a Woodsman, my knowledge of Yehuli prayers?

There's a pressure in my chest like something trying to gash right through me, and I almost let instinct take over, that snarling animal's desire to live. My legs twitch faintly, shackled with cold. And then, with a flood of warmth, I think of Gáspár. If I'm to save him and everyone else, this is the only way.

Something tugs on me from below, just the faintest pull, like a thread lacing around my ankle. The cool suspension of the water is gone. For a moment, relief tastes as heady as swallowed wine—and then I'm hurtling downward, like a lobbed knife, still wrapped in skeins of velvet darkness.

Light rushes back at me. The force of it peels back my eyelids, and I see only the blur of white sky, smudged with gathering storm clouds. A coil of pine fronds flashes across my vision, and finally I land with an agonizing thud against something quite solid, my arms and legs tangled in the needly branches of a very, very tall tree.

I don't have time to feel relief. I sway precariously with each howl of wind, demanding that I straighten my legs and crawl to safety, or else plummet to the ground in a twisted heap. I am still drenched, cold water crystalizing on my hair and cloak. As I brush needles from my face, I see that the tips of my fingers are already swollen and blue. My heart stammers, skipping its beats.

*Move,* I tell myself, forcing my numbing fingers to flex and grasp. *Move or die.*

With great care, I crawl from the web of branches that

cradle me toward the fat bulwark of the trunk. When I reach it, I wrap my arms around its girth and cling to it fiercely, wind stinging my eyes.

As I hold to the trunk, the wind battering me from all sides, the cold water hardening on my skin, I think that I have made a terrible mistake. The turul isn't for me to find—me with my half-tainted blood, with my malice for my own people. How many times did I rail against Virág's stories, only to ask them to save me now? I feel as hollow as a gutted animal, nothing left in me but fear and regret over my own reckless bluster.

But Katalin's vision can't be wrong. I brace myself with the thought, downing it like a sip of wine I want to swallow over and over. The wind bristles over me, carding its fingers through my stiff, freezing hair.

I dig my fingernails into the bark, scrabbling for purchase. And then I see it: an amber tail feather, the sharp crescent of a beak that gleams like molten gold.

All my breath rushes out of me, and then it's only adrenaline that moves my limbs. I heave and strain and shimmy my way up the trunk, my vision surging away and then billowing back dizzyingly. I don't know how high I am, just that the white clouds are so dense I could believe them to be the snow-packed earth, and that the tree is spiraling up into them, cutting through them as if with a knife.

With every move, I remind myself what I have to lose if I fail. I imagine Yehuli Street littered with tiny fires, the doors flung open to reveal black and empty houses. A caravan of Yehuli winding toward the Stake. Boróka's wolf cloak matted with gore. Virág folded in on herself like a conch shell, pitiful and tiny in death. Even Katalin a bluish corpse, blood drying in ten perfect daubs at the ends of her bare fingers.

And worst of all, Gáspár: his throat open under Nándor's knife, eye like an empty inkwell, vacantly black. The thought maddens me with grief and I jerk myself up onto the next branch, ignoring the blood crusting on my lips and the twanging pain in my muscles.

When I do, I am eye-to-eye with the turul.

I half expect it to flutter away, or screech in protest at my intrusion. I feel stupid and clumsily human, an unmoored trespasser in this celestial world. But instead it perches on a thin branch, its head cocked to one side so it can look at me. Its eye is black and shiny enough that I can see myself in it, warped and small, like something trapped at the bottom of a well. I wonder if it looked at Vilmötten the same way.

Nothing survived the journey with me, not the hunting bow or even my dagger. This is Isten's very cruelest joke, certainly: that I will have to use my magic to kill the turul. I raise my hand, and I feel Ördög's threads give a twitch of resistance. My determination puddles out of me. I can't do it.

Stories are supposed to live longer than people, and the turul is the most ancient story of them all. Tears go running hotly down my face. Maybe killing it will save this generation of pagans, but what about the next? When the fabric of our stories thins and wears, the people will be alive, but they won't be pagans anymore. And that, I realize, is what Virág always feared the most. Not our deaths, or even her death. She was afraid of our lives becoming our own. She was afraid of our threads snapping, of us becoming just girls, and not wolf-girls.

But I have never been one of them, not wholly. It's this thought that guides my hand to the turul's breast. It gives a trill, a peculiarly small sound, and its chest swells, feathers shifting like a quiver of dancing flames. If anyone is to kill the turul, perhaps it ought to be me, because of my tainted blood and my treacheries, not in spite of them.

Blood leaks down my fingers, sudden as spring. The turul wilts into my outstretched arms. From far, far below, someone screams.

I want to cling to the tree until my body freezes there,

like a gruesome mortal lichen. Something in me has snapped; I can feel it. In my mind I can see Virág's hut, where I first heard the story of the turul, just the smudged shape of it. And then the image curdles and blackens, as if someone has taken a match to parchment.

But my journey isn't over. With trembling fingers, I pry loose a thread from my dress and use it to wrap the turul's claws—scrolled tightly, stiffening in death—and then string it around my neck. It hangs down my chest like a gory talisman.

I can't see the ground from here, only the fretwork of branches, needles bristling in the wind. Tears rim my lashes, blurring my vision. Saltwater tracks across my cheeks. All I can do is take one trembling step at a time, bracing my boot against the frost-limned branches. Another gust of wind howls past me, nearly snatching the turul away and up into the sky. I clutch it to my breast, a sob coiling in my throat.

Down, down, down. The moments trickle past me like water. Even my journey through Ezer Szem didn't feel so long, my shoulders tensed with the knowledge of my destiny, with the knowledge that each step brought me nearer to death. Now my fate stretches out in front of me like a road in the dark, no pools of torchlight, no signal fires. I don't know what waits for me at the end of this climb, if what I have done is enough.

Pine needles plaster to the blood on my face. The ground and the sky are both the same color, pure white, and I can't tell if I'm getting nearer. I can feel the trunk begin to thicken, its knots growing fat with moss. My feet make their landing on a thin, willowy branch and it snaps, sending me careening through the fronds of pine, my vision smearing brown and green and white, until I manage to catch myself again. My heart is pounding a ragged melody.

And then, finally, black shapes in the distance. The silvery veil of Katalin's hair, the brown hood of Szabín's cloak.

Tuula's skirts pooling around her, a bright spot in the snow. The bear. I can just glimpse Gáspár, standing, shifting, and my whole body slackens with relief. Seeing him sharpens my focus, whetting my intent. I hold tight to the trunk and lower myself to the next tier of branches, snow shaking out under my feet.

Something else: more black smudges ghosting over the lake. I hear the heavy galloping of their horses, the rattling of chains, and my boots slide off the branch beneath me. Pine needles snatch at me as I fall, swiping across my cheek, catching on the fur wolf cloak. I scarcely have time to panic before the ground flies up at me.

When I land, pain echoing through my elbows and knees, I am staring at the black suba of a Woodsman.

There are twelve of them and twelve horses, and ropes and chains and a team of oxen dragging a wooden cart with a cage. The Woodsman before me bends down, and I recognize the mangle of his nose. Lajos. He takes the turul, where it is half-crushed under my chest, easily snapping the thread that tethers it to me. I make a low sound of protest, but the words get caught in my throat, blood pooling under my tongue.

Bierdna honks pitifully as the Woodsmen throw chains over her huge shoulders. Two of them close on Katalin, axes drawn. I search for Gáspár, stomach reeling with horror, and find him being ushered toward the cart, wrists bound behind his back.

Just like that, our days of searching, our nights spent huddled in the cold, Zsigmond and Yehuli Street vanishing behind me—it all turns to ash in my mouth. Lajos dusts the snow off the turul's red feathers, then wraps it in burlap and stows it away.

Blood is dripping into my eyes. Some branch must have thrashed my forehead on the way down. Another Woodsman lifts me from the ground and coils rope around my wrists, my whole body throbbing with the ache of the climb and the fall.

"What does Nándor want with the turul?" I manage, blood slurring the words.

"Nándor?" Lajos gives a gruff shake of his head. "We're here on the king's orders, wolf-girl."

I'm not sure whether to laugh or to weep. Through the bars of the cage, I see Gáspár lurch to his feet, reaching for me. And then the edges of my vision swell with blackness, and in another moment, I can see nothing more.

# CHAPTER TWENTY-THREE

I am half-deaf by the time we reach Király Szek six long days and nights later, between the rattle of the cart's wheels and the thundering of a dozen horses, hurried and whipped so brutally by their Woodsman riders that their rumps are raw and gashed, all the sounds swelling up around me like the press of a hundred people in a crowd. I push myself as far to the corner of the cage as I can, avoiding everyone's gaze except Gáspár's, who rides alongside the cart sullen-faced, after initially refusing the dignity of a mount. When I woke again, I gave it my best jabbering effort to convince the Woodsmen that I'd forced Gáspár at sword point to come with me, and that he was innocent of any crimes against the king. The lie tasted like nothing, as slick as swallowed water.

"You shouldn't have said that," Gáspár had fumed, and of course he wasn't really angry at me for lying, only angry that I'd somehow cheated him out of his proper atonement. Even stripped of his Woodsman suba, he still clung to his Patritian morals, only now I was the object of his misguided nobility. "I shouldn't be walking free while you're in a cage."

"You're a prince," I said dimly. "You shouldn't be chained up with wolf-girls and Juvvi and a runaway Daughter." From her side of the cage, Tuula scowled at me.

"What part of being a prince," he'd said, "means that one should try and shirk the consequences of their mistakes?"

"Ask your father," I said. "He does it all the time, and he's the *king*."

Gáspár had fallen silent after that.

Now I think I do understand that real, ravaging Patritian guilt. It feels less like a weight and more like an absence. Like the Woodsmen with their missing eyes and their missing ears and their missing noses, something vital has been cut out of me.

There is also the fact that my magic is gone.

I had tried, of course, to kill Lajos when he came around the cart reluctantly to feed me. But I succeeded only in wrapping my sore fingers around his wrist and holding it limply, like a child pestering her mother. No invisible threads laced into my skin, no Under-World power staggered through me. Lajos shook off my grasp and shoved me away from him, and I stared down at my pitiful bound hands in a numb sort of disbelief. Katalin watched with pursed, twitching lips, even her eye looking trapped behind three neat wounds running from her forehead to her jaw.

"Have you lost your magic, then?" she asked briskly, sounding as impatient as Virág when I came to her moping over some small injustice. "I did say the gods would find a way to punish you."

"What about you?" I bit out. "You haven't even tried to heal yourself."

"And I'm not going to, but not because I *can't*," Katalin replied. "I want her to feel guilty every time *she* looks at me."

She nodded at Tuula, who made a noise in the back of her throat. "Who says I'm interested in looking at you?" Tuula muttered.

No one in the cart has spoken since then, even though a storm passed during that time, leaving us soaked and shivering and staring stubbornly at the floor, refusing to even huddle together in furious silence. Gáspár passed me a fur through the bars of the cage, and Katalin sparked up a tiny fire in her palm, but I am almost relieved when we reach the gates of Király Szek, if only because the clouds thin and quiet overhead.

As we clatter through the main gates and into the marketplace, Gáspár draws his horse to my side of the cage.

"I won't let my father hurt you," he says. "Not again, Évike. I swear."

"I don't think you have the power to make that promise," I say, and it nearly guts me, the way his face falls.

A part of me feels numb even thinking of my fate, that the king might decide to punish me for stealing his seer and trying to take the turul's magic for myself. My own life seems so pitiful in comparison to the hundreds of others who circle me; I am one small star in a huge and brilliant constellation. All I can hope is that him having the turul will give him enough power to stand against Nándor, to keep the Yehuli and the pagans safe. That our sacrifice will be enough.

People pour past us, stopping to gawk and gape. Király Szek's peasants look no richer or cleaner for the turul's death, despite all their railing against the poisonous influence of our pagan magic. Two Woodsmen have to clamber down from their horses to throw more ropes over Bierdna, anticipating the bear's panic, but she shuffles forward, her eyes black with their animal dullness, and none of Tuula's fire. Tuula hunches in the cart, avoiding the gazes of the Patritians, and Szabín puts one bracing hand on her shoulder.

As we pass through the marketplace, air roiling with smoke and paprika smell, I push myself to my knees and peer through the bars, hoping to catch a glimpse of Yehuli Street. Of Zsigmond's house. I can't smell any pig's blood, and the windows are yellow with light. The relief that goes through me is enough to make my eyes mist. We clatter into the courtyard, right to the mouth of the barbican, where the cart grinds suddenly to a halt.

One by one, the Woodsmen yank us out of the cage, checking to make sure our bindings are still tight. I want to tell them there's no use binding my hands, because I couldn't forge a blade *or* turn their axes to dust even if I thought it would help, or if I were simply feeling rash and vengeful, but I can't find my voice.

"We're meant to take the wolf-girls right to the king," Lajos tells Gáspár. "The others can go to the dungeons."

"So we can rot there until some tribunal packed with Patritians finds us guilty and the king has our heads off?" Tuula asks. She straightens, and Bierdna gives a low, shackled growl. "Is that your god's justice?"

"Keep your mouth shut, Juvvi scum," Lajos snarls, jabbing her with the blunt end of his ax.

"My father could be convinced of your innocence," Gáspár says evenly, though there's a pulling between his brows. "Once he has the turul, he—"

Tuula interrupts him with a laugh. "And you, the false prince, Fekete, think you can comfort me? You let them take your power from you, hang you in a Woodsman's suba, and send you into the bleak wilderness while the king sits in his castle tending to his bastards like pretty sheep? I'd rather die with a blade in my hand, or at least with fire in my heart, than live as the shadow of a shadow."

Gáspár doesn't reply, his mouth quivering, but Tuula's words kindle a simmering anger in my belly.

"Leave him alone," I snap. "You'll only shorten your life here in Király Szek if you can't stop yourself from snarling like an animal."

The hair on Bierdna's back is bristling. Tuula's lips twist with a smile.

"I never thought I'd see you so toothless, wolf-girl," she says. "Lying with a Woodsman has snuffed all your flame."

Before I can reply, Lajos jerks his head. The rest of his retinue circle Tuula and Szabín like black birds, crowding them toward the barbican. It takes another four Woodsmen to wrangle the bear, dragging her into the palace hall. Her claws leave long gouges in the stone floor.

We don't make it very far down the corridor when a figure crosses through the archway. The collar of a blue dolman parts like two strewn tulips over the pale column of his throat. Nándor.

Seeing him stops my heart. He strides toward us, lithe as a mountain cat, parting the gathered Woodsmen. For a single panicked beat I think he's approaching me, but he pauses before Szabín, instead, clasping his hands over his chest.

"It's been a long time, sister," he says. "You look less holy than when I left you."

Szabín's lips tremble, but she doesn't reply, only lifts her chin to meet his eyes.

"Cavorting with Juvvi, I see." His gaze flickers to the bear, pitifully muzzled. "I thought better of you—you always seemed to have greater devotion than the rest."

He flicks off her hood and runs his knuckles gently along her cheek, the gesture wavering somewhere between loathing and tenderness. Szabín shivers, and I see Tuula's chest swell like she wants to speak, but there is still a Woodsman's ax at her back. Relief pools in me, seeing her submission. Though there is little love between us, I don't want to watch her die. Bierdna growls, one yellow tooth sliding over her lip.

"And you." Nándor turns to me. "I don't know how you managed to survive, but I suspect you had help from my traitor brother. Either way, now that your bargain has been broken, I suspect you're not much longer for the palace, or this mortal world."

I have been afraid of Nándor for a long time, but only in

a hazy, indistinct way, the same way that I feared the Woodsmen as a child before I knew the fate of the wolf-girls they
carried away. Now I cannot look at him without imagining
the wound on his chest knitting itself shut again, flaps of skin
stitching up the horrible gash that I'd left. The gash that ought
to have ended his life. I feel like I have been plunged into Lake
Taivas again, this time going stiff in the black water.

Gáspár moves to my side, but before either of us can reply
Nándor is gone again, his footsteps vanishing down the corridor. My breath shudders out of me. Before, when I had my
magic, I could have at least tried to fight him. Now I can do
nothing while the ice closes over my head.

The Woodsmen lead Tuula, Szabín, and the bear to the
dungeons, and Lajos nudges Gáspár, Katalin, and me toward
the Great Hall. I can scarcely feel the floor under my boots. If
Nándor is right, I may not leave this chamber alive, even with
Gáspár at my side. What can he do to halt the swing of his
father's blade?

King János sits on the dais, crown of fingernails resting on
his head like a stag's weathered antlers. My eyes go at once
to the smears of blood dried into its ridges and grooves, small
details that I have come to recognize, though I don't wonder about them anymore. My mother's fingernails are there
among them, but she's gone now, just like my magic.

The king's beard has been braided, almost lovingly, and I
can't imagine who has done such a thing. Certainly not Nándor, who spoke so openly of his attempt to kill me in front of
Lajos and the other Woodsmen. It frightens me to think that
there are only King János's weak chin and dull-eyed rambling
between Nándor and the throne.

There's a wet gasp from the corner of the room and I twist
my head to see the Érsek, puddled in the shadows to the left
of the dais, nearly invisible until he patters forward into the
light. In the mound of his brown robes, he looks like a sleepy-
eyed animal peering out from its burrow, head bobbing on his

wattled neck. He blinks at the king, and then at Gáspár, and then at me.

"I saw a bear in the courtyard, my lord," he says.

"A bear?" the king echoes.

"Do not concern yourself with the bear," says Lajos. "My lord, we found it. We have the turul."

He reaches into the cloth bag he has slung over his shoulders and pulls the turul from it. Its amber feathers are matted from the long journey, drained of all their previous luster, stiff and cold after six long days being dead. Lajos bows, then lays the turul at the king's feet.

King János has the look of a half-starved man at the feast table. The eyes of a besotted man at the bedside of his lover. Very gently, he reaches down and lifts the turul, holding it up to the scant candlelight.

"Finally," he whispers, and then even more quietly, as if he doesn't expect anyone to hear: "To *Kuhale* and back."

He uses the Old Régyar word for the Under-World. Old Régyar is the tongue that was once shared between Southerners and Northerners, before the Southern tongue split off, a branch fallen from a mighty oak. We all still know the language, or at least a few adages and rhymes, but Old Régyar is on its way to extinction: by the time Virág is dead, it will be all but forgotten. The king is not nearly as old as Virág, but I wonder if his wet nurse sang to him in Old Régyar. He is old enough for that.

"Will you have a feast tonight, my lord?" the Érsek asks. "To celebrate this boon?"

"Yes," the king breathes. "Yes, a great power is nearly upon me."

He passes the turul off to a serving girl, who scurries quickly out of the hall with it. The rheum in the king's eyes seems to lift. His gaze is clearer and sharper than I have ever seen it when he turns to me.

"Wolf-girl," he says. "My Woodsmen tell me you were the one to find the turul."

I glance toward Lajos, who is glowering at me. There's no use in lying. "Yes."

"And you stole my seer, *and* my son, in order to do it."

Gáspár opens his mouth to argue, but I speak first. "Yes."

The king draws a breath. He rises from his seat, stepping off the dais, and comes to stand before me. I watch his hands, waiting for him to forge a blade and put it to my throat. Waiting for him to use his stolen magic to kill me.

"Father, please—" Gáspár starts.

"Quiet," the king says. "You do not need to beg for the wolf-girl's life; I don't intend to end it."

I ought to feel relief, but I can only manage a short, bitter laugh, remembering how I stood in this same hall before, the king's sword angled over my head. Remembering how it rusted away to nothing in my hand. I'd felt suffused with power then, manic with it, freer than I'd ever imagined I could be. The girl in my memory is a miserable fool for not seeing all the sheathed daggers, for not knowing how to maneuver around the pits in the floor.

At the very least, I will leave this room with my life. That was all I wanted when the Woodsmen took me—to survive— but somewhere in the time since I left Keszi, I have begun to wish for more. For the gentle embrace of my father, for a quill and ink I could use to write out my own name, for stories that didn't make me flush with apology for daring to speak them. For a man who kneels with my name on his lips. I think that I sealed the turul's fate the moment I started wanting any of it. I would have done whatever it took to keep it all from falling out of my hands like leaves.

"Perhaps it was not your intent." The king's voice jerks me back to the half-lit room. "But you have helped to deliver me the greatest prize. And for your aid, my son, I will reward you—a place in my hall permanently, and no more Woodsman errands."

A swallow bobs in Gáspár's throat. King János leaves

me, and puts both hands around Gáspár's face, cupping his cheeks. Almost imperceptibly, Gáspár flinches. I wonder if he is remembering his father's heated blade swinging down at him. I wonder if it is possible, to be comforted by the same hand that struck you. Certainly I craved Virág's gentleness as much as I loathed her cruelty. Nose to nose like this, Gáspár several inches taller than the king, I can see no mirror between them. Gáspár must take after his mother alone.

It is another moment before Gáspár speaks. "Thank you, Father."

His words, low and deferent, are more than King János deserves. An old bitter part of me wants to hurl the king to the floor and see how it looks when he's the one kneeling, at the mercy of his ill-treated son and two wolf-girls. But Gáspár has no appetite for vengeance, none of my own perverse spite. He stays still and silent until his father's hands slip off his face.

"Is that it, then?" I ask. "Now that you have the turul, will you let the seer go, and stop taking wolf-girls?"

The king's gaze drifts over Katalin, landing on me. Something kindles in his eyes, like a match being struck.

"Leave us," he says. "I will speak to Évike alone."

"My lord," the Érsek protests, but the king silences him with a glare. Lajos prods Katalin from the room, and Gáspár follows, brow furrowing with concern. I suspect he will wait nervously on the other side of the door. Only when the chamber has been emptied does King János speak.

"I did not intend to be a cruel king," he says.

This nearly sends me to hysterics. "No? What was your intention, when you cut out your son's eye? When you had twelve wolf-girls killed so you could steal their magic?"

"Careful, wolf-girl. I can still take your head too."

"If it weren't for me, you'd never have gotten the turul," I say. What's the use in being docile now? Smiling pliantly and serving him dutifully didn't stop the king from betraying me. No bargain can last between a hawk and a mouse. "Now that you have the power you wanted so desperately, will you finally leave Keszi be?"

"There is nothing more your village can offer me," says King János.

"Except the legitimacy that our pagan myths and pagan ways grant you." My voice is sour, like I have tasted a peach with a blackened pit. "And, of course, our magic. Once you've ended the war with Merzan, you believe the peasants and the counts will rally back to your side?"

"They will," he says. "I'm certain of it. And I know you worry over the fate of the Yehuli, too, but I have no desire to see them banished. They provide important services to the city, and they have lived in Király Szek for a very long time."

Just like Jozefa said. I think of the star-dappled temple ceiling and the gold-wreathed columns. I think of Zsigmond. If keeping the king on the throne is what will ensure his safety, and the safety of everyone on Yehuli Street, then my magic is a very small sacrifice to make. If killing the turul is what keeps Keszi safe, how can the gods fault me for what I've done? Better King János than Nándor. Better to kneel than to die.

Even as I think it, I know it is a Yehuli thought. One that Virág would try and scrub from me like she would a stain on her skirt.

I don't speak. There is nothing else to say. Finally, King János steps back up onto the dais and returns to his seat.

"I would like it very much if you attended my feast tonight, wolf-girl," he says. "After that, I'll no longer have any need of your services. You'll be free to go."

I don't swallow my laughter; the king can punish me for it if he likes. I have been in Király Szek long enough to know when a trap has been laid at my feet.


In the dim corridor that leads to the king's Great Hall, Katalin stands straight and tall, like a winter bird on its branch. The drench of candlelight makes the wounds on her face look wet and lush, but her silvery hair has been braided back so that not even a strand obscures them. Her finely shaped chin is raised haughty, high. Her straight-backed certainty ought to be a comfort to me, but I have only recently begun to think of her as an ally, not an enemy, and in comparison I feel as whimpering-weak as a struck dog. If she can walk into the king's feast with scars on her face and still manage to look down her nose at everyone, I'm a coward for wanting to hide in my wolf cloak. When Katalin sees me putting my hood up, she marches over to me and locks her hand around my wrist.

"Stop it," she snaps. "You're acting like a child."

"How else should I act, now that my magic is gone?" I have no words to explain the emptiness that I feel, now that Ördög's threads have shriveled up like flowers in the frost, leaving me bereft. I'm just as weak as the day I left Keszi.

Katalin fixes me with an icy stare. One of the cuts has dragged down the corner of her left eye and dyed the white of it with a needle-prick of blood.

"So you don't have your magic," she says. "That never stopped you from being wicked and spiteful before."

I give the scar on my eyebrow a pointed rub. "*You* made me that way, by tormenting me every chance you got."

"Fine—are you asking me to torment you again?"

"No."

"Well, then, stop looking like Virág has just given you a lashing," she says. "There's no reason to feel guilt over what you've done. I would've done the same."

"And what if Isten punished you for it?"

She snorts. "You are starting to sound like a Patritian."

Face flushing, I begin to formulate a reply, but Katalin pushes through the doors to the Great Hall before I can say another word. Mute and cowed, I follow her.

The feast is nothing like I expect. There's no gouged pig, no plucked swans, no red-currant soup with clouds of sweet cream. No carafes of coveted Ionik wine. There is only one silver dish and a single goblet, and they are both set out in front of the king. His guests are strewn like precious stones around the empty tables, jeweled silks gleaming. Their eyes dart up to the dais, then back to their neighbors, sharp and bright as blade points. I catch whispers of their conversation as I walk.

". . . don't approve of it, not one bit . . ."

". . . cavorting with *pagans*, for saints' sake . . ."

". . . rather the Érsek, if anything . . ."

A pang of worry makes my footsteps falter, but only for a moment. King János was certain he could silence his detractors once he had the turul's power. But until he makes a demonstration of its magic, their whispers will go on unstemmed.

The king's dais has been set with a long table, and Nándor is seated beside him. Gáspár sits to his father's left, and when he sees me starts to rise, but I give my head a quick shake and he sinks down again. I don't want more gazes drawn my way. The king's younger sons, Matyi among them, line the table to its end. A group of Woodsmen press along the far wall, and beside them, the Érsek, as squint-eyed and blank-faced as ever. A thrill of loathing goes through me, something old and perfunctory, scarcely less rote than the instinct to breathe. Nothing will ever stop these Patritians from bristling at me, from wrapping their red belts tight to keep me away.

The wooden doors push open. A small, pale-haired serving girl carries a silver tray, her arms trembling under the weight of it. She lays it in front of the king and removes the lid. Inside, garnished with sprigs of elderflower and fleshy red slices of pomegranate is the turul.

It's been perfumed with herbs to mask the faintly rotting smell, and its feathers seem to have a renewed, if artificial, glow. A fine layer of gold leaf is plastered to its wings and breast, not quite the right shade for its amber plumage. It lies flat on its back, wings stretched to their downy tips, as if it's just been shot out of the sky.

Seeing the turul like this makes my stomach turn as hard and tight as a stone. Virág would weep, I think. She would throw herself in front of the king and beg to be taken instead. For all that I railed against her, she loved us all more than she loved any one of us, and much more than she loved herself.

I do none of it, but I move closer to Katalin, the fur of our wolf cloaks brushing.

The king raises his knife and fork. I see the gleam of the silverware, the gleam of his hungry gaze, and I realize what he means to do. Bringing a hand to my mouth, I lean over, gagging.

"Quiet," Katalin whispers, but in a way that's more comforting than chiding, and nothing I would have ever expected from her. I stand up again, my vision starry at its edges.

King János doesn't slice into the bird like a piece of roast pork. Instead, he takes the delicate tines of his fork and plucks out the turul's eyes, one by one, rolling them onto his plate. The eyes are iridescent in the candlelight, like two shelled insects. He spears one and holts it aloft, throat bobbing under his gray beard.

And somehow this is worse than watching the shorn wolf howl out its death, worse than watching the deer go limp under a Woodsman's knife. I have delivered the king this feast. I feel as if I have offered my own arm to King János and told him to begin cutting wherever he liked.

The room is silent, like a long-held breath. Suddenly, Katalin reaches out and grabs my hand, fingernails carving tiny sickles into my skin. I tamp down my surprise and cling back. We hold on to each other as the king puts one of the turul's eyes into his mouth, chokes, and then swallows. I don't see whether he chews.

"Are you all right, my lord?" the Érsek asks in his reedy voice as the king's face turns violet.

"I can feel it," he rasps. "The power of it, running through me."

He spears the second eye with his fork and puts it in his mouth. This time, he swallows it whole.

The king's own eyes are moon-wide and just as bright. He pushes up from the table with such force that he flips it over and sends it tumbling down the dais, the tray and turul clattering to the ground with it. Guests flutter and start. King János stumbles forward, his head twisting madly, his gaze following the path of a ghost that no one else can see.

My legs are trembling with such ferocity that I think they might give way beneath me. Katalin sucks in a sharp breath, her grip on my hand tightening. The king is thrashing about the Great Hall, spittle foaming on his lips.

"I can see it," he whispers, eyes flashing. "I can see it all. What will be. What might have been—"

He stops, a cough shuddering out of him, and a stream of rosy blood dribbles down his chin.

"Father," Nándor says. He is standing now, too, behind the mess that King János made of the table. "What do you see?"

"Too much," the king says. And then he screams so loudly and terribly that it cuts the air like a blade gashing through silk, and it's all I can do not to press my hands to my ears to blot out the sound, because the least I can offer the dead turul is to hear it. He drops to the ground on his knees, screams ebbing to whimpers.

How long have I wanted to see King János kneel? Now it feels like a trickster god's perverse joke, that I can't watch it without wanting to retch. Gáspár moves to his father's side, but even he can't disguise the look of revulsion on his face. Tears have dried in salt streaks on the king's face, and there is spittle crusted in his beard. He wails and weeps, and I can only wonder whether this happened to Vilmötten, too, when the turul gave him the gift of sight. This was never in any of Virág's stories.

Suddenly, the clamor of the king's sobs is knifed through

with a laugh. A high-pitched, pealing laugh that I would know anywhere, for how often it rang in my ears while I snarled and thrashed. Katalin's whole body is shaking with that laughter, and her mouth is wide open enough to show the pearls of her perfect teeth.

"How dare you—" one of the Woodsmen begins, but Katalin pays him no mind. She lets go of my hand and picks her way across the room, a streak of pure white among all the wood and silk and stone. There's a smile gracing her scarred and lovely face. When she reaches the king, she lowers herself beside his crumpled form.

"You're weak," she says. There's a vicious, satisfied gleam in her eyes that I would have thought reserved only for me. "You don't deserve this power, because you're too feeble to survive it. Could you stand it, a new vision every night? Never knowing what kind of horror it would bring?" She laughs again, as bright and clear as a bell. "You're weaker than every wolf-girl you ever brought back to Király Szek, and you're far, far weaker than me."

"Please," the king bawls. "Please . . . I just want it to end."

In spite of all the pagan blood he's spilled and even my mother's fingernails on his crown, I feel a prickling of pity. King János is still a man, after all, guilelessly mortal, and in the end less a tyrant than a fool. The king reaches up with feebly spasming hands and starts to claw at his own eyes, fingers slipping into the sockets and then pulling. Someone in the crowd shrieks like a sparrow hawk. I search for Gáspár and see the horror flashing in the one eye he has left, almost as if he's having a vision of his own.

And then the king sprawls forward, Nándor's knife in his back.

# CHAPTER TWENTY-FOUR

At first there is no sound, and then only the scything of blades. The Woodsmen on the wall lurch forward, axes drawn, and descend on the dais like crows over carrion. They have their weapons at the throats of the princes, including Gáspár, before the guests can even start clamoring for the door. A black shadow washes over the threshold: more Woodsmen, their blades flashing, barring every exit.

Nándor removes the knife from his father's back with a gentle twist.

"My dear friends," he says, voice rising over the sounds of their screaming and the winking of jewels on fingers and throats as the guests roil together in the terrible hot hall, "there is no need to be afraid."

"You've killed him!" someone cries. "The king is dead!"

"Yes," Nándor says. Blood has begun to seep down the stone floor, like tributaries on a map marked in red ink. "And now a new rule can begin."

"But the laws of succession—" another guest starts.

Before they can finish, the Érsek hobbles up to the dais, robes trailing through the king's blood. Seeing him pick his way around King János's body like he would a puddle of muck in the road is what finally jolts me from my stupor. I let out a half-mute stammer of protest, unheard over the clamoring guests. The Woodsmen have grasped Katalin, jerking her arms behind her back.

"The Patritian laws of succession are subject to interpretation by the church's authorities," the Érsek coughs out. "The Prinkepatrios has chosen me to interpret his laws, and so I have chosen a new king, to lead our nation out of darkness."

"Isn't it convenient," Gáspár says, straining against the knife at his throat, "that Godfather Life has changed his views on the rule of succession to put you in power?"

He speaks to Nándor, voice lancing through the crowd's uncertain tittering. A word floats up from the throng, its three hard syllables like dropped stones. "*Fekete.*"

Nándor's face is as pale as Saint István's marble statue, smooth and unweathered by time. "Convenient? No. This is a burden that the Prinkepatrios has placed on me, brother. I don't presume to argue with His judgment. Do you? Do *you*?" he presses, turning to the men and women gathered in the hall. "Those who have been loyal to me will receive many blessings, and a great bounty in heaven. And those who defy me—well, you defy the will of God."

The dagger of his stare cuts right to Gáspár as he says it. The crowd murmurs again, someone choking out a sob. Some unnamable black thing is pooling in my belly, an awful oily mingling of fear and dread and utter, complete despair. The turul lies in the spill of King János's blood, eyeless.

There is a rustling behind the row of soldiers guarding the threshold, and the line breaks to let another Woodsman through. The front of his dolman is gashed, his face blood-flecked. He is dragging something behind him, a mangle of ruined flesh and torn silk, sinew stretched like pink cables over a gutted chest. It's not until I see the yellow curve of a bear's claw that I recognize it as Count Korhonen.

"Apologies, my lord," the Woodsman pants. "Furedi and Németh managed to escape and flee to their fortresses."

Nándor's gaze flickers to Count Korhonen's body, over the arc of his collapsed rib cage. His eyes are glazed, slick, like stones in the riverbed.

"No matter," he says. "I will send the Woodsmen to root them out and bring them to kneel before me, or else die."

"We have put the other Woodsmen in chains," the panting soldier goes on. "After a week in the dungeon with no food or water, I suspect they will be clamoring to embrace their new king."

*The soldiers, the soldiers, where are the other soldiers?* I wonder desperately. The Woodsmen are all raised in the strangling grasp of the Patrifaith, but the soldiers of the king's army are ordinary men, with wives and sons and daughters, less likely to want to bleed for the lofty ideals of princes and kings. But then I remember that every legion King János could scrape together is in Akosvár, a seawall against the tide of the Merzani army.

"Good," Nándor says. "For if they don't, they can join the demon Thanatos."

At the sound of his name, a shudder runs through the crowd. The men and women give full-bodied quakes, like the word itself is a ghost to be exorcised. I squeeze my own eyes shut, wishing the star-daggered blackness would swallow me. When I open them again, Nándor has leapt back up onto the dais, running his hand down the edge of his father's throne with the hungry gaze of a dog in heat.

"Ah, my lord," the Érsek says. "What is a king without a crown?"

Nándor blinks, then looks back at the priest. His eyes rest on the Érsek for one long moment. "Of course."

Then he leaps down the dais and snatches up the king's crown of fingernails. My heart thrashes like willow branches in the wind, my throat and stomach burning. Nándor gestures to the nearest Woodsman, the one who dragged in Count Korhonen's body. "Sir, if you please."

The Érsek wheezes out a protest—it's *his* duty to crown the king, after all—but the Woodsman comes forward and clasps his hands.

"Megvilágit," he whispers. A fist of flame closes around the king's body, orange fingers catching on his ruined dolman, his blood-slick mente. It spreads sickly, like a strewing of lambent petals, gleaming red and gold. The smell of burning hair fills my nose, along with the ugly char of bone. I almost retch.

Nándor tosses the crown into the fire. It chokes and splutters, and for a moment burns a bright, sharp blue, streaming up nearly to the ceiling, where the chandeliers groan and sway. When it calms and cringes orange again, the crown is nothing but ash. Sad embers crawl over the stone floor like blinkering fireflies.

My mother's fingernails, the fingernails of eleven other wolf-girls—gone, and all their magic with them. My bargain with the king and his promises to keep the Yehuli and Keszi safe are smoke in the air.

"A true king's crown is no hideous thing, suffused with pagan magic," the Érsek proclaims, with as much gravity as he can manage in his thin voice. "The crown of a true king is a beautiful thing to look upon, and it is forged in pure gold."

All through the room, hands grasp at iron pendants. Voices weave and tangle like a thousand dark threads. They lace around his ankles and shoot up, up, up through his arm and coil in his mouth, until the words that leave his parted lips are echoed by a hundred others.

"Bring him," Nándor says. The smile on his face is blissful and horrible.

He gestures to the Woodsmen guarding the door, and they

part again, this time for another man to stumble through. He is slight of build, dressed in plain merchant's clothes, with limp gray curls and a stubborn mouth that is better suited to frowning than smiling. Zsigmond.

Until now, my panic has been a caged thing, manacled by the knowledge that I am surrounded by Woodsmen on all sides, and that my magic is gone. Something looses in me and I am screaming, all that numb terror burst like a bloodletting, plunging through the crowd toward the dais. The Woodsmen are on me before I can make it within steps of Nándor. The blade of an ax presses between my shoulder blades, and someone jerks my arms behind my back.

Gáspár lurches forward, the Woodsman's knife drawing a line of blood along his throat. "Don't touch her—"

"Quiet the wolf-girl," snaps the Érsek.

Lajos stalks forward and claps a heavy gloved hand over my mouth. I keep screaming anyway, until he pinches my nose shut and I turn light-headed and dizzy. Tears cloud my vision. All I can see is Zsigmond's doomed march up to the dais, knees quaking. When he gets there, he bows his head and kneels.

Nándor returns him a flimsy smile, then turns to address the crowd. "The Yehuli are a blight on our city, friends," he says. I choke against the hot press of Lajos's hand. "But I am told there is no finer goldsmith in all of Király Szek."

Perhaps there is some seed of truth in it, but what is truer than anything is this: Nándor wants to wound me in whatever way he can. I struggle to meet Zsigmond's eyes, and when I do, I see that he is crying too. Quiet, dignified tears, nothing like my own.

"A crown, then," he says to Nándor, voice low and rough, "for our new king."

A wooden workbench is brought for him, and on it a gleaming block of gold. There are no tools, not even a hot kettle with a flame hissing under it, but Zsigmond doesn't ask after any. He steps forward and puts his bare hands on the gold, palms flattening against it, feeling its shape and its heft. Then, without a word, he takes a finger and traces something onto its surface, once and then again, and it's three times before I recognize what it is: *emet*. Truth.

He traces and traces until the gold turns to something like clay in his hands. He holds it in a way that reminds me of Virág kneading dough. Sweat pearls around his hairline, dampening his curls. And then, into the soft gold, he traces something else, letters I don't recognize at first. But he traces them so many times that eventually I can make out the shapes of the kaf and the tav and the resh and the little dots and dashes that fill in the rest of the sounds. He is tracing the Yehuli word for crown.

It seems to come into the shape almost by itself, as though he's imbued the gold with its own sort of mind, a lumbering cleverness, the way the rabbi did the clay-man that he carved up from the riverbed. The crown is a thick circlet with a domed top, lined with filigree plates and strands of gilt beads that hang down and finally, at its peak, the three-pronged symbol of the Prinkepatrios. My father traces more words, words that I don't know, and they etch delicate patterns into the gold, the heads and shoulders of saints and feathery outlines of holy fire. When Zsigmond finishes, he's panting.

Nándor leans close to the workbench, candles casting the crown's golden light along the curves of his face. He runs the pad of his thumb around the edge of it, tracing the shapes of the saints, every filigreed frond of flame. He smiles again, but he does not put it on.

"Stories of Yehuli craftsmanship have not been exaggerated," he murmurs. "And you, Zsidó Zsigmond, are gifted even for your kind."

"Yes," Zsigmond says evenly, placing one trembling hand flat on the workbench. "I have upheld my oath and made your crown. Now you must uphold yours: leave the Yehuli be."

The word *oath* strikes my heart like an arrow. I strain against Lajos's grasp, but it's useless, and I'm far too late, anyway. Far too late to have told Zsigmond what he needed to know: that you should never strike a deal with a Bárány.

Nándor's gaze travels lazily to the Woodsmen beside the dais.

"Soldiers," he drawls, "seize him."

They have Zsigmond's arms behind his back before I can even scream again. By the time they are dragging him away, Lajos has pinched his fingers over my nose once more, leaving me breathless, head throbbing and vision warping as tears burn salt trails down my cheeks. Putting my faith in King János was like boarding a ship with green rot in its hull and hoping that it wouldn't sink. But Zsigmond making a deal with Nándor is like asking the river for mercy as its black water fills your lungs.

I think of Yehuli Street, looted and empty, Jozefa and Batya fleeing as torchlight shines bright on their terrified faces.

The Érsek ambles toward the dais. "But won't you let me crown you today, my lord, in the sight of all your honored guests?"

"No," Nándor replies, and the Érsek gives a little shudder, as if unmoored by his defiance. "No, my coronation will take place tomorrow, and it is my dear brother who will place the crown on my head."

He has all four of his brothers at blade point but it's Gáspár he addresses, Gáspár he bounds up the dais to see. He leans close to him, their noses nearly touching. From my vantage point they look like skewed mirror images of each other, Nándor's face washed and pale, no more than a vague, jagged shape under ice.

"Never," Gáspár says, his throat bobbing beneath the Woodsman's blade.

"I suspected you might refuse," Nándor says. "You would easily offer your own life as forfeit, being the gallant

Woodsman that you are, but what about the lives of your brothers?"

He shifts toward Matyi, who is shivering in his bright-green dolman, eyes pressed tightly shut. Gáspár flinches, but he doesn't rise to Nándor's threat. Blood from his earlier wound is gleaming ruby-bright in the hollow of his collarbone.

"If you do as I say and place the crown on my head, I will take your other eye and let you leave with your life, so long as you never return to Régország again. Perhaps the Merzani will welcome their blind, half-breed son back home."

Gáspár swallows. "And the wolf-girl. Évike. You won't lay a hand on her."

As Nándor's head swivels toward me, so does every gaze in the room. A smile curves over his face, thin and red as a knife wound.

"That I will not swear to you, brother," he says. "Tomorrow, at my coronation, the wolf-girl will die by my hand, and a hundred more deaths will echo in its wake, for my first act as king will be to destroy the pagan villages in Ezer Szem."

There is no strength left in me to scream, but a sob tears out of my throat, my breath hot in the shell of Lajos's hand.

"Now," Nándor says, rising, "there is the matter of our dear Érsek."

The Érsek blinks at Nándor, perfectly sedate. "Yes, my lord?"

"What am I to do with you?" Nándor tilts his head. "What shall I do, when *I* am king of Régország, with an archbishop who helped murder the last two kings of Régország?"

This time there's no sleepy blinking, no slow, animal twitches. The Érsek stands suddenly stiff and tall, his eyes bright.

"Yes, my lord," he says, without coughing or wheezing once. "I awaited a *true* king, one who would earn my loyalty and the blessing of the Prinkepatrios, one who I would never think to betray."

"And I'm sure you swore that same oath to my father, after you helped him murder Géza," Nándor says coolly.

Silence blankets the Great Hall like new fallen snow. I think of the statues in the courtyard, of Géza with his beard as long as dripping moss, of how he was called Szürke Géza, or Géza the Gray, even though he never lived past middle age.

"Never, my lord." The Érsek's voice is silken. "I am loyal to you, now and always. I only helped your father murder Géza because I could sense his weakness, and I helped to murder Elif Hatun because King János *asked* me to."

"Elif?" Gáspár rises to his feet even as the Woodsman's blade draws a jeweled collar of blood around his throat. "Elif Hatun, the queen?"

The Érsek dips his head. "It was a quick poison, procured from a Rodinyan apothecary, which mimicked the symptoms of a fever. King János asked that I use it on his father, and then again his wife."

"Enough," Nándor says. A rosy flush has come over his face, the color of dawn at its earliest hour. "Do you think I care for the life of my weak-willed grandfather or that Merzani dog?"

For a moment, I think that Gáspár might lunge for him, and fear coils hard in my throat. *Please,* I want to say, though Lajos's hand is still pressing hard over my nose and mouth. *Please don't be a lofty-minded martyr.* Nándor's eyes are as pale and hard as bits of ice, and the whole room is roiling with its piety.

"Nándor," the Érsek croons. It's a terrible sound, like the braying of a mule. "My child, remember what we have done together. Remember who breathed the power of the Prinkepatrios into you, when the cold had stopped your heart beating—"

"You have done nothing," Nándor snarls. "*I* was blessed, and you merely brought me to this city so that I might make it holy too."

"No, Nándor," the Érsek says. "I brought a frightened

peasant boy, his skin still marbled blue from the cold, and I made you into the people's hero. You should not have lived at all, but Godfather Life took mercy on you and then I took His mercy and molded it. Can a saint ever be holier than the one who consecrated him?"

The Érsek's boldness is almost to be admired. As if in agreement, Nándor doesn't move, not really, but a tremor goes through him, like lightning fissuring across a still, black sky. The hall is lush and heavy with silence, a rain-swollen cloud near to bursting. Finally, Nándor lifts his head.

"I'm afraid," he says, "that your time as archbishop has come to an end."

I recognize the look in his eyes, despite all their snow-frosted sharpness. It's the look of a child who's grown too tall and strong to be cowed by his father's whip, the look of a dog who has been lashed one too many times.

For one suspended instant, I really do believe he will let the Érsek live. Perhaps he will strip him of his title and his brown robes and banish him, like he plans to do with Gáspár. In this fleeting second of frozen time, I am convinced that Nándor will choose mercy.

Then the whisper of a prayer glides off his lips.

There's a sound like ice breaking and the churn of freed water. The Érsek's neck snaps back at a gruesome angle, but he's still alive; there's a hazy gleam of terror in his eyes as he's lifted off the ground. An invisible hand drags him forward before dropping him into the vacant throne, bonelessly limp. Nándor prays again, something longer this time, with the cadence of a song, and a great iron crown glimmers onto the Érsek's head.

The Érsek whimpers, perhaps garbling for a prayer of his own, but only spittle foams at the corners of his mouth, dyed the pale red of diluted blood.

I try to close my eyes, but some perverse urge keeps them open. I know that whatever happens now, my imaginings will only be worse. The crown gleams with a smoldering heat, rippling like glass in the sunlight, shiny enough for Nándor's face to pool warped and smiling on its surface. The Érsek screams hoarsely as the hot iron sears through his skin, down to the white dome of his skull. Blood rises in the riverbed of his throat and bubbles out of his ears.

The hall fills with retching and sobbing, the cobbled noises of horror. Some of the guests scramble for the doors, but the Woodsmen are packed shoulder-to-shoulder in the threshold like sentries, looks of blank, stupid devotion on their faces.

The skin of the Érsek's forehead melts and crumples over his eyes. He can't even scream anymore, for all the blood in his mouth.

In another moment, it's done. The Érsek's body topples out of the throne, a mound of blood-drenched brown robes and stinking flesh like warm pink candle wax. Nándor bends delicately over the corpse.

"Do not be afraid, good people of Régország," he says, lifting the Érsek's iron chain off his body and winding it around his throat, instead. "I am both royalty and divinity now."

Water skims across my skin like the edge of a blade, hot and cold at once. I look up from under my damp hair at the Woodsman who holds the now-empty bucket. It's a Woodsman I've seen before, one with a missing ear. The absence of it makes his head look lopsided. Like a tree with branches but no roots.

"What's the point?" I ask through chattering teeth. "I'm going to die tomorrow."

"The king wants you to look clean," the Woodsman says. "I don't ask questions, nor should you."

"He's not the king yet," I say.

When I've been cleaned to Nándor's satisfaction, and even my wolf cloak brushed and made to shine, I'm brought to my old bedchamber. I try, in a hopeless and perfunctory sort of way, but the iron bars on the window hold fast, the door is tightly sealed, and my magic is well and truly gone.

I want to cry again, only because it seems the proper thing to do. But all my tears have been ground out of me, like dead skin scrubbed off a wound. Instead I fold myself against the eastern wall, where the sun will rise tomorrow on the day of my execution, my face flush against the cool stone.

The memories of my mother's comforts are distant and removed, the tenor of her hushing and the feel of her palm on my forehead nearly lost to me now. But I do remember Virág's comforts well. Her six-fingered hands could comb through my hair as nimbly as a squirrel leaping among the branches, and on the days I came to her hut weeping, she sat me down by the hearth and brushed my hair and braided it until all my tears had dried. The memory seems as pale and hollow as the inside of a conch now, drained of all its warmth. I think of Zsigmond holding me to his chest, but that memory feels twice-removed, too, like I'm remembering a ghost. Tomorrow, he will likely be dead, too, and all of Yehuli Street abandoned.

This is the wretched state of my mind when the door swings open. Two Woodsmen shoulder through, carrying another man between them. He is bare-chested, his blood leaking onto the stone floor. Gáspár.

I lurch to my feet, heart throbbing its jagged beat, but before I can manage a word the Woodsmen have hefted him onto the bed. Then they turn on their heels and vanish, the door thudding shut behind them.

Gáspár lies facedown, unmoving. The expanse of his back is etched so thoroughly with lash wounds that it's a fretwork of flesh and blood, gleaming braids of red stitched through with pink. The sight of it, and the copper stench in my nose, and the faint moan that feathers through his parted lips—it all makes my chest ache unbearably. And then I do cry, tears stinging the corners of my eyes, as I take Gáspár's head into my lap and brush back the curls from his sweat-damp forehead.

After a few moments, his lashes flutter and he looks blearily up at me. "Did he hurt you?"

"No," I say, and laugh at his absurd unselfishness in spite
of myself. The laugh sounds all wrong, like a river bubbling
over and flooding someone's sod house. "He won't hurt me
until morning."

He lets out a breath, and very slowly, his arms move to
circle my waist. Pain draws deep furrows on his brow. I've
never felt so limp and miserable before, paralyzed by my love.
This is the feeling, I think, that keeps mother deer loping after
their feeble and defenseless fawns. A mad thing, really, that
makes you so terribly attuned to mortality, to the soft places
where throats meet jaws, to the hawks circling overhead and
the wolves lurking just beyond the tree line. I lean over and
press my lips to his hair.

"Will you tell me a story, wolf-girl?" he mumbles against
my thigh. In his mouth the epithet is toothless, even tender.

"I think I am all out of stories now," I confess.

His soft laugh warms my skin through the fabric of my
dress. "Then let's just sleep."

We don't, though. Not yet. We sit. We breathe. We speak
in hushed tones, as if there were someone else here we might
risk waking. I do tell him the story of the rabbi and the clay-
man, in the end. I tell him about Queen Esther too. We stumble through some Old Régyar. I let Gáspár teach me a few
words of Merzani, and they coat my tongue like a sip of good
wine. We hold each other all through the night, until the sun
rises.

# CHAPTER TWENTY-FIVE

I wake sometime in the morning, when the sky is as pink as the shell of an ear, delicate and raw. The stretch of bed next to me is cold, the sheets streaked with old blood, and Gáspár is gone. Futile panic rises in me. I throw off the covers and run between the window, still gridded with its iron bars, and the door, sealed as tightly as before. As the last bit of moribund hope leaves me, I stand in the center of the empty room and wish I could make all the stone crumble, the floor collapse, and the roof cave. I would bury myself in the ruin, if only I could bring the Broken Tower down with me.

The door opens with a shuddering metallic sound, the scraping of its iron grate against the stone floor. I see Lajos's wreck of a nose before I see Katalin's face—her wounds, now black and scabbing, her eyes furiously blue. He shoves her through the threshold, and she stumbles forward into my arms.

"The king wants both of your hair braided," Lajos says shortly. He jerks his chin between the two of us; it's mounded white with scar tissue.

"Why?" I ask. My voice is hoarse with all the hours of whispering.

"In the pagan way," he says, and closes the door behind him.

"And why should we?" asks Katalin, once she has righted herself, even though Lajos is long gone. "If they're going to slit my throat, I don't much care whether there are pretty ribbons in my hair."

I think of Gáspár's back, latticed with its gruesome lash wounds. "They'll find some way to punish you for your refusal, you know. The best you can hope for is a sweet, easy death."

Katalin's jaw unlatches. "What have they done to make you so meek? If I knew, I would have done it long ago."

That kindles an old flame in me, and my face grows warm. "And for what? Why did you hate me so much? Was it because I didn't stay down when you shoved me, or because I didn't swallow every insult you hurled at me? Did you sleep more soundly at night when you knew that I was weeping in *my* bed, three huts away?"

For a long moment, Katalin says nothing. There is a faint rosiness to her cheeks, and this, I realize with a morose satisfaction, is more than I have ever managed to fluster her before. I am ready to consider it a perverse victory in the hours before my death, but then Katalin turns me around and starts running her fingers through my hair.

I'm afraid to speak, afraid to imperil this precarious moment that seems hesitantly to approach camaraderie. I think of Virág's hands, supremely agile with their six fingers, threading my hair into dozens of intricate braids as thin as fishbones. I think of Zsófia shrouding me with her silver dye. I think of the way that they trussed me for the Woodsmen like a prized pig, fat under the farmer's blade.

"Your hair is impossible," Katalin huffs, but she finishes my last braid and ties it off with a strip of brown leather.

"It's finally done now," I say, my gaze fixed dully in the middle distance. "I'll die in Király Szek like I was supposed to."

Katalin makes a halting sound, and her fingers tense against my scalp. "I never wanted you to die for me, idiot."

"It certainly seemed like you did," I say, "given how much you tormented me."

"I wasn't the best—"

"You were *terrible*," I cut in.

Katalin gives her head a dignified shake. "Do you know what Virág always told me, when we were alone? *A seer never trembles,* she said. Stupid old bat. She was always kind to me, but that's because she *had* to be; I was the next táltos, and I was supposed to take her place. She forced me to swallow every vision like it was sweet wine instead of poison, and said that it was kindness. She had no reason to be kind to you, with you being barren and all, but she was, anyway—between the lashings, at least. I hated you for that."

I manage a short, humorless laugh. "So you were cruel to me because she was kind?"

"Silly, isn't it? Virág told me I should be ready to do anything for Keszi, to die for my tribe. You were part of my tribe. A wolf-sister." She tries out the word, chewing on her lip. "I should have tried to protect you too."

Something unravels in me, like thread. I press my face to her shoulder, to the soft white fur of her wolf cloak, just below the curve of its frozen jaw.

"I could burn this whole tower down, you know," she says. "And both of us inside it."

I think of my own fleeting desire to see the Broken Tower crumble. But it would be a weightless gesture, a shout without an echo. They would only build it up again, or fashion something new from its ashes. Even smashing Saint István's statue or snapping his saintly finger bones would be like kicking a lone rock down a dark abyss. Just the way that killing the turul hadn't killed us, hadn't killed everyone in Keszi, the Patrifaith would survive some shattered marble and ruined stone.

"I would rather die by steel, I think," I tell her. "It's quicker and cleaner, and I won't have to smell my own burning skin."

"I suppose that's fair enough," Katalin says. Without forcing me from her shoulder, she starts to sing. A low song, sweet and brief, one that Virág often used for a lullaby. For a moment I think she's forging a blade, but it would be as useless as a fire; we might kill one or two or three Woodsmen, but it would never be enough for all of them.

When Katalin's song is done, there's a small silver disk cupped in her palm, slick enough to be a mirror. Holding it up, I see that inside is the wavering reflection of a perfect pagan girl, myths and stories and magic braided into her hair, history in the flash of her eyes and the set of her jaw. For better or worse, no one would guess at the taint of my father's blood.

The door opens again, Lajos and the two other Woodsmen behind it. There is rope for our hands, pulled tight enough to burn the pale skin on the inside of my wrist. The Woodsmen take us down the castle's serpentine hallways for the last time, through the smolder of half-lit torches, and out into the courtyard.

There's no stale air from the marketplace drifting over the palace gates; the stalls have all been shuttered for Nándor's coronation. The foul cobblestones have been scrubbed of their muck and laid over with lush woven rugs, in wine-dark violet and evergreen and gold. Garlands of white and purple flowers trim a makeshift dais, their delicate petals curling up in search of a cloud-wreathed sun. They are early crocuses, which bloom only on the southern slope of a single hill in Szarvasvár.

The dais has been built to hold a new throne, one of freshly burnished gold. I wonder if Nándor had my father make it, too, standing over him with a lash in hand. The back has been wrought into the shape of a three-pronged spear, each prong sharpened to a glistening point, like a jagged golden tooth. It has been draped with a great tapestry that bears the seal of House Bárány. So that Nándor can claim the throne under the Bárány name, even though he is a bastard by Patritian law. Seeing it fills me with a turbid, manacled fury, but it's nothing compared to seeing Nándor himself.

He ascends the dais in all the heat and clamor of the crowd, his admirers with their faces shining as bright as coins newly minted. They pelt him with woven laurel crowns and bouquets of tulips that they must have paid for in blood, because the Merzani are burning all the flower fields on the Great Plain. His dolman is pure white, like the sky in deep winter, and over it is a red-and-gold mente, with furred sleeves that hang nearly to the ground. They sweep through tulip petals, which are strewn over the dais like pale-bellied carps beached on the shoreline.

A coterie of Woodsmen rings the dais in a black collar, pushing back against the teeming of the crowd. On the dais is another man, wearing a dark-blue mente, a lone feather pinned to his chest.

Count Reményi holds the crown on a red satin pillow. I scan the crowd in a blind panic, searching for my father's face among the shining hundreds, and find him flanked by two Woodsmen. I cannot imagine why Nándor hasn't killed him already—perhaps he wants Zsigmond to see what it looks like, when a Patritian king wears his crown. A beat of relief goes through me before I remember that it's all for nothing. Nándor will slit his throat as soon as the crowd disperses; maybe before, if he wants to make a show of it. I expect there will be a thousand eyes on me when I die.

At last I see him. Gáspár ascends the dais in his black dolman and suba, looking every inch a Woodsman again. All he's missing is the ax at his hip. His movements are stiff and considered; I can see him wince when he lifts his arms to take the crown from Count Reményi. I feel a twinge of phantom pain go down the backs of my thighs, where my scars are a pale mirror of his fresh and lurid wounds. It is so achingly, viscerally wrong to watch him stand there beside Nándor in his brilliant red and gold, like seeing both the sun and the moon in the sky at once—Isten drawing up the dawn with one hand and painting midnight with the other.

Lajos maneuvers Katalin and me through the crowd, toward the very base of the dais, so close that I can taste the pollen-sweet scent of the spring crocuses on my tongue. I meet Gáspár's eye, glittering wet in the meager sunlight, and I can see all my painful, ruinous love reflected back. There is another world in which we might have stayed in the cradle of tree roots forever, our words rising in cold whispers but our hands and mouths warm.

"Good people of Régország!" Count Reményi cries out— once, twice, until the sound of the crowd simmers low and then goes silent. "We are gathered here to crown our country's next king. He is heir to the throne of Ave István, blood chieftain of the White Falcon Tribe and all its lands, and blessed by the gentle hand of the Prinkepatrios. Kneel for him and for your god."

I recognize the words from the Saint István's Day feast—it was how Nándor introduced his own father. As he speaks, Count Reményi unfurls his white-feathered cloak, the cloak of Akosvár and the White Falcon Tribe, the same one that Reményi himself wore that very night. Now he drapes it over Nándor's back, and I inhale a sharp breath. Even after all his heated ramblings about the perversion of our pagan ways, he will take his throne by Isten's rite.

Count Reményi gives Gáspár a vicious nudge, leaning close to whisper words that I can barely hear: *"Say it."*

Gáspár steps forward. His face is hard, but his gloved hands are trembling.

And then Katalin screams.

She slithers boneless to the ground, thrashing and wailing. Suddenly oblivious to the threat of Lajos's ax, I kneel down beside her, trying to turn her over clumsily with my bound hands. Her eyes have gone blank and white.

"What is the meaning of this?" Nándor cries out. The crowd lurches toward her and then shudders away again, craning their necks to view the commotion, and then leaping back in revulsion when they do.

"She's having a vision," I grit out between my teeth. "It will be over in a moment."

There is the barest sheen of sweat on Nándor's forehead; I have never seen him look so close to alarm. He turns to the crowd again, their fear swelling like a pulse of torchlight, almost visible.

"Don't you see?" he crows. "Pagan madness and pagan magic! Once I am king, there will be no more dark horrors making their home in our Patritian land, no more cloaked servants of Thanatos leading us down to our doom."

The veil of white vanishes from Katalin's eyes. She sits up, straightening herself, and amidst all the tremulous rumbling of the crowd, sets her lambent blue gaze on Nándor.

"They're coming," she says. "The pagans. All of them, from all the villages. They're going to storm the capital."


The only word for it is chaos. Nándor rallies the Woodsmen to him at once, and they ascend the dais, making a bulwark around their almost-king. Gáspár hurls the crown away from him and it clatters onto the cobblestones; a bald man in stained linens leaps upon it, covering the crown with his body while a dozen more haggard and desperate peasants claw their way toward it, just for the chance to touch something made of gold.

I've lost sight of Gáspár behind the bastion of Woodsmen, and I nearly lose Katalin to the furious roil of the crowd. I cling to her as best I can with bound hands, huddling under a fretwork of flailing limbs, occasionally catching an elbow or the toe of a leather boot. My stomach turns over on itself, a mirrored churning of the throng.

I wonder what kind of future Virág has seen: Woodsmen thundering through Ezer Szem, axes slicing through fern and bramble and then through human flesh, before they can sing a blade or an arrowhead to life, or light one hopeless fire. Nándor at the helm, like a ship's figurehead carved in ivory and gold, his pale hand closing around her throat. I know what choice she has made. She wants to die fighting.

Deaf to everything but the torrent of blood in my ears, I lurch to my feet, hauling Katalin up with me. I shove my way through the crowd with half the savageness of a real wolf, trying to find my father. When I do, it's because I slam hard into his back, and nearly topple both of us to the ground.

"Évike," he gasps, gripping my bound hands. "We have to flee this city at once."

I shake my head mutely, thinking of that star-dappled temple ceiling, heavy with all its histories. I think of the white columns like cracked ribs, and all the pale rubbed spots on the benches where so many men and women and children have sat, generations wearing through the wood varnish.

"There's no shame in fleeing, when it's a choice between that and death. More than anything, God wants his children to live. To be good, and to survive."

His words make my throat close, something raspy and hot rising in it. I remember that he whispered the true name of God in my ear, like it was the best and truest story he ever told, and only a secret because you had to be sure you were ready to handle it gently, the way a doe noses its newborn fawn toward the softest grasses.

"You go," I whisper. "I have to stay."

"Where you go, I go," my father says.

"Please," I say. "Take Batya and Jozefa and the rest and leave Király Szek as quickly as you can."

Zsigmond doesn't reply. He begins to undo the bindings on my hands. I remember the pressure of his fingers from when he taught me to hold a quill. Then he reaches up to cup my face.

"My daughter," he says. "Do you remember the true name of God?"

I roll its syllables under my tongue, tasting them like I would a bite of bread or a sip of wine, measuring their heft. "I do."

"Then you have the strength that you need."

He kisses me once on the forehead, and then lets go. I watch him vanish through the crowd, eyes blurring over the shape of his retreating back. I reach up to wipe my tears, still tasting God's name on my tongue. In the story, Esther went to the king, even though she knew she risked her own life, and the rabbi made his clay-man even though he knew he might be punished for it. Whatever strength and shrewdness they had, I have, too, as long as I can remember how to make the letters.

When Zsigmond has gone, I lift my chin and try to peer over the city gates, to the crest of the tallest hill beyond. There is a line of pale wolf cloaks glimmering along the horizon.

It must have taken them seven days, all the warriors in all the villages of Ezer Szem, riding as straight as a dagger toward the capital. Easy once they made it out of the woods, gliding through the yellow grass of the Little Plain, past villages that shuttered their doors and hid their children's faces as the convoy went by. Hair braided with bramble and eyes gleaming with singular, ill-omened purpose.

I can't hear it, but I know that they are singing as they descend, singing their way into oblivion.

Katalin is still beside me, her head ducked low under the lattice of reaching arms. I loosen her bindings and drag her through the crowd, cutting a narrow path to the barbican.

"Are you mad?" she spits. "We're going the wrong way!"

"I'm not leaving them," I say, though my words are nearly swallowed by the din.

I know the way to the dungeon well enough to walk it blindfolded, and even now the castle is empty, its hallways hushed like a cold hearth, until we turn the corner. The next corridor is painted in blood. It's caulked onto the walls and smeared into the stone floor, in a gruesome trail that leads to a heap of bodies beneath a carved archway. Blood crusts on the black wool of their cloaks, bruises fresh on the skin of their shaven heads. Woodsmen.

Ice in my veins, I kneel beside the nearest one and examine his wounds. He's been cut several times in the torso, clear through the fabric of his dolman. Broad, deep slashes that cleaved off whole hunks of flesh—cuts made by an ax, not a sword. Tiny grains of dark metal are flecked all over the ruptured skin. They must be the loyalist Woodsmen, the ones who refused to yield to Nándor, though I don't know if he only lied about imprisoning them, or if his rebel Woodsmen just had them killed anyway, against his orders.

One of the men still has a bow strapped to his back, and I find a quiver of arrows nearby. I pick up both and hold them to my chest with shaking hands.

We descend the stairs by muted torchlight. Tuula and Szabín are huddled in their cell, and Bierdna is an unmoving mass of matted fur, looking already half-killed. When Tuula sees me she stands slowly, rousing the bear too.

"Are you here to execute us, wolf-girl? Has the king finally given the order?"

"The king is dead," I say.

Tuula draws in a quick breath, eyes wavering uncertainly.

"The pagans are coming," I tell her. "Everyone from Keszi, and all the other villages. It's madness. You have to leave."

"Will they win?" Szabín asks.

I'm so taken aback by her question that it takes me a

moment to answer, and with a snarling anguish I reply, "I don't know." I look to Katalin.

She shakes her head. The vision must not have gone that far.

Tuula's expression is unreadable. "So are you here to free us, wolf-girl?"

"Yes," I reply, swallowing around the hard thing in my throat. "Katalin . . ."

I turn to her expectantly, but all she does is scowl. "I still haven't gotten an apology from the Juvvi girl, for setting that feral beast of hers on me."

"*Please*," I bite out. "Katalin, please."

I don't care how pitiful my wheedling is; desperation has chilled me like a fever, a cold sweat thickening on my brow. If I cannot save my father, if I cannot save Virág or Boróka or Gáspár, wherever he is now, at least I can do this.

Muttering unintelligibly, Katalin pushes past me and bends at the door of the cell, examining the lock. Her singing comes in stops and starts and grudging half-whispers, but when she finishes, she's holding a small brass key in her hand.

"There," she huffs, pressing it into my palm. "Now I won't hear any more recriminations about my cruelty."

My relief is fleetingly sweet. I turn the key in the lock and swing the cell door wide open, and then the door to Bierdna's cell too. With a tightness in my chest I watch Tuula stroke the bear's furry head, carefully loosening her chains and removing her muzzle, while Bierdna twitches her wet nose with contentment.

"Thank you, Évike," Szabín says quietly. I think of how I hated her then, those days in Kaleva. My mind filled with mean thoughts about what an imbecile she was to think she could live peacefully with a Juvvi girl, when there were a hundred years of ugly history between them, and plenty of fresh blood besides. Perhaps I was only castigating myself, miserably aware that I was falling in love with a Woodsman.

"There's an easy path out of the city," I tell them, shaking my head. "Through the Woodsman barracks."

"No path will be *easy*," Katalin says. "The pagans have surrounded the city from the north. If you want to leave, you'll need to go through it."

I look down at the bow I snatched from the Woodsmen, knuckles whitening. "I suppose you aren't leaving, then."

"No," she says. "There will be nowhere to go back to unless we win, just a blood-soaked clearing in the forest and a cluster of burning huts."

I'm not clever enough, not well-versed enough in battle tactics to have a good sense of the odds. I only know there are so many wolf-girls who will die, no matter how the sword of fate swings, in the end. I know that Gáspár is still here—I must believe he's alive, until the moment that I see light drain from his eye—and if I leave him I will be as unmoored as a ship set loose with no captain, a compass point spinning on and on and never finding its true north. And I know that Régország will not be safe for anyone I love unless Nándor is dead, and his memory drowned out by the sounds of a hundred voices shouting.

God's name tastes sweet on my tongue. I lead the way out of the dungeon, down the labyrinth of hallways, to the door that leads to the Woodsman barracks. Tuula and Szabín and Katalin take swords from the weapons rack, blades flashing silver as fish tails. I add as many arrows as I can find to my quiver, breath clouding in the damp air. There is a pale light at the end of the tunnel, like an unblinking eye, and once we're all girded in our iron we follow it, toward the roaring and snarling of battle ahead.

# CHAPTER TWENTY-SIX

The mouth of the tunnel opens up under a mounded hillside, cached by bramble and wildflower brush, not far from the Woodsman stables. No sooner have we mowed our path through the coiling bracken than I feel something wet and hot splatter my face. Scarcely more than a yard away, a Woodsman's limp body slides off its horse, chest gashed open to the red curve of muscle and crumpled white scaffolding of bone. I reach up to touch my face, and when I look down at my fingers again, they're stained dark with blood.

A girl in a gray wolf cloak stands over him, brandishing a long thin sword. Her black hair waves like a flag of war, braids streaming down her back. Zsófia. I start to move toward her, the first syllable of her name on my lips, but before I can say a word a Woodsman sails by on horseback, his ax cleaving her head from her body.

The seconds seem to pass in sluggish agony, dripping like molten steel. Katalin flies down the hillside, fast as a flung spear, toward the Woodsman. Tuula and Szabín follow, the bear thrashing through the ferns and briar, lips pulled back from her long yellow teeth. Several feet away, where her head landed, Zsófia's eyes stare up at me still shining, pearly with suspended terror.

Zsófia who tormented me, Zsófia who sang slurs at me, Zsófia who helped dress me in white for the Woodsmen— now dead by the arc of their ax. It feels like I have brought this fate upon her, as if all the hatred that ground my teeth at night somehow transmuted to real power. I open my mouth to whimper, to scream, but someone claps a hand over my face and drags me down into the bushes. Limbs flailing, I claw myself free and crawl away, only to turn around again and see that my attacker is Boróka.

"Évike," she gasps, and throws her arms around me.

I squeeze her so tight I think my nails might pierce through her tawny wolf cloak, and when we break apart again tears are stinging the corners of my eyes.

"I thought you were dead," she whispers. "When I saw you there, in Katalin's cloak, your hair dyed white . . . I should have tried to stop them."

All I can do is shake my head; the memory of it feels long faded, like a scratch that has healed to a small blue scar. The only thing that's real now is the scything of blades and the flurry of bodies and the iron tang of blood in the air.

"Please," I say. "Keep your head down until the fighting's over—"

Boróka gives a breathy laugh. "You can't ask that of me."

I knew it would be her answer, but it guts me all the same. I reach up and take her face between my bloodied hands, and she lets me, for a brief and aching moment. But then a Woodsman lunges toward us, hard-eyed with loathing, and she leaps up and draws her sword to cut him down. In another moment, she has vanished into the throng.

A line of wolf-girls rims the top of the hill, fire-makers lobbing their balls of flame. Small fires are burning all over the battlefield, flecks of orange light dappled through the brush. Then there are forgers, wielding their sung blades, sometimes two at once. And laced among the mottle of wolf cloaks are the Woodsmen, their cloaks dark against the winter-bleached grass. Futilely I search for Gáspár among them, though I know he would not cut down a wolf-girl, nor one of his own Woodsman brothers. Still I cannot imagine he would flee from battle like a coward, or look on like a grim-faced tactician, coldly weighing the odds. If he has thrown himself into the morass of the fight, it is only to seek out his brother.

Farther down the hill, I find my mark: a bright pulse of white amidst the churning bodies, a shirt of mail over his dolman and a golden sword in his hand. Nándor. The hilt of his sword is teethed with pearls, his auburn hair blowing back from his face as he plunges through the briar on horseback. Not his horse—mine. The shining pale mare I'd ridden from Keszi, her mane now neatly combed, wearing the gilt saddle of a royal mount.

I clamber to my feet and nock one of my arrows. Woodsmen are darting through my line of sight, black smudges like soot on skin. I loose my arrow and it pierces a Woodsman's chest, just below the hollow of his throat. He coughs blood, but men don't die like rabbits and deer. He drops from his horse and lumbers toward me, unsteady on his feet, and doesn't fall until I put another arrow into him. This time it lands right at the center of his chest, where his heart sits winged by two lungs.

In the madness and the blood steaming in the air, it's impossible to tell where the scale will tip. Impossible to tell whether pagans or Patritians are winning. All I can see are wolf-girls puddled in their bloody cloaks, and Woodsmen lying limp, run through with swords. Their bodies are near identical, one black suba over another. I drop to my knees again and paw through the nearest pile of corpses, praying and praying to whichever god might answer that I will not find Gáspár among them. These dead Woodsmen are faceless, pockmarked with missing ears and noses and eyes.

When I look up again, I spot her, sailing down the hillside in her white wolf cloak, hair the color of snow. I've never seen Virág move this way, with the agility of a fox, or at least a woman less than half her age. Her forehead has more lines than I remember, like the hard mud in a dried-up riverbed, and yet there is youthful vigor in her movements. The last time I saw her, she was handing me off to the Woodsmen, a perfectly serene cant to her chin. But now my mind crowds with other memories: Virág pulling me onto her lap, her stories wafting through her hut like wisps of smoke, Virág braiding my hair and covering my ears with her six-fingered hands when the thunder was too loud and too close for me to sleep.

It is a mangle of what I feel for Gáspár, like a Woodsman's severed nose or my lopped finger, small and ugly by comparison. But love, I think, all the same. It's that ugly and awful love that sends me skidding down the hill after her, just as Nándor jerks his horse's reins and turns her way.

Their blades meet, but there's power behind Nándor's swing that she hasn't yet seen, that she doesn't understand. With the force of the impact Virág topples off her horse, sliding to the ground with a guttering thud.

I scream her name, but either Virág doesn't hear or she doesn't care enough to turn. Nándor's lovely face is blood-flecked, and there's a sheen to his gaze that looks half-mad. His eyes are nearly as white as Virág's hair, the pupils shrunken and colorless. He seems to scarcely even see Virág as he leaps from his mount, sword smiling down at her. He will kill her the way the Woodsmen have killed all the other wolf-girls, without ever knowing their names. He will never know the stories that live in her marrow and blood, will never know how once, when I was bitten by a snake in the woods, Virág sucked the venom out of the wound herself, extra eyeteeth gritted against the skin of my wrist.

She'll die the way the turul did, as if it were just any bird to be eaten. That's all I can think of as I throw myself between her and Nándor's sword, its blade burying itself deep through the muscle of my left shoulder.

Nándor blinks as he pulls the sword from me, as if he has just woken from a deep slumber.

"Oh, wolf-girl," he says, almost wistfully. "You must have learned this sort of stupid nobility from my brother."

And then he's gone again, swallowed up by the fray. The pain is like the lick of a thousand heated blades, and my heart gives a stubborn, feeble quiver. My vision tunnels, plunging me into darkness and back out again. Through the feather of my lashes, Virág's face is hovering over me.

"Why did you do that, you fool of a girl?"

Blood burns in my throat. "Why did you save me, way back then?"

"Perhaps I saw that one day you would save *me*," she says. Her face ripples like a reflection on water.

My vision is narrowing again. "So then you know why I did it."

She always knew everything before I did. As she mutters something unintelligible, Virág's hand is on my wound. The pressure is unbearable at first, another fiery ribbon of pain. Then it begins to recede, in throbbing increments, the blackness clearing from my gaze. I think I hear the whisper of a song on her lips, but when I pick my head up again and the world comes roaring back, I realize it's not a song at all.

"Honorable girl, foolish girl," she's murmuring, almost with the rhythm of a prayer. "Both of us will live to see another winter."

There's an odd tightness in my shoulder as Isten's invisible needle works through my wound, guided by Virág's hand. I try to stutter out a thank-you, but Virág's mouth only twists into its familiar scowl, the same face she made at me whenever I cursed or lied or burned her broth.

"There," she says. "What you have given won't be forgotten."

A tremor goes through me, and I shudder with the pain's vicious ebbing. "Won't it all be forgotten, if we die here today?"

"We won't die," she says. "Isten won't allow it."

I wonder if her vision showed her that too: the Woodsmen spent, the pagans victorious. It seems too much to hope for, too simple and neat. The hillside is littered with bodies in wolf cloaks. But by my hasty count, there seem to still be more of us standing, and fewer Woodsmen.

A gleam of white catches the corner of my eye. Nándor is stumbling up the hill, swordless and blood-drenched, his dolman hanging half open. He reaches the mouth of the tunnel and lets the darkness swallow him. Wounded, but alive. And seeing how wounds mean very little to him, I know he'll only return to fight again unless something is done. I rise to my knees, shocked by how light I feel, how strong. I give Virág a hasty kiss on the cheek before scrambling up the hillside after him.

I follow a trail of blood through the empty Woodsman barracks, down the corridors of the palace, and out into the courtyard, still arranged for Nándor's coronation. Pale flower petals have peeled off the dais, floating through the air like listless snow. The tapestry is still draped over the burnished throne, its tassels fluttering in the wind, and the cape of white feathers is abandoned on the cobblestones, as sleek and flat as a spill of water frozen over. Nándor is limping down the makeshift aisle, blood splattering with each heavy-footed step. I hear him whisper something to himself, too low to make out, and then his back straightens, as if his spine has been fused with steel. His gait grows steadier as Godfather Life heals him.

Breath held, I nock my arrow and draw the bow string. I have to land a killing blow.

Before I can loose my arrow, Nándor turns. His face is cracked like a porcelain bowl, torn up by a terrible snarl.

"I thought I killed you, wolf-girl," he says.

I am standing precisely where my father stood that first day in Király Szek, boots slippery with pig's blood. "I thought I killed you once too. You aren't the only one who can survive certain death. I suppose I am as blessed as you are."

His eyes have turned that eerie sheen of white again, and for a moment it stuns me. I don't think he ever managed to exorcise his death. Ever since that day on the ice, I think he has grown up beside his own ghost. Why would he need to bleed like Gáspár when he has already made the greatest sacrifice of all?

Nándor gives a laugh, but it comes out short and choked. "You can't really think you can kill me now. Whatever gods or demons that answer your prayers—well, they are no match for mine."

I don't know if he means the Yehuli god or Isten or both. I swallow around the name of God in my mouth, tasting its syllables like sweet juice on my tongue.

"No," I say. "I think I can kill you without their help."

In the instant that I let my arrow fly, Nándor whispers another prayer, and I'm blasted back across the courtyard. My head hits the stone so hard that I feel my molars loosen and taste blood along the line of my gum. My arrow spirals off somewhere in the distance, and my bow clatters to the ground, far out of reach.

Nándor kneels over me, straddling my chest. I reach up with one hand but he's faster and stronger and his hand closes over my throat first. I gasp, lips parting as I strain for breath, and then he sticks his hand into my open mouth, tugging one of my loose molars free with two fingers.

I scream, the sound muffled by his tight grip on my throat. His hand is bloody up to the wrist. He examines my tooth, pearl-bright between his finger and thumb, with an almost innocent curiosity. Maybe he's thinking precisely what his own father thought—that there's power in that tooth, like the power the king sought in every wolf-girl's fingernails. For a moment I remember my mother, fox-red hair flashing as the Woodsmen crowded her into the mouth of the forest. Even after everything, I will die here in the capital just like she did, torn to tiny pieces. Nándor tosses the tooth away, and it skitters across the cobblestones.

"I will enjoy killing you, wolf-girl," he says. "This time, I'll make sure it sticks."

He reaches into my mouth to pull another tooth. The pain comes in one sharp burst, blooming like a rose. Blood streams from my mouth, dark spots clustering in the center of my vision. I can still feel the name of God there, bearing down against my tongue. Nándor might be stronger than me, purer than me, but that's something he can't ever know.

Nándor holds another one of my teeth up to the light, smiling and smiling. He doesn't notice that my right hand with its four fingers has started inching across the cobblestones, toward where his palm is pressed flat to the ground. He doesn't notice my slow, tremulous movements, doesn't notice my finger tracing the Yehuli word for *dead* on the back of his hand in blood.

A shimmering heat branches from my fingertips and crawls up his wrist, through his arm, over the curve of his shoulder. It sears right through the white silk of his dolman, and peels back his skin as if it were pale fruit. Nándor screams and topples off me, clutching his arm to his chest. The whole length of it is black with burned flesh, flaking like the curled edges of parchment set alight.

"Witch!" he gasps, staggering back. Whole hunks of muscle and sinew are falling away, leaving open long stretches of charred bone.

I can't move from the ground, and I can hardly breathe for the blood in my mouth. Even the Yehuli magic, with all its knowledge and certainty that cleared a swath through the blackness of my mind, seems unreachable and distant now. Winking away like a dying star. Before Nándor can lurch toward me again, his name rings out through the air.

"Nándor!"

He turns, swaying on his feet. Gáspár strides across the courtyard, still in his Woodsman garb. Relief floods me like a rush of clear spring water, and I nearly surrender to the darkness entirely, so woozy with the joy of seeing him alive. He's unhurt—but unarmed. There's no ax glinting at his hip.

"Brother," says Nándor. A half-smile quakes onto his face, eyes too bright again. "If you're here to rescue your pagan concubine, I'm afraid you've come wholly unprepared for this battle."

"Leave her be," Gáspár says. His gaze flickers to me briefly, just one caught-breath moment that loops between us like black thread. "You're going to lose, Nándor. Most of your Woodsmen have already been slain, and it will take weeks for the rest of the army to make its way here from Akosvár. If you surrender now, and call off the rest of your Woodsmen, I will spare your life."

Nándor laughs and it's an awful sound, like water breaking over rocks. "I don't need your mercy, brother. You're unarmed."

Gáspár doesn't reply. Instead, he walks over to the statue of Saint István, with its blank marble stare, still wreathed in white flowers. Gáspár draws the sword out of Saint István's hand—the real sword, rust-flecked—and holds it up, a silvery bolt against the cloud-dark sky.

"Megvilágit," he says, his voice as clear as a bell. And then a flame bursts across the blade.

"You dare wield the sword of a saint?" Nándor snarls.

"I wield the sword of a *king*—my sword by right," Gáspár says. "I am the only true-born son of Bárány János and heir to the throne of Régország."

Nándor's colorless lips curl. "You've never managed to best me before."

"I've never really tried," says Gáspár, and for the briefest moment I see his lips twitch too. "This time, I won't show you any restraint."

Nándor growls out a prayer, and a sword glimmers to life in his good hand, coin-shiny and as bright as gold. When their blades meet, flame against steel, it is with a gonging sound that echoes somewhere deep in my chest. Their battle dance is almost too fast for my eyes to follow, and nothing like their previous dalliance, with wooden swords. All the playful cunning has drained from Nándor's gaze.

"And why do you think the people of Régország will ever welcome you as their king?" Nándor spits as his blade darts toward Gáspár's left shoulder. "A mutilated half-breed, tainted by his mother's foreign blood and poisoned by his love for a wolf-girl. Is it any wonder why Father balked at handing you the crown?"

I don't expect Gáspár to rise to his taunting, but a volley of fury goes through me, and I push myself up onto my knees.

"The crown was always mine," says Gáspár evenly, between breaths. "I only lacked the strength to claim it."

"Strength?" Nándor crows a laugh. "You had the kingdom's finest tutors, and all of Father's kindnesses—"

"Kindness until he cut out my eye," Gáspár breaks in, but his voice is measured in a way that Nándor's is not, matching his pace and his blade's steady scything. "Kindness until he banished me to the Woodsmen."

"The day he cut out your eye was the happiest of my life," Nándor says, face shining with a jeweled dampness. "I remember it well. I had come from the chapel with the Érsek, and I still had a child's mindless zeal, eager to show Father some new trick of swordplay. But when I came to him in the hallway, he brushed right past me and took you inside. I was weak enough that I sat there outside the hall and wept at his rebuff, until I saw them drag you out with blood running down your face. And then I was the most elated I've ever been."

Nándor's recounting of it makes me bristle with rage. I can see the blood soaking through the back of Gáspár's dolman now, his lash wounds opened over and over again with every roll of his shoulder, every leap and lunge. Slowly, my mouth still aching, I get to my feet and limp toward my abandoned bow and quiver. My bloody fingers close around the bow's grip.

"You've been lied to all your life." Gáspár advances on Nándor with a series of quick jabs, sending him stumbling back several paces. Nándor's left arm, ruined by my magic, flaps between them like a flag of surrender. "Made to fit some false sainthood—"

"False?" In the lick of orange light cast by Gáspár's sword, his eyes look like they are pooling with fire. "You've seen what power I have. Real power, by which I have claimed the crown. By what right do you claim the throne of Régország?"

"Birthright," Gáspár answers. "Blood."

And then he cuts his flaming sword across the flat of Nándor's blade with such force that he knocks it from his hand. It sails across the courtyard and clatters onto the cobblestones at the foot of Saint István's statue.

The shock creeps onto Nándor's face in slow, bitter increments, like the trickle of snowmelt. What little color there was vanishes from his cheeks, and his jaw goes slack. For a moment it seems impossible that I ever thought he was beautiful. He looks like a river carp, pale and belly-slit.

"Meghal," Gáspár says, and the flame of his blade snuffs out. He lowers his sword as he paces toward Nándor, who has backed nearly to the barbican.

"Brother—" Nándor starts. He splays his palms, raising his arms over his head. By the time Gáspár reaches him, his hands are up, and he is cowering. "I ask you now to show mercy . . ."

"I don't want to kill you," Gáspár says. His face is hard, his heated sword point mere inches from the curve of Nándor's throat. "It's not worth blackening souls for—mine or yours. If you surrender, call off your Woodsmen, and repent for your sins of violence and patricide, then I will make you the same offer that you made me: live in exile, in the Volkstadt, and never again take up arms against Régország."

As silence swans over the courtyard, a memory prickles at me. We are standing in Kajetán's tent, the headman's knife cold against my tongue. Gáspár had been keen to spare him then, too, despite all his gruesome treachery. I realize now that it was more than the Woodsman oath that stilled Gáspár's blade. It was his own private vow, a constellation hung with a hundred starry virtues and lessons, and he followed it like a ship's captain charting a course across the wine-black sea. Its stars had been gleaned from old tomes in the palace archives, from the stories of his wet nurse, from the Merzani proverbs that his mother whispered into his hair. From the lectures of the Érsek and his battalion of tutors, even from his cruel and inconstant father.

How had he managed to swallow it all and not die of poison? When Merzani words clashed with their Régyar cousins inside him, how was he not cut up by their sibilant swordplay? For so long I'd thought my mixed blood a curse, blamed it for the absence of Isten's magic. Watching Gáspár now, offering his traitor brother mercy, I think that blood cannot be either blessing or curse. It can only be.

Wind sweeps white petals into the air. In the distance, there is the sound of blades singing, metal rasping. Gáspár holds his sword without trembling as a swallow ticks in Nándor's throat. For a moment I think he will acquiesce.

And then his lips part with the utterance of a prayer.

Gáspár's sword, Saint István's sword, shatters like window glass. In the same instant, a small dagger gleams into Nándor's hand. The panicked, animal part of me, that pure

race of adrenaline, is what nocks my arrow and draws back
my bow string, but before I can shoot, Nándor has his good
arm wrenched around Gáspár. His dagger is at his throat.

"I warned you, wolf-girl," Nándor says. Each word is a
plume of frosted breath against his brother's cheek. "I warned
you that it would not be so easy to kill me."

Bow string taut, I meet Gáspár's eye. Where my love
immobilized me before, making me flounder with hopeless
weakness, now it coats me all over with iron. Nándor draws
a line of blood along his brother's neck, tongue curling in the
nascent shape of another prayer.

This is a power I've always had, one that I've earned, one
that can't be taken from me by some capricious god. The
wood rough against my palm, the tail of the arrow brushing my cheek. It does not matter whose histories sing in my
blood.

I let my fingers slide off the bow string. My arrow looses
through the air, quick as a wing beat, and buries itself in Nándor's throat.

He coughs. He chokes. Blood wells in his mouth, bubbling
over his lips in place of a prayer. He lets go of Gáspár and
falls to his knees, grasping at his own neck as blood gathers
at the site of the wound. Gáspár stumbles toward me, and we
both watch as Nándor splutters out his last, wordless breaths.
Ruby-bright droplets limn his collarbone, like icicles on eaves.
I think of the shorn falcon, screeching and flapping its wings
as it died inside its gilded cage, and it pleases me that Nándor
will not have the dignity of last words.

When Nándor finally does topple over, his eyes are as
clouded as two bits of sea glass, and his mouth and chin are a
glut of red-black blood.

Gáspár's shoulders rise and fall in the silence, and I let my
bow drop to the ground. He starts to speak, but I grasp the
collar of his suba and it hushes him.

"Don't," I say. "A king shouldn't begin his rule with a

blackened conscience. My soul is perfectly content to bear the burden of it instead."

He lets out a breath that is half a laugh, though there is a peculiar grief threaded under the sound. It swells in me, too, the acknowledgment of something lost. The hazy, half-dreamed future where he writes poems from the cloistered safety of his Volken hermitage, and I am either his scullery maid or his bride.

"If there is anyone I would damn my soul for," Gáspár says, "it would be you."

I echo his laugh then, and he kisses me gently on the mouth. In another moment, the courtyard will flood with survivors, limping Woodsmen and wounded wolf-girls, and curious peasants who dare to pick their way through the wreckage. Someday an archivist will shelve a book about the siege of Király Szek in the palace library, and it will document the lives lost, the ground gained, the treaties signed, and the maps redrawn. But it will not say anything about this: a wolf-girl and a Woodsman holding each other in the blood-drenched aftermath, and the clouds cleaving open above them, letting out a gutted light.

# EPILOGUE

The woods are restless today, with the snickering of elms, the low, mournful murmur of the willow trees, and of course the anxious whispers of our cowardly poplars. I pick my way through the copse, taking great care not to trip over the lumpy fretwork of their roots, and I rest my hand against the trunk of an oak to feel its timbered heartbeat. My own heart is quivering, like something ready to leap.

As I tread back to Keszi, I see the long tables dragged out and dressed in red cloth, piled high with root vegetables, potatoes the size of a fist. There's an edible garland of rawboned carrots and pearl onions, and the smell of gulyás rises like plumes of smoke. I lean over a pot bubbling with sorrel leaves and boiled eggs and listen to the sizzle of hot dough. The vinegar smell of pickled cabbage leads me to Virág's hut, where she is holding court around her hearth, most of the village's small children in attendance.

Her six-fingered hands are animated, alive, tracing the contours of a story I've heard half a hundred times before. The children are chewing plates of cabbage and summer's last plums, mouths stained purple. I recognize one girl among them: no more than seven years old, with a snarl of dark hair, an orphan. Her mother was struck down by some ghoulish sickness that resisted even Boróka's efforts.

I crouch beside her on the dirt floor. Her face is pinched in the firelight, a furrow deepening between her brows as Virág speaks. With the story of Csilla and Ördög, Virág has perfected her theatre—she knows precisely when to pause for the whispers and gasps, and what parts will make her audience fall silent, shuddering in fear. The little girl is staring intently at the banked fire, watching embers eat away at the wood.

"You don't *have* to listen, you know," I say to her softly.

My own hand is splayed on the ground beside her, missing its fifth finger. Her eyes go to it, tracing the absence. She looks between my hand and Virág's.

"What happened?" she asks in a whisper.

"I'll tell you, if you like," I say, and she nods, so I do. Virág frowns from the other side of the fire; I can hear the echo of her scolding looped through my mind. She thinks I am raising a generation of happy masochists, scarcely better than the Woodsmen. I reply that when summers are long and food is plentiful and mothers stay alive until their daughters are grown, no one will be desperate enough to lop off their fingers or their little toes. Besides, she is happy to try to argue her end; I will not stop speaking mine.

By the time I've finished talking, the little girl's eyelids are heavy. I hand her to Virág, who tucks her into bed, my old bed, for a nap. She kisses me briskly on the forehead, a swallowed rebuke on her tongue, then chases me out of her hut.

Villagers have begun to gather around the long tables. Katalin is bent over a pot of sour-cherry soup, precisely the color of a midsummer sunrise. When she sees me approaching, she looks up, lifting the corner of her mouth that's stippled with scar tissue.

"They're almost here," she says. "I've seen it."

I can hear the thundering of footsteps before I see them, like some giant heart is beating under the forest floor. The trees heave themselves up out of the ground, with the groaning sound of a thousand limbs being wrenched, scattering dead leaves and seed hulls and small sour green apples. When they bed down again, there's a narrow path snaking between their huge trunks, just wide enough for a man on horseback to walk through.

A moment later, the first Woodsman emerges from the tunnel. His horse's dark coat is marbled with the late-afternoon sunlight. He pauses at the mouth of the woods, and behind me the throng of villagers presses in, waiting and watching as another Woodsman breaks through the tree line.

The wind whispers through the leaves, and the last horse trots through. On its back Gáspár sits slightly taller than his men, dressed in a black dolman with a fine embroidery of gold. A matching crown rests on his head, hammered thin into a circlet of gilded branches. He meets my gaze and I stare back, holding him there for a moment before letting him go.

"The king is here," Boróka whispers, leading two young boys to the front of the crowd. "Do you remember all the stories?"

I must have told dozens of them, to anyone who would listen, feeling sometimes every bit as stubborn and ornery as Virág, miffed when my audience's attention drifted or when their eyes glazed over important details. If I live to even half her age, I worry that I will eventually inherit her temperament.

"The black king," says one of the boys. "Fekete."

"He fought his usurper brother with a flaming sword," says the other boy, and they both stare up at Gáspár, slack-jawed.

"It's about time," Virág grouses. "The stew is nearly cold."

It's no easy thing, Woodsmen and pagans sharing a feast table, the precarious inauguration of a new tradition. We have

already killed three sheep in a sacrifice to Isten, and the
Woodsmen clasp their hands to thank the Prinkepatrios for
his bounty before picking up their knives to eat. It helps that
they have brought carafes of wine in their saddlebags, and
sachets of spices, and even skeins of dyed wool for weaving.
Virág leads Gáspár to the head of the feast table and then sits
at his elbow. We eat and drink until our lips are wine-stained
and our bellies are too full under our tunics.

When evening lies over Keszi, the deep velvet blue of a
rich man's dolman, we push back the tables and one of our
men starts plucking his kantele. It's easier now that everyone
is pink-cheeked, a little unsteady on their feet. We all know
the same dances, even these city men and their king, the way
that we all can recite the same nursery rhymes in Old Régyar.

I take Boróka's hand and we spin together, laughing and
dizzy, watching Gáspár turn to a dark blur in my periphery.
He stands stiffly outside the dancing circle, speaking in hushed
tones to Virág. When the song has quavered to its end, kantele
strings twanging, I make my way over to him. My vision is
still gleefully muddled.

"Won't you join us?" I ask. "Or is there some grim prohi-
bition on kings dancing?"

"There's no time for dancing in Király Szek," says Virág,
only the faintest lick of true bitterness in her voice.

We get our news third- or fourth-hand in Keszi, from mes-
senger hawks whose wings don't tire on their long journeys
from the capital, or from runners who can gulp enough courage to brave the dark tangle of the woods, but still I know
there's much work to be done. Király Szek has been flooded
with war refugees from Akosvár, and the Merzani are still
hungering along the border. But the surviving counts have
been convinced to try for peace, and there are Merzani envoys
in the palace now, hesitantly beginning armistice talks. The
bey has warmed considerably to the idea, now that Régország
has a king who is of Merzani blood. Gáspár has started to

make arrangements to settle the refugees around the country, and new villages have sprouted up in all four regions. Some have even taken up residence just outside Ezer Szem, and there's a Woodsman guard stationed there permanently, to make sure the forest creatures don't do them any harm. Once, when there was a particularly bad attack, Virág even sent a few wolf-girls through the woods with their forged blades and healing magic, to keep the new villagers safe.

"We can find time," Gáspár says, lips twitching. "Particularly if my new council wills it."

In the full-moon light, the trees cast a cobweb of shadows over Keszi. Virág leaves us, padding over toward the hearth. She circles the fire and takes one last sip of wine. Gáspár's face is limned with silver, same as it was any night we spent on the ice or in the woods together, our bodies curled in twin crescents under the white eye of the moon.

"And tell me," I say, feeling something hot rise in my throat, "how is the new council faring?"

This king's council is not like the last. There are still the four counts, one from each region (though Gáspár has replaced poor dead Korhonen, and exiled scheming Reményi) and a recently appointed Érsek, who is young and vital and sharp-eyed, with none of his predecessor's cloaked wickedness. But now there are other members, too, chosen to represent Régország's smaller factions. Factions that live in the icy fringes of the Far North, or in the dark belly of the woods.

"Well, Tuula and Szabín have started their journey toward the capital," he says. "And we've fished half the river clean in preparation for hosting the bear. The Yehuli have held their own debates for weeks, finishing in a small election, to choose their representative. It should please you to know that Zsigmond's arguments won out."

The thought floods me with such joy that I laugh, heady with relief. In my absence, my father will have a new way to fill his days, sitting on the council of the king, and perhaps even a woman to come home to at night. "Batya will be pleased."

"She's already sent a basket of bread to the palace, in gratitude." Gáspár's smile is gentle, eye pooling with moonlight. "Now we're only waiting for our last."

In a way it was like being cast out again, when all of Keszi voted for me to be their voice on the king's council. Perhaps still some of them only relished the idea of me spending so many weeks gone in the capital. But most, I think, have given up their old cruelties, as I have abandoned my perverse grudges. Some of the girls who tormented me are mothers now, and when I pass by them running after their daughters or showing their sons how to weave, I see that they don't pull their children away from me. I see that they are teaching their children to be kinder, even if sometimes their lips still twitch with the beginnings of a slur, or the scarcely fettered desire to scowl.

"Did you worry I might not come," I ask, "if you didn't bring me?"

"Of course not," he says. "I didn't want you to go through the woods alone."

We have crossed so many miles together, only to end up back here. When our eyes first met at the edge of Keszi, me costumed in my lying wolf cloak, and him burdened by his Woodsman's suba, I could not have guessed that our journeys would bring us to this place again, the very same spot in the clearing, with so many new words blooming inside us.

"One day when I come for our council meetings," I begin carefully, "you will have a new bride. You must."

A shadow casts across his face. There is that blade sharpening over our heads, counting down the moments to its fall. I have tried not to think of it, during the days that I waited for him here, my skin singing with anticipation. I will try not to think of it during the nights we spend together in my new hut, or on our journey back to Király Szek. But I think I must say it now, or else choke on the swallowed pain.

To my surprise, Gáspár only lifts a shoulder. "Perhaps. Perhaps not. If the king has no true-born son, the crown will fall to a brother, a cousin, an uncle. The line of succession is more like a long thread that spirals across our family tree. I can always name another heir."

It is enough for me to hold on to, hope as thin as the knife's edge hanging above us. I will grasp it even if it cuts me; I will keep it from falling. When winter is one long haze of white, snow weighing down your roof and the cold lining your marrow, it is the dream of a green, bright spring that keeps you from despair. I kiss him just once, on the left side of his faintly smiling mouth.

"There's one more thing," he says, and reaches into the folds of his cloak. "From Zsigmond."

He hands me a package wrapped in brown muslin and looped with twine. I loosen the bindings and peel back the cloth to see a thick scroll of parchment, a large inkwell, and two fine feather quills. The sight of them makes my chest swell and, unbidden, tears leap to my eyes.

"Thank you," I say.

"I only brought them," Gáspár says. "When we get to Király Szek, you can thank Zsigmond yourself."

I grip the quill tightly in my fingers, still warm with the heat of Gáspár's hand. Virág has gathered another audience by the fire, all the men and women who haven't retired already to their huts. The Woodsmen stand by their horses, faces grim with uncertainty.

"Well, now you'll have to stay for the story," I tell him, arching my brow. "Once Virág has started, she doesn't take kindly to interruptions." Gáspár looks like he might protest, so quickly I go on, "I've spent quite enough time in your world. You can linger for a bit longer in mine."

His eye widens; for a moment I can see the early traces of a flush along his cheekbones and the tips of his ears. But he follows me across the clearing, toward the bright whorl of flame and Virág sitting before it. We pad down beside Katalin, who is seated shoulder to shoulder with Boróka. The fur of their wolf cloaks bristles, white stroking tawny. On the ground, their fingers are a whisker's breadth apart.

"I will tell the story of Vilmötten and his journey to the Under-World," Virág says. "How he met Ördög and his half-mortal wife, and came back to the Middle-World with both a blessing and a curse."

Katalin groans softly, but Virág quiets her with a glare. Gáspár's face is hesitantly open, like the very first crocus to bloom. I unfurl one of Zsigmond's long scrolls and dip my quill into the fresh ink. There are Yehuli letters stamped onto the side of the inkwell, and I can read them all. Long fingers of flame reach for the sickled moon. Sparks wink against the night sky. Virág starts to speak, weaving the story of Vilmötten into the air like two dovetailing tree roots, or like a river carving through the land, and I put my quill to the page and write it down.

# PRONUNCIATION GUIDE

## A

**Akosvár (AH-kosh-vahr)**—the southernmost region of Régország, formerly the land of the White Falcon Tribe

**Anikó (AH-nee-koh)**—a healer girl from Keszi

**arany (UH-ran-yah)**—gold

## B

**Balász (BO-las)**—a man from Kajetán's village

**Bárány (BAH-ran-yah) Gáspár (GASH-par)**—the true-born prince, a Woodsman, the son of Bárány János and his deceased Merzani queen, also known as Fekete (FEH-keh-teh)

**Bárány Géza (GEE-zah)**—the third Patritian king of Régország, the grandson of Saint István and the father of János, also known as Szürke (SOOR-kay)

**Bárány János (YAH-nosh)**—the king of Régország, the great-grandson of Saint István

**Bárány Tódor (TOO-dor)**—Régország's second Patritian king, the son of King István, founder of the Holy Order of Woodsmen, and conqueror of Kaleva

**Batya (BAT-yah)**—a Yehuli woman from Király Szek

**bey (BAY)**—the sovereign of the Merzani empire

**Bierdna (bee-erd-NAH)**—a bear

**Boróka (BAH-roh-kah)**—a pagan woman from Keszi

**boszorkány (BAH-sahr-kahn-yah)**—witch

# C

**Csilla (CHEEL-ah)**—in pagan mythology, the wife of Ördög and the queen of the Under-World

**Count Furedi (FOO-reh-dee)**—the count of Farkasvár

**Count Korhonen (KOR-ho-nen)**—the count of Kaleva

**Count Németh (NEE-meth)**—the count of Szarvasvár

**Count Reményi (REH-meen-yee)**—the count of Akosvár

# D

**Dorottya (DOR-ot-yah)**—a woman from Kajetán's village

# E

**Élet River (EE-let)**—meaning "life," the largest river that bisects the country of Régország

**Elif (UH-lif) Hatun (ha-TUHN)**—King János's deceased Merzani wife

**Érsek (EER-shek)**—the archbishop

**Eszti (ES-tee)**—a girl from Kajetán's village

**Évike (EE-vih-kay)**—a pagan woman from Keszi with Yehuli blood

**Ezer Szem (EH-zer SEM)**—a forest in Farkasvár, where the last pagan villages sit

# F

**Farkasvár (FOR-kosh-vahr)**—the easternmost region of Régország, bordering Rodinya, formerly the land of the Wolf Tribe

**Ferenc (FUH-rents)**—a Woodsman

**Ferkó (FUHR-koh)**—a Woodsman

# H

**Hanna (HA-nah)**—a woman from Kajetán's village

**harcos (HOR-kash)**—warrior, soldier

# I

**Imre (IM-ray)**—a Woodsman

**Írisz (IH-rees)**—a pagan woman from Keszi

**Isten (ISH-ten)**—in pagan mythology, the father-god and the creator of the world

**István (ISHT-vahn)**—the first Patritian king of Régország, widely regarded as its founder, and a saint

# J

**Jozefa (YO-zeh-fah)**—a Yehuli girl from Király Szek

**Juvvi (yoo-VEE)**—an ethnoreligious group who mainly reside in the northernmost areas of Kaleva

# K

**Kajetán (KO-yeh-tan)**—the head of a small village on the Little Plain

**Kaleva (KAH-lev-ah)**—the northernmost region of Régország, formerly an independent kingdom

**kantele (KAN-tuh-luh)**—a stringed instrument, famously played by Vilmötten

**kapitány (KO-pee-tan-yah)**—captain

**Katalin (KOT-oh-lin)**—a pagan woman from Keszi and a seer

**Keszi (KEH-see)**—one of the pagan villages in Ezer Szem, located closest to the edge of the forest

**király és szentség (KEER-ai EESH SENT-sheg)**—literally "king and holiness," used as a colloquial expression "royalty and divinity"

**Király Szek (KEER-ai SEK)**—the capital of Régország

**Kuihta (koo-EE-tah)**—a monastery in Kaleva

# L

**Lajos (LOY-osh)**—a Woodsman

**lidércek (LEE-der-tsek)**—monsters common to the forest of Ezer Szem

# M

**Magda (MOG-dah)**—Évike's mother, a pagan woman

**Marjatta (MAR-ya-tah)**—Nándor's mother, a Northern woman

**Matyi (MAH-tee)**—King János's bastard son

**meghal (MAY-khal)**—literally "die," an incantation to put out fire

**megvilágit (MAG-vee-lah-geet)**—literally "illuminate," an incantation invoking fire

**mente (MEHN-tay)**—an overcoat

**Merzan (MEHr-zahn)**—the empire to the south of Régország

**Miklós (MIK-losh)**—a Woodsman

**Mithros (MEE-thros)**—a hero and savior figure of Patritian lore

# N

Nándor (NAHN-dor)—King János's eldest bastard son

# O

Ördög (EUR-deug)—in pagan mythology, the god of death and of the Under-World

# P

Patrifaith (PAH-truh-fayth)—the state religion of Régország
Patritian (pah-TREE-tee-ahn)—a follower of the Patrifaith, or relating to the Patrifaith
Peti (PEH-tee)—a Woodsman
Prinkepatrios (prink-eh-PAH-tree-os)—the father-god of the Patrifaith, composed of two aspects, Godfather Life and Godfather Death

# R

Rasdi (RAS-dee)—a Juvvi woman of lore
Régország (REEG-or-sahg)—a kingdom bordered in the west by the Volkstadt, in the east by Rodinya, and in the south by Merzan
Régyar (REE-jar)—the language and people of Régország
Riika (RIK-ah)—a serving girl in the palace of King János
Rodinya (ro-DIN-yah)—the empire to the east of Régország

# S

Shabbos (SHA-bus)—a Yehuli day of rest
suba (SHOO-bah)—a woolen cloak worn by the Woodsmen, historically associated with the farmers on the Little Plain

**Szabín (SAH-been)**—a former Daughter of the Patrifaith

**Szarvasvár (SAR-vash-vahr)**—the westernmost region of Régország, formerly the land of the Deer Tribe

# T

**Taivas (TA-ee-vas)**—literally "sky," a lake in Kaleva

**táltos (TAHL-tosh)**—a seer, typically the headwoman of a pagan village

**Thanatos (THAH-nah-tos)**—the demonic entity of Patritian lore, responsible for tempting humans to sin

**turul (TUH-rool)**—in pagan mythology, a hawk that gave Vilmötten the gift of sight

**Tuula (TOO-lah)**—a Juvvi girl from Kaleva

# V

**Vilmötten (VIL-meu-tun)**—in pagan mythology, a mortal man who was given the favor of the gods and went on to become a heroic figure

**Virág (VEE-rag)**—the táltos of Keszi, a pagan woman and a seer

**Volkstadt (FOLK-stat)**—the kingdom to the west of Régország

# Y

**Yehuli (yeh-HOO-lee)**—an ethnoreligious group who mainly reside in Király Szek

# Z

**Zsidó (ZHEE-do)**—the name for the Yehuli in Régyar

**Zsigmond (ZHIG-mund)**—a Yehuli man from Király Szek, a goldsmith

**Zsófia (ZHO-fee-ah)**—a pagan woman from Keszi

# ACKNOWLEDGMENTS

This edition comes four years after the initial publication of *The Wolf and the Woodsman* and was made possible by the passionate and enduring support of readers, both new and old. My deepest gratitude you all.

Many thanks as well to my editor, David Pomerico, for saying yes all those years ago and for continuing to champion this book. Thank you to Liate Stehlik for helping to give *The Wolf and the Woodsman* a second life. Thank you to my agent, Sarah Landis, for supporting me so faithfully and believing in me so unshakably.

And thank you to artists Mary Metzger and Kris Cooper, who conveyed the beating heart of the story through their work on this beautiful edition.

# ABOUT THE AUTHOR

Ava Reid is the #1 *New York Times* bestselling author of *A Study in Drowning, Lady Macbeth, Juniper & Thorn,* and *The Wolf and the Woodsman.* She lives in the New York City area.

Website: avasreid.com

Twitter: @asimonereid

Instagram: @avasreid